Advance Praise for
Acts of Omission

"This is a book that should be read by every trial lawyer, everyone who wants to be a trial lawyer, and everyone who wonders what it takes to be a trial lawyer. Bostwick spins a powerful, informative tale drawn from real life. The courtroom scenes leap off the page and will have the reader cheering for justice."

—WALTER H. WALKER III, Bestselling author of *A Crime of Privilege*

"This book is a movie! A page turner! I couldn't put it down! The author's concise, lyrical, and romantic prose, powerfully captures INJUSTICE, crime, greed, and court room drama. With careful detail, and clear insight, the author lets the reader into the mind of personal injury lawyer Matt Taylor, who, with great stakes, fights for, and wins justice. Beautifully written, this is the kind of book you keep in your book case to read again, and again. This author has written a masterpiece! An author to watch."

—BARBARA ROSE BROOKER, Bestselling author of *The Viagra Diaries* and other books, Professor of Creative Writing, San Francisco State University

"This is more than a good read; it is a masterpiece of courtroom drama, life of a trial lawyer, intrigue, intricate relationships, love, and one man's perseverance for justice. Bostwick nailed it!"

—WILLIAM WHITEHURST, Past President of The International Academy of Trial Lawyers, The Texas Trial Lawyers, and the Texas Bar Association

"It is a story that best highlights what a lawyer can do if he or she wants to get into the ring of justice. Every young lawyer should read this."

—JOSEPH W. COTCHETT, Author of several widely-read law treatises and the recent bestselling book, *The People vs. Greed: Stealing America*

ACTS OF OMISSION

ACTS OF
OMISSION

JAMES S. BOSTWICK

A POST HILL PRESS BOOK

Acts of Omission
© 2019 by James S. Bostwick
All Rights Reserved

ISBN: 978-1-64293-261-4
ISBN (eBook): 978-1-64293-262-1

Cover design by Cody Corcoran
Cover art by Sung Kim
Author photo by Marti Phillips
Interior design and composition, Greg Johnson/Textbook Perfect

Post Hill Press
New York • Nashville
posthillpress.com

Published in the United States of America

"We are all advocates. Whether in the courtroom or in our daily lives, we all have unique and powerful voices. Whether we affect one person or a nation of people, our voices can be heard, one word at a time."

—NOEL M. FERRIS, Esq. Dean's Address to the International Academy of Trial Lawyers, March 20, 2015

This book is dedicated to the memory of Noel Ferris, trial warrior extraordinaire—who left us too early. She was built of steel, but always led with her heart.

1

San Francisco, 1984

The trial was over. Matt stared at the implacable gray wall in front of him, unwilling to turn the ignition key and break the stunned silence that had followed him from the battered courtroom to the empty garage. It was remarkable how quiet it could get when a jury said "no" to parents who had lost their only child. Matt couldn't exorcise the expression on the faces of his clients when the verdict was read. They were completely shattered. There was nothing Matt could do to ease their pain. Now, they had to put their lives back together and he had to find a way to pay the rent.

Jamie had been alive when Jim and Mary Olsen first came to talk with him about the drug that had destroyed their son's liver. Their doctor had received no warning from the manufacturer that the medication he ordered for Jamie had previously caused the death of several children. In Matt's office, the little guy had been so excited about riding in a genuine cable car. After two years of Matt beating his head against the company's corporate brick wall, the case finally got to trial. By then, Jamie had died. Matt never had the chance to give him the model cable car he bought him for his seventh birthday.

On the eve of trial, the pharmaceutical giant finally made a reasonable offer. Matt had advised his clients to settle. Mary would have been happy to have the case over, but Jim wanted retribution. Matt pulled out all the stops to give them the justice they deserved. His clients had depended on him, and he had lost.

His stomach twisted. He hated to lose and knew this case would continue to haunt him. Scenes from the trial were going to replay in his head forever. Losses left a void that his victories never quite filled.

Five o'clock. Emily, his office manager, would be anxious for him to get back to the office. He needed to deal with a pile of work and clients who had felt neglected during the trial. He thumbed through the stack of papers Emily had given him to go through—anything to take his mind off what had just happened. It was mostly bills, of course. He saw a circled note about some new case she wanted him to call a lawyer about. She had underlined the words "game changer." Yeah, right—he had heard that before.

He turned the key and the Blazer jumped to life. He headed home to change his clothes. Work could wait. He needed a dose of The Bridge.

* * *

Matt parked next to the St. Francis Yacht Club. He stretched by the seawall, savoring the panorama and acrid tang of the moist air. The pastel city cascaded down the hillside to meet the white-capped bay. Fleets of sailboats wheeled around their marks, their crisp Dacron sails thundering in rapid succession. The competitors heeled, close hauled, into the northwesterly gale. They angled toward the Golden Gate Bridge, its massive columns silhouetted by shafts of sunlight. Further down the beach, sailboards skimmed between the racers and the ferryboats, a kaleidoscope of dorsal fins dodging back and forth across the wind.

A tendril of fog extended under The Bridge, tentatively testing the resolve of the warm afternoon. All around him people were running, walking, or bicycling to and from the distant towers. The balmy weather had obviously put a serious dent in the city's afternoon workforce. He felt the darkness coiled within him gradually begin to release as he ran toward the dying sun.

He recognized runners and walkers he literally only knew in passing. Most runners, he had noticed, acknowledged only other runners, and walkers other walkers. Seldom did cross-breed socialization occur. Their dogs were more egalitarian.

A running magazine pundit had once opined that this stretch of beach had more beautiful women per mile than anywhere except Malibu. Today, Matt could almost believe it. Running through the pain of three exercise-free weeks of trial, he gradually became anesthetized by his surging endorphins.

Near the end of his run, he saw his favorite fantasy approaching. He'd first noticed her a few months ago. She usually wore shapeless winter sweats. At first, he almost didn't recognize her in the colorful Lycra. A large-brimmed running hat pulled low over sunglasses couldn't quite conceal her prominent cheekbones, smooth olive skin, and elegant nose. He smiled at her as she passed, but, for naught. She acknowledged no one as she ran—at least, never him.

Well, given the reality of his life, why should she? He was a divorced father, close to forty, with more gray hair than he would like. He hadn't been in a serious relationship since his marriage. He'd cobbled together a reasonably successful law practice, but he always seemed to be on the edge financially. Now that he had lost this case, he was going to be well over that edge.

Matt collapsed on the grass. As his breathing quieted, he stared across at the uninhabited headlands rising serenely above the bay. His dream in going to law school and representing injured people had been to make a real difference. He had been so ambitious, so ready to take on the world. Now, the only thing he cared about in his life was his son. Maybe he was just really tired.

Matt decided his fantasy runner should be a model or an actress. He wanted her to love the mountains as much as he did. Perhaps she also had studied ballet, loved dogs, cooked Cajun cuisine as a hobby, and was a Class 5 whitewater kayaker.

On the other hand, with his luck, she was probably married, had several kids, and hated lawyers.

* * *

Matt let himself into his apartment, poured a pitcher of ice water, and dropped into his favorite chair on the deck. The gray mantle was starting to win its daily skirmish for control of the bay. In the misting twilight he could just make out the burgeoning lights in the flats of the Marina District below. He let the gusting air cool him down from his run.

After his shower, he hit the button on his answering machine. Most of the calls were predictable: a few friends checking up on him, a call from Lena, a woman he had been seeing, and the standard four calls from his ex-wife, Susan, worrying about money and their son Grant's schedule. There was also a message from Emily.

"Hi, Matthew; that verdict was bull. I think it was that squinty-eyed accountant they picked as foreman—a ringer. I know you're thinking about running away—don't, or our house of cards will tumble for sure. We knew it was tough. You did everything you could and then some." The air pent up in his chest escaped slowly as he listened.

"Don't forget to call Fred Stadahl. He called a bunch during the trial and said he was anxious to talk to you about a 'dynamite' new case. I left you a note about it but I know you never read those. He was being sort of mysterious about it. Said his home number's listed in Marin County. Well…see you in the morning."

Matt stared at the floor for a moment as the machine recycled. He wanted today to be over, but he should call the man and at least accomplish something positive.

Stadahl answered on the first ring. "Matt, how the hell are you? Damn sorry by the way, I heard your case didn't go so well."

Matt never failed to be surprised at the efficiency of the trial lawyer gossip network. "'Bout as bad as it can go—but then it's always a roll of the dice."

"Ain't that right—just can't predict 'em. Leave anything on the table?"

"The drug company offered two hundred fifty thousand dollars to settle just before trial."

"Hell, the case could have gone into seven figures, no wonder you went for it."

"Yeah, well thanks, but what the hell—that number looks pretty good right about now." Matt sat slumped, his head resting on the back of the chair. "How's it going for you? I heard things have been a little rough lately."

"Fucking understatement. You hear what that asshole, Sal Conti, did to me? Law partners for ten years and he locks me out of the office—I'm talking personal papers, photos of the kids…. Not to mention my *files*; I had to get a goddamn court order to get the files so I could represent my clients!"

"Good Lord, the man's really out of control—but then hasn't he always been? When you're called the 'Prince of Personal Injury' and the newspapers love you, I guess you think you can call the shots."

Stadahl growled in agreement. "Yeah, like that young lawyer he met back east during that huge case—hired the kid away from another firm on the spot. The poor bastard sold his house and moved wife and kids to San Francisco to go to work for the world-famous Salvatore Conti."

"Oh shit, I think I remember that…"

"Guy shows up for work Monday morning and Sal throws him out in the street—says he's changed his mind. 'Go back to Boston,' he says. 'Got my own damn problems,' he says."

"One cold son of a bitch. Well, guess you can't say you weren't forewarned, can you? You think you can work things out with him?"

"Nope, fucking dogfight all the way—and he owns this town—the courts and the media." They both thought about that in silence for a moment.

"Enough about my problems. I was calling to see if you'd be interested in handling a case I took with me when I left."

"You're not handling it yourself?" Matt's curiosity was piqued. Most of Matt's cases came to him by referral from attorneys who were not trial specialists, but Stadahl was a trial lawyer. He could try the case himself, so why offer it to Matt?

"I can't handle it because I will probably be a witness." Fred got right to the point. "This may not be the best time to talk to you about a new case, but I have to find this client a lawyer soon because the statute of limitations is about to run."

"Fred, if the statute is about to expire, there won't be much time for investigation." Matt grimaced. "I just lost a case, remember—I can't risk jumping into a case with time problems."

"Look, I've never sent you a case before, but I always figured you were the one I'd go to if my family had a problem.... These people really need help, Matt."

Matt pinched the bridge of his nose with his fingers. "What kind of a case is it, Fred?"

There was a brief pause at the other end. "It's a malpractice case—the client's a young man that lives in San Diego. He was hurt in a crash and the hospital missed the diagnosis."

"Okay—well that doesn't sound so complicated. What's our time problem and how bad was he hurt?"

"To cut to the chase, Matt, I'm talking about a *legal* malpractice case." Stadahl took a deep breath. "The kid's paralyzed—and the defendant is Salvatore Conti."

2

Matt headed east from the San Diego airport to see the young man Stadahl had told him about. Matt was startled at the changes since his high school days. He could scarcely recognize the old landmarks. Matt had been back a few times over the years, but things had always seemed the same. He had put in so many hours on these roads, restlessly looking for whatever it was that teenagers sought.

Coincidentally, the family he was going to see lived in El Cajon, where Matt had spent his high school years. He stopped along the road that skirted the granite rim of the pretty valley, and looked with amazement at how the sleepy town had been transformed by the burgeoning growth of the past two decades.

Emily's instructions led him to a neighborhood that would once have been considered expensive, given its vantage point gazing down on the hot dusty valley. The Gleason residence, which looked like it had once been well maintained, now had a distinct aura of neglect. As he approached the front door, he could see a well-tended rose garden through the traditional southwestern breezeway. Obviously, it was a lack of time and money, not of care, that accounted for the deterioration of the home's appearance.

The face that greeted him was friendly and inquisitive, but there was evidence of sadness and lack of attention around the edges. Debbie Gleason was about fifty, with dark, soulful eyes and a luminous smile. You could see kindness and a loving nature, but hovering in the background was a sense of loss and despair. Matt was skilled at reading people, but this was no challenge—she wore her feelings like the jacket of a book.

Her son, Todd, was still at his morning therapy, so she offered tea. A few questions revealed that Todd's father had left about three years earlier, ostensibly to seek work back home in Georgia. Matt guessed he didn't plan to send for them or return. Matt knew that many families were torn apart by a devastating injury to a child.

Money arrived only sporadically. They survived on meager savings, now pretty much exhausted, and the income of Todd's older brother Bob, who had moved back in to help when Todd came home from the rehabilitation center. Debbie took care of her son most of the time. Matt asked what Todd could do for himself and what had to be done for him. The answer was damn little of the former and a lot of the latter.

Todd was a complete C6 quadriplegic. This meant that he had partial movement of the hands and no strength in portions of the upper extremities, including the muscle groups such as the triceps, that would allow him to push up and transfer himself to or from bed or chair. If a patient can't transfer himself, he can't live independently. There was no feeling from the mid-chest down, no ability to move the legs, and no ability to control either his bladder or his bowel function.

Debbie's twenty-year-old son would forever need the care he had required as an infant. His mind and desires, however, were those of a perfectly normal young adult.

Matt was trying to figure how to inquire more about the family situation when Todd arrived with his brother. Todd was painfully thin, with an aesthetic face and a tentative but mischievous, grin. He seemed shy, but his eyes danced with interest and curiosity. In contrast, his brother was sullen and soon left the room.

Todd suddenly spoke. "So why are you here? What kind of a lawyer are you, and why isn't Mr. Stadahl here?"

Debbie Gleason reproached her son gently with her hand on his shoulder as Matt explained his purpose for visiting. He noticed Todd stiffen at her touch and sensed an undercurrent of resentment. No wonder, Matt thought. This young man is at the age where most of his friends have escaped their parents. Todd remained totally dependent on his mother for even his most basic bodily functions.

"Fred Stadahl asked me to check out if your case was handled correctly by the Conti office. There is a possibility that they missed some things. To do that, I need to know the answer to a few questions." Matt lifted out a notepad. "For example, how did you originally employ Mr. Conti, and who did you understand would do the work?"

The young man looked over to his mother and the two of them remembered together. Debbie answered first. "Mr. Conti had us come up to his office in San Francisco in 1981. We got to meet him personally and he had us sign a contract. We never saw Mr. Conti again until the settlement." Debbie's soft mouth tightened perceptibly. "It seemed to us that all the work was actually done by Mr. Youngstone—even though Mr. Conti had agreed he would handle the case personally."

Todd nodded in agreement and added, "Mr. Youngstone was very nice, but seemed awfully new at this to us—he never seemed to be sure what he was doing. The case settled six months before trial."

"Why did you settle for only six hundred fifty thousand dollars when I heard the policy limit available was one million dollars?"

Debbie put her hand over her mouth in obvious surprise. "Mr. Conti told us about the offer himself. We thought six hundred fifty thousand dollars was the entire amount in the policy! Actually, that was the only other time we saw Mr. Conti."

Matt could see his own shock at this revelation mirrored in their faces. He plowed ahead. "One of the things I also wanted to ask you is whether you could move your arms and legs when you first got to the hospital and if so, when it was that you lost the ability to move them."

"All I can remember is waking up the next day and being paralyzed. I felt like I was just a head and there was nothing else to me, like the rest of me had been amputated." He stared down at his offending body resentfully. "I guess they might as well have for all the use it is to me." Then, as quickly as the shadow of a cloud could pass on a windy day, his face brightened and became animated. "What I'm really wondering is when I'm going to get some sensation and some motion back in my legs. Do you know how long it should take?"

Matt was stunned. Did Todd really still not understand his condition was permanent? "Todd, I haven't really been over all your records yet, but I was told it has been about four years since this happened. Has there been any progress or return in the last year or so?" Was this lack of candid medical advice or simple denial?

"No. There hasn't been any return since I first woke up in that bed. That's why I'd like some more money, so I could go to one of those places where they do special therapy."

Matt caught the look of infinite sadness on Debbie's face as she turned away. The air in the room felt thick as Todd continued to talk. Eventually Matt sat forward and looked directly at the earnest young man. "If I do decide I can represent you, I will always tell you my honest opinion, like it or not. Some of the things you've told me concern me very much. For now though, I think I'll just do some more homework before I say any more."

Todd Gleason soon excused himself, claiming that he needed to take a nap. After his mother had gotten him into bed, she came back into the living room. She sat down in the opposite chair with a sigh. Her hair was askew and a light sheen of sweat shone on her face.

"My son knows what your opinions probably are, Mr. Taylor, and so do I. Todd still has a hard time facing reality." Debbie Gleason appraised him. "We both appreciate your sensitivity in holding back your thoughts until we know you better and you have had a chance to prepare us to hear them. You've made it clear candid opinions will come with the territory if you can help us. That will be a refreshing change."

She laughed and he could see a hint of the beautiful young woman who must have enchanted many suitors once in some Georgia town. "Mr. Stadahl said there might have been a medical malpractice case, that the doctors may have missed Todd's broken neck. He said he discovered it too late to sue the doctors and you were going to see if Todd could sue Conti for that." She looked down at her worn hands.

Matt sat forward. "I'm just starting my investigation. It's really too early to say." Then a resolute expression came into her mobile features and she looked him straight in the eye. "If you don't think we have a good case, then you just tell us. We'll just do as we have been and we'll manage just fine."

He stayed for another hour or so, talking with Debbie and learning more about Todd. She told him that her son had been an artist of remarkable ability before he was injured. When she proudly showed him Todd's work, the obvious talent reminded him of Matt's brother Alex's work as a youngster. "Debbie, this work is great! Todd needs to develop this." He saw the look on her face and moderated his enthusiasm. "I know it's hard for him, but with some occupational therapy, he might be able to learn to use those hands better."

She tried to smile at his encouragement. "Well, maybe one of these days we'll be able to get him more therapy." He resisted the impulse to suggest that the lawsuit he was contemplating could provide the funds. Instead he just nodded in support.

He found it easy to relax and enjoy her warmth and gentle southern hospitality, and eventually he allowed her to cajole him into staying for lunch.

* * *

On his way to the car, he saw Todd's brother, Bob, come out from around the garage. He had obviously been waiting for a chance to talk to Matt alone. The sullen attitude had been replaced by a tentative hope in his nervous glance. He scuffed the baked dry earth.

"My brother likes you, Mr. Taylor. He really hopes you can help him out."

Todd wasn't the only one looking for a lifeline. Todd's brother had the look of a trapped animal searching for a way out of a cage. It wasn't hard for Matt to get him to spill his heart out.

"The actual fact is, you know, that I was planning to get married before I had to move in and help them out. I mean, who else was going to do it? Now I don't know if I can get married. I'm getting the feeling I may be stuck here forever. It's beginning to drive me crazy, you know?"

The intensity of the plea engulfed Matt like the cloying atmosphere of the east county afternoon. He wasn't sure whether the trickle of moisture down his spine was from the spring sun or the pressure of this family's need.

"Also my mom…she puts on a good show but this is killing her, you know what I mean? She has to care for Todd night and day, you know, so she is up several times at night to turn him and calm him since he always has trouble sleeping. I mean, her back is going out from having to lift him all day long, and she hasn't had a vacation or a day off forever!"

Bob's words rushed on. "Whenever I can help, she has to use that time for shopping and other chores. I mean she hasn't seen a friend for months. I think the strain is really getting her down. I'm sort of worried about her, you know, and if she has a breakdown, or her back goes out…." Bob heaved a sigh. "Well, then it will just be me—and if I can't work, we'll lose the house. I don't know, what I'm saying is you've got to find a way to help us." He looked at Matt apologetically. "I'm sorry, I mean…do you think you can?"

* * *

The droning of the packed Friday afternoon commuter lulled Matt as he nursed a beer sandwiched in his middle seat. He thought about the family he had just met. They really didn't have any idea whether there was a case or why he had been there at all. They were spending their energy just making it through each day. In the process, they showed more raw courage than many people society viewed as heroes.

Debbie was an incredible woman She had given up her entire life and devoted herself to her son. Somehow, she had retained her grace and sense of humor, and didn't show a hint of resentment for what life had dealt her. She managed, much like the way his mother had handled the situation with Matt's brother. Todd was an artist like Alex had been. The boy reminded Matt of his brother in so many ways. He had to be careful not to let that similarity affect his objectivity.

Conti had settled the auto accident case for only six hundred fifty thousand of the insurance available. Matt could not understand why they hadn't insisted on the entire one million dollars. Too much work for too little money, Matt surmised. So Todd ended up with around three hundred sixty thousand after fees and costs and before he paid the remaining medical bills. That's why they were out of money.

As far as the "special therapy" Todd wanted, the few medical records Matt had seen made it clear that Todd was a permanent quadriplegic. Some of these "special therapy" places promised the impossible to desperate people willing to pay anything for a bit of hope. The worst ones put injured people with no reasonable hope of improvement on rigorous and expensive programs. They then blamed the families for the patient's lack of progress, saying they must not have tried hard enough. Matt could imagine the impact it would have on this family if they were given false hope and then were told that they were responsible for the resulting failure.

Matt reflected on his week. After the devastating verdict, he should probably be conservative and pull back—both in his business and his personal life. He was certainly on the edge in both. This Gleason case could turn out to be a bottomless pit of money and time. The risk was huge and the thought of taking Conti on in San Francisco, the famous lawyer's personal fiefdom, was intimidating to say the least. Jake, his best friend, had strongly advised him to reject the case when Matt told him about it. He pointed out the kid had been drunk, the accident itself likely caused the paralysis, and Conti was a dangerous foe in many ways.

Matt pulled at his beer thoughtfully. Stadahl was passionate about the case though, and even said he wouldn't ask to share the fee if the case was successful, because he expected to be a witness when it went to trial. The records he had sent over did raise several questions in Matt's mind about the care. There were doctor's notes about movement of Ted's arms and legs for the first few hours and there were also some missing x-rays. Then there was this family. Matt didn't know how they would manage if they didn't get some help. At this late stage, if he didn't take the case it was unlikely anyone would. Matt had the feeling the Gleasons would give up on the idea of further lawsuits if he said no.

He stared out the window at the swirling fog as the plane touched down in San Francisco.

3

Driving north into Marin through the rainbow tunnel, Matt felt the weight of the week slipping away. A CD of Metallica at high volume and the start of a weekend in the mountains was the right formula to improve an attitude. Everything would be right with the world when he had picked up his son and they were really on their way to the cabin. His ex-wife had complained about the fact they would miss one of his little league games by going this weekend. He figured they would more than make up for that with some special time together. Grant lived with him every other week, but the trial had cut into their time dramatically. Susan had never really cared that much about the cabin anyway.

Upon reflection, he was glad his friend Lena hadn't been able to come with them this weekend; she had a major work project that she had to have ready by Monday. This way it would just be the two of them entertaining Jake and his new girlfriend for the weekend. Jake dated a lot, but never seriously. This was the first time he could remember Jake asking to bring a friend for the Taylor "seal of approval." Matt was intrigued.

Matt shared space with Jake's law firm in an old brick building on the north waterfront under Coit Tower. While Matt loved the character of the post-gold rush ice house with its pre-earthquake brickwork, twenty-five-foot ceilings and massive beams, the primary reason he rented space there was Jake Orlov. Matt and Jake had been close since law school. Orlov and Harsh primarily represented insurance companies, while Matt spent most of his time on the opposite side of the fence, representing people that were injured.

Matt headed east toward Vallejo and I-80 on the Black Point cutoff, his tow-headed son chattered on about his week. People said they looked a lot alike, but Matt thought they were wrong. Grant's fine features and quick easy smile were more like his beautiful mother. As he listened to his son, his thoughts drifted back to Todd and Debbie Gleason. Suddenly he was flooded with a rush of gratitude that this wonderful little creature sitting beside him had his health.

* * *

They turned off Highway 89 and started up the canyon that would take them to the cabin. When they pulled onto the dirt road that started the property, Matt put his SUV in four-wheel drive. There was no snow left down here now, but the roads were muddy and there was no point in taking a chance. They wound up the hill and around the corner, pulling up to the front. It looked like Jake and his special friend hadn't arrived yet.

As they got out, they both stood for a moment and let the chilly alpine air revive them. The cabin was situated on a knoll, with the dark shadow of Lake Tahoe spread out below them. The massive peaks of the Desolation Wilderness loomed behind. The wind was blowing through the pine trees surrounding them with that peculiar roaring sound Matt always found strangely reassuring. They both relaxed; they were home.

Carrying in the few grocery items, they began the ritual of opening the place for the long weekend. The cabin was built of sierra granite and rough-hewn cedar. Inside were mostly honey-colored pine walls and floors with massive hand-hewn beams. Pictures of ancestors covered some walls; others held western oil paintings or colorful native weavings. The cabin was furnished with an eclectic mix of primitive furniture and huge, inviting upholstered pieces. A person walking in for the first time would sense the love and care of generations. The living room looked down on the lake while the kitchen and dining areas looked to the rear to a magnificent view of the wilderness. It was all pretty much as his father and grandfather had designed and built it in the late thirties before the war broke out. The only exception was the kitchen, which Matt had remodeled.

Soon Matt had a fire going in the living room and in the dining room/kitchen area. Grant switched on the hot water and turned up the thermostats in the areas that would be in use. The place had just begun to take on its usual welcoming glow when they heard Jake yell for help carrying things in from his car. He had assigned himself the task of bringing groceries for the three-day weekend and had obviously taken the job seriously. Jake and his friend each had three bags and there were several more in the car.

As Matt set down the last of the provisions in the kitchen, he turned to meet Jake's friend, Adrianne. She gripped his hand firmly, gazing directly at him with a friendly and open manner with eyes that were a startling shade of green. She had a wonderful smile from a full mouth and the slightest hint of a southern drawl in her greeting. Thick, dark hair with auburn highlights surrounded intriguing features.

The preliminaries over, they made drinks and set about preparing a late snack for the new arrivals. Adrianne pitched right in, while Jake supervised and provided a little background on his newest companion. She was in her late twenties, was from Atlanta, and had decided to relocate to California. She had been in the Bay Area for about six months, and was working through an agency doing temporary secretarial work. Jake had met her in another lawyer's office several months ago. Adrianne, in an obvious effort to change the subject, asked about the history of the cabin.

Grant, obviously taken with their guest, proudly undertook to give the background. "My great-grandpa bought this land back in the twenties and he came up here with my grandpa when he was little. They used to camp out here a lot and sometimes they would have a trailer. When my grandpa grew up, my great-grandpa had the cabin built. All the land around is what they call 'wildness,' so no one can build here anymore. So we'll never have any neighbors! Dad says that this will always be Taylor land and I'll be the fourth generator to own it."

Matt and Jake laughed, but Adrianne took pains to reassure the chagrined youngster that his story had been great. She explained the difference between the words *wilderness* and *wildness,* as well as *generation* and *generator,* and then, after they ate, enlisted him for a guided tour.

While they were gone, Jake looked at Matt and raised his eyebrows with a tilt of his head in an obvious inquiry. Matt gave him a thumbs-up. Such questions were unusual for his friend. Jake was clearly taken with Adrianne. When the two explorers returned, Matt told Grant it was time to say goodnight.

While Grant got his ritual back scratch, they had their usual discussion of important matters of the day. "Dad, I think that Adrianne person is nice. She's fun to talk to—she doesn't treat me like I'm just a kid. I think she's really pretty too. Do you think she's pretty?" Matt agreed with him that, yes, she certainly was.

* * *

The fire and the margaritas warmed everyone as they sat in the living room and allowed the silence of the mountains to envelop them. The wind gusted in the pine trees and whined under the eaves. The heavy beams of the cabin creaked and sighed in protest under the pressure of the cold wind outside.

Matt watched Jake and Adrianne gradually unwind from the pressures of the week. He had often marveled at the response his friend's good looks and Slavic intensity elicited from the other gender. Matt and Jake presented quite a contrast. They both were just over six feet in height, but Jake had dark coloring and full, powerful features. On the other hand, Matt had sandy hair and a chiseled facial structure, more in keeping with his Nordic heritage.

Matt smiled as he thought back on his friendship with the complicated man sitting across from him. They had met during the first week of law school. Both of them were broke so they relied on hard work and loans to make it. Matt had no help from his divorced parents. Jake and his parents were emigrants, arriving shortly after the war in the late '40s. His parents had never learned English. Jake never had anything he hadn't kicked and scratched for—sometimes literally.

Jake had always been there for him: class notes and study advice when Matt needed it (all too often) and eventually a safe haven when he finally quit the old firm (at Jake's urging). A few cases tossed his way, many lucrative recommendations, and months when Jake would wait for or forgo the rent payment had pretty much made the difference for Matt's new venture. Jake had also provided emotional support when Matt and Susan finally called it quits. Matt couldn't have developed his practice or kept his emotional stability without his friend's support. Matt didn't have many male friendships. This one he cherished.

Breaking into Matt's musing, Jake asked how he was doing now that the trial was over. Matt tried to describe the emptiness the loss left in his soul—the void that reassurance and rationalization could not fill. He also articulated the feeling of freedom he always experienced when the weeks of concentrated effort were over. Ordinary things took on the aura of a special occasion because of the sudden absence of the consuming effort necessary during trial.

Jake explained to Adrianne that Matt suffered from what he liked to call the "Steven Wallace syndrome." "Matt was the fair-haired boy for his boss when he was with the old firm. Wallace, before he semi-retired, was probably one of the best trial lawyers in the state, maybe the country. The man was consumed by trial—nobody worked as hard getting a case ready as Wallace did and his results showed it. He and a few others like Melvin Belli and Salvatore Conti had the biggest civil verdicts in the entire country. Wallace taught Matt everything he knew. I think he wanted him to take over the firm when Wallace quit."

Matt shrugged in embarrassment.

"The prodigy threw cold water on the old man's parade though. Matt didn't like some of the people he would have as partners and he wanted his own shop; he wanted to come out with the rest of us and learn to starve. Matt has managed a few great verdicts along the way too, but the good cases are harder to come by when you aren't with a famous office anymore, aren't they, buddy?"

Matt got up to stoke the fire, hoping the subject would change. He freshened up their drinks and asked more about Adrianne's background. She ignored his question and asked him to talk about some of his interesting victories. Matt explained there really wasn't much worth telling. It was mostly all legal stuff, which most non-lawyers find quite boring. He was startled when Jake burst out laughing.

"I guess I didn't mention earlier why Adrianne is working temp jobs! Adrianne graduated at the top of her class from Duke Law School. She worked a few years in her mother's insurance defense law firm in Atlanta before deciding to chuck it." He kneaded her thigh. "She headed west to 'find herself' and also, I suspect, to get away from some guy that Mom had picked out. She plans to take our bar exam this summer and join the hordes of other young lawyers who can't support themselves in this lousy profession."

Matt stared at her, startled by this revelation. "Adrianne, if you really want to hear something interesting, ask Matt about the case he was offered against Sal Conti. He's probably not going to take it, but it makes great gossip."

Hearing the name Conti, she sat up and gestured in excitement. "That guy came to Atlanta a few years ago after a big plane crash and actually set up shop in the lobby of one of the hotels. All the victim's families were staying in the place. Everybody was so impressed with his reputation." She evinced disgust. "I thought he was nothing but a glori-fied ambulance chaser."

"Once he signed up those poor clients, no one ever heard from him again. My mom's firm handled part of the defense of the case and the other attorneys from his office didn't seem to know what they were doing. Every-body was totally appalled." Adrianne lifted her wine enthusiastically. "So tell me about your case. I'd love to see someone hang this guy out to dry!"

Matt sat forward. "I had an opportunity to see the medical records this week and found them quite interesting. Todd was clearly able to move his arms and legs when he got to the hospital, but he was unconscious from a head injury and smelled of alcohol, so it was difficult for the doctors to do a thorough exam." Matt could feel his animation increase as he talked about the facts.

"The first x-ray reports indicate he had no skull fracture. The radiolo-gist read the neck x-rays as not a problem. The neck x-ray films themselves are now missing. Todd became conscious about six hours after he was admitted. At that point, he complained he couldn't feel or move his legs. I think there are some serious questions about the medical care. For example, even if the films were negative, shouldn't they have stabilized his neck?"

As they discussed the case, Matt was impressed with her knowledge of this area of the law. She made sensible comments and asked perceptive questions. "My father did some medical malpractice defense before he started teaching law at Emory. He said lots of mistakes are made in the E.R, especially in those smaller community hospitals. Of course, they would use that against you—that they're not as sophisticated as a trauma center." As she asked questions, she stood and began to pace. Her expression became more intense and her features quite animated as she emphasized a point. Matt found himself responding with growing enthusiasm.

"You're letting this visit to the family fuzz up your thinking!" Jake scoffed. "Just because he has serious medical problems doesn't make this a case worth pursuing. The boy probably moved his arms and legs because of reflexes; that doesn't mean he could've moved them on his own if he were awake. The spinal cord was probably already damaged when he got to the hospital. Besides, if the kid was drunk then this is all his fault anyway."

Quite naturally, Adrianne began to moderate what was fast becoming a debate between Matt as the advocate for the case and Jake as the detractor. "I'm surprised at your cynicism, Jake. We're all opposed to kids drinking and driving, but Todd wasn't the driver. Besides, how he managed to get himself hurt isn't really the issue, is it?"

Adrianne gave Jake a look. "Just about everybody in an emergency room with an injury has done something dumb—that's how people usually get hurt! The doctors are still supposed to do a reasonable job treating them."

"I don't know about when or how you can move if you've injured your neck; a doctor can answer that for you." She had a pensive expression. "If they said he didn't have a broken neck when he came in, and later they found he did…then, unless he fell out of bed in the meantime, it sounds to me like someone was pretty damn wrong!"

Jake turned to Matt. "You'll never prove that a lawyer has an obligation to know what these docs are supposed to have done. All he was hired to do was sue for an auto collision." He waved his arm dismissively. "Was he also supposed to sue the car manufacturer because the seatbelt hadn't been invented yet when they made that old Chevy he was driving? Your case is as far-fetched as that would be." Jake stood up. "Anyway, it's late; I think I'll hit the sack."

"It is a bit late." Adrianne set down her drink. "I think I'll turn in also. Matt, I know it's a difficult case, but it just doesn't sound right. What happened to this teenager—to this family, really—is wrong. I think lawyers have an obligation to do more than just get their client the easy money."

She put her hand on his arm. "Conti certainly didn't have to sue everybody in sight just because Todd was badly injured. But if this boy didn't have to end up paralyzed, and the doctors caused it, then I think his very famous and expensive lawyer should've figured that out. Maybe you're the guy to take him on."

After she said goodnight, Matt thought about her comments. Her analysis had clarity and common sense. As she walked away, he also had found himself again impressed with the way she carried herself. Even at the end of a long evening and after a few drinks, she moved gracefully. Her long, slim legs were encased in tight black leggings tonight instead of the colorful Lycra running tights she had been wearing when he last saw her at The Bridge. He certainly hadn't been close to reality in his fantasy about her. Except for one thing: now he was quite sure she had never noticed him from behind those sunglasses.

4

Matt always woke early in the mountains and Grant usually slept in. Quietly, Matt pulled on his running shorts and shoes and went outside. The damp chilled his bare torso, but he felt invigorated by the crisp air and the tangy pine smell of the still morning. He knew he would be warm soon enough when he started his run up the fire road behind the house. The blue jays and the squirrels scolded him as he stretched.

The lake was absolutely flat, a huge gray mirror as far as the eye could see. Wisps of fog hovered randomly, obscuring the distant features of the far shore. He looked around at the granite range soaring toward the sky behind the cabin. The early morning sun illuminated the massive upper cliffs and high mountain bowls rising out of the shrouded morning darkness. The pine-covered canyon pointed like an arrow from the cabin toward the wilderness beyond. As always, the scene replenished his soul and made his spirits soar.

As he walked toward his running trail, he caught a glimpse of vivid pink out of the corner of his eye.

"Beautiful morning in your paradise!"

Guests seldom got up as early as he did, so he was surprised to see a familiar vision of Lycra and Adrianne's cheerful face grinning at him. She was leaning against the rail post of the porch. There was something about the way she was looking at him that suddenly made him grateful for all those hours of arduous exercise over the last several years.

She tossed her head up. "I thought I might be able to find a running partner if I got out here early enough. Although I'm intimidated with the looks of that trail you're headed for—I hope it levels out pretty soon."

"Oh, it's not so bad, I guess, it sort of levels out each time you get to the point you think you're gonna need to call an ambulance. So how'd you know I was a runner? What tipped you off?"

She laughed and pushed off the porch, heading for the trail head. "I could always claim it was your lean, well-muscled look, but actually it's the fact that I see you running out to The Bridge often in the afternoon." She pulled her hair back into a tight ponytail. "You always seem to be in another world when you run by. I was pretty sure you hadn't noticed me."

He barely managed to hide his surprise. Inside, he felt pleased she had noticed him—and a bit dishonest for not having admitted he also had recognized her.

The fire road quickly diminished to little more than a wide trail winding up the west side of the canyon. He was soon concentrating on sucking as much of the thin air as he could manage. He asked her questions—very short ones. She, on the other hand, chatted like she was on a picnic as they scrambled up the mountain.

"My folks hated it, but before law school I decided the Peace Corps was the way to learn something. Went to Nicaragua. That was something else! Learned more than Spanish, I can tell you."

"Hot-blooded Latinos?"

She gave him a sidelong frown. "Huh? Oh, no—well, that too, maybe. No, I meant how people are treated in the third world by their so-called leaders and by our government. Unbelievable."

"So what next?"

Her stream of conversation seemed unaffected by the climb or the altitude. "After that, I travelled in Europe, also Syria, Egypt and Turkey. Ran out of money fast, so I worked where I could, mostly teaching English as a second language. My Spanish and French helped there."

He couldn't let that one go without an inquiry. "I thought you said you were traveling alone mostly. How could you travel in the Middle Eastern countries without a male escort?"

"It wasn't that bad. Mostly people treated me very well. In the primitive areas I had problems a few times, but nothing serious. Also, sometimes when I was going somewhere way out, I would connect with a group. It was worth the risk to really get a sense of the local culture and to see some special archeologic sites."

She had graduated from both summer and winter Outward Bound survival courses, loved to ski, and had even tried ocean kayaking a few times. To Matt's chagrin, he noted that any questions that touched on more personal matters were deftly turned aside in favor of general information.

They came around a bend in the trail near the head of the canyon, and Matt veered off along a ridge to a large outcropping of rocks. He led her through a series of boulders and around the last pockets of snow. They worked their way up a fissure, using hands and feet and pushing against the rock with their backs. At the top, they only had to skirt another large boulder and the whole Tahoe Basin was laid out before them. The sun was just rising above the rim of the eastern mountain range and the flat promontory was flooded with its welcome warmth after the chilly canyon.

"Is that your cabin way down there? It looks so small and isolated from up here! This has to be one of the most spectacular places in the world!"

She wasn't very familiar with the area, so he pointed out Emerald Bay and showed her the white streaks that were the Nevada ski areas of Heavenly Valley to the south and Incline to the east. He also described the areas of the wild forest below that made up the twenty-acre parcel of land surrounding the cabin.

They sat comfortably in silence for a while soaking up the sun and the vista below. "So tell me, Matt, what're you going to do about this Conti case anyway? I woke up still thinking about it this morning and can't get it out of my head. I just have this gut feeling that something bad happened to that kid. I'd sure hate to see you drop the thing without trying to help them."

Matt shivered despite the warmth of the sun. It was easy to think he should give it a shot, but taking on a case of this magnitude with his small shop and shaky financial circumstances would be foolhardy. He had several cases that needed work and nobody but himself to get it done.

On the other hand, as Stadahl had pointed out, none of the larger firms would touch a legal malpractice case like this one and it was late in the game with the statute of limitations about to run. The legal community wouldn't like proving that a lawyer had an obligation to discover and investigate any other possible causes of the injury. Nobody would want to take on Salvatore Conti as well. He was one of the most famous lawyers in the country and could bury an adversary financially. He could ruin an enemy in the press and had a reputation for fighting dirty.

"I don't know, Adrianne. Like Jake says, it's a tough case and it would take a lot of time and money to do it properly. I would hate to take it on and not be able to do it justice. One thing about a legal malpractice case, if you're claiming someone else did something wrong, you sure better do everything right yourself!" He sighed. "Like you, though, I have a hard time putting that family out of my mind."

"Jake says there's only one guy with the guts and ability to take it on—that's you. He also says you won't be able to do the case without help." She faced him directly. "He thinks I should hire on to work for you and help out."

"I kept Jake up last night talking about this case. In addition to getting quite irritated with me, he told me a bit about your up and down finances. Don't get mad at him—I wheedled it out of him." She gave him an imploring look. "I'm admitted to the bar in two other states, so I could even make appearances if admitted for the case. I have a little experience in this area of law, but what you really need is a grunt lawyer. I might have to take a few weeks off to study for the bar this summer, but I've done it twice before. The rest of the time I'll be available. Besides, I'll be cheap, I promise."

Matt wondered when she had an opportunity to think about all this. The most he had managed to do in the few hours since their conversation last night was sleep. She was looking at him with an eager expectancy in those big green eyes that made it difficult to avoid saying yes. Her plea was obviously sincere.

He thought back about his conversation with Emily before his trip to see the Gleasons:

"Things are damn tight. Payroll is Friday, the rent will be due, and two of the experts for the arbitration next week want their fee in advance or they won't show up. Most of the other pressing bills are partly paid or put off for a week or so. We need some cash, Matt. Can you get the settlement check on that Simpson case or settle something else soon? Otherwise, we'll have to go into the line of credit."

He shifted uneasily in his chair. Maybe it would all just go away if he ignored it. "I don't want to go to the bank unless we get desperate. The Simpson check might be in by Thursday, if I can get hold of Ed and get him to send us the releases. After that, there are two little cases close to wrapping that might tide us over 'til I get something bigger to happen."

She sat up in her chair. When her eyes narrowed along with her mouth, she was really quite intimidating. He swiveled his chair away from those accusing eyes.

"What do you mean 'get desperate'? All that may get us through temporarily, but we have lots of expenses coming up and not a hell of a lot on the horizon. Don't forget you're going to have to pay your alimony and child support out of what little savings you've got left."

Matt gave Adrianne a look of indecision. "There's no question that if I took it on I would need help. This case would be a bottomless pit for energy and resources. I don't have much money right now and the cases that could bring in some money need a lot of work. I'm really not sure it makes sense to take it on."

They stood to climb back down toward the trail and then walked pensively for a while. She stopped and leaned against a tree to stretch her heel cords for the run down, then put her hands on her hips.

"Look here, you need help, and I need a job that doesn't bore me to death. I live pretty cheap, and I have savings from my work in Georgia so money's not much of an issue. The days you don't need me I can earn enough as a temp to get along fine. You have to wait to be paid if you take the case, so I will too. You pay me what you can, if you can, and I'll wait 'til the end like you." She gave him a salesman-like grin. "If you win, pay me something extra. If you lose, the experience alone will be worth the price." She became serious. "I want to have a chance to work with you on this."

He shook his head. She was smart, capable of pressing for what she wanted, and willing to gamble—all necessary qualities for an effective trial lawyer. "So's that supposed to be an offer I can't refuse? Okay, *if* we take the case—I'll think about it. Meantime, if you're planning to run down this mountain, you'd better get at it. I'm sure Jake is convinced I've dragged you off to some secret cave by now. Don't wait for me; these football knees won't take running downhill. I'll be along shortly."

She gave him a radiant and somewhat triumphant smile and headed down the mountain. He watched her disappear down the trail and sighed to himself. He had actually said if *we* take the case. There were good reasons, which had nothing to do with his finances, why he shouldn't work with this intriguing woman. The trouble was, he couldn't figure out how to get out of it gracefully, and he really did need the help.

5

Matt surveyed his motley crew with a certain degree of trepidation. This small and eclectic group was his secret weapon.

It was hard to describe Emily to anyone and do her justice. She was obviously Irish, both in appearance and temperament. She had a law degree but refused to practice. "Too confrontational," said she, proceeding to spend her life *in the face* of everyone with whom she dealt. This self-proclaimed shrinking violet was loud, difficult, as unbending as a railway spike, and by far the best thing that had ever happened to his law practice. The clients loved her; she could charm any judge's clerk and was smart as hell. Better yet, most of the time she put up with his eccentricities.

Emily should have been married and the mother of at least six kids. She tolerated most adults, but was crazy about any kid who came through the door. Though she never complained, Matt knew she was frustrated. Things hadn't worked out as she had dreamed they would. So she put her heart into being his secretary, personal assistant, law clerk, receptionist, business manager, and psychotherapist.

Then there was his paralegal, Mary Beth. Tall and gaunt, she sported frizzy brown hair and Coke-bottle glasses that made her eyes look huge and myopic. About fortyish, she lived for her work and politically was somewhere to the left of Lenin. She hated institutions and, happily, insurance companies fell into that category. She had apparently decided to classify

Matt as a proletariat and had proved to be fiercely loyal to him for the last six years.

One of the marvels of modern professional life was that Mary Beth managed to work in relative harmony with Matt's investigator, Clint Staley. No one knew enough about Clint to have discussed politics with him. It was, however, generally assumed that in a former life he probably had been a spy for Attila the Hun. This guy probably could have successfully investigated Howard Hughes. Actually, he may have, because no one knew what he had been before and you didn't ask. Outside of the office, his past and present life was a blank. Nobody knew whether he was married, or what he did with himself when he wasn't working. To say he was private was a considerable understatement.

Clint was a huge, laconic man with a lantern jaw, a shock of unruly black hair, and a lumbering gait. He looked deceptively slow, both mentally and physically. He wasn't. Matt had hired him based on a tip from a friend who was a federal prosecutor. His friend had said not to ask questions, to just hire him.

Matt's surreptitious check turned up little or no trace of any background. Soon, though, he had stopped worrying about where the big man had come from. It turned out he was good. He could charm a witness or, if necessary, scare them. He had "friends" who could make things happen. He could find anybody or anything. So who cared where he came from?

"Listen up, guys. This is basically an early war council for this Conti thing. I know we usually have these things in the middle of a case or just before trial, but this one could be lots of work—it looks complicated and an early jump may help. Because the statute is about to run, we have to file it while we investigate whether we want to continue with the case." There was a series of good-natured groans. Emily looked pointedly at Adrianne with a question mark in her expression.

"You've all met Adrianne." Matt waved in her direction. "She'll work on all our cases, but mostly the Conti case." They all nodded their welcome to her. Mary Beth's face registered relief at the thought of much-needed help. Emily's expression held reservations, and Clint's look was, as usual, impassive.

Emily held up her hand for attention while she made a point. "Look, I've talked to these folks. They're real nice people. Since they're what this is all about, not that pompous ass, Conti, I suggest we make it a point to call this the 'Gleason' case or 'Todd's' case from now on rather than the 'Conti' case." The moment of silence from all made it clear that her point was well taken.

For the next hour or so, they talked about the facts of the case and kicked around some theories of potential responsibility. Matt noticed that Adrianne mostly listened as the team warmed to the subject.

"Emily, we need a package of fee contracts and medical record authorizations prepared and sent down for the family's review. I'll talk to them about all that. The fee should be the standard one-third if it settles out of court and forty percent only if we go to trial. As usual, you are going to be the primary liaison with the clients and the one responsible to answer any questions." He held up an index finger. "Remember, though, I think it's important that they not feel isolated from me. If they want to talk to me, don't over-protect me."

She gave him that look, the message clear: *So who was it that thought we should use their name—and what have I been doing all these years, anyway?* He smiled to himself. If he didn't make a big deal about it, she would think he had ignored her.

"Mary Beth, you should prepare subpoenas for Conti's entire case file as soon as we've filed the complaint with the Superior Court and served Conti and his firm. We're going to want every last paper they have. When we get it, keep the original as it arrives as evidence." Matt explained: "If we find out they pulled something out of the file, then we will be able to prove it." He went on. "Break down a copy of the original file into categories so we know everything in it, can find it and will know everything that's missing."

She took careful notes as he continued to itemize her responsibilities.

"In the meantime, take his medical records and prepare a chronological summary of what happened to him from the moment he came through the E.R. door to the moment they found out he was paralyzed. Get the records of every place he has ever been treated before and after this happened—summarize them as well. Pick out his main treating docs and we'll go talk to them. Do the same with his teachers, his minister, and his close friends. I want to know everything there is to know about this kid, his background, and his family."

Matt saw Clint sitting there staring out the window like he would rather be elsewhere. "So what do you think about all this, Mr. Staley? You have anything to contribute?"

He kept perusing the view for a moment, then spoke in that low rumble that passed for a voice. "I have a few things I'd like to check out. For a start, I'll see if there was anyone else in that E.R. that day. Then I'd like to see where the x-rays went, and maybe check out the whereabouts of a few ICU nurses." He looked around slowly. "Seems to me that we need more info about the original accident. I'd also be interested in the recollection of the ambulance people about whether he could move his arms and legs. That'll keep me busy 'til there's more to go on."

Matt quietly sighed in relief. Clint was notoriously picky about what he worked on. If he didn't like a case, he would only do what he was specifically assigned, or disappear to work on one of his other client's cases. His attitude indicated he was intrigued. That was good news, not only because his effort would be greater, but also because he had a bloodhound's nose for good cases.

He addressed the newest member of the team. "Adrianne, you've got to find every case in any jurisdiction where a lawyer got sued for missing another theory of liability while handling a case. We have to know if there's any case precedent, good or bad. Look at things like whether to sue for negligence or breach of contract, or both. Also check out the measure of damages. For example, do we have to show we could have actually collected a big verdict against the doctors or hospital? I don't want to do all this only to find out that Conti doesn't owe anything because some doc was broke or uninsured."

She appeared intrigued.

He checked off another line on his list. "At the same time, I need you to be drafting a complaint to file with the Superior Court to get our lawsuit going before the statute of limitations runs out next week. Then, when we get the file from the Conti office, I want you to get to know it backwards and forwards so you can help me figure out whose testimony to take."

He looked around at the pensive expressions. It was obvious his crew was a bit stunned by the quantity of work necessary at this early stage. The enormity of the task facing them over the next year or so, if they really took on this case, was now beginning to sink in. "My job for now will be to work on understanding the medicine and seeing what some experts think. This case won't be worth a damn unless we can show he didn't have to leave that hospital in a wheelchair."

6

It was always impossible to find parking at the medical center during the day. Even after giving himself an extra fifteen minutes, Matt was still going to be cutting it close for his appointment with Harvey Goldbaum, Vice-Chair of Neurology. He stood at the elevators as the crowd of hopeful riders continued to expand beyond any reasonable chance of fitting into one that would eventually arrive. In exasperation, he finally headed for the stairway to walk the six flights with the residents and interns who knew better than to wait.

He had first met Harvey Goldbaum ten years ago when the opposing attorney had called the expert as a surprise in a case that had been going well. The guy was a devastating witness. He had white hair even then, a distinguished career, and was polished on the stand. His testimony had almost destroyed Matt's case, but he had been honest when pressed. After that experience, they often worked together on cases.

Matt and Harvey now spread Todd Gleason's E.R. records out on the conference table in the small library used by the neurology department. "I didn't have a lot of time to go over these before you came over. Since you have a time problem, I figured we could go over them together."

The doctor rubbed his hands together gleefully. "It's fascinating that the real issue here is a lawsuit against Salvatore Conti rather than the doctors— must say, I've never particularly liked him. But, setting him aside, I expect you want to know whether the nurses and doctors treated the patient right in the first few hours before they figured out he was paralyzed."

"Well, yes. I figure he was moving his arms and legs when he came in and became paralyzed later." Matt pulled out the summary he had prepared to help himself. "Also, they missed the fact he had a broken neck. To a layperson, that doesn't sound like great medicine."

"Matt, you of all people know medicine is never that simple." The neurologist pulled out his smelly pipe and began fiddling with it as he formulated his thoughts. "A spinal cord can be damaged with or without a fracture. A person with a seriously damaged cord might still move his legs because of reflexes. A cord can be injured and quit working immediately, or it can be injured and take some time before voluntary movement is lost because of later swelling." He lifted his shoulders helplessly. "Sometimes treatment by the doctor will help, and sometimes the best treatment won't do any good. Unfortunately, there are still many things we don't understand about how the spinal cord works."

Matt should have known it would be complicated. He pulled out the record and pointed to parts of it. "What about this though? The nurses say the patient is 'thrashing about.' The emergency doctor says that Todd could 'move his legs to deep pain.' When the neurosurgeon came in, he says 'the extremities moved when stimulated.'" Matt tapped the records. "Why isn't that evidence that his cord was still working? It was six hours later before the nurses wrote that he had lost his sensation and the ability to move."

The neurologist sighed; apparently, lawyers only want to hear good things about their cases. He reached for a book on the shelf and in a few minutes had it open to a schematic drawing of the spinal cord and the nerves radiating to the extremities.

"Look here, you could cut the cord at the level of the shoulders and the person's brain would have no ability to voluntarily move their legs. On the other hand, there are nerves still connected in a loop below the cord. With deep pain stimulation, these nerves may cause reflex movement of the legs on an involuntary basis."

This was becoming extremely frustrating. Harvey was having so much fun arguing the defense case that he was forgetting the reason for the meeting. Matt held up his hands in supplication. "Look, I know there's a lot they can and will say in their defense. What I need to know first is, do you think they did anything wrong?"

The doctor did not like to be rushed when he was torturing an attorney. His next comments were grudging. "Well, I must say, the comments in the records look to me like he could voluntarily move his legs when he got to the hospital. For that reason, I do think he became paralyzed later." The doctor's expression became serious. "This was probably preventable. Remember, though, what is written is very ambiguous.

"Also remember, the doctors don't write down all of their impressions and observations, and they should be in the best position to know what the boy's condition was." He jabbed the pipe stem in Matt's direction for emphasis. "I think one of the most compelling bits of evidence suggesting that his cord was functioning at the time of the doctor's exams can be inferred from what is *not* written down after the exams. Can you see what I mean?"

Matt suddenly realized what the neurologist was hinting at. He jumped to his feet and began to pace. "I see what you mean. They had to have concluded that his cord *was* functioning or they would have diagnosed a cord problem. They must have seen enough when examining him to convince them it was working!" He stopped. "Wait a minute—can't they just say that a cord problem never occurred to them?"

The professor grinned around the pipe with which he was now industriously polluting the atmosphere. "Sure, they'll probably say that." The doctor was pleased with himself as he continued. "This boy was the victim of a serious auto accident. He came in with evidence of head trauma, meaning the significant bruise on his head." He gestured with his pipe and smiled. "They did say 'rule out cervical fracture.'"

Matt considered this information thoughtfully. "Now we're talking; I can work with that!" He wrote some notes to himself and then looked vacantly at Goldbaum. "There's one thing I'm not so sure I understand. Where exactly do the reflexes they noted fit in this picture?"

Once again the professor, Harvey opened the records to the pertinent pages and pointed to the entries in question. "The reflexes are a complicated subject I need to explain. The short version is that his knee and ankle jerks were depressed on admission. That could either mean head injury or spine injury, or it could be explained by the alcohol. They will say it was the booze."

"What it boils down to is this. The case is complicated and the defense has a lot to talk about. On the other hand, with evidence of a head injury, they have to rule out a neck problem." Matt looked at his hastily scribbled notes. "There is enough evidence of some type of nerve problem when they examine him, that they have to do more to figure out why, and they have to protect his neck while they're doing it. That's where they blew it."

"You have the basics." The professor set down his pipe and seemed to set the game-playing attitude aside. "I think it may be a good case. I'll help you, but my effectiveness might have become limited. We've done a lot of cases together and for that reason, the jury may not value what I have to say."

They spent another hour going over details of the records and trying to improve Matt's understanding of the medicine. When Matt finally left, he was full of energy. Problems or not, he was getting excited. The case had possibilities.

7

Emily dropped a stack of papers on the corner of his desk. She stared out the window while Matt finished the phone call.

"All right Jeff, I understand...you'll recommend one hundred sixty-five thousand. Yeah...okay...on the strength of that, I'll go to my client... Right, I'll try to get authority to wrap it at that figure. This all presumes they'll go along with your...Well, I don't want to get my client thinking the case can be settled unless...okay—good, sounds like we can put this one to bed...Right, call me when you can confirm."

Matt hung up the phone. He smiled broadly as he arched his back up over the chair, stretching toward the high ceiling. "Sounds like Molly Peterson's case will be settling out. Thank our lucky stars they didn't take the deposition of our last expert." He winked at Emily. "The offer would have plummeted if they'd figured out what a flake he was. She'll be happy with that figure, and we'll have some time for something else, rather than getting ready for trial."

"There's nothing lucky about it. You orchestrated the whole damn thing—brinkmanship I'd say." She let out her breath. "On the other hand, who knows what we didn't know about their case?"

She looked down at her stack of papers. "I figured it would settle. The costs are about fifteen thousand dollars and there's a one-third referral fee due to the guy who sent the case in. We'll end up with a net of about thirty-three thousand dollars—I've already spent it." She flipped a sheet of paper toward him. "Here's a spreadsheet showing what we need for the next two months."

"Well," He leaned across the desk to take his copy. "We've been in the soup before. Something usually works out."

Her face brightened as she pulled a report out of her stack. "Speaking of working out, look at this! Clint's investigation on that Bergeson thing turned up some great stuff! He found two eyewitnesses the police missed. They both say our light was green."

"Seems one of them's a nun who was doing door-to-door church solicitation." Emily's smirk hovered. "Clint talked to all the neighbors, and then went to all the convents in the area! Guy's a miracle worker—pardon the pun.

"I don't know what's eating Jim Olsen lately." She stabbed her pencil at the list. "We filed their notice of appeal, but he's acting weird—and I haven't been able to talk to Mary in a long time either. That's unusual."

"Give them time—they're blown away by the verdict. Probably don't feel like talking. You blame them?"

Her expression was shadowed with concern. Finally, she moved on, thumbing through her stack, getting his thoughts, and bringing him up to date. "Also, we sent the contract down for Todd Gleason to sign. You said you wanted to talk to them. Better get at it so we can get his case filed. Mary Beth talked to them and the people you suggested. Here's her preliminary memo."

None of the information in the memo surprised him. Todd was trying very hard and having a tough time. The father was a jerk and had ripped off most of the money Conti got them. Debbie came off as a saint.

After Emily left the room, Matt picked up the phone and called the Gleason home. Both Debbie and Todd got on the line. While they were very gracious, Debbie got to the point quickly.

"Mr. Taylor, we've got your contract, but we want to hear what you think of Todd's case. Going through a lawsuit is tough. We don't want the trauma of it if we don't have a reasonable chance of winning."

Matt watched a sailboat slowly negotiate the space between the piers across the street as she talked.

"Also, what's our responsibility? What do we owe if we lose?"

Her questions were just like those Jim and Mary Olsen had asked. Choosing his words carefully, Matt said, "This isn't a simple rear-ender we're talking about. We've checked things out enough to feel the case should be pursued, but the whole process of developing a case like this is one of constant re-evaluation."

In the pause, there was a hesitant cough and then Todd's thin, reedy voice came through. "You said it looks *good* though, the case? Does that mean that...well...that the doctors...?"

Matt's head rested on the back of the chair and his eyes searched the shadows in the heavy beams overhead. "Todd—the bottom line is yes. We think they could have prevented your paralysis." Matt listened intently to the silence. "I know that's tough to hear. We can't be positive at this point, but the first expert thinks it should be pursued. He thinks more could have been done." He watched the fading glow of twilight toward the east bay. "We think Conti should have figured it out and filed...Look at it this way: I'm going to have to invest a lot of time and money to work the case up. If I didn't think we had a good shot, that would be stupid—bad business."

Debbie Gleason broke in. "Isn't that our financial risk in the long run?"

"Technically, yes. You're supposed to reimburse my expenses win or lose, but you can't afford it. So—don't worry. If things don't work out, that's my problem. I won't try to collect from you."

He massaged his temples thinking about the more than one hundred thousand dollars he would probably need to invest. He couldn't leave it at that; it really wasn't that simple. "If we lose, you also could have to pay the costs of the other side...that's tougher. I can't pay that, and their costs might be steep. Often they don't try to collect costs, and sometimes an arrangement can be made to waive them."

"Can we plan on them waiving?" There was apprehension in Debbie's voice.

Matt placed his pen directly in the middle of his yellow pad. "No...I can't guarantee that. Basically, there are no guarantees in lawsuits—it all comes down to what the jury thinks—and they're darn hard to predict."

He could hear them whispering to each other as he stared into the growing darkness over the bay. When Debbie spoke, her tone was decisive. "We have decided to put ourselves in your hands. We met you and liked what we saw and heard. We trust you will do the right thing. We'll send the signed contract back today." A stab of excitement quickly found a home in the pit of his stomach as she continued. "Try to keep us informed as things go along, please. We know you're busy…we won't bother you unless it's important."

* * *

Adrianne was bent over her desk scribbling on a legal pad when he looked in her office. "They gave us the green light—it's time to jump on the merry-go-round."

Adrianne sat up and wheeled her chair around to face him. "Then let's kick some ass. Let me show you the research I've done."

When she was halfway through her analysis, he began to relax. Her work was solid. Finally he had some help he could depend on. He stood and stretched. "Let's call it a day. Tomorrow you can tell me what you've found on collectability of any verdict."

"I looked at that just this morning. The cases are all over the map. There's no Supreme Court case on point, but there is a recent appellant-level case." She turned off her light and walked toward the door with him. "It looks like in the case against the lawyer, you have to prove what you could have gotten from the medical defendants—but probably the trial judge would deal with that after the trial is over."

"So, no matter what we get from a jury, the most we can actually collect from Conti is what the doctors or hospital would have been able to pay if Conti had sued them and won?" Matt rubbed his chin. "So we have to be sure we can show that the medical defendant with the biggest insurance policy was the one responsible."

She pointed her index finger at him and dropped her thumb like the hammer of a gun. "Yeah—the hospital. Unfortunately, that may be pretty damn difficult."

"So we could win the case big and collect zip against Conti unless we get the jury to blame the right medical defendant…and they're not even parties in our case." Matt looked down at her as they locked the outside door to the office. "That gut feeling I told you about is beginning to feel less like instinct and more like the flu." They both laughed.

The tension from the other day had disappeared. Her analysis was right on. She was going to be a valuable member of the team.

8

The burly investigator was in what might even be called a good mood when Matt met with him that morning in Matt's office. "There are a few leads I'm checking out, but I can't say I'm too optimistic at this point." His long legs terminated in scuffed black ropers that were planted casually on Matt's desk. His gravelly voice was muffled by the mouthful of sticky donut he was wolfing. "The best lead so far has to do with this kid lawyer that worked on the case in Conti's office. Word has it he was the old man's fair-haired boy 'til shortly after this case came down. All of the sudden his ass was fired—cold turkey."

"Maybe he's pissed and will help us?"

"Don't know. I'll check it out—if I can find him. I think he's somewhere back east."

Matt jabbed his pen at the papers on his desk. "Those x-rays, they're important—any luck?" The big man just looked at him with disgust.

Emily stuck her head in the door. "Boss, Mr. Murphy wanted to talk to you before Conti's deposition starts—should I bring him back?" Emily had barely had time to utter the words when Conti's attorney strolled through the doorway behind her. He blithely ignored the venomous look she shot him as she left.

As Matt stood up to greet him, he noticed the man's eyes wandering over his desk. Murphy was always on the lookout for anything that might help his case—all the better if it was none of his damned business.

Matt knew from prior experience that Lew Murphy was a master at reading documents upside down.

"Getting a bit desperate for cases, are we, Matthew? Thought I'd see if I could talk some sense into you before you start rattling my poor old client's cage." The nattily attired defense attorney levered his lean body into the other chair opposite the desk. He made a point of ignoring the hulking investigator sitting next to him.

Clint exited the office with an expression that suggested his olfactory senses had been offended.

"Hi, Lew. I've always felt it must be tough for you insurance guys who can't pick and choose your clients like we can." Matt studied his opponent while they killed time waiting for Conti's grand entrance. Murphy was about sixty, graying and with an open face and an easy grin. You had to look closely to see the shrewd and calculating intelligence behind the affable manner with which he all too often charmed the jury. He was usually reasonable to deal with up to a point, and then he became as tough and unbending as a hunk of concrete rebar. Sometimes when Matt looked into his grey eyes, they looked as flat and cold as cheap pewter.

"What's this case all about anyway? Sal was hired to represent this boy for an auto case—and he got him a bunch of money. So what's the beef?" Murphy also liked to play dumb. He would be asking similar questions a year from now. In the meantime, he would develop some stealth plan of defense you might never see coming until you were decapitated.

"We think old Sal missed one hell of a medical malpractice case." Matt responded. "When my kid chose your client, he wasn't exactly picking a bush-leaguer. Don't you think most people would expect the Prince of Personal Injury to be able to figure out his client was done in by a bunch of doctors?"

The defense lawyer smiled in appreciation of the gauntlet that now lay between them. His face never changed its friendly expression. His tone remained mild. "This man is very powerful, Matt. He has wrecked the careers of more lawyers than you and I would ever imagine. I like you. It would be sad to see him destroy you too."

Ah yes, there was that look Matt had learned to expect.

* * *

Matt had expected an entourage and was not disappointed. The distinctive high nasal tone of the notorious advocate's voice had betrayed his entrance. He was admonishing his canine companion in his usual stentorian fashion. Unlike criminal cases, taking the testimony of the parties under oath long before the trial commenced was standard in civil cases. Witnesses and experts were also deposed in order to discover as many facts about the case as possible before trial. The theory was that the process reduced gamesmanship and, hopefully, encouraged out of court settlement before the more extensive expense and risk of trial. This would be the first of many depositions in Todd's case.

Emily was almost apoplectic in Matt's doorway. "For heaven's sake, it's bad enough he's forty-five minutes late and had to bring his secretary and his wife. The damn dog is just too much! It'll probably pee on the carpet, or worse!"

"Now Emily, you mustn't discriminate against Fido, or whatever its name is, just because you're a cat lover. Open your mind to all species like the true egalitarian you claim to be." Matt grinned at her wickedly. "Now go and greet Mr. Conti and the various species he has brought with him, in a properly gracious fashion. Take him and Lew up to the conference room and offer the rest of the team coffee in the reception area—except for the dog, that is."

As she stomped out, Matt decided he would make a few calls. If Conti was making a point by being late, then it wouldn't hurt the man to cool his heels for a while.

9

Everyone was waiting when Matt finally strolled into the room. He had told Adrianne to go up early and lay out their materials on the far side of the large conference table. With this setup, Matt could concentrate on the witness and Conti had to look directly into the glaring light of the day. Matt didn't care about a view of the bay when he was working.

The seventy-eight-year-old defendant was sitting at the table pretending to look through some papers. He was heavier than Matt remembered and wasn't wearing his age gracefully. His thick jowls spread over his collar and his girth was only restrained by the vest of his traditional black wool suit. A slight rise of the bristling white eyebrows betrayed an awareness of Matt's entry into the room. He strode up to the aging lion and introduced himself, holding out his hand.

His arm hung in the air for a long moment. The florid face shifted its gaze slowly from the papers to his hand and eventually to Matt's face. The eyes were black and hooded. They studied him for a moment then, in dismissal, shifted back to the papers. "You're late. Let's get this over with."

Matt smiled and took his place directly across from his subject. "Could you swear the witness please, Ms. Reporter?" The court stenographer had Conti raise his hand. In a grating, high-pitched whine, he swore to tell the truth and then stated his name.

The litigator picked elaborately at lint on his food-stained vest in an effort to convey his lack of interest as Matt started. "Mr. Conti, I'm going to talk to you a bit about the deposition process. I'm also going to give you a few of the ground rules so you will know what to expect during the procedure."

"This is all written up into a booklet by the court reporter, do you understand that?" The old man continued to industriously address his housecleaning. "You are required to answer all questions with an audible sound that can be properly interpreted by the court reporter. Do you understand that, sir…Mr. Conti, do you understand the question?"

The voice came out as a growl. "I was teaching such things when you were still in diapers."

"Yes, sir, but we will still require a proper answer to my question for the record—that is, if you understand it." Murphy nudged his client and Matt was rewarded with a nasty look and a "yes" that sounded like the man's pet asking for a bone.

Matt continued to take the famous trial lawyer through the explanations normally reserved for those unfamiliar with the procedure. After a while, he was pleased to see the complexion of his adversary begin to compete with the hue of his bright red tie.

When Matt judged that his quarry was sufficiently irritated to have his judgment somewhat impaired, he struck for the heart. "Mr. Conti, can you describe everything you remember personally doing on Todd Gleason's case during the course of your firm's representation—that is other than signing him to a fee contract and collecting the check at the end of the case?"

The man's brows crashed together in anger. "It's been years since we handled that case. I can't remember any details about it at this point in time."

"Then if I understand your testimony correctly, you cannot remember personally doing anything on Mr. Gleason's case at all. Is that correct?"

"No, that is not correct." The witness shifted in his chair and looked pointedly out the window. "I am sure I did many things on his case."

Matt inclined his head sympathetically. "Perhaps you could give us a list of the things you are sure that you did on Todd's behalf."

There was a long pause as the witness tried to formulate an answer. "I supervised the case at every stage. That is a very important part of the processing of such a case." Matt looked at him expectantly letting the silence encourage him to list additional efforts. "I made sure that the work was done correctly and made suggestions at every point as to how to proceed with the case."

Matt tapped his pencil thoughtfully. "So you did none of the actual work on the case yourself, that you can remember now?" There was a pause during which the man's jaw muscles jumped in repressed fury. The only sound in the room was the soft click of the steno machine as the reporter caught up with them.

"I can't remember."

"Yes, as I understand it, you can't remember personally doing any of the actual work on his case?"

The dark eyes glared at him from under the beetling brows. "That is correct."

Matt shuffled through some of the papers in front of him. Now he had the bastard's attention. "In reading your letterhead, I see that the lawyer you assigned to the case was the youngest on your staff, is that correct?"

"Yes, but I had the greatest of confidence in him. He was quite brilliant." His hands flew out to the side in a dismissive fashion.

"Had he ever handled a quadriplegic case or any other case with such serious injuries before, to your knowledge?"

"I can't remember, but he was very capable."

"He was only six months out of law school at this point in time, was he not?" Matt regarded the ceiling absently. "That would make it extremely unlikely he had ever handled a case with this serious an injury before, correct?"

His jowls quivered irritation. "Yes, but then he was working under me."

Matt leaned forward and stared at the witness. "Quite true, you are the person who was personally responsible for overseeing everything that Mr. Youngstone did on the case, correct?" Sensing the trap, Murphy quickly interjected an objection, but Conti ignored the lifeline and bulled ahead.

"Yes, that is true. I supervised him very carefully."

"That would be required in a major case such as this, would it not? Namely, that all the activities of the young lawyer assigned to the case be closely supervised by a senior attorney such as yourself?"

Lew Murphy suddenly thrust his hand in front of his client. "I object; there is no such requirement in the law that has been established."

The advocate sat back in his chair, his face flushed under the shock of white hair. Ignoring his lawyer's attempt to advise him of the danger ahead, he angrily blurted his answer. "Yes, and I did just that." Murphy sat back in frustration. His client had just voluntarily established the first element of the standard of care the jury would later use to measure his conduct during the trial.

"I think it's time for a break. My client needs to visit the facilities more at this point in his distinguished career." With that declaration, Murphy stood up and practically dragged his client out of the room.

* * *

Adrianne caught up with him as he went into his office to check his messages. "I can't believe what happened up there! First you get him to admit he didn't do anything on the case. Then you get him to admit to standards we'll later kill him with. How the hell did you manage that?" Her green eyes were sparkling with the excitement of the chase.

Matt sat on the edge of his desk and rolled his neck to loosen the knots of tension. "He thought he had intimidated me, so he got impatient and let his guard down. Sometimes the lightning bolt approach works and sometimes it doesn't. I got lucky."

She crossed her arms and leaned on the door jam, studying him. "I don't know how much luck was involved. As obnoxious as he is, I'm starting to feel sorry for the bastard."

He returned her look. "Don't waste your time. The man's an old war horse and will cut our hearts out in a minute—if we give him half a chance. We'll make our points here and there, but Sal and his entourage are going to make the rest of our day as difficult as they can—not to mention the next several months—and Murphy's no pushover."

* * *

When they resumed, both lawyer and client were subdued. The witness looked at Matt warily. "Mr. Conti, did you commit to Todd Gleason that you would personally handle any aspects of the case?" The witness stared at a point just over Matt's head in thought.

"No, I did not agree to personally handle any aspect of the case."

"Do you ever agree on certain cases to handle them personally rather than assign them to an associate?" Conti was now looking down at his fingernails, inspecting them carefully.

"Rarely. I believe I've made such a commitment a few times. On this case I did not, however, and I would never have considered doing so." He pulled out a nail clipper and began to pick at his nails.

"When you do make such a commitment to a client, would you intend to honor it, or would it only be intended to convince the client to sign the agreement?" The defendant raised his head from his manicure and looked down his nose at Matt.

"I don't know how you practice law, young man, but when I make a commitment I keep it. Under those circumstances, I would take the depositions, make the appearances, and personally handle all important aspects of the case. I didn't do those things in this case because there was no such agreement—period."

Matt studied his adversary for a moment. When Conti shrugged and went back to his grooming, Matt looked over at Adrianne. She opened her briefcase and took out a small file and handed it to him. He showed Conti a document. "Perhaps you could tell us if this is your signature on the original contract with Todd Gleason?"

"Yes, of course it is. Why are we wasting time with such questions anyway?" Conti looked over at his attorney in feigned exasperation.

"Patience, Mr. Conti, I have something else I wanted you to look at here somewhere." He rummaged in his file for a moment. "Yeah, here it is. Could you identify the signature on this document please?"

Murphy grabbed the piece of paper out of his client's hand and snapped. "Let me see that." As Conti started to answer the question, his lawyer grabbed his arm and whispered fiercely in his ear. He then waived the document at Matt. "On behalf of my client I demand to know where this letter was obtained."

"We simply requested the file of the attorney who referred the case to Mr. Conti's office in the first place. Among the papers it contained was this letter from Mr. Conti to this attorney."

"Now let's get back to the questions at hand." Matt looked the witness directly in the eye. "Is that your signature? Mr. Conti, do you remember sending this letter in which you agree to personally handle the case?"

Conti stretched his neck and pulled vigorously at his starched collar. Then he sat back and folded his arms across his chest. "I did not send this letter and did not sign it. As I said before, there was no such commitment."

"Then how do you explain this letter, which is written on your letterhead, and which appears to have your signature?"

The witness made a serious effort to look both bored and exasperated. "Obviously, someone in the firm signed my name to the letter without my knowledge. They are used to signing my name and I suppose they simply decided to tell the attorney I would do parts of the case. I made no such commitment. Besides, the letter is directed to another attorney—not the client. This is completely meaningless."

Matt stared at the deponent across from him as the man casually resumed his assault on his nails. The man had no shame.

"Perhaps you could explain to us how it came to be that the letter is in the file of the referring attorney but not in the file we subpoenaed from your office?"

In the ensuing silence, the witness intently studied his handiwork. Matt heard a fly buzzing as it crashed repeatedly against the window. Finally the old man answered. "We have a busy office. Obviously, the letter was simply misplaced."

"How many other documents do you suppose have been 'misplaced' from your original file on this case, Mr. Conti?" During Murphy's lengthy and outraged objection, Matt and Adrianne smiled at each other from across the room.

* * *

"I heard the unmistakable tones of the press's favorite ambulance chaser today. How'd the depo go?" Jake dropped his body onto the couch next to Matt. Matt's feet were on the coffee table in the middle of the reception area, and his body was sprawled as he let relaxation gradually replace adrenaline.

Adrianne was curled up on the opposing couch with her head propped on her elbow. "I thought it went very well, most of the time. Matt caught him in some things that oughta hurt 'em—on other things, Conti just stonewalled. That is, while he was kind enough to grace us with his presence."

"Yeah, I thought I heard him leaving awful soon. I was surprised you were able to wrap it up that fast."

Matt pinched his eyes. "Wrap it! It was wrapped alright, but not by us. Tell him, Adrianne."

"Jake—that bastard just stood up in the middle of a question and announced he was leaving." She sat up with a look of pure disbelief. "We thought he wanted to take a break—but, he was quitting! He just walked out. Even Murphy was flabbergasted."

Matt looked at them. "The best part of the day was when I unloaded a document on him that Adrianne found in the referring attorney's file." He stared at the beams overhead. "An hour and a half of depo and then the son of a bitch just split. Said he wasn't in the mood to answer any more questions!" He shook his head. "This is gonna be a messy case."

10

It was said the elevators traveled over forty-five miles per hour on their trip to the top of the Bank of America World Headquarters. Matt's stomach had always agreed with that estimate.

Matt's old office still looked expensive and sterile. On his way down the hallway, he saw a few of the old-timers and waved hello. He noticed most of the people had their heads down as they scurried about in the rabbit-warren atmosphere of the big, busy firm.

Steven Wallace waved to Matt as he was ushered in, and then continued his phone conversation. Matt caught something about oil and tuned out. He had heard such conversations for years sitting in the old man's office waiting to get his ear. Everything the man touched turned to gold. The brilliant trial lawyer was virtually retired now and living off his investments.

As Wallace finished his call, Matt thought back on his relationship with the remarkable man sitting across from him. The only person at his former office that had been unhappy about Matt's decision to strike out on his own had been this man, his mentor. On the other hand, for all the years they had worked together, the man had never displayed any degree of warmth to Matt or anyone else, other than the necessary courtesy of the workplace.

The office was huge, with a breathtaking view of the North Bay. Any layperson seeing this man would have assumed he was a banker or accountant. He dressed conservatively and had a mild manner. While extremely intelligent and articulate, he seemed a bit shy and even ill at ease. No one would ever peg him as one of the few top trial lawyers in the country. But then, the public didn't realize that good trial lawyers were seldom flamboyant anymore. Most of them were just very careful and thorough businessmen. Conti, the subject of this visit, was a notable exception to that rule.

"Matt, sorry about the call, had to finish up a few details on a deal we're putting together. How's your son doing?" Wallace spent a few minutes on the social amenities and then quickly got to business. "Tell me something about this case you want me to be an expert on."

"I represent a young man who is a quadriplegic from a neck fracture. He was in a vehicle rollover, but we think he actually became paralyzed because of poor medical care at the hospital. We are suing the lawyers who handled the auto case but missed the malpractice case and blew the statute of limitations. Obviously, we need a top-notch legal expert to testify."

After they talked about the details of the case, Wallace sat back. "I don't really like your case all that much. The medicine is going to be tough, of course, but mostly I think the idea of holding all attorneys to this standard is a bad one. Next thing you know, you are going to be the one that missed a potential case, or someone will say you did. It's a high standard to hold us all to."

Matt couldn't quite believe his ears. He had not expected the old man to be a pushover, but he had championed the rights of injured people for years. "Steven, you are the one who taught me professionals should meet very high standards—especially when they are dealing with a serious injury. This young man lost his chance for a reasonable existence. You, of all people, know what his life will be like with no money."

The balding litigator stared out the window. Matt remembered he often refused to look a person in the eye, especially if Wallace thought they didn't like what he was saying. "Matt, a law office isn't perfect. If no one saw anything unusual and no one mentioned anything unusual to the attorneys, then they just may never pick up the other possibility. That doesn't mean they should be liable."

"That is quite a different standard than I've seen you apply to physicians and architects over the years." Matt tilted up his chin. "We both know that someone should have read the records. If the records had been read, the question why he lost his movement later should have been raised."

"The other thing is the defendant." Wallace turned to him. He suddenly looked much older than Matt had remembered. "Conti and I were struggling in this field when you were in kindergarten. Sure, I know his style's different than mine, but we're in all the same organizations. I see him at meetings. I just can't testify against him.

"You should think about that. If you go on with this case, you may never get into any of those special trial lawyer groups. You have to be invited to the good ones, you know." Matt sat in stunned silence while his former mentor continued. "Or worse could happen. He can be a mean and vindictive man; you need to know that."

Matt made a sound like someone punched him in the stomach. "All these years I thought you meant it when you got upset about the doctor's' 'conspiracy of silence.'" Matt stood. "I can see now it wasn't the principle at all—you were just upset they were getting in your way." He strode toward the door as Wallace rose. "Don't bother—I know the way out."

As he rode down in the elevator, he thought back on the conversation with Wallace. It was ironic. The man had just shown more loyalty to a lawyer he had disliked for years than he had ever shown to Matt. If Wallace had been that loyal to Matt while he had been working his heart out at the firm, he would probably still be a partner. Guess it was a good thing he hadn't.

What the hell was he going to do for a good legal expert?

* * *

Matt pulled up to the Julius Castle restaurant. He was shown to the table where Adrianne looked up from her menu. "So, I heard this is where you and Jake used to sneak for occasional lunches. I'm impressed. The waiter has been very attentive. He obviously doesn't realize I'm just a lowly peon in your office."

Matt looked around and saw his favorite waiter miming his approval with movements of his eyebrows that only a Frenchman could manage. "Lovely, yes—a peon, never."

"You heard me. Seriously, this place is spectacular. Didn't even know it existed—at least the best view of any restaurant in the city. I hope the food is as good."

"It definitely is—especially if you order the cold poached salmon. And the Caesar salad is to die for." Matt looked out at the bay from the old mansion's window. He missed the regular lunches here; it had been too long. The restaurant was perched high on a cliff right under Coit Tower in a beautiful old Victorian at the end of a cul-de-sac. It looked out at the northeast waterfront, with a commanding view from Alcatraz to the Bay Bridge.

The sunny day was fast darkening as heavy clouds scudded in from the north. The water was dramatic, colored gray in marching patches with bright, interspersed areas of blue-green. Directly in front of them was the foaming line of the ebb tide snaking across the water toward Treasure Island. In this perpetual skirmish, the brown of the delta met the blue of the ocean in an elusive contest for supremacy. The scene fit his mood.

"Didn't go so well with Wallace I see."

"It's that obvious?" Matt was startled by her perception. "I can see I'm going to need to work on my poker face before this trial."

"We've been working together for several months now." She looked up from her menu. "I'm beginning to recognize your moods—though you're still pretty good at hiding things."

"He copped out on me. I thought he would be upset at this and anxious to help. Instead he was worried about setting a tough standard and hurting his relationship with Conti."

She could see he was deeply disappointed. "Matt, you've told me a bit about Wallace. He's about retired now, right?" She leaned forward intently. "Look at it from where he stands. He has a great rep—he's fought his battles. Now he wants to enjoy his status—leave the clashes to other, younger warriors. Can you blame him for a little caution at this point in his life?"

"You're probably right." Matt was chagrined to realize she was a hell of a lot more sensitive to his old boss's position than he had been.

"There is probably some sort of empathy with Conti too. She softened her gaze. Their ages are similar—their careers are winding down. Don't you think?"

"No question about it." He colored as he thought back on his parting comments to Wallace about the "conspiracy of silence." "I was probably a bit hard on him, actually."

"Hey, he's been around. Of all people, he should understand your passion. Your position *is* right, remember? I'm sure he knows it."

He was suddenly hungry. "Let's order. I'm famished." As they made their choices under the waiter's attentive guidance, Matt glanced at her surreptitiously. The more he dealt with her, the more he became impressed with her insight and judgment.

"How'd I get so lucky to have a fancy lunch with the boss?"

"Well, you managed to settle that Barstow case—against all odds—so a bit of a celebration was in order." He handed the menus back. "Also, we've been working pretty hard these last few months and things have been pretty austere. I thought we needed to look at where we are—and relax a bit." He gave her a warm glance. "You've been a great help getting some of those other orphan cases moving too, not to mention Todd's case. Getting you specially admitted to work on those cases was a godsend."

"Do you mind a question?" She collected her thoughts. "Things are going to heat up pretty soon in Todd's case—aren't the depos and the experts going to get super expensive—soon?"

"You got that right. My plan is to try to turn over a couple more of the cases you've been helping on in the next few months. My Marley case also if we can hold these trial dates. We have a special assignment in Todd's case, so we may have a trial date about March or April next year."

"Maybe you should stop paying me for now." Her expression showed concern. "I can make it okay. I'm learning so much I should pay you! I'll be done with the bar in a few weeks. Then I can be even more help."

"Thanks, but I'd prefer to pretend I can afford you. You're valuable and should be paid. I've got a bit more room on my line with the bank, then these cases should kick in some cash."

He watched the waiter's table-side artistry with the salad for a moment and then said: "Let's let the office go while we eat—okay?"

She raised her glass and smiled in agreement. "Tell me something about Lena. How long have you two known each other?"

"I guess it's been about two years now." He sat back. "I met her at a party that my landlord threw on the Fourth. It's been stormy—but interesting—ever since."

"How so? You seem to get along well enough, at least on the surface."

"Oh, yeah—there are some good things and a few minuses here and there. She seems to want more out of the relationship right now than I do."

"Maybe you're just not ready yet." Adrianne twirled her glass absently between two fingers. "It hasn't been that long since your divorce—has it?"

"Long enough!" His laugh was a short bark. "That divorce was happening for years before it was a reality. No, I'm just not sure I feel quite as strongly as she does about the whole thing. I'm ambivalent, even though sometimes it's great. She can be a hell of a lot of fun."

"So what's wrong? She is smart, pretty and fun. Sounds like a good package to me."

"I dunno. Yeah, right, I should know myself better. I'm just bothered by the contents; something's missing."

Matt pushed back his salad. "Anyway, enough about me. How are you and Jake doing?"

She sat back with a slight knot between her brows. "We're fine, I guess. Why would you ask me? He's your best friend, isn't he?"

"Jake isn't the most communicative of friends under any circumstance." He chuckled wryly. "He is particularly silent about your relationship. Though, it's rather obvious to me he's totally taken with you."

"I'm surprised he's so quiet about us with you. I was actually hoping you could give me some insight." She blew out her breath. "You're right, I think he also holds back a part of himself. There's the Jake I can touch and talk to—then there's a hint of something walled off. I thought it was just me—maybe it's hidden from everyone." She bit her bottom lip. "He's so mercurial—one minute he's got the energy of ten men and then he's just disconnected—unreachable."

As the main course was served, they watched in silence. Matt glanced at her sympathetically. "It has a lot to do with how hard it was for him as a child, I suspect. He and his family have never had an easy time of it. His parents escaping and then coming here as refuges after the war—he was born during all that too."

She tried her salmon. "I know a little bit about his background. He's told me some about his immigration and how hard his folks worked to provide. I suspect those tough times are a big part of what drives him."

Her profile was pensive as she studied the view. "Sometimes I think he is almost obsessive about me—and that I somehow represent what was unavailable to him as a child. I think he sees me as one of the privileged. If he can own me, he can own all of them."

"I'm sure you're wrong." Matt searched her expression. "He's dated many so-called 'privileged' types—but you're different from anyone I can remember him dating. Of course, he's been with beautiful women; most of them have been intelligent and perceptive. But you confront him on his own level. Hell, emotionally you exceed his level! Maybe he's just intimidated. Don't be upset at him."

There was something disconcerting in the intent way she searched his eyes. "Thank you very much!" Suddenly she gave him an easy smile. "It's nice you're worried about your friend. Don't be. He's a special guy."

Throughout the rest of the lunch, their conversation meandered from one subject to another. As they enjoyed the meal, Matt reflected on her description of her relationship with Jake. She certainly seemed challenged and baffled by him. On the other hand, he had found himself listening intently for any evidence that she was truly in love with Jake. He had been startled to find there had been no suggestion of anything deeper than affection in her words or her tone.

11

The crew all gathered in the conference room upstairs for the update. The atmosphere became somber when he described his recent court appearance when the judge had set an early date for disclosure of expert witnesses in Todd's case.

"I just don't get it." Mary Beth threw her pencil in disgust. "Usually the court sets disclosure of experts for just before the trial date—hell, we won't have even finished our depositions. The damn judge is trying to make things difficult for Todd just 'cause he knows Conti. The establishment screws the little person again!"

"Wait a minute—don't count us out yet." Matt looked at the glum faces. "I just got one lawyer to review the case—I got a good feeling about this guy. We also have an expert radiologist, though he said it's difficult to say much without the films. We really need a good neurosurgeon; that's the key."

"I talked to the perfect guy, Matt." Mary Beth said. "I told you about him last week. He's Chief of Neurosurgery at some hospital in Burbank near LA—seemed very excited about the case."

Matt glanced at Clint. "When you told me his 'requirements' I thought I'd check this guy out, Mary Beth." Matt looked around at the group. "This is something for us all to learn from. The guy wanted a retainer of ten thousand dollars to look at the materials and said he would charge fifteen hundred an hour for review and twenty-five thousand a day for testimony.

I had heard some of these guys actually charge like that, but the jury would expect him to be neurosurgeon to the president to justify rates like that. I asked Clint to do some digging—he found some interesting stuff on him."

"Seems this guy is a part owner of this 'hospital' and named himself Chief of Neurosurgery." The big man just stared out the window while he gave his laconic report. "He mostly does back surgery and there have been quite a few complaints about how quick he is with the knife. Most of the rest of his income comes from testimony in court. Oh, and he was charged with perjury once—he got off by promising never to testify in the state of Kansas again."

During the pause, while the group absorbed the information, Matt shoved his chair back and crossed his legs. "Anyone have any thoughts?"

Mary Beth cleared her throat. "I didn't think they could use something you were just charged with against you if you weren't convicted. If so, maybe he'd do if we couldn't find anyone else?"

Matt glanced over at Adrianne. She was sitting at the end of the table with a thoughtful expression on her face. She reluctantly spoke up. "I just don't like the sound of this guy. To me he just smells bad—if he stinks to us, what will a jury think?"

"I feel the same way." Matt was pleased at her analysis. "This guy could hurt the case if any bad stuff comes out. Besides, if we can't find a good neurosurgeon, I'd rather forget the damn case than use a hired gun."

"Then prepare yourself for an unpleasant conversation with our client." Mary Beth's response was weary. "I've tried fifteen different neurosurgeons. Our friend in LA's the only bite so far. They all dislike lawyers, and none of them want to testify against another doctor—even if the doctor isn't being sued. That's why I got excited about this last guy."

Matt sat in silence for a while as they all racked their brains for a lead. Suddenly it struck him that he had once had a very pleasant conversation with a neurosurgeon at Stanford that had seen Grant for headaches. It was worth a try. "I'll follow up on a few leads for now, Mary Beth. In the meantime, you keep trying to get us an E.R. doctor."

Emily came in and sat down. She looked as if something was seriously disagreeing with her digestion. "You want to tell us what's bothering you, Emily?"

"I got a call from the defense attorney in the Olsen case." She looked around a little desperately. "He said he'd like you to call him as soon as you have a chance."

He smiled at her and relaxed. "Is that all? He probably wants to discuss waving their costs in exchange for a waiver of our notice of appeal. That would be good news, Emily!"

She didn't look any happier. "He said he couldn't talk to us any more about the case because we don't represent the Olsens anymore! He really wants to talk to you right away. He didn't want to tell me what this is about, but I kind of insisted." She looked at the floor. "He said the Olsens are going to sue you because they claim you never told them about the offer of two hundred fifty thousand dollars before the trial."

There was a stunned silence as the group absorbed the news. "But that's crazy. Of course I told them about it. Not only that, but I told them to take the money and run. He's got to have that wrong."

"That's not all, is it, Emily?" Clint's gravelly voice startled everyone as they sat looking at Emily. "Why don't you tell us the rest?"

"Unfortunately, Clint's got that right." She spoke with repressed fury. "It seems they're being represented against you by that asshole, Conti."

12

They dragged the boats off the rack and down to the water. It was going to be a great day on the river. It was only half past nine in the morning and Matt could feel the swell of the Indian summer warmth already. All around them were boaters with their uniform of waterproof paddling jackets, life vests, helmets and aqua socks. The kayakers could be distinguished by the tight spray skirts that drooped around their waists like large rubberized diapers.

As they suited up for the river, Matt looked around at the milling boaters. Mostly, they were novices, putting-in on the river here at Coloma to make the bunny run to the take-out at Lotus. The more expert paddlers would show up later when they had finished the Chili Bar run that started farther up the river. No one had yet had time to finish that run. The slanting rays of the morning sun threw a glowing haze over the scene where they hit the fine dust stirred up by the activity. God, Matt loved the crisp, sweet smell of ozone on the river.

After an hour of lessons for Grant and Adrianne, they threw the boats back on the Blazer and headed for the put-in at Chili Bar. Grant and Adrianne would be the shuttle-bunnies, taking the car back to the take-out at Coloma, while Matt and Jake ran the river. As they wound leisurely up the river through the rolling hills of the gold rush country, they pointed out places of historical interest to Adrianne. Grant's enthusiastic description of some of the old mining sites resulted in a suggestion that the two of them do some exploring and find a place to have a picnic while Matt and Jake made their run.

Boats finally in the water, Matt and Jake peeled off into the current. Matt decided to stay behind and let Jake lead. Jake had a tendency to do wild things and sometimes needed someone to pick up the pieces. The first rapid came up fast and they both eddied out to work their way back up and play in the moderate surfing wave it had to offer.

Soon they were back in the flow, heading for the next series. This one had some great play waves, with boaters dancing in and out of the churning maelstrom. Matt positioned himself for a good-sized one. Driving with his paddle, he ferried his way out and over it. He hung with his bow pointed up river and rode down the wave. Leaning to the side, he let the boat turn across the curl. Then, hollering, he pivoted in full circles as he surfed on the bucking curve of water. Finally, he shot out of its embrace into a calm stretch, relaxed at last and grinning like a fool. Controlling the exhilarating power of the river surging under him blew all the anxieties and concerns right out of his head. He felt completely rejuvenated.

Halfway down the river, they beached the boats on a sand bank and picked a flat rock for a break. The searing sun dried and baked the cold out of Matt as he let the roar of the river seep into his soul. As warm as the day was, the daily release came from the bottom of the dam and the water was extremely cold. Matt watched a hawk soaring on the thermals and felt his own spirit rise and fly with the winged hunter.

Jake had been awfully quiet the last few days. Matt studied his morose companion. "Things going alright, Jake? You seem a bit disconnected."

He gave Matt a sideways glance. "Yeah, things are alright I guess."

Matt just kept looking at him. Finally Jake broke the silence. "I guess I could use a few more cases in the office right now. Things have gotten a bit lean and it's getting hard to make the overhead."

Matt heaved a rock into the river. "You're not alone. I've just about exhausted my line of credit and only have a few cases that are close enough to bring in anything. But that's always the way it is for us plaintiff types. You're on the insurance company teat. I haven't seen you get in a financial hole before."

"Yeah, well, if you hadn't taken on that Conti case, you'd be doing okay. It's expensive and it's taking too damned much of your time. Now, you're going to get sued for your trouble."

As they sat staring into the swirling current, Matt thought about his friendship with Jake. When Matt needed someone to listen, Jake had always been there. At least, he had been until the last few years when it seemed he had started drawing into himself. Matt wondered if a good relationship would help his friend.

"How are things going with Adrianne? She going to be the one to get you to settle down?"

Jake shot him an enigmatic look that seemed almost angry. He then looked down and said nothing for a long moment. "I don't know where she is. Sometimes I think everything's okay and then she pulls back. It's like there's a barrier I can't get through."

Matt rolled a couple of smooth pebbles around in his hand. This was a new experience for Jake. The women in his life had usually wanted more than Jake was willing to give.

"You ever consider it's maybe you? You've become a pretty closed person in the last few years. Maybe she just can't get close to you." He punched his friend in the shoulder.

Jake shook his head morosely. "It seems like the harder I try, the less interested she is. Then I get mad and take off for a while and that doesn't help either."

Matt hadn't heard his friend open up this much in a long time. He could feel the pain underneath the irritation. "Maybe you need to step back and look at yourself—at where you're coming from. Think about what it is that makes her so special."

"You know what's so special about her." Jake looked askance at him. "I see you looking and watching." He leaned back on the rock. "I introduce her to anyone and she's a hit. She's well bred—you know what I mean?"

"Yeah, but keep in mind—she may not be responding all that well to your enthusiasm about her bloodlines. She may be more concerned what you think about her character than her social skills."

Jake jerked his head impatiently. "These *are* important things I'm talking about—they *are* aspects of character—and they show you a lot about her."

Matt groaned inwardly. They certainly showed something about Jake's value system. Perhaps Adrianne was feeling more like one of Jake's trophies than a significant other. In any event, Matt decided any more thoughts were better kept to himself.

Warmed and rested, they geared up to finish their run. Matt followed again and watched with growing concern as Jake threw his boat recklessly into difficult spots he should be avoiding. The river wasn't a place to act out; it could be very unforgiving. At least Troublemaker, the next rapid, was the last. Adrianne and Grant would be up on the rock overlooking their run of the final rapid.

Matt carved out of the current into the eddy where Jake was waiting for a boat full of rafters to lumber by. Jake was red-faced and snarling. "Look at those assholes taking up the whole river—that last bunch of rubber duckies almost ran me down when I was playing in that wave back there."

Matt reached over and grabbed his arm. "Cool it, Jake. Use your damned head. They can't maneuver so you've got to stay the hell out of their way." He shouted to be heard over the roar of the water. "Stay right when you hit Troublemaker; that back curl on the rock bank to the left looks bad."

Jake glared at him and jerked his arm away. "Watch your own ass—I own this river today." He abruptly peeled out into the current and headed directly for the narrow opening between the undercut rock wall and the pillar of granite in the middle of the channel through which most of the river had to funnel to reach the calm of Coloma beyond. Intent on his approach, he hadn't looked to see if the river was clear before he committed himself to the current. Too late, he heard the shouts of the next big raft that was also in mid-flow and bearing inexorably down on him as they approached the dangerous chute. There wasn't room for both of them.

For an instant, Jake tried to back-paddle to see if the fast-moving raft could forge ahead. He quickly realized the huge raft was too close to him. He then drove his paddle into the water furiously, trying to hit the opening first. Sliding just in front of the raft, he hit the wave that was curling off the wall at an angle. His kayak started to tip. Instead of leaning into the wall and stroking through the curler, he panicked and leaned away. The boat instantly rolled over.

Matt could see Jake's helmet go under and then everything was obscured by the massive bulk of the raft. The paddlers aboard the rubber boat were yelling and shouting but there was nothing they could do. Their own panic and confusion caused them to hit the opening poorly and they hung up for what seemed an eternity. Finally they pivoted around the barrier rock and shot free toward the calm below.

Matt looked anxiously for Jake or his boat, expecting that he had probably been spit through the chute upside down and should now be rolling up in the calmer water beyond the rapids. He couldn't see him. Suddenly he became aware the people on the cliff above were shouting and pointing directly below at the rapid itself. Craning his head as he jockeyed to maintain his boat's position in the eddy, he was stunned to see the hull of Jake's plastic kayak upside down and bent around the finger of rock in the middle of the whitewater chute. If Jake hadn't been able to bail out of the boat, then he was pinned underwater with the full force of the American river holding him in an airless prison. From the shouts of the people on the bank, Matt had to assume Jake was still in the boat.

The force of the river could pin the strongest man against the hull of his boat forever. Jake would be dead in minutes if he didn't get help. Matt was the only person on the river that could get to him in time. There was only one thing he could think of that might work. He would only have one shot at it.

Pivoting his boat, he arced out into the current and paddled directly for the wall. When he hit the side-curler that had thrown Jake, he threw his body toward the face of the cliff and drove through the wave with his paddle, pulling with all his strength. He slammed through into the hole and immediately leaned to the right, frantically pulling to catch the backflow of water immediately behind the rock that Jake's boat was embracing. He was lucky as hell to make it. It was usually damned near impossible for him to catch an eddy like this in the middle of a class four rapid.

Paddling up the eddy as far as he could, he put his bow against the side of the rock, trying to keep his boat from catching the current that would tear him away from his goal. The grab loop on the nose of Jake's boat was just a few inches from his hand. He stroked hard and just as he reached for it, he could feel the current grab the bow of his boat to peel him away from Jake forever. At that second Matt lunged over toward the rock. Just as his head was going underwater, he felt the strap hit his hand. Grabbing it, he quickly jammed his other hand through the open loop. Clutching the strap desperately, he felt the river dragging him and his boat away from the rock. He knew if he lost his hold, he would never be able to work his way back up the river in time.

Groping down with his other hand, he finally found his spray skirt and jerked at it frantically until it came loose. He felt his boat being stripped away from his body by the current. Now he hung from the strap in the flow of the river, bouncing against the rough granite. His hand was so numb he could hardly feel his fingers. His arms felt like jelly and the chill of the river was beginning to numb his lower body. Bracing himself against the rock, he pushed his feet and arms out while he put all his weight on the strap. He thought he could feel the boat move slightly.

He knew he couldn't hold on much longer. Heaving on the grab loop, he threw himself out sideways from the rock to improve his leverage. Now he thought he could see Jake under the water with his back arched against his boat by the river's flow. He had definitely felt the boat move that time. The thought of Jake and how long he had been without air filled him with a rush of adrenaline. Furiously jerking and heaving, he got himself up on the rock and pulled directly to the side. He could feel the strap begin to loosen in its mounting with each frantic effort.

The boat had pulled around a few feet but was still jammed tight against the rock. He realized he could use the force of the river, but to do that he would need to go underwater. Taking a deep breath, he went under using the weight of his body to pivot the nose of the boat down into the river. He was now flailing in the current like a fish on the end of a line. With the stern out of the flow, the river could now push only on the bow and maybe Jake could get a breath. Matt continuously heaved on the loop by violently flexing his arms, but as the river tore at his body and drove air from his lungs, he was losing his strength. Gradually, he could feel the boat scraping and bending as the river buffeted it. Finally, just as he was convinced either he or the loop attachment must fail, the boat broke loose and the current tumbled them toward the calm below.

Suddenly it seemed like there were helpful hands everywhere. As he thrashed around to look for Jake in his boat, he felt an arm slip around him and Adrianne's voice in his ear. "Ease up, Matt—they've got Jake out already; let me help you to the shore."

After Matt got Grant to bed, he pulled a beer out of the refrigerator and poured a glass. When the phone rang, he let the machine screen the call. He heard the distinctive voice of his friend MJ and picked up the receiver. She was a lawyer he had worked with several years ago. Over the years she had gravitated to the top of his list of favorite people. He saw her often when she wasn't eliminating depraved elements from the Oakland scene. She was a very successful prosecutor, and Oakland was a fertile territory in which to ply her trade.

"Did they let you out of your cage for the weekend, Bocci—or are you investigating me for something this time?"

"Matt, are you doing alright? I got worried about you when I heard about this—at least you sound cheerful enough."

Matt dragged the phone out on the deck along with his beer and settled on the lounge chair. "Oh—it wasn't all that big a danger. I was only mildly heroic—sounds worse than it really was."

"Are we talking about the same thing?" Her voice sounded puzzled. "I'm talking about the article in the newspaper today—you did see it, didn't you?"

He immediately got a feeling in his stomach very similar to when your airplane hits wind shear. "I actually haven't the slightest idea what you're talking about. I've been out of town all day on the river."

"Pull out your newspaper then—but I'd suggest you sit down before you read it. Salvatore Conti called a press conference and said he was filing a case against you for negligent and unethical conduct. Said you purposely withheld information about a settlement offer from some clients in a case you recently tried. He said he is going to push the Bar Association to investigate you and he is going to personally do everything he can to see to it that you lose your license. Just off-hand, I'd say he's out for blood. I also think it's going to be on the ten o'clock news."

They talked for a few more minutes and agreed to catch up the next day with details of the Olsen case and the reasons Conti was out to get him. Then he hung up to turn on the TV. Matt went and got the paper and read the story grimly while he waited for the local news to come on. Eventually the commentator led into the story. "Today the Prince of Personal Injury turned his formidable guns on one of his own brethren of the bar with claims of fraud and unethical conduct. Calling a news conference, he accused one of the city's young trial lawyers of failing to tell his own clients about a settlement offer he had received from the defendants in a lawsuit he was handling for them. The lawyer, Matt Taylor, then lost the case in trial. The lawsuit concerned a child who died from complications of drug therapy."

The familiar broad features of Salvatore Conti filled the screen in front of Matt. He stood next to Jim Olsen as he talked. "The sad thing is that most lawyers work very hard—quietly sacrificing for their clients and acting at all times in a professional manner. At the same time, an unsavory few manage to give our great profession a bad image in the mind of the public. This scurrilous and greedy conduct of Mr. Matt Taylor has not only brought shame on his profession, but has brought my clients—people who put their faith and trust in him—to the veritable brink of bankruptcy."

The commentator signed off with a brief description of the circumstances of Matt's case and the fact that the jury had decided against the Olsens.

Matt took his beer out to the deck and looked out at the twinkling lights of The Bridge and Marin beyond. There was no wind and it was crystal clear. The last vestiges of twilight had left the sky with vague hints of deep cobalt over the western horizon. The night was still; even the traffic seemed hushed except for the faint lonely wail of a distant warning horn.

Matt suspected if he attempted any public response to this beautifully orchestrated attack, he would end up sounding as lonely and ineffectual as that lost horn in the night. No one, in any event, could effectively compete with Conti's command of the media, and any action by Matt would probably just add fuel to a fire that would hopefully burn itself out if ignored. Unbelievable. Only Conti could get the papers and TV to spend any time on a lawyer bitching about some other lawyer. It was just Matt's luck to hit a slow news day.

13

Strange-looking equipment chortled and belched at Matt as he wandered deeper into the bowels of Stanford Medical Center. Open doors gave him brief glimpses of *Star Trek* control panels or, for a brief terrifying moment, even transported him back to high school chemistry lab. Huge containers lined the halls, flashing lights and humming foreign tunes. They were probably controlling temperature and humidity for esoteric medical experiments. Matt imagined Petri dishes full of strange viruses bubbling in preparation for injection into an unsuspecting bunny. He wondered how many Peter Rabbits he could save if he unplugged a few of Doctor MacGregor's contraptions. Actually, those huge freezer-like containers probably just contained Eskimo bars for the lab nerds' late afternoon snacks.

At the Stanford doctor's office, his receptionist said, "Doctor Wilmont will be along in a while; his surgery went a bit longer than expected." Magnified eyes behind thick lenses contemplated him in narrow disapproval. "I don't suppose he will mind if you wait in his office, though you might be more comfortable in the hallway?"

"Thanks, I'll just sit here and look at some papers. You think he'll be long?"

"The doctor never hurries surgery; his patient's well-being must always come first." She hesitated a moment. "Aren't you the one they talked about on TV…?" Matt just stared at her—she knew who he was; he didn't feel like making it easy. She closed the door.

The dingy little office looked like it had been arranged by a hurricane. The awards, if not the office, were about what you would expect from the Chief of Neurosurgery of Stanford University.

Matt had just eased a pile of *Neurosurgical Archives* from a chair to the floor when the door burst open. "Just throw those anyplace—gotta clean this place somehow before they move me into the new quarters. Elsie! Coffee, quick—you like yours black? They're still closing that guy upstairs, I guess—what a mess. Luckily I got paged out or I'd still be picking stuff out of the kid's head."

The doctor collapsed into his chair. "Been over most of that stuff— looks like they screwed up big-time down there with this kid. I don't know the surgeon—Escobar? Kid clearly had some deficits when he came in. Seems like you got a case here."

Doctor Edgar Wilmont was about fifty with dark curly hair receding in the middle and graying at the temples. His eyes and his body seemed to dart about the room as he fired bursts of verbal energy in Matt's direction. Suddenly he hunkered in his chair, his feet pulled under him and his knees under his chin. "I can't stand those long hours in the OR anymore; this is the only thing that relieves my damn back."

"That's great, Doctor Wilmont. We thought it might be a good case, but you never know until it's been reviewed."

Wilmont nodded in agreement. "Yeah, most of the time they don't go to trial if I say they screwed up. Let me finish looking at the records. Wish I could see the originals of the films. Anyway, this kid's got an indication of head trauma in this accident. The radiology report says 'correlate with clinical data.' That means, 'what's the damn physical exam show?' The kid had signs—I'm telling you—they screwed this up."

Wilmont leaped up and began pacing like a caged cat. He was lanky and graceful with barely restrained energy. His full features met at an axe-head slab of a nose. Matt had to restrain his growing excitement. This guy could be good in front of a jury—real good. Better play devil's advocate a bit to see how his opinion held up. "Could they have prevented his paralysis, though? That's what's always worried me."

"Here's the thing. We know that he had an unstable fracture at C6 from the films taken after he was known to be paralyzed. When he's first examined, the spinal cord is telling us it's in trouble with the changes in reflexes." He stopped and held up one index finger. "But he can move those legs some. Now they'll say that's just reflex movement—but not if the doctors don't say so—by that I mean they need to document it in the medical record!" He raked his fingers through his beard. "If it's not documented, then it doesn't exist. You've got to assume this kid's got spinal cord function until you prove he doesn't."

"Then why did he lose the function and how could they have prevented it?" As he watched the professor become more animated, Matt could begin to see why he had gotten awards for his teaching.

"You see, that cord's a bundle of nerves that will probably get over the bump it got when the neck got broken in the accident. We know that because if it were hit hard, it would have gone into shock and probably shut down completely."

He continued. "They'll fight you on it—but they really should have to help this kid out—his life's going to be terrible."

"That's something I meant to explain. The case against the docs is dead—the lawyer that handled it blew the statute of limitations. I'm after the lawyer."

His huge grin split his face. "Well, hell! That's even better! Who's the sorry son of a bitch we're going to torpedo?"

"Sal Conti."

His lower lip reached for his nose. Matt saw his eyes flash for a second and then go flat. "Conti, huh? That's heavy stuff. The guy is nobody to mess with...but...I suppose you know that." He turned toward his dirty window and stared out at the dead plants. "So, what else can I tell you about this case?"

Matt spent another hour getting an education to help with the upcoming depositions of the doctors involved in Todd's care. On the way out, Elsie stopped him. "Here's the doctor's fee sheet. I think its self-explanatory. You can leave the ten thousand dollar retainer check with me." Matt felt a part of his gut start toward the floor. He had been told to bring a check, but no amount. This one he was writing with a casual flourish might rebound like a cartoon character when it hit the bank.

* * *

"The guy was right out of central casting. He'll make our case—'course we'll probably go broke before we get there. Why the hell do all these doctors think we're made of money…they try to pay their malpractice insurance on every case they look at. Hell, this guy doesn't even have an overhead—the university pays for everything."

Emily just looked askance at Matt. "So you expected what? That he would donate his time because you're such a nice guy?"

She was right, of course. He always felt shocked when the costs of a case started to mushroom. But nothing changed; the only chance you had to win one of these things was to do it right—spend whatever it took. "Yeah, we've done it before and we always find a way. Only this one's extra big and complicated. We'll have fifteen experts before we're done, and they'll have at least that many."

"Yeah, so get real. How the hell're we gonna manage this with our cash flow—even if everything we have in the pipe comes through?"

"We'll find a way, my dear, we'll find a way."

"While we're finding a way to manage that, *my dear*, let's look for a solution to this Olsen mess." She tapped her pencil on the desk and stared at him for a while. Getting no response, she sighed and headed out of his office to go back to work.

Matt was still watching the wind whip the fog into a gray froth just outside his office window when Adrianne slipped onto the couch in his office. "How're you doing? That thing on TV wasn't a very pleasant way to come home, after everything else this weekend."

"I'm okay. It isn't such a big deal. As soon as I remind the Olsens what really happened, I'm pretty sure the whole thing'll die a natural death."

She opened the file she had carried in with her. "I looked through what I could find of the Olsen file. I couldn't find anything about that offer to settle the case at all. Did the defense really make one?"

"Yeah, they made one alright—just a few days before the trial. I was pleased as hell. I even drove up to the Olsens' place in Marin and talked to them about it over the weekend. Mary Olsen wanted to take it and be done with the case. Jim, though, he said no way. He wanted blood." He expelled his breath slowly through his teeth. "I can't imagine they'll go through with this when the facts come out."

"But how are the facts going to come out—in a deposition, or maybe a trial? I think you can plan on these people saying there was no offer that they knew about." She thumbed thoughtfully through the file. "It's not good that there's no letter to them or memo about it in your papers."

"Look—I told them about it, okay?" Matt shifted irritably in his chair. "For Christ's sake, I *wanted* to settle the damn case—the law was bad, the chances of winning slim at best."

"Hey! I'm on *your* side, okay? I'm just saying it would be nice to have something to show them—make it easier, that's all. Maybe someone knows that you told them? Was someone else at their house?"

"Nope, no memos, no witnesses—they're just going to have to believe me, I guess. Let's drop it." He sat forward and hunched his shoulders then. Restless, he moved to the couch.

She smoothed the fabric under her hand absently. "I can hear Conti now: 'So, Mr. Taylor, you're an experienced lawyer, a man who presumably knows the value of a letter or a memo to document what has taken place— and you would have us believe you actually *recommended* a settlement—but never even put it in *writing*? Not even in your own file at work?'"

"Not so great, I guess." He swiveled his body around, laying his knee up between them. "So what do you suggest—can't change the facts. You think I'm screwed?"

"Maybe we should make sure he can't say that." She patted the file. "No one has seen this—right? Let's just document what happened—now. You know, lay it out—describe it in detail."

"Nothing we say this long after the fact is going to help anything. They'll see right through that, I'm afraid."

"No Matt, don't be dense. I mean *backdate* it—for the first day of that trial. And don't look at me like that! Hell, they're lying and cheating and Conti's out for your ass. You gotta do what you can to protect yourself."

"You're crazy! That's not only wrong, it's stupid! For one thing, I don't even type those memos—Emily does—and we're not getting involved in a conspiracy."

"She already is—she and Mary Beth came to me this morning—they're pissed at the Olsens and know what happened. Emily said, 'So what's the difference when I type the damn thing? It happened—it's all true; this just helps show it.'"

"Look, I appreciate the effort to help, but—no way." Matt planted his face in his hands. "Somewhere down the line, one or more of us will have to testify—*under oath*. They're sure to ask when it was prepared. I guess the bottom line is—it's just wrong. I wouldn't feel right about it."

"Well for God's sake," Adrianne's teeth were bared in frustration. "At least talk to Mary and try to get her to bring Jim around before this goes too far, or let Clint do it."

"You know the answer to that—she's represented by Conti now. I can't talk to her and neither can Clint. Conti would go straight to the Bar—*just* what we'd need at this point."

"While you're wallowing in the goody-two-shoes role you've picked for yourself, you might want to give some thought to the other people who are going to be affected by a trip down the tubes with you." Adrianne stood, her face stony. "Emily for one, and many clients, starting with Todd Gleason. Conti's certainly not bothering with ethics!" As she stalked from the room, he heard her muttering something under her breath that sounded like "…done right…do it yourself."

He shoved the stacks on his desk to the side. No damn room on this desk anymore. How the hell was he supposed to get anything done with all this going on anyway? Swiveling his chair around, he watched gray wreaths swirl around corners and billow over the roof-tops, scattering the sun, the wind driving icy fingers of moisture deep into the body of the city. Usually he welcomed the inevitable sweep of the fog returning after a few teasing days of late summer heat. Today the chill seemed to reach through the window into his mind, filling it with uncertainty.

The phone startled him from his reverie. It was Emily. "Some guy named Willistin called from the Bar Association, boss. Says he's going to come by tomorrow to pick up the Olsen file—seems they've been asked to do an investigation. I suggested he talk to you, but he said, 'Just have it ready.' He's one cold son-of-a-bitch."

14

There were four of them on the other side of the huge conference table. They were lawyers from two different firms and claims representatives from two different insurance companies. Each was stamped from the same cookie cutter, Matt thought: short haircuts, thin ties, and drab dark suits. The only attempt at unrestrained individuality was a pair of white gym socks sported by one of the insurance claims guys. He probably wore dark socks only when he had on Bermuda shorts.

Matt had them out-numbered, though. On his side of the table sat his client, Edna Mae Marley. About ninety-five pounds of gnarled and weathered obsidian, she looked at the arrogant kids across the table with eighty-plus-year-old eyes that had seen it all. She had buried three husbands and raised six kids, some now in medicine, some in jail, others in various places in between. She was the emotional bulwark for sixteen grandchildren. They had all been loved and most raised in the old Victorian she had owned for fifty years in Oakland. All of the mementos and treasures, all the memories of a life time had been destroyed in a matter of minutes when her home blew up and then burned to the ground in front of her eyes. At least her little dog, Sadie, wasn't likely to have suffered for long.

She couldn't replace the furniture she had lovingly restored with her own hands, the photographs, the paintings done decades ago by now deceased (and some, famous) friends, but she could expect reasonable compensation from the gas company that had "repaired" her lines that morning and the city whose inspector had approved the work.

Matt had just finished explaining most of this to Judge Armister "Army" Brewster. Matt had known Army when he was the presiding judge of the Santa Clara County Superior Court before he retired to found the Judicial Arbitration and Mediation Service. JAMS was an extremely successful group of former judges who rented themselves out to litigants for help in dispute resolution.

Army flashed his famous grin at Bronson, the utility company's lawyer. "Compelling situation. I'm sure, as usual, you've brought your checkbook?"

Bronson had all the endearing characteristics of a reptile: shiny hair combed tight to the skull over skin that reflected light like the barrel of a Smith and Wesson. He sat with coiled tension, his eyes never seemed to blink. His handshake, like his soul, was cold and scaly. He was smart and tough, but Matt couldn't imagine a jury relating to the man.

"My client's position is simple. We performed the job correctly. There is no evidence that the explosion was caused or could have been prevented by our work, and it was thoroughly inspected by a competent city employee. The fact that the valve the plaintiff has mentioned is very old is irrelevant and so are the other instances of similar valve failures. The complaints she had made about gas smells in the meter area were all investigated and unsubstantiated. She has the burden of proof as to how the explosion occurred."

The judge turned toward Matt. "Any observations?"

"Sure. The gas company is hoping the jury will have no common sense. The type of valve in question was put in before 1920. It has been implicated in many leaks over the years—and four explosions. The company had many opportunities to replace this one when they came out to check her complaints of smells and inordinate gas use. We think they just over-tightened the old valve and split it. An hour later, it blew."

The judge turned toward the last pair. The city attorney looked about sixteen. If he shaved at all, his razor probably lasted a good year. He had curly hair and nervous, washed-out eyes. The city must have figured they would rise or fall with the gas company and could save an experienced lawyer for another case. "The inspector filled out his job card and everything checked out. Also, the city has immunity for inspections even if we do it wrong."

Army thumbed at his file and looked puzzled. "Gee, why was it that the job card wasn't found by the fire inspectors until a month after the explosion? Wouldn't it normally be put in the file at the end of the workday? There's an exception to the rule of government immunity if the job isn't performed, or if there's willful misconduct by the inspector, isn't there?"

His willingness to embarrass the kid was not a good sign. Army's attitude suggested they had taken a hard line in their confidential papers submitted just before the hearing. Matt wondered what had changed since they suggested the mediation a month ago.

Judge Brewer looked around the table thoughtfully. "Matt, why don't you let me talk to the defense privately, and then you and I can have a talk."

Matt's gut tightened. For some reason, this was going the wrong direction. Maybe they had discovered new evidence or had a better explanation for the explosion than yet disclosed. Whatever the reason, if today was unsuccessful, he would not see the fees and reimbursement of costs he and Emily had counted on from this case. He would also have to fit this trial into a schedule that was already jammed next month. Emily was going to be very unhappy with him. It wouldn't be the first time.

An hour later, Matt followed Army Brewster back into the conference room. The judge didn't waste any time coming to the point. "I don't think we're going to be able to settle this thing today—you may have to try it, Matt."

The judge looked at him for a minute. "There's stuff going on that doesn't have anything to do with this case at all, as far as I can see." He pulled absently at his lower lip. "How do you think this thing with the Bar is going to come down? You know, the offer Conti says didn't get communicated to those clients?"

Matt forced himself to expel his breath gradually. "I think it's all a mistake that should be cleared up quite easily, once I have an opportunity to give my side of the story. Hopefully in a proper legal setting, rather than on the nightly news. What does *that* have to do with Edna Mae's loss of all of her worldly possessions?"

"Like I said, I don't think it has anything to do with it." The judge sat up in his chair, his eyes searching the corners of the room. "But these guys have it figured that it's going to impact your practice, and maybe your ability to try this case. Or at least finance it." He looked back to Matt. "They say the talk is the Bar is really going after you—after your ticket. These guys think you may not even be on this case when it goes to trial."

Matt fought the rising flush. He suddenly felt like he had stepped into a sauna. "That doesn't make any sense at all! Worse things get done to clients every day—not to mention that the whole thing is not even true. What the heck is going on?"

"You know what's going on—the whole town does. When you sued Conti, you took on a vengeful, egotistical man—one who has a lot of influential friends who can make things happen—bad things. It's Salvatore, Matt—he's calling in all his markers. He's after your ass, big-time." The judge's eyes glinted like ice crystals in the night.

"Judge, I didn't..."

"Matt, for Christ's sake, I know you wouldn't file a case unless it was a good one—and I'd love to see you stick it to Conti. Also, I'm damn sure you'd always tell a client what's going on. That's not the point here. This isn't about what the facts are. It's about power and survival. Just like those lawyers in the other room, the people who are after you don't give a shit what really happened. They smell blood. Maybe you can stop this before it gets any worse. Don't be stubborn. Get out of the Conti case now."

Matt knew the judge just wanted to help. He certainly meant well, but the judge apparently didn't know Matt very well at all. "This guy's pushed people around for too many years. It's time somebody tried to put a stop to it. Besides, this kid I represent needs a chance at some kind of a reasonable life. Somebody's got to give it a shot."

"Somebody else can represent the boy, Matt. Refer it to an attorney from L.A. You could even get a referral fee." Seeing Matt's expression, Army Brewster seemed to deflate in resignation. "Well, you're nothing if not predictable."

15

Adrianne pulled at the cloth compartment on the back of the seat her long legs were crushed against. "Matt, I swear, if I see another damn article about the Olsens, I'll write a letter to the editor!"

"Well, they say you've got to get your publicity where you can—and Lord knows, Conti's getting lots of it."

"Yeah, and I'm getting so sick of it I might have to make use of one of these barf bags." She and Matt were crammed, with the other cattle, in tiny seats far to the back of a PSA shuttle flight to San Diego.

"Where do you get most of your cases, anyway? Could this start affecting your business?"

"Oh, I doubt it. Most of them come from other lawyers—guys I've known and worked with for years—though I did get a call from a referring attorney last week that worried me a bit." She leaned closer toward him to hear over the engines and to escape the corpulent body that was overflowing the seat next to her. "He'd been called by Conti's investigator. Wanted to know if we'd told the clients about the offers in a case I tried for him a year or so ago."

Her eyes got even larger than usual as she absorbed that information. "But that's horrible. I mean, what business is it of theirs? What was his reaction?"

Matt made a grab for the coke the stewardess was hanging precariously over Adrianne's head before the plane could hit another bump. Then he replied. "He told them to stuff it, of course—but I think he was really bothered. They can always go direct to the client. Actually there was really nothing to find out. We doubled the offer with the verdict and the client was well-informed."

She sipped at her drink and nodded. "Sure—but he's nervous at the whole idea of them sniffing around clients asking questions—right?"

"You got it. I doubt I'll see another case from him for a while…if ever. The trouble is that the whole town is talking about this—like those defense lawyers in Edna Mae's case." Matt moved his seat back the two inches he was allowed. "That's not all. Our insurance carrier on the Olsen case called and said they'll provide us a defense but they're reserving on coverage."

Adrianne eased her hip toward the aisle and angled her head at Matt. "So that means they will only pay for a defense lawyer and not for any judgment?"

Matt nodded in agreement with her analysis. "Yeah, they said they just cover negligence. They're arguing this case's allegations constitute an intentional act and so isn't covered."

"That's ridiculous!" Adrianne slammed the heel of her hand on the armrest. "You're accused of not telling clients something they needed to know about. How could that be anything but a plain old professional-type screw-up which should be covered?"

"Yeah. I think they're just playing hard ball. They'll probably cover eventually."

They stared out the window for a few minutes, glumly contemplating the ripple effect on his practice. Matt felt like he was being attacked from all sides. The night before, Grant's mother made it clear what her thoughts were. The conversation had turned downright nasty:

"For God's sake, Matt—what you are doing is stupid and meaningless. You had things going great. Then you lost that Olsen case and you took on this ridiculous case against one of the best lawyers in the country. Now you are going to lose your license and be sued for a ton. On top of that, your clients and referring attorneys are dumping you."

"Susan, that's just plain not true. I've lost cases before—you know what this business is like—it's unpredictable. Nobody's going to jump ship, and

the case against Conti might be dynamite. You should see this great expert I found."

"That's just bullshit. I talked to Jake the other day and he said you were in deep—up to your neck. He thinks you're making bad decisions. Instead of worrying about your son, not to mention me, and working on some cases that can make some money, you're chasing some god-damned windmill."

"You don't chase a windmill—you tilt at it."

"Fuck you, Matt—I'm sick of having money problems."

"Lighten up, Susan—we have these cashflow valleys all the time. I always pay you—eventually—every dime."

"Yeah, well I'm sick of all this crap. Especially when you're intent on ruining everything we built together. I talked to my lawyer. She says you have to pay or I can garnish your cases. You either pay me what you owe me in ten days or I'm going to court—and remember, in this state you're stuck paying both the lawyers."

"Go ahead—file, I'll represent myself. If the judge can't wait for me to earn something to pay you—I'll just go bankrupt. For a change, try to 'do lunch' every day with your friends on a salary you've earned yourself."

"Fine, Matt—go for it. My lawyer says I'll have preference in any bankruptcy. I'll take the cabin and sell it. Then I won't need you anymore. Be my guest."

Adrianne shifted around so she could cross her legs and lean on his armrest. "Have you had a chance to talk to these guys you're deposing yet?"

Matt huffed in disgust. "No way. I tried to talk to them before their depos—but Murphy had already convinced them to refuse. He's told them I'm the enemy. That way he can represent them, tell them what to say and—more important—what *not* to say." It was standard operating procedure. In a medical malpractice case, Matt often couldn't even talk to the doctors who were treating his client. The doctor he was suing or his lawyer always made sure of that. This trick of the trade made the cases even more difficult if you couldn't find out what the treating doctors would say about your own client.

"Is that going to mess up your chance for good testimony?"

"Hard to say. Could be bad, could even be good. At least the doctors won't know what to expect—so it'll be harder for them to sandbag me."

"Why would they do that? They aren't even defendants—they can't get hurt. Conti's the target."

"They will pretty much take it personally no matter what."

She sat quietly for a while and then looked amused. "Must say, pretty much fits the personality traits of most doctors I've known. Particularly reminds me of a certain former fiancé."

Rousing herself from her thoughts, she turned to him. "Changing the subject for a moment, let's talk accommodations."

"That's all set up; I had Emily get us a couple of rooms at the Travel Lodge out in El Cajon."

"Matt, have you ever stayed at the Hotel Del Coronado out on Coronado Island? I hear it's fabulous. I had a friend who stayed there on her honeymoon."

"Oh, it's great alright—I stayed there a few years ago for a few days when I was celebrating a verdict." He looked at her sideways. "I just figured the Travel Lodge would be more convenient since it's near the hospital where the depos are—not to mention quite a bit cheaper."

"Would you do me a favor, Matt? If you don't mind driving a little farther in the mornings, I'd love to stay at the Del. I'll pay the extra expense with my savings. I've asked Jake to take me there but he never gets around to it."

She was obviously excited at the prospect, so what could he say? The place was expensive though, and he couldn't let her pay. "Frankly, I doubt they have any room. I think they're usually booked way ahead." He started stowing things in preparation for the landing.

"They do. I checked. Actually, to be honest, Emily and I conspired to cancel the Travel Lodge reservations quite a while ago and I guaranteed a couple of nights on my credit card. I thought you might be reluctant to let me pay."

She put her hand on his arm. "Wait, listen before you decide. You can reimburse me what the Travel Lodge would have cost. You've been killing yourself…depositions, three or four court appearances a week. Things have been pretty bad on all fronts. You deserve a little something special. Besides, there's a little good news we need to celebrate." She gave him a big smile.

"You will probably find this hard to believe, but this morning I got news that I managed to pass the bar exam!"

Matt clapped his hands in delight. "That is incredible news! Fantastic! If we were on the ground, I'd hug you!"

Her expression softened. "I'll take a rain check on that." Her head assumed that inquiring angle which was becoming familiar. "So—you were worried?"

"No! No... I'm just really excited for you—that's great news!" His excitement faded slightly. "I guess you'll be looking for a real job now that you're going to be legal and all?"

She gracefully eased her seat back. "I thought I already had a real job."

"Sure you do—but I mean one where...well...you know, this was just temporary." His face suffused with heat. "You have a career ahead—and there are a lot of places out there that can pay you a real salary and give you some kind of a future. I can't right now." He held his hands out sheepishly. "I guess that's evident enough with all these problems."

She looked at him for a long moment, her eyes hidden in the shadows of the overhead spot. "So what are you planning to do about all this? Are you going to back off a bit and let the pressure ease up—or keep beating your head against this wall?"

"I probably should." He looked out the window, trying vainly to penetrate the encroaching evening's darkness. "My friends tell me that most of this is just to pressure me into dropping the Gleason case. One guy has a backline of info the rest of us mortals just have to guess at. He thinks I may get in over my head in this whole deal."

"So what do you think?"

Matt looked at her. The angles of her cheekbones were highlighted in the overhead light. "I seldom do the smart thing."

* * *

The room upgrade was obviously a direct result of the assistant manager being quite taken with Adrianne. Since the bellman was thirty seconds late, the young manager decided to escort them to their rooms himself. They walked through a lobby paneled with dark Victorian mahogany. The moonlight streamed through huge paned windows framing a lush, softly-lit central courtyard. The mesmerized manager dumped Matt at his room and then, purring about various hotel amenities, walked Adrianne to the corner suite next door.

Amused, Matt dragged his own bag into his room, hung it, and threw open the drapes and window. The crisp tang of the sea billowed into the room with the soft onshore breeze. He could see the bluffs of Point Loma straight out his fourth-floor window, its outline etched by the gleam of the full moon. To his left, he could see a sliver of the Pacific, breakers rolling sedately in the warm calm of the southern California evening. With his head hanging out the window, he almost missed the pounding on his door. He pulled the hall door open and stared, puzzled, at an empty hallway. In between the continuing knocks, he could faintly hear his name being called. It finally dawned on him the sounds were coming from the inner door to the suite next door.

Adrianne grabbed his arm and pulled him into her room. "Just look at this incredible place—and the view! All this for a two hundred fifty dollar reservation and a few strategic bats of my eyelashes!"

It was a huge corner room with west windows overlooking the ocean and the same view as his on the north side. "The bathroom has a Jacuzzi you could have a party in."

She let his arm go and gave him an impish grin. "The bed's got some interesting features too. Must be the honeymoon suite." He checked it out and began to figure out why the manager had given her the room. There were controls right next to the bed for the drapes, lights and music.

"Hey! Stop hyperventilating and check out this night air."

The balcony had wrought iron railings and comfortable chairs. There was a whiff of jasmine mixed with an earthy southwest coast aroma he remembered from childhood. The soft sound of small palms rustling completed his feeling of homecoming. They stood together for a long while in comfortable silence, their arms propped on the rail, allowing the mantra of the ocean to gradually dispel weeks of tension.

Eventually, she turned away from the view. "I just have to get my feet in that sand before I can sleep. You game for a walk?"

As they walked through the massive lobby, they could hear the sound of a blues singer in the bar. From the noise level, the place was popular. Heading to the lower level, they discovered it took them right to the boardwalk. The sounds of the music faded and they had the beach to themselves.

She swung her shoes in her hand and delighted in digging her toes in the cooling sand. The mellowing breeze fanned her hair into a dark crown edged in silver. He watched as she hung her head back and stared up at the ebony blanket enfolding them, smiling in recollection. "When I was a kid, I used to spin with my head back like this and make a million stars become whirling circles of light." She sank to the sand. "I'd end up falling on my back and still they'd spin over my head…I loved that feeling."

He traced the highlights of her features, watching them alternate from warm and glowing to faint and mysterious, as small clouds scudded across the moon. "I remember that as well. I wish I could recapture the feeling that it was warm and safe to be a part of a world that was spinning out of control." He sat next to her on the warm sand.

She rolled over and propped her head on her hands and looked at him with a question in her eyes. "So you are scared by all this—it does get to you."

"Sure. I don't like to admit it—I shouldn't, I suppose—but those stars are whirling around me and it's not fun anymore…. My world is out of control and sometimes I get a sick feeling in my gut."

She watched his face for a while and then looked out at the moonlight skittering toward them over the undulating sea. "That's certainly reassuring. I'd begun to wonder if you were really human under that veneer of self-control. If you can get involved enough to be scared, maybe there's hope for you after all."

He followed her gaze toward the glimmering ocean. Why did people have this unrealistic view of him? Of course he got scared just like anyone else. There just wasn't any point in being too obvious about it. Especially when he had to be a consummate poker player to even survive in his business.

As they walked back toward the rooms, he thought more about her remark. He wondered if she was talking about something more than just his legal problems.

When they got to the rooms, the only key they had was hers. She let them in her room and they walked toward his open door. In the entrance to his room he turned and looked at her. She was standing a few feet away, her hands in her pockets and a flush on her face from the wind and the night air. Her eyes were searching his face. He clutched for the safety of his door.

"'Night, Adrianne. Let's meet for breakfast at seven."

Her eyes crinkled with warmth. "'Night, Matt—sleep tight."

He quietly closed the door from his side. He listened but could not hear if she closed her door. Stripping off his clothes, he laid on top of his bed and let the breeze from the window gradually cool him. He pillowed his head on his arms in the dark room and stared at the ceiling. Lord help him, he was crazy about her.

16

He could have been cast as a South American hitman. Coal-black hair combed tight to his skull, deep-set eyes, and his face hollowed and pitted under high, angular cheekbones. The look he gave Matt was icy, opaque. Doctor Alejandro Escobar had been raised in Guatemala and obtained his medical degree at the University of Michigan. He had taken a neurosurgical residency in New York. He was brilliant, articulate, and as cold as the concrete floor in the hospital basement where they were taking his deposition. His eyes were the same dirty grey color. Matt wondered how he had ended up in this eastern San Diego County backwater. They had spent quite a bit of time on the preliminaries. An hour into the process and they were just getting into the meat of the case.

"So, would you be good enough to tell us what abnormal findings you elicited during your neurological exam?"

"There were no abnormal findings."

The man's affect was flat as he basically said black was white and then retreated behind his shield of superior knowledge. Well, Matt thought, there were a couple of ways to play it. Either way, this guy had obviously decided to make him work to get there.

"What about the depressed reflexes, doctor? Those are abnormal, aren't they?"

The surgeon stared back coolly. "Not necessarily."

"So normal patients have reflexes like these?"

The skin around his narrowed eyes was grainy like the skin of a reptile. "They do if they're drunk."

"How did you know he was drunk?"

A small smile with dead eyes. "He was a teenager in an accident with another teenager and he smelled like a brewery—most of his admitting symptoms fit. His labs showed a blood alcohol level."

Matt stared for a moment at the colorful print hung on the wall over the doctor's head. "Tell me, doctor, do people who have been drinking sometimes get injured in accidents?" The amusement drained from the neurosurgeon's expression and a shadow slid across his face. "Don't you understand the question? Let me put it this way: Todd had evidence of a blow to the head—he was poorly responsive, he had depressed reflexes. For the boy's safety, isn't it important to rule out a neurological cause of those symptoms before you assume it's just alcohol?"

Matt knew the guy could fight him for a while, but he would have to make some concessions here if he wanted to keep his credibility. Matt would learn a lot about him by the way he handled the next few questions.

"Counsel, this kid had been drinking." The surgeon sniffed the air arrogantly. "The films of his head were negative for fracture and so were the cervical spine films. His pupillary response was normal for someone who had been drinking. If we treated every drunken teenager as if they had a neurological injury, we would never get anything done."

The guy was tough as nails. Many witnesses would have made some concessions here. "Doctor, can you have a head injury from a blow to the head and not have a fracture?"

"I suppose it's possible," The witness shifted in his chair, his voice still flat. "But not very common."

"Can you have an injury to your spinal cord with spine x-rays that do not describe a fracture?"

"Highly unlikely, and not too relevant anyway." The neurosurgeon sat back and looked more comfortable. He was in charge after all; no reason to worry. "If you have an injury to the cord with no instability of the spine, there is little you can do about it anyway—so observation would be the treatment of choice."

"Did you personally look at the spine films or did you rely on the reading by the radiologist?"

The doctor started slowly turning a pencil in his hands. "Doctor Moore was an extremely competent radiologist—I didn't need to see the films."

"Yes, but did you look at them yourself?"

"No."

Matt considered his next approach. "Tell me, doctor, if you are in an accident after you've had a couple of beers, a rollover like this one for example, and you receive a blow to the head—can that cause you to have an injury to the spinal cord? Just hypothetically?"

"You mean just generally can that happen? The answer is yes."

"If you have a cord injury after an accident like this, can that cause you to have depressed reflexes?"

"In theory, yes." The pencil began tapping on the table.

"Can it cause you to not be able to move in response to commands from an examiner?"

The doctor sat up slightly. "I suppose so."

"And what is a positive Babinski sign, doctor?"

The doctor's eyes flickered toward the attorney sitting next to Murphy. He cleared his throat. "That's a sign of long-tract problems in the brain or in the cord. That is, damage in the neurons that go from the brain to the extremities...but it also can be found when a patient has been drinking."

"And when their cord has been damaged from trauma?"

The doctor sat back and crossed his arms over his chest. The knuckles of his hand were white where he was clenching the pencil. "That too."

Matt's gaze shifted into neutral space. "Not every kid who comes into the E.R. after drinking has evidence of a blow to the head and all these symptoms as well, do they?"

"No."

"Well then, with this lesser number of ones who do, isn't it important to make sure that they don't have a cord injury before you just assume it's all related to drinking?"

"It is and we did." Escobar's pupils looked like burnt match heads. "This kid could move his arms and legs and had negative films of his neck. It was obvious that he did not have a cord injury when I saw him."

Staring at the ugly print, Matt visualized that moment when fishing and you lay the fly in just the right spot at the apex of the riffle—the big one you've been working rises and then hits for a split-second...*wham*! You set the hook. Playing the fish after that was the fun part.

One of his big problems had been to prove that Todd's cord had not already been irreparably damaged before he ever got to the hospital. They could have argued that with a damaged spine, nothing the doctors did could have made any difference. They could still try that defense, but now they would have to argue with the treating doctor. He could see by the rising color of the attorney's face sitting next to Murphy that he was just getting it. Escobar didn't have a clue yet, but he knew something had happened. Now to work on the rest of it.

Kevin Andersen, the lawyer beside Murphy, had been quietly turning ever darker shades of crimson as Matt continued to ask questions. Finally, he broke in angrily. "That last question was argumentative. We object. Doctor, don't answer the question."

"Kevin, it may or may not be argumentative, but he's a percipient witness and you can't instruct him not to answer. Besides, Murphy is the defense attorney here—not you. It's tough enough to have to deal with one of you at a time."

Andersen was huge, a former linebacker for Cal and normally pretty calm. He was big enough that he didn't usually have to get excited to make his point. He had no hair to speak of and a big square-jawed look about him. He had graduated, top of his class, from Boalt Hall Law School at UC Berkeley and had done medical defense ever since. He was one of the best. "I can instruct him because I represent him. I'm associating into the case to represent all the medical defendants."

"You can't do that—they're not defendants. The only defendant here is Conti."

Andersen swung his chair to the side and tilted up his chin, defiant. "Then why are you treating them like defendants? I represent them and Conti as well—Murphy will handle the legal malpractice part of the case and I'll handle the trial of the underlying medical malpractice case. Now stop whining and ask a proper question."

Good Lord, thought Matt. They were pulling out all the stops to defend the case. He had never heard of hiring two attorneys to defend one legal malpractice case. At least that meant they were worried.

* * *

Matt walked in the hotel room and threw his briefcase in a corner. After this day, what he needed was a shower. Stripping off his tie and shirt, he started the water. As Matt let the hot water scour away his day, his mind started to relax. What a day! These two defense attorneys were going to drive him crazy. It was going to be fun to spend the evening with Adrianne. He could talk to her about cases and the law. She understood and cared—not that he really wanted to talk shop with her. Shoving his head under the faucet, he let the noise of the water fill his brain. The stinging flow couldn't wash her out, though; Adrianne kept floating to the surface of his mind like an answer that bobbed to the surface on the base of one of those old magic eight ball toys.

He sighed and turned the water off. Somehow these feelings about her had to get shifted to a different plane. She was just a person he could relate to and admired. It wasn't uncommon to have that kind of reaction when you work with people every day. Working together simply built bonds of respect and friendship that shouldn't be misinterpreted. It wasn't anything more. He stared at himself in the mirror as he buttoned his shirt. It couldn't be—she was Jake's girl.

She let him in almost the instant he knocked. "About time! You take more time showering than some of my girlfriends."

He dropped his body gratefully onto the massive couch and propped his feet on the coffee table.

She perched at the other end with her feet tucked under her. "Okay, you first—how'd the depo go?"

He reached over and poured some wine from the icy bottle. "Unfortunately, all in all, the guy was pretty impressive. Good credentials, articulate, and about as hard to break as a manhole cover." He chuckled. "Looked a lot like one too, now that I think of it."

"It became obvious that those x-rays are very important." He spun the stem of the glass absently in his hand. "I hope you and Clint have been able to find out something about them."

"Not a darn thing." Her expression shadowed in frustration. "Clint has talked to all the former employees and I tried to find the widow of the radiologist. She still owns a house in town, but no one has seen her in several months. Clint totally bombed out."

"Where is he, by the way? I thought he was going to have dinner with us."

"He had to go back for some hot stakeout he's working on—films of a client's errant husband or some such thing." She squinted with distaste. "I don't know how he can stand that stuff he does. In the meantime, I guess you're stuck with me for the evening."

"Tough duty. Better fortify ourselves." As he poured himself another glass, she answered a knock on her door.

"Jake!" She pulled him into the room. "What a great surprise—I thought you were in Phoenix taking depositions."

"Yeah, so did I, but it cancelled so I thought I'd swing down here and see you." He looked up from her and caught Matt's eye. "Hey there, buddy, how they hanging? You two are pretty slippery. I thought you were staying at the Travel Lodge." He looked around and whistled. "Pretty nice digs for a hard-up PI lawyer."

Adrianne gazed at him quizzically. "This is my room, Jake, I just got upgraded." Jake eyed her, his mouth a thin seam. She gestured at Matt. "We were just debriefing each other on the day. Both of us pretty much struck out."

His expression chilled even more. "Frankly, I'm not all that interested in hearing about that case." He looked toward Matt. "So where's your room? Did you get upgraded also?"

"Just a regular room, Jake, that's it right there."

Jake seemed to notice for the first time that there was a door opening into the adjoining room. "Well, that's pretty damn cozy."

Matt stared at his friend. So that was it. He was jealous! Matt felt stupid. Of course, Jake was very perceptive. He must have been sensing something. "Come on, man, the rooms were just handed out by an assistant manager who had the hots for Adrianne. Luck of the draw."

"Yeah, lucky for whom?" Jake's jaw was taut.

Adrianne looked at him, her eyes searching his face. "I suppose I should be complimented that you care enough to make a scene, Jake, but you aren't giving either one of us much credit, are you?"

Jake's knuckles were white where he was holding the wine glass. Matt could see the obvious anger, but what bothered him the most was the fear and uncertainty in his friend's eyes. He knew Jake well. He wasn't going to back down for a while. He needed some slack. "Jake, why don't the two of you take our reservations and go to dinner? Have a nice evening and talk things out. I've got some work to do for tomorrow anyway."

Adrianne looked helplessly at Matt. "Sounds like the best plan, Jake. I think we need to do some talking."

Matt stepped around his friend and into his room. He heard the door on the other side close and the lock snap decisively into place. He turned his own lock. He could hear nothing from the other room.

17

He looked around the dining room after finishing his meal. The steak had been good and the wine even better. Actually, he had consumed a few more glasses than he should have. Now that the other diners had thinned out, he could hear the faint sound of a blues melody. He should check out that singer before he called it a night.

As he ambled down the hall, the music increased in volume. The bar was packed with happy blues lovers. The singer had lazy eyes and a voice that slid warm fingers around his soul. He navigated through the smoky haze to the bar. After shouldering in far enough to get a shot of Bushmills, he searched in vain for a place to light.

"Hey, Good-looking, pull up a chair, we can find some room." He turned to a flash of white teeth in a pretty, tan face surrounded by a riot of curly blonde hair. Matt grinned. "Well, that sounds pretty good!"

"My friends will be back in a minute—visiting the facilities. I'm Marie." He told her his name and she leaned close, talking into his ear to be heard over the music. "We saw you at dinner—you looked sad sitting there by yourself."

"Just lost in my thoughts, I guess." The other two arrived back at the table and introductions were made. As they talked around and over the music, he discovered that Marie was celebrating her twenty-fifth birthday, that Sonia was married, though she obviously didn't want to be, and that Amy was a dancer and visiting from San Francisco.

The band took a break and they could finally talk without yelling at each other. Shortly, they were laughing and teasing each other like old friends. Marie and Sonia lived in San Diego. They were characters; they had a certain raucous wit and an interesting depth of knowledge. Amy was more reserved; she had a lithe grace and dark eyes that took in everything.

After the next set and another round of drinks, Marie and Sonia left to make a call to Sonia's husband. When the band came back the singer filled the room with her magic sound. Amy's eyes searched the room and eventually found Marie and Sonia in deep conversation with two men at the bar. It seemed contact had been made. She bent to his ear. "Matt, you want to walk on the beach? We will be able to hear each other. It doesn't look like my friends are coming back any time soon."

They took off their shoes and left them by the beach entrance of the hotel. The night was sultry and still, the only sound the drifting melody from the bar and the measured cadence of the surf. Matt shoved his hands deep in his pockets. They talked as they enjoyed the feel of the sand.

They reached the fence for the military base and turned around to start back. By the time they were approaching the hotel, they were well into each other's history and both enjoying the company. They slowed their pace and she slipped her arm through his. Amy had just told him of an amusing experience when she had first started skiing. They both roared with laughter, supporting each other. Matt looked up to help Amy step onto the boardwalk and suddenly saw Adrianne standing a few feet away in the shadow of the building. She had obviously been standing there for some time, watching them walk up the beach.

Matt opened his mouth to say something, but the look on her face stopped him cold. Her eyes glistened with what looked like moisture in the moonlight. She held his eyes for a long moment and then turned on her heel. Jake was not with her.

Amy dropped his arm. "Well, that was interesting."

Matt stared after Adrianne and then turned to Amy in chagrin. "It's a long and complicated story—and I'm not sure I understand it well enough to tell." He looked after Adrianne's retreating back in confusion.

Amy took his hand gently. "It was a real pleasure meeting you, Mr. Matthew Taylor. Goodnight now." She leaned over and gave him a feathery-light kiss on the cheek and then was gone.

* * *

After dinner when he got to the room, he found himself purposely making noise and hoping he would hear a knock on the adjoining door. Before he turned in, he put his ear to the door—nothing. He thought he had heard Adrianne's door shut when he was in the bathroom, but he wasn't sure. Resisting the temptation to knock or call, he crawled into bed. She might be asleep, or worse, Jake was probably there.

He laid there watching the gauzy, billowing curtain intermittently obscure and then reveal the dark headlands to the west. As he waited for sleep to overtake him, his thoughts kept returning to the room next door. What was happening in there? Was she alone? What if she knocked on his door? What would he do? He turned away from the window in an effort to get comfortable. She had never given him any reason to think she was interested in him. This was all a fantasy constructed by his overactive imagination. Not to mention too many drinks tonight. He rolled again and crushed the pillow into better shape. It was too darn hot. Should he close the windows and turn on the air? He had a big depo tomorrow, the E.R. doctor in Todd's case. Forget all this—get to sleep.

The clock glowed in the darkness—two a.m.. He had been pounding this pillow for an hour and gotten nowhere. His mind was like a video stuck on repeat—playing scenes with Adrianne over and over in his head. Was that a noise he heard next door? What was *she* doing? What was *she* thinking? He visualized her in his mind. She was lying alone in the bed, staring out at the moonlight. She rose and walked around the room, leaned against the open door to the balcony.

He heard a soft knock—was it his imagination? No, there it was again—soft, intimate. Then he saw the doorknob between their rooms turning, ever so slowly. His breath caught in his throat, what should he do? His heart drummed against his chest. The door slowly opened. Ethereal fabric blew through the door ahead of the night air. A slim white figure slipped through the opening and stood wreathed in moonlight, silk rustling, diaphanous in the wind. She said nothing; her eyes held his with a singular intensity. After an eternity, she moved gracefully toward his bed. He felt paralyzed. She slowly reached out to him.

The harsh buzzing of the alarm dragged him from his sleep. His eyes frantically searched the room—empty. Bright sun pushed him from the tangled bed sheets and impelled him toward the shower. Just a dream. His head was pounding; his mouth tasted terrible.

The coffee shop was full of people, but no Adrianne. He called her room. It rang and rang, and then the operator cut in. "There's no answer, sir. What guest are you calling?" He gave the name and room number. The operator came back on the line. "I'm sorry, sir. That guest checked out last night."

* * *

Matt and Adrianne found each other at the airport terminal. They walked silently toward the gangway, each absorbed with their own thoughts. Adrianne had arrived just before the flight was called. She had said little but hello, her demeanor distant. They took seats in the back of the plane, choosing a vacant row. Adrianne took the window and Matt the aisle, the empty seat between them a buffer.

After the takeoff, Matt sipped at a cold beer and gradually screwed up his courage. "So where'd you two go for dinner last night anyway?"

She looked down at her hands and then glanced toward him, her eyes opaque. "I'd really rather not discuss it, Matt." Sipping her coke, she briskly changed the subject. "What we should discuss is how my day went today. It was quite productive, actually. I talked to some nurses at the hospital. Nothing concrete yet, but some leads on the widow and a couple of former nurses. Clint's going to check them out."

Then they sat in an awkward silence. She had certainly made that clear. Well, it was about time somebody did. Their relationship should be one of business—period. It would be better for both of them, and much less confusing to him.

"How did it go with the E.R. doc?" Adrianne turned from the window view, her manner subdued. "What was he like?"

Matt looked up from the airline magazine he was pretending to read. "He was tough as nails—a young, buzz-cut, Marine type with no sense of humor. Though he might've been pretty honest if they'd let him answer any questions. I wasn't allowed to get much of substance—damn irritating, really."

"Irritating, you call it!" Red spots appeared in her cheeks. "I don't know how you can stand it—they're just being nasty and obstructive. I've seen lawyers do it to you before. That's not the way the law should work."

"Some lawyers are just like that." He was at least pleased to see some thawing of the cool demeanor. "I guess they feel that the protection of their client comes before anything. Many agree." Matt looked at her helplessly. "So what can you do? You complain to the court and *possibly* get a favorable ruling—you go back and by then they've just told the witness how to answer the questions anyway."

She gave an unladylike snort. "So are you just supposed to let them get away with it?"

He stuffed the magazine back in the seat pocket. "Essentially—but they lose in the long run."

She nodded as if to herself. "Each time they use tactics like that, they lose a little more of that essential element that makes the practice of law a noble thing."

Matt felt an inner thrill. There again was that confirmation. She was one of those who really cared about it also. He smiled at her profile. "Bingo. Hovering over all that we do is that old-fashioned concept called justice. Abuse it and you lose it."

18

"Ready about! Hard over!" Matt released the jib sheet and ducked under the crashing boom as the boat reeled in response to Jake spinning the wheel. Quickly, Matt grabbed the starboard sheet and hauled the flailing jib taut just as the main took the full force of the thirty-five-knot wind with a crack like thunder. The graceful giant heeled sharply into its new tack, the sleek bow crushing each attacking wave.

Matt braced himself and looked almost straight down to where the lee rail was half-obscured by the roiling water of the bay. Above him, the mast was straining like an archer's bow, the restraining blocks deep in the bowel of the hull groaning and cracking with the tension. The main was practically lying on the water. How could anything manmade withstand such force? The bow plunged again and the wind whipped a torrent of icy foam over both of them.

He felt on edge—like the sailboat—balanced between the power of the wind and the stolid weight of the keel. He was dependent on the singing strength of thin steel mast stays for his balance. Adrenalin surged through his body. He wanted to howl into the teeth of the wind.

Then, the heavy calm was almost intrusive as they glided into the lee of Angel Island. They shed wet jackets and relaxed as the temperature jumped ten degrees and the sun warmed their backs. Jake tossed Matt a beer and laid his head back on the mahogany trim of his sailboat, his face turned to the warm October sun. "So—how's things?"

Matt closed his eyes and let the warmth soak into his skin. "Okay, I guess—a little tight right now."

Jake took a long pull at his icy beer. "Yeah—Emily told me you wouldn't be able to make the rent this month. Pay it when you can."

"It's pretty frustrating. I can't get anything to trial. If I can't drag their feet into the fire, they don't pay. I'm behind on everything."

Jake loosed the mainsheet and angled the rudder to best take advantage of the warmth of the sun. "Is Susan being difficult as usual?"

"Yeah, going to go to court this time, she says." Matt looked back at the city glowing in the golden light of the fall afternoon. "How're things with you?"

Jake kept playing with the rudder as he squinted toward the sun. "Great! Everything is just fine. Couldn't be better."

Matt studied his friend's bland expression. That was always Jake's standard answer, no matter how bad things were. "You and Adrianne alright?" Jake's gaze flickered toward Matt, who added, "I mean—things were pretty noisy in your office the other day."

Jake's slitted eyes returned to his lazy duel with the elusive sun. "She's just boning up on her argument techniques—woman's got some moves though, I'll give her that." He drained the beer and flicked open another. "How 'bout Lena? She got you pinned down yet?"

Subject closed and changed—classic Jake. No point in chasing him. It never worked. "She's still working at it. The latest is she wants me to see her psych-therapist with her."

Jake's eyes abandoned the tell-tales and scrutinized Matt. "Why the hell would she want you to do that?"

Matt downed some more of his beer. "Who knows? Probably wants to enlist her shrink's help in getting some sort of commitment."

Jake held up another beer and Matt shook his head. "You're crazy if you go. Be like choosing the door with the lion behind it—on purpose." Jake set the can aside for himself. "Like they say, 'just say no.'"

Matt sat back and looked at the lush woodland a few hundred yards away. The sun was just skimming the top edge of the island. As they coasted along, the brilliant light passed through the trees on the crest and flashed like a strobe on the lens of his eyes. "Probably right, but hard for me to do. I feel I owe it to her to talk it out. If she needs moral support— that's okay too."

"Figure out what you're going to tell her?"

Matt could see the indistinct outline of his friend in the flickering light. "Got no idea." Why didn't he know what to tell her? It would be easy to let himself get serious about Lena. She had a great mind. They laughed together and had much in common. She at least tried with Grant. Lord knew their physical relationship knew no bounds. Most people would be happy with less. It was easy though, to get along when things were great. How about when the bills couldn't be paid? Would she be there when the sex got too familiar? Would he want her to be?

"How's that Conti case coming?" Jake studied his beer. "Got any experts yet?"

"Got some great ones, actually—going to shake up the opposition." As he told Jake about the experts he had found for the case, Matt mused. Jake was drawing him out, saying nothing about himself, and, as usual, it was working.

As they passed beyond the sheltering mass of land, the rigging began to clatter its call to action and the tell-tales sprang to life. Soon the sails began to resonate, cracking in response to fitful eddies from the dragon's breath just a few short yards ahead. They could feel the deck beneath them stir, groaning and flexing, its sinews sensing the test to come. Quickly they hauled on slackened sheets, stowed anything loose, and braced themselves. Seconds later the boat staggered under the impact of a freight train of moist sea air, rushing from the cold Pacific to feed the hot inland valleys. As the sails gulped huge draughts deep into their bellies, the formerly-wallowing platform was again transformed into a soaring bird of prey.

They were aimed like an arrow at the heart of the white village tumbling down the cliffs of the Marin headlands. Sausalito looked as if it had been scoured and burnished by the wind. They sped into the setting sun with seagulls dancing and pirouetting in the fading light.

19

The crew sat in silence, looking at their notes. These office meetings used to be fun. Emily finally looked over at Matt and cleared her throat. "Mary Beth will be here soon. She's on the phone—why don't we get started?"

He looked at his dispirited group. They needed to meet periodically and update each other on information and direction, but lately it had all been negative. Today was no exception. Two cases they had been depending on for cash flow had come up for trial last week. One got continued because a defense expert had to have surgery. The other was bumped because there were no courts available. No trial, no settlement offers. It was frustrating. There was no way to anticipate or control such random events. He looked at his list, trying to emphasize something positive.

"Edna Mae's fire case starts Monday and we're getting close to being ready. Thanks to Clint, Mary Beth and Adrianne, we've got a shot at that one. If we can get a courtroom, maybe we'll make a few bucks."

Emily shuffled her papers and looked around the small group. "No money for the costs though. I hate to sound like a broken record, but we need some cash for the experts and to prepare the exhibits—not to mention jury fees."

In the glum silence, Adrianne spoke up quietly. "I have a short-term solution, I think." They all looked at her expectantly. "I've been working on that Logan motorcycle case. Clint found a good eyewitness and I've been sweet-talking the claims guy on the case. I arranged to meet him at lunch with Jake a few weeks ago. Anyway, he's offered two hundred twenty thousand dollars."

Matt could feel his jaw unhinge. Most female lawyers wouldn't admit to the value of using their feminine attributes. Here was one that openly described using them—to great advantage. "That's a hundred thousand more than I thought we would get a year from now!"

She bobbed her head at his excitement. "That's why I told him that we would recommend it—if he could have the check and release here by tomorrow." Matt's face split in a big grin. She mirrored his expression. "He thought he could do that."

"Saved by the cavalry!" Emily exchanged a high-five with Clint and looked at Adrianne with giddy gratitude.

Invigorated by the news, they whipped through several more items on their list. They spent a few minutes finalizing the disclosure of experts in Todd's case, which the court had ordered for no later than Monday. Then, Matt inwardly braced himself and said, "I got another call from an attorney who has sent cases in for years. He asked about the Olsen situation." He could see the tension oozing back into the faces around him. "I hope I made him feel better about what's going on. Anyone else get any calls?"

Adrianne reluctantly looked up from her notepad. "Mrs. Andersen called in that missed-diagnosis breast cancer case you signed up last month. She was asking lots of questions I didn't like."

"Such as?"

She let out a deep breath. "Such as—can you change lawyers if you've already signed a contract?"

Matt folded his arms across his chest and studied his notes.

Adrianne searched the faces around her in the dead silence. "Hey, lighten up. I think she's still in the fold, guys."

"She may be, but there're others who aren't." Emily bounced her pen on her tablet. "Len Davis sent us three cases last year. He said no more—at least 'til he and his clients can see whether the Bar is going to dump on us."

They all stared at the tapping pen, mesmerized by the nervous cadence. Clint's gravelly drawl broke into their thoughts. "Just gonna get worse—'less we do somethin' about it." He spit into a paper cup and moved his wad of tobacco to the other cheek.

Matt looked at the big man's coiled bulk and felt a stirring of interest and hope. "What did you have in mind?"

As usual, Clint had immediately commanded everyone's attention. "Not just sittin' on our butts." They all waited while his tongue milked the chew. He spit again. "First thing's I visit that feller what called you and said he had some info—next we turn over every rock 'til we find somethin' on those Olsens."

Matt had been taking a very passive approach to the whole situation. If the laconic PI thought they should go on the offensive, that was good. "I thought that call was just a crank."

Clint adjusted his cud and shook his head deliberately, his long curly hair swinging next to his face. "Yeah, but I rang the number again—this time the guy answered. He still wants to meet you—alone."

"That doesn't make any sense—why can't he come here or write you?" Adrianne sat forward on the couch.

Matt looked at her concerned expression and then back at Staley. The PI's piercing eyes were just watching Matt impassively. "I think Clint's right—let's pull out the stops. See what you can find on him, Clint. Let's set up a meeting with this guy."

They went through the rest of his list and then they talked about the trial Monday. Matt told them about some ideas he had for presentation of the evidence. "I think I'm going to put the head guy from CG&E on the stand right out of the blocks. Catch them by surprise."

Emily laughed in appreciation. Adrianne just looked puzzled. "But will the jury get the impact of his testimony before they've heard your experts? Will they even know enough at that point?"

Clint broke in. "They'll figger you'll put him on near last—he won't be coached. Bump him a bit when he's off balance and you might hit pay dirt. It's good."

The tension had Matt's back and neck in a Gordian knot. Matt closed his notebook and stretched. He looked up and saw Mary Beth standing in front of them. Her face was pale and she had a wild look in her eyes. "What's the matter, Mary Beth?"

Her hands were visibly shaking as she turned the paper in her hand over and opened it. "You won't believe it. It's hard to imagine, but they've done it to us bigtime."

"Spit it out, M.B." Emily grunted impatiently. "You're not making any sense."

She looked around in a daze. "Our experts—they've taken a hike. Every damn one of them but Goldbaum. We're screwed."

"Calm down, Mary Beth." Matt leaned forward and waved at Emily to keep her mouth shut. "Tell us what experts you're talking about."

Her eyes cleared as anger replaced the dazed look. "I was confirming each of the experts we are about to disclose, getting dates for their depos and clearing the trial date. Each liability expert I called—all of them—said they couldn't testify for us, period. No explanation, no recourse, nada." She looked around at the blank faces and realized no one was connecting.

She took a deep breath and let it out slowly. "I'm talking about Todd Gleason's case, guys. We're supposed to disclose our expert witnesses in the case the day after tomorrow, and somehow Conti got to them. They've all pulled out—no experts, no case."

20

Nothing they did helped. Matt talked to each of the doctors. He pleaded, cajoled, even yelled at them. They were cold, sympathetic, or apologetic, but the net result was the same—they were out. The neurosurgeon at Stanford was typical. It seemed the chairman of the Department of Surgery had made it clear. The university didn't want him testifying in the case. Conti was an alumnus, big contributor, and so forth.

The timing was impeccable. If Mary Beth hadn't called, they would have disclosed these people without knowing of their change of heart. Matt figured the court would have difficulty believing they all just pulled out. They made a hasty appeal to the court for extra time anyway. The judge reacted predictably, ruling in favor of his old friend Conti, and inquiring snidely from the bench whether Matt had ever really had any experts who intended to testify. The ruling was, "Disclose your experts in a timely fashion or plan on summary judgment being granted in favor of the defense."

The whole thing had been carefully orchestrated. Contacting disclosed experts was unethical conduct, but these had not yet been disclosed. Putting pressure on the bosses of as yet undisclosed consultants was just plain old dirty pool. Murphy, who successfully argued against Matt's motion for more time, had taken Matt aside and disavowed any complicity in "the case of the disappearing experts." He had looked very embarrassed. But how in the world had they found out who his experts were?

Matt pulled out all the stops. Everyone in the office called and Fed-Exed records all over the country. Jake suggested several good names. Unfortunately no one wanted to get involved in a case without the chance to review everything and think long and hard about it. They finally found a trial-worn radiologist who gave a tentative yes, and then a brand-new E.R. specialist who was real excited about the prospect of testifying in his first case. He had only practiced for a year. They still needed a nurse and a neurosurgeon. It was Friday afternoon and they were at the end of their rope. Disclosure was Monday.

A very tired and discouraged group of people sat staring at each other. Matt looked around at his loyal crew. They had done nothing else for the last forty-eight hours but look for experts. Normally this process took months. He ticked off their options on his fingers. "One. Name the people that finked out on us—try to replace them with another name later. Two. Name someone who has never looked at the case—and replace them later if they won't come through. The judge will reject the first two options, by the way. Three. Find two people in the next two hours. Four. Give up." He gave a crooked smile. "Want to vote on it?"

Clint pulled his can out of his hip pocket and took a pinch of chew. "It ain't right. They're not going to get away with this screw-job—I'm just not gonna let them do it to that nice family." He stuffed the brown lump down in his cheek. "Got a name. Good nurse. Don't ask how I got her though." Matt looked at Adrianne who had her head cocked to the side, looking at Clint in bewilderment. The burly investigator looked at the faces around him and spit into his cup. His mouth turned up slightly at the edges. "They can put some pressure on folks—well—so can we."

Matt's gaze went to the ceiling. What the heck did Clint mean? Who had he pressured? What had he done to get this person? What if the defense found out about it—whatever it was? Knowing Clint, they probably never would.

"At this point, we're not going to send any gift horses to the dentist, Clint. Give Mary Beth the details. Problem is—all this is for nothing without a good neurosurgeon." He stood up and shrugged. "Back to the phones."

* * *

When he got to his office, Adrianne followed him in and sat down on the couch. He sank slowly into his chair and closed his eyes. He just couldn't be positive anymore. This expert thing was devastating. "I gotta say, I'm pretty discouraged. Hate to admit it, but it looks like they're going to get away with this. Hard-ball is a game I'm used to, but this is more like World War III—and we just got nuked."

"Is it the insurance carrier? If so, why are they acting this way? It's just a lawsuit—they get them every day."

"No, they're probably involved in all this, but this is the monstrous ego of Mr. Conti at work. He's never been sued, and he's acting way more childish about it than most doctors." Matt pressed his fingers into his temples. "Doctors being weird about it, that I can accept to some degree—they're afraid of what they don't understand. But Conti sues people for a living—this reaction is sick."

Adrianne sat forward. "Busman's holiday syndrome."

"More like Rommel responding to an attack from a boys' school with a full division of tanks and phosphorus bombs."

"Not a good metaphor." She followed his pacing. "He may be Rommel, but I think he's scared that you're Patton."

"I have an idea for our elusive surgeon." She tapped on her front teeth with her nail pensively. "I don't know if it'll work, but I called my mom today and she gave me the green light."

Matt stopped pacing and sat down next to her. "I'm all ears, but what's your mom have to do with your idea?"

"Henry Roberson's an old family friend—I think he saved my grandmother's life years ago." She took a deep breath. "Anyway, my mom has used him as a witness a few times and she said he's good." Matt nodded encouragingly. "The thing is, he's pretty old, like eighties I mean, much older than Conti, and I just don't know whether it would work. I mostly think of him as a sweet old man who's always come to family get-togethers."

She stuck out her hands defensively. "Now, I have no idea if Doc will do this, or how good he'll be if he does. But we seem to be down to the short strokes."

"What's to lose at this point—right? Any idea is worth a shot." Matt leaned his elbows on his knees and watched her. She was very nervous and intense. She had, obviously, gotten very worked up about this situation, and had beaten the bushes vigorously. Adrianne's concept of fair play had been violated. She was angry and determined to not let them get away with it. Matt sat back. "Well, he might be fine. He is a neurosurgeon though?"

"Oh yeah, I forgot to mention that part. He's an emeritus professor now, but he was chairman of the Department of Neurosurgery at Emory University until about ten years ago—and, decades ago I think, he was the same at Harvard. He was a big wheel. I didn't want to say anything until I saw what you thought."

Hope and energy coursed through him. "Wow, that sounds fabulous. What do we have to do to see if he'll do it?"

"Basically send him the records and the depos. I talked to him at noon and he said the case sounded interesting. He also said we could put his name down in our disclosure—subject to his review of the file, of course."

"You're brilliant!"

She looked over at him, her cheeks were flushed with excitement. "I love it when you look happy. Not often lately."

"Hey, you two, what are you so happy about?" They looked up to see Jake leaning in the doorway.

Adrianne stood and went over to him. "We've been busting our tails to solve this curve Conti threw at us, and we think we just might have done it."

"I'd have thought it impossible for you guys to fix this problem." Jake whistled softly. "No wonder you're so excited. Any of those guys I suggested work out, Matt?"

"Hey, they were appreciated, we tried them—every damn one. No luck though, just too short on the notice. I think Adrianne may have saved the day in the meantime."

"Well, good for you, sweetheart." Jake looked down at Adrianne with a soft, loving expression. "Sounds like a night for celebrating."

She looked up at him and slipped her arm through his. Jake waved at Matt. "Well, we're off for the weekend, old buddy. See you Monday."

"Okay guys, have fun." He watched them walk across the office, arms around each other. Looked like they were finally getting it back on track. That was great for both of them—about time. He sat there in the silent office. So—if it was so great for them, why did he have a sick feeling in his gut?

21

In the Alameda County Presiding Judge's courtroom, the restrained energy and tension were palpable. Apprehension and anticipation crackled in the air between somberly uniformed gladiators armed with heavy briefcases. Their honed witnesses were prepared for the thrust designed to gut their opponent's case. Who would be picked for battle? If picked, for whom would the thumbs be turned earthward, their case defeated, the client's hopes draining like lifeblood into the sand of the legal arena?

Ninety percent of the suits were blue; the rest brown, colors they had been told from legal puberty would project warmth and sincerity. Red ties flashed here and there, intended to subliminally project power and strength. Occasionally a grey suit would enter, obviously either poorly trained or planning to try its case before a judge rather than a jury. Small knots of old pros murmured to each other, their conversations punctuated by bursts of laughter intended to demonstrate their state of confidence and relaxation.

All a veneer of deception, Matt mused, his experienced eye knowing to look for the shaking hands, the flickering gaze, and the brittle edge to the merriment. All of them, especially the pros, were wound to the breaking point, either by careful preparation or by an uncomfortable awareness of a lack thereof. Soon the battle might be joined, years of effort, and the economic or emotional life of their client in the balance. Fifty cases were set for the Monday morning cattle call, the master trial calendar. There were only five judges available. Many cases would settle, but most would be bumped for another call—months later. Five lucky, nervous groups of litigants would finally face some form of justice, meted out by twelve people, most of whom thought they hated lawyers and lawsuits but, despite monumental efforts, had been unable to avoid serving.

Matt was nervous too, but not for lack of effort. Other than the expert problem with Todd's case, he'd done nothing else for two weeks but prepare for Edna Mae's trial. He looked around at his fellow supplicants to the blind lady's altar. He understood them and fought with them as a brother with his siblings. Tough-talking, hardworking, and hard-playing, they were as competitive as most professional athletes. They were a study in the art of intimidation. Matt thought it was interesting though, that what drove many of them, beyond the money, even beyond the pure competitive urge, was a basic fear of failure. He knew old war horses who had tried two hundred cases, big and little, won and lost, but every time they stood to pick a jury, they were as nervous as a kid giving his first speech. They were the dangerous ones.

"All rise, the Superior Court of the County of Alameda is now in session, Honorable Charles Dunken presiding." The mass of humanity rose and then sat. Dead silence fell over the big old courtroom. With some presiding judges, you could hardly hear the calendar call for the murmur of voices, but not in Judge Dunken's courtroom. He'd been presiding judge for a year and he ran a tight ship. Matt's case was fifteenth on the list and the ones ahead of his case were falling like kamikazes. Some were continued, others had been settled. After number fourteen, there was still one judge left.

The clerk intoned, "*Marley v. California Gas and Electric, et al.*"

Matt and the other lawyers leaped to their feet. "Ready for the plaintiff, Your Honor, Matthew Taylor appearing." The others gave their appearances for the record.

The judge looked up at the four attorneys with a frown on his ruddy face. "Here again? Can't you guys get this case settled? Go see Judge Harmond and give it another shot. If not, you're assigned to Judge McGee to start picking a jury at eleven this morning."

Thank God. He had a courtroom and a good judge. Matt felt a thrill of anticipation flash up and down his spine. That charge of current through his body reminded him there was another wonderful thing about what he did—it was exciting and a heck of a lot of fun.

They spent an hour with the settlement judge and then Matt was sent out to caucus with his client, Edna Mae. "The bottom-line is, they say they'll give us a hundred thousand right now and not a penny more. They don't guarantee that amount will be there much longer if we start the trial."

She looked at him from a face that had seen many chances come and go over the years. The skin was tired, but the eyes were crackling with wisdom and energy. "So you think they mean it when they say the offer may not be there much longer?"

"Sometimes they do. I can't guarantee they won't withdraw it, especially if things don't go well for us. But I suspect it's a negotiating ploy. If things go as we hope in the trial, then maybe there'll be more."

She nodded thoughtfully. "Well, I can't do much to replace my house for that kind of money. I say, let's see how it goes."

Matt went back in and told them it was time to pick the jury. Most of the money was coming from the City. The gas guys obviously weren't too worried yet. He needed her to sign a letter about the rejected offer, especially after the Olsen problem, but he thought she had made the right decision. He had a few things up his sleeve.

As they picked the jury, Matt thought about his opening evidence. He had arranged for his first expert to sit just outside the courtroom so the defense would assume he would be the first to testify. If the timing went right, he might be able to surprise them and catch the gas company's big man unprepared.

Sure enough, the voir dire questions for the jury went fast and then Matt gave an opening statement designed to be short and punchy. The defense said they would do their opening statements when he finished with his witnesses. He loved it when they made that mistake. This way he had the jury's attention first. With any luck, he might have managed to do enough damage to convince the jury before they had their say. Sometimes they had a specific reason to reserve their statement until later. Yet, most of the time it was just lazy lawyering.

Judge McGee looked deliberately around the quiet courtroom, his white hair askew and his pale blue eyes squinting over his reading glasses. His eyes finally came to rest on Matt. "Mr. Taylor, you may proceed with your first witness."

Matt moved from behind the lectern where he had kept his notes for the opening statement. "Thank you, Your Honor. Plaintiff will call to the stand Mr. Stan Carson, California Gas and Electric, Vice President for Engineering and Service."

A startled look passed between Carson and Berl Bronson, the utility's attorney. Bronson flashed a venomous look toward Matt and then shuttered it quickly when he caught his opponent's amused gaze.

"Please approach the witness stand and be sworn, Mr. Carson." The tall, overweight engineer put his hand on the Bible. Matt could see a slight tremor in his hands and a thin film of sweat on his forehead. The corpulent body eased into the witness chair and the clerk adjusted the microphone.

Matt paused at his table and left the participants hanging in a pregnant hush. He loved this moment. The subject was in position, brush and color at hand. All that was necessary was a stroke of artistry and a touch of inspiration, and the outline of the case would begin to emerge. Sometimes the ultimate result was what you intended, possibly even brilliant, sometimes an unappealing failure. The plaintiff had the first, unique opportunity to create an image of the case on the blank canvas of the jury's collective mind. He let his gaze wander slowly around the huge old oak-paneled courtroom. He looked toward the jurors, and eventually allowed his gaze to rest on Mr. Carson. Sure enough, after a moment of heavy silence, the witness dropped his eyes to his hands. It was time.

"Mr. Carson, as the head of service, you become aware of all gas explosions and fires of gas origin in the Oakland area, do you not?"

The witness sucked in air and looked like a man with a sudden pain in his chest. It was supposed to start easy and build, not open with a roundhouse punch to the heart. He made a visible effort to calm himself. "Yes, I suppose they come to my attention at one time or another—most of them, that is."

"Well, actually, aren't they *all* required to come to your attention? So you can take steps to change any dangerous situations?"

"Yes." His back straightened.

Matt waited a beat. "How many have there been in Oakland in the last ten years?"

"Objection, Your Honor—that's over-broad and doesn't have anything to do with this case."

"It does seem a bit all-encompassing, counsel." The judge said to Matt. "The objection will be sustained."

Matt smiled as if he had planned the objection and the ruling. "Thank you, Your Honor. Mr. Carson, how many houses have there been that the fire inspectors felt involved explosions and/or fires in the vicinity of the riser from the street near the meter, that is, on the high-pressure side of the meter, like in this case?"

"Objection, Your Honor," Bronson said confidently. "Same grounds."

Matt started to respond. Judge McGee held up his hand. "Overruled. Proceed, counsel."

Carson looked toward Bronson and then back at Matt. He swallowed. "I don't really have those figures at my fingertips." Matt just looked at him steadily while Carson searched the ceiling in the silence. "Well, probably, on average about twenty a year, or about two hundred."

Matt turned to look at Edna Mae. "Ms. Marley's house would be one of those included in that statistic—is that correct?"

"I presume so."

"Now, Mr. Carson, can you tell me how many of those houses, that are included in that statistic, are homes that are over sixty years old?"

Carson's knee began bobbing slowly above the witness box rail, as if he was exercising his foot. "That would be very hard to say."

"It would be most of them, wouldn't it?" Matt asked with his head cocked.

Carson shifted slightly in his seat. "Probably."

Matt pulled a folder out of his briefcase and opened it, looking at a document. "Wouldn't the actual number be ninety-three percent?"

The milky eyes shot toward Bronson and back to Matt, then they were inexorably drawn down to the folder that Matt was holding. "Ahhh…yes, that does sound familiar." Matt looked at his folder again. "That's around one hundred and eighty homes damaged or destroyed?" The round face was getting ruddy, and Matt could see the sheen on his forehead growing. After waiting a moment, he prompted, "That's just arithmetic, Mr. Carson, but really what I'm interested in is how many of those homes had this old cutoff valve that Ms. Marley's house still had in the riser?" Carson just sat there looking at the folder held in Matt's hand. "Or, if it's easier for you to answer this way, how many of these old homes that had these gas fires we're talking about had been upgraded with the new safety valves that have been available in the last twenty years?"

"Objection! That's three questions—which one is the witness to answer?"

The mouth of the judge curled just a millimeter. His tone was dry. "I suspect counsel will be content if the witness addresses himself to the last one attempted." He looked toward the wilting engineer. "Mr. Carson?"

Carson's knee was bobbing faster now, and Matt could see white around his knuckles where the CG&E manager was clenching his hands. "Not very many. We only upgrade those that have remodeling work done on them. It's way too expensive to come out and upgrade the hundreds of old homes that aren't having work done on them."

Matt allowed himself a quick glance at the jury. They were watching Carson intently. Six African-Americans, three Latinos, and three Caucasians—a typical Alameda County jury. All but three of them lived in old houses. Matt doubted many of them had done much remodeling recently. "Let me change the subject a bit, Mr. Carson." The man sat back and his expression as well as his knee relaxed. "Tell me, you are also involved in service and engineering for San Francisco County, are you not?"

The small, close-set brows developed a small worry wrinkle just between them. "Yes, that is part of my territory."

Matt looked back down at his folder and picked out a sheet with figures on it. "Is it true that in San Francisco County there have only been twenty gas-related fires traced to the high-pressure side of the meter in the same time period?"

119

The knee was suddenly back at it. Carson cleared his throat. "I think the stats are something near to that."

"Gee, Mr. Carson, I'm surprised by the degree of difference between the two cities."

"Objection! Mr. Taylor's state of mind is not at issue in this courtroom."

The corners of Judge McGee's mouth turned up more obviously this time and he leaned back in his chair. "You might try framing your thoughts into a question the witness can answer, Mr. Taylor."

"Of course, Your Honor. Mr. Carson, do you know why there is such a large difference in this important statistic?"

Carson's plump cheeks looked like a small bellows as his breathing rate increased. "I'm not sure this particular statistic is all that important myself…" Out of the corner of his eye, Matt could see Bronson frowning at the witness. "…but, I suppose it has to do with variations in regulations and probably just random discrepancies."

Matt paused a moment to let the answer sink in and then spoke slowly. "'Random discrepancies'—you mean like—it's just a matter of *chance*? The difference in this *non-important number* is around *one-hundred and sixty homes* that were either severely damaged or *destroyed* like Ms. Marley's home. You think this is a matter of *chance*?"

"Objection! That is argumentative in the extreme."

The judge sat up. "It only sounds that way because it is repeating what the *witness* said. Overruled."

Matt stole a look at the jury; they were all staring at Carson. They also seemed quite interested in why the stats were so different. "Mr. Carson?"

The knee was pumping and the sweat was starting to soak his collar. "Well, chance is really only a small factor. The biggest factor would be PUC regulations."

"Ah! You mean the Public Utility regulations that provide that you should replace all those faulty old valves in San Francisco?"

Carson studied his hands. "Yes."

"Tell me, Mr. Carson," Matt came out from behind the rostrum. "Who asked the Public Utilities Commission to pass that regulation for San Francisco?"

The witness searched the courtroom for help. There was none. "We did."

"Who was that again Mr. Carson? Was that your company? The same people who can't afford to replace these valves in Oakland?"

Bronson started to rise and then he saw the judge was looking at Carson for an answer. The judge lived in Oakland also. He slumped back down in his chair. Carson sighed and seemed to deflate. "Yes, we did ask for that to be passed."

"By the way, did you ever ask for a similar regulation for Oakland?"

"No." Carson's tone was resigned now.

Matt stood by the jury railing and looked at the jury full on. "Tell me, Mr. Carson, where does the president of CG&E live? Oh, and while you're at it, you might tell us about the residence of the senior vice-president, senior corporate counsel, and even yourself?"

The courtroom was absolutely still. In the hush, the only sound was the soft clatter of the court stenographer's keys as she caught up to Matt's last question. Even though Carson's voice was a whisper, everyone could hear his answer. "The ones you mention all live in San Francisco."

Matt kept looking at the jury. He added very quietly. "And do you all live in houses over sixty years old?"

Matt never looked at him again. He was just looking at the jury when they heard the answer. "I think so."

There was a snap as the judge closed his notebook. "Is this a good time for our evening recess, Mr. Taylor?"

"Yes, Your Honor."

"Okay. Ladies and gentlemen, remember not to discuss this with anyone or to form or express any opinions until all the evidence is in. We'll reconvene at ten o'clock tomorrow morning."

* * *

The next morning, leaving the courthouse, Matt thought back on the cross-examination. Clint had done some digging and had learned about a study done by the gas company several years ago that compared explosions in areas that had the old valves with areas where they had been replaced. The results strongly suggested the old valves were in fact dangerous and that the new valves should be installed in all homes. To save money though, the company had staged the replacement process, with certain areas getting priority. The information was a devastating indictment of the company's willingness to leave certain communities like Oakland at risk. Carson had realized, with all of that knowledge, the folder Matt held must contain a copy of the report and had decided to tell the truth. Happily, Carson had *not* called his bluff and discovered that Clint had been unable to get a copy of the actual document itself.

A pleasant surprise had awaited them the first thing this morning. California Gas's new offer of five hundred thousand dollars for a total settlement of six hundred thousand dollars had resolved the case and made Edna Mae a very happy woman.

22

"That info about the explosion report made a huge difference, Clint. I can't figure out how you got it—but thank God you did!"

The investigator's profile was chiseled, with sharp angles in the faint dashboard light and the shadow of a day's growth on the cheeks jutting from under the long curly hair. He grunted an inaudible response and kept his eyes on the dark street ahead.

"Well, anyway, she's looking forward to building a new house and the settlement's going to make a big difference for us the next few months." The car had a personality much like its owner: rough, rusting exterior, new tires, with the soft growl of a powerful and carefully tuned engine hidden within. The interior was casually trashed but everything important looked to be in place and ready for use. Maps organized in a container, a radio tuned to police bands, mic attached, the sawed-off handle of a baseball bat peeking from beneath the seat. Matt was sure there was more lethal defensive equipment in the bulky side pocket mounted on the door near Clint's left hand. He was just as sure there was a permit.

The huge hands had a deft and gentle touch on the wheel as he guided the car through the quiet night on the south Potrero Hill streets. The car jumped off and turned like a heavy, but surefooted, quarter horse. "I don't know that it was really necessary for you to come along, Clint. This guy sounded very reasonable on the phone, and the info on Conti sounded great. Hope the two of us don't scare him off."

The piercing gaze speared him for a moment and then he slowly moved his plug to the other jaw. "I still think I should meet 'im. As for my comin' along—if he's legit, he shouldn't mind a witness." He pulled the dirty old cup from the niche where he had jammed it between the seat and the console and spit the collected juice. Matt shuddered inwardly. He could never get used to the filthy habit. He had always wondered if the gumshoe ever accidentally drank out of any of the old cups and bottles full of the nasty stuff he left around everywhere.

"I think it's just up here a few blocks." Matt looked again at the address he had written down during his last conversation with his anonymous benefactor. The guy had told him a lot already and really seemed to hate Conti, but didn't want to get personally involved. This meeting in an empty lot was kind of strange, but the voice had explained that this was the only way he could feel safe about giving him the important documents and maintaining his anonymity. Apparently they were going to speak and hand material through some kind of a hole in a fence.

Clint wheeled slowly around the last corner and coasted to a stop with his headlights shining near the empty lot just ahead. They were on a cul-de-sac just at the southwest base of Potrero Hill, about two blocks from the freeway. The heavy fog dampened most of the sound from the busy highway. Most of the houses were dark or had a dim metallic light flickering from their televisions. There was an old torn mattress at the side of the lot and the abandoned, rusting carcass of an old Dodge was barely visible back among the bushes swaying against the rotting wooden fence at the outer limit of the headlights. There were no people in sight. It wasn't the kind of neighborhood where folks would be likely to take an evening stroll with the kids.

"I guess I'm happy to have the company after all."

Clint's grizzled head nodded abruptly and his eyes continued to quarter the area carefully. Matt strained to penetrate the darkness but could see little movement in the lot except for the bushes whipping erratically in the heavy, damp air. At the far end of the street, a single, weak streetlight swung on a wire with the wind, causing the shadows below to jump and sway, playing tricks with his vision.

"Well, nothing's going to happen unless I go back there where he said he would be, so I better get at it." Matt pulled at the door latch and started out, but an iron grip pulled him back.

Clint's eyes were hooded in the dome light. "I've already told you I don't like this. It doesn't past the smell test at all."

"Yeah, I know—but I've got to try. The stuff he's told us has been good and it all checks out. This could be what I need to get this whole Olsen mess to go away. This Conti thing scares me, Clint. The man's after my ass. I need leverage."

The curly head shook once and then he reached under the driver's seat and pulled out a short club. "This thing's weighted. Stick it in your back pocket under the jacket. I'll stand by the car where I can see you. Keep me in sight."

Matt's hands were clammy, but the wrapped adhesive grip clung to his hand when he took it from Clint. He crammed it in the back pocket of his Levis and pulled the leather jacket down so it was hidden. He felt slightly foolish, but the weight of the club was reassuring as the car door closed behind him.

Broken glass and old tin cans crunched under his feet as he walked back into the lot. Once Matt was out of the car, the wet chill quickly penetrated his jacket and sweater. Smoky billows of fog swirled around him and quickly muffled the sound of Clint's engine. He looked back and could just see the investigator's bulk through eddies of moisture-laden air drifting between them. He whirled and almost fell when a sudden screech stabbed through the night. Then he realized it was just a prowling tomcat. The rush of adrenaline left him weak. He was obviously pretty jumpy.

He scanned the bushes ahead and the old wreck, looking for the opening "Ricky" had described. All he could see between the whipping shrubbery were the boards of an old fence leaning crazily in several different directions. The empty windows of the old vehicle stared at him malevolently. The streetlight, dancing in the wind, caused dim forms to move deep in the shadowed interior of the battered hulk. The wind whispered, rattling branches against the fence and rasping an occasional metallic tone from the car. He reluctantly moved closer to the bushes and peered within.

Sure enough, just to his right behind a thick shrub, he could see a grated opening in the fence just barely glinting in the dim light behind the car. He relaxed, there it was after all. Behind it, he was sure, waited Ricky, probably just as spooked as he was.

In the distance behind him, Matt heard a heavy thud and then the sound of running steps fading into the night. He turned and looked toward the car. All he could see was the reassuring glint of headlights gleaming through the heavy gusts of fog. He looked harder. Something was wrong. He realized there was no bulky figure standing by the car. Suddenly the world went dark.

The headlights had gone out. Matt felt a gust of panic and he spun in a quick circle. Nothing, no sound. He could feel his heart thudding under his ribs. Gradually his eyes adjusted to the dark and the same surroundings took shape in the faint light thrown by the lonely streetlight. Where was Ricky? Where had Clint gone? He looked back toward the car and thought he could just make out the outline of a dark shape lying on the street beside the car. Was that Clint? He had better take a look.

"Matt…over here, Matt. I've got the stuff. Take it quick." The voice was a sibilant whisper. Matt was hardly sure he had not imagined it over the sound of the wind and the branches.

Matt looked toward the fence. "Ricky? What the heck is going on here? Where are you?"

There was a quick shuffling sound behind him and he instinctively ducked and turned. The blow slammed into his left shoulder. His arm seemed to go dead. Matt staggered back and his foot caught in a root. He fell heavily. A weighty boot crashed into his chest and he curled into a ball, covering his head with his arms. There were grunting sounds as kicks rained on his back and side. Searing pain jammed through his body and he felt a heavy sickness deep inside.

A grating voice rasped from the night. "Get the asshole's head. Go for the brain bucket." A sudden blind fury flooded through Matt. He was going to take a piece of them with him. He kicked the side of his shoe suddenly toward the sound of the voice and was rewarded with the solid crack of contact with bone and a shriek of pain. "Fucker kicked me. Harvey, do him—kick his ass inside out!" Matt rolled to the side and pulled the club from his pocket. The outline of a knee appeared and he swung at it frantically. He missed the knee but connected with hard bone. An animal growl exploded from over him and something smashed heavily into his head.

His head splintered with pain and his body was flung to the side. Matt rolled with the momentum and staggered to his feet. He felt a blow coming and hunched his head quickly under his shoulder. The shock threw him to his knees and the club fell from nerveless fingers.

"Brain him, Harvey!" Matt looked up at the vague mass standing over him and watched helplessly as the man raised both arms over his head. Desperately, Matt threw his body forward and rammed his head directly into the man's groin. Fetid breath gusted over him and the man fell to the ground retching. Matt felt the club under his hand and swung it in a vicious arc toward the man's massive head. The weighted end connected just as the first man's boot smashed into Matt's side. He felt something give way and a compelling weakness flowed through his entire body. From a great distance, he felt the first man's steel-toed boot glance off his head and then saw it carefully drawn back for the coup de grace. As if in a dream, he saw the huge, familiar figure of Clint appear. The body the boot was connected to suddenly disappeared. There was the sound of heavy grunting blows and then silence.

As Matt slipped slowly down a darkening well from consciousness, he thought he heard a familiar whisper from behind the rotting fence. *You're lucky this time—get smart, mutt—if there has to be a next time, you're gonna get dead.*

* * *

Grant and Susan were framed in hospital green. The color of the institutional walls did wonders for her complexion. Matt had hated that color ever since those months of visits with his brother. Lord, everything in his body hurt.

"How come you have that funny sound in your voice, Dad? I can hardly hear you."

"He's just having a hard time getting in enough air to talk right, dear. The doctor said it is very painful to have broken ribs." Susan had brought Grant to the hospital personally. "You might ask your dad why he persists in doing stupid things—like going into the worse part of town to explore empty lots at night." Matt shook his head at her comment and felt fireballs go off in his brain. Having her around could be more painful than the bruises—you couldn't take a pain pill for that.

Matt squeezed his son's hand. "Your mom's right—it was pretty stupid to put myself in a position where that sort of thing could happen." He could see Susan nodding her head. "If Uncle Clint hadn't shown up, I would probably be a lot worse off right now."

There was a rap of knuckles on the door and a huge mass of tangled hair peeked around the door. "Speak of the devil. Come in—come in."

Clint and Adrianne crowded into what was left of the small room. "Adrianne. You know Grant, of course, but I don't think you've ever met Susan." The two women nodded neutrally.

Clint immediately started talking. "You look pretty good for a guy with four broken ribs and a bruised kidney. 'Course, that bandage you're wearing over most of your face and head may account for some of the improvement." It was quite a bit of humor for the taciturn investigator. Grant began grilling Clint on the fight, leaving Matt to occasionally shovel words into the silence between his mismatched guests.

Finally Susan stood and gestured to Grant. "Let's go, Grant, we have to get some dinner." She looked in Adrianne's general direction. "Nice to meet you. Clint, thanks for saving this guy—we've gotten sorta used to having him around."

He got a gentle hug and a big wave from Grant as they headed out the door. Adrianne waved at Grant and then stared after closed door with an enigmatic look. Matt looked from her to Clint and moved his eyebrows, that being one of the few parts he could move without pain. "So what have you found out?"

"They're local thugs. Possibly connected."

Matt looked back and forth between the two of them. "Connected?"

Adrianne sat on the end of the bed. "Gang members. They're some kind of local rank and file. Of course, all they are giving is name and serial number—no rank. But the cops know them—and they aren't just errand boys, either."

"Jesus, you mean I was going at it toe to toe with gang types?" Matt shivered involuntarily and winced at the wave of pain. "What the hell would they want with me?"

Clint looked at him quizzically. "Come on. You're not that dense. The word on the street is that this was just a warning."

"These guys wouldn't say anything." Adrianne looked toward the silent PI and then back to Matt. "Say *you* attacked *them* actually. Cops wouldn't comment much either, but Clint is looking for a connection."

Matt looked back at her. He hadn't told anyone about the whisper just before he passed out. At first he thought he might have just imagined it. "Maybe it's all a coincidence. What kind of egomaniac would call out these kind of thugs just because he got sued? It's a ridiculous concept."

"Don't be stupid—you know it's the only thing that makes sense." Clint made a sound of disgust in the back of his throat. "This whale you got by the hind flipper's got an ego to match that blubber."

"Maybe it's time for a reassessment." Worry pinched Adrianne's features. "Taking some risks on time and money is one thing. This is getting downright scary."

Matt studied the cold rain driving against the Med Center windows. "What did happen over there by your car? I thought I saw somebody lying on the ground."

The big shoulders hunched. "Luckily, I heard something just before they jumped me. One lost an argument with a size twelve. The other took off. I was stupid enough to chase him for a block. By the time I got back to check on you, the smaller one of the assholes was just about to dropkick what was left of your hairdo."

The sound of a throat clearing brought him back to Adrianne. Those intense irises were locked on to his. "You're avoiding the issue, Matt. Promise me you'll think about what we've said." He shifted uncomfortably in the silence, unable to keep eye contact. Finally she rose.

They stopped at the door and then they both looked back at him. "Hey, okay! I got the message. I'm no hero, guys. Thanks for coming."

* * *

The gusts drummed the rain in volleys, rattling the window against the empty silence of the hospital room. An acrid antiseptic sting teased his nostrils. Gang members, for God's sake! That was serious. Those guys could take care of him easy…if they really wanted to. Would Conti go that far? The answer had to be *yes*. Lawsuits, bar complaints even…and now a contract beating. It would be easy to get out after this. The Gleasons would certainly understand, and the case was problematic anyway with all the experts cutting out. He had a dozen battles to fight that weren't this dangerous—winnable ones—cases that wouldn't get him disbarred or killed. Maybe a bit of discretion would make more sense for a change.

He searched the room, desperate for distraction. No book—TV sounded terrible—maybe he could call somebody. The phone jarred him out of his thoughts. "I'm downstairs—can I come up?"

He should have known Lena would show up fast. "Yes, of course. I was just sitting here thinking about you."

It didn't take long for her to bounce through the door. "Care packages! Chocolate chip cookies, your shaving kit, clean underwear and a couple of books. Did I forget anything? They didn't fight me very hard on the visiting hours." Her lips were warm against his and her face cold from the icy wind. "Hmmm—I've missed that. You taste yummy for an invalid!"

He felt guilty. Just a few weeks ago he had gone to her shrink with her and it hadn't gone very well:

> *Her therapist cut her off. "Listen to him, Lena. Sit back and listen to the man."*
>
> *Matt searched for the right words. There was no easy way to put it. "There are lots of things about you that I love." Her expression softened. "But I'm not in love with you, Lena." She took on the look of a doe transfixed by headlights. "I'm not saying it won't happen someday, but that's not how I feel right now."*
>
> *"You don't know what you think." Dark, angry spots appeared on her cheeks and her hands trembled. "I can tell how you feel. I know. You couldn't make love to me like that if you weren't in love with me."*

"Yes, what we have is special, but that doesn't make up the whole package. There's more to the kind of love that will make me want to commit for the rest of my life than wonderful sex and great compatibility."

"What more for God's sake?" Her hands jammed together and tears glistened. "That's more than most people have their whole lives."

"True enough—more than I ever had with Susan." Matt tried not to let the compassion he felt show. "But I want more. I don't know if I'll ever find it, but I'm not ready to stop trying."

"That's stupid fantasy!"

Monica's quiet voice cut through the ensuing silence like a blade. "Listen to the man, Lena. He's being honest with you. That's a rare commodity—respect it. Listen, and think about it."

"But what more?" Her voice was plaintive.

Matt raised his gaze from his clasped hands and spoke softly. "I want a partner, Lena. I need a real partner."

Lena gave him a soft kiss. "Was this little episode more work by your fat nemesis?"

"Apparently so." Matt eased his arm around her gingerly. They listened to the storm raging outside their window.

"Getting serious." Her fingers traced lines absently on his chest. "What are you going to do about it?"

"I don't know." He softly expelled a pent-up breath. "Maybe it's time to rethink my involvement in this case."

She pulled her head back to look at him. "Really? Well that's good, I guess...I haven't ever been that excited about your involvement in this one...but..." She searched his eyes for a moment then laid her head back down on his shoulder.

"But what?"

Her fingers twirled his golden hair that wasn't covered with bandages. "I guess I'm just a little surprised, that's all." He waited for her to collect her thoughts. "You don't seem like the kind of guy to let people push you around." She scratched her fingers lightly over his chest. "It's kind of like our relationship. I may decide to dump you, but I'll be damned if I'll let you make that decision for me." She grinned at him. "I figure you're a lot like me that way."

"Well, I'm not exactly in the same league with local gangs, Lena. I don't really know how to prevent them from pushing me around."

"Gangs?" She sat up abruptly. "That's a bit more complicated, I guess." She squinted in thought. "Look…there has to be a way." She took his hand. "Isn't there any way this can be turned around and used against him?"

He fixed on the driving rain. "You've got me pegged alright. It rankles to be bullied into quitting. But it may be the right decision, even if for the wrong reasons."

"Look." The blue in her eyes glinted in anger. "If I wasn't able to get you to quit this case, I'll be damned if I'll let them scare you off. I'm sure we can figure a way to turn this against them."

Next thing he knew, she had changed the subject and was expounding on some adventure of one of her girlfriends. He listened with amusement, but his mind kept coming back to her words about the case. He found himself thinking about Todd and Debbie and wondering what their life would be like if he did drop out. They would never find another lawyer willing to pick up the file at this point in the process. Of course, if he kept it and lost, they would have to find a way to survive anyway.

The room seemed awfully quiet when Lena finally left. He sat in the dim light, the lonely splash of the waning storm punctuating his thoughts. Finally, he reached for the small voice recorder in the drawer beside the bed. He pushed the button on the side and listened again to the chilling words the machine had caught, words that had already become an unwelcome part of his dreams.

"You're lucky this time—get smart, mutt—if there has to be a next time you're gonna get dead."

He shuddered as the evil voice whispered into the hush of his room. Slowly he switched the machine off and picked up the phone. "Clint? Can you drop by tomorrow? I've got something I'd like you to hear."

23

The ornate old elevator rose slowly in the heart of the Mills Tower building. Matt's glance caught Howell Muskind watching him with a hint of appraisal. Matt's former schoolmate was not weathering the years very well. Grey thinning hair, shaggy at the collar, a heavy paunch and vague, red-rimmed eyes swimming in a sallow complexion were not particularly reassuring physical attributes. Howell specialized in legal malpractice cases and had been assigned by Matt's insurance carrier to represent him in the case Conti had filed for the Olsens. He was also going to help him with the Bar complaint, since the two matters were so closely intertwined.

"How long do you expect this to take, Howell?"

The thick defense attorney's expression was careless. "Hard to say. I understand they treat this first Bar complaint meeting like a preliminary hearing in a criminal case. Depends a lot on what's said. This guy Robert Willistin is handling the complaint."

They were soon ushered into a large conference room with a nice view of the building's central ventilator shaft. A few minutes later, Willistin entered the room and introduced himself. He was closely followed by Conti and Jim Olsen. Not a particularly auspicious beginning to find the three of them in tandem.

Willistin sat at the head of the table, his greeting smile a thin extension of nonexistent lips. Thin dark hair was carefully combed across his forehead, starting from a part just over the ear. His gaze shuttled around the room like flat rocks skipping across a pond.

His look rested briefly on Muskind. "You've had an opportunity to review the complaint?" Not waiting for an answer, Willistin scanned the group, his eyes moving restlessly. "This is intended to be an informal session where we can discuss all the evidence and hear everyone's position." His eyes finally centered on Matt. "The ultimate goal, of course, is to determine if a discipline hearing will be in order."

Conti studiously scanned some documents, a satisfied smile on his fleshy lips. Matt broke into the ensuing silence. "Who makes that decision, if I may ask?"

Willistin placed his palm flat on his chest. "I will be making that judgment…well, at least the recommendation. The ultimate decision itself is made by the Chief."

Muskind held up his stubby finger. "And the only check and balance for this Star-Chamber process is an appeal to a Supreme Court that is so overworked it can barely look at ten percent of what it's asked to consider. True?"

Willistin's face narrowed. "Those attorneys who follow the rules usually have no complaints."

Matt watched the Bar prosecutor preen and shuddered inwardly. This pompous bureaucrat had his hands at the throat of Matt's future. The smug glances between Willistin and Conti were not very reassuring either.

"Mr. Conti, perhaps you could summarize the complainant's position?"

The trial lawyer roused himself from feigned boredom and slowly looked around the room, milking the moment's drama. "It's all rather straightforward. My clients had a terrible tragedy visit their lives. The worst that can be imagined. They looked to the system for justice. They put their lives, their emotions, and their financial future in the hands of this man right here." He gestured carelessly toward Matt, not bothering to look at him. "They trusted him, relied on him, depended on him to obtain this justice for them, and he violated that trust. In doing so he destroyed their lives and their faith in the system."

Leaning back with a hint of triumph in his eye, Conti finally looked at Matt. His expression exuded contempt. "It's simple. If he tells them about the offer, they would grab it. But then, of course, Taylor would get a small fee. But *lie* to them—and he might hit it really big. If he loses? Who cares? He's got other cases."

Matt felt a familiar throbbing start deep in his head. First, the man hires people to kick him in the head and then does it again—with words. But he had to give the old bastard his due. He was good. It was time to shift the focus. If his lawyer wasn't going to do it, perhaps Matt had better.

Matt spoke quietly, but his intensity sliced into the hush following Conti's statement. "I'm the one who's being accused here. I'd like to have Jim and Mary Olsen tell me that I never told them about this offer." He leaned forward and drilled the side of Olsen's averted head with his eyes. "I want to hear from them. Not the lawyer I'm suing for malpractice. I'd like to hear from your wife, Jim, that I didn't *beg* you to take this money. And where *is* Mary, by the way?"

Willistin frowned at Matt but then looked toward Jim Olsen. "Well, Mr. Olsen, *did* you have any idea that there had been an offer in this case?"

Olsen hadn't given Matt more than a quick glance since he came into the room. Now he was looking down at his hands. Matt's gaze burned into him. It's one thing to have your lawyer write it or say it for you, he thought. Try looking me in the eye and see if you can say it.

Olsen licked nervously and glanced involuntarily toward Matt. He flinched from the intensity he found. The old war-horse sitting beside him immediately sensed the hesitation and broke in smoothly. "Now we all know how difficult this is—after the loss of your son and then that terrible verdict. Just calm down and help me answer a couple of brief questions for Mr. Willistin."

Conti shuffled a few papers to take the focus off Olsen and let him calm down. "Now. Did Mr. Taylor ever tell you about the offer of two hundred fifty thousand dollars?"

Olsen slowly expelled a breath and kept his eyes on his hands. "No."

"Would you have accepted the offer if you had known about it?"

"Yes."

"Is the reason you would have accepted the money offered because you were in debt caused by the extensive medical costs from the care of your dying son?"

"Yes, we owed a lot of money to the doctors and hospitals." Olsen was starting to relax with Conti doing all the talking. The silver-headed advocate spoke gently, a sad look coming over his face.

"Has Mary Olsen had a hard time with all this? Is that why she's not here?"

"Yes, this whole thing's been a great strain on her. I'm afraid she's going to have a nervous breakdown."

"And what is your present financial condition?"

"We are essentially bankrupt—thanks to that man sitting right there!" Even his own lawyer turned to look at Matt as his former client pointed an accusing finger directly at him. Matt felt sick inside. The whole process was a farce. Olsen hadn't even been put under oath and Conti was supplying the questions and the answers. The worst of it was that this whole business of the Olsens' finances was obviously irrelevant, but Willistin was eating it up. Meanwhile, Matt's own representative was sitting on his hands.

Willistin turned to Matt. "Mr. Taylor, I know you claim to have told the Olsens about the offer. Let me ask you this: Did you put this in writing to them or document the conversation in a memo to your file?"

Matt stabbed a look at Olsen. He enunciated each word slowly and deliberately. "I was dealing with people I thought I knew very well—we spent days, weeks together. I didn't think I needed to write letters or memos to cover myself. I trusted these people."

Olsen's eyes skittered away. Conti's high grating voice cut through the silence. "Come on, we're talking basics here. Everyone knows competent professionals put important information in writing to the client *and* put a memo in the file!"

Willistin cleared his throat. "Well, Mr. Taylor? That's pretty standard, isn't it?"

Matt stared steadily at the side of Olsen's head. "If you're used to practicing law in an adversarial position with your own client—I guess that would be necessary. From now on, I guess I'll have to make it my standard."

Conti grunted and spoke *soto voce*. "If there's a 'from now on.'"

Matt told himself to be patient. The Olsens had filed a lawsuit against him as well as the Bar complaint, so they could eventually be questioned under oath. That is, if the Bar didn't take Matt's license away in the meantime and make it all moot.

24

Matt stirred the fire with the poker and threw another log on the dying flames. Settling back in the wing chair, he draped his leg over the arm and let the warmth chase the chill from his body. The northeast corner of the flat shivered and quailed in the icy blast funneling through the Golden Gate. Sheets of rain pummeled the windows, viciously punctuating his wandering thoughts.

Nothing had gone right lately. Lena would say his karma was off kilter. Everybody had strong feelings about this case. Adrianne was worried he could be seriously injured if he continued, and Lena now argued that if he gave up he would be bowing to the pressure of a bully. Jake thought Matt was going to go bust. Matt didn't want to quit, but he wasn't very sanguine about his chances of success.

He smiled inwardly at his sudden pessimism. He knew from experience that most cases were cyclic and, typically, at about this point in a file's development, the initial tide of optimism would be at full ebb. This one was certainly no exception, though in some respects the lawsuit itself was gradually developing a vague shape. Through the fog of conflicting facts and opinions a form was emerging, its outline still amorphous, but with possible substance at its heart.

At this stage of the process, it was as if they were poised at the summit of a mound of preparatory material, about to choose from blind paths to an obscure destination. The inexorable slide toward court would develop increasing momentum and inevitably conclude in triumph or disaster. The expert depositions that would fill the next months before the trial would be critical to any chance of success. They still had not found the nurse on duty that night and, without the missing x-rays, they were stuck with an ambiguous report of the cervical spine that gave each side an equal advantage. In other words, it was like any other big case at this stage—exciting, scary, and a roll of the dice.

The fire had taken the chill out of him and the room. He could feel himself relax as the wine took hold. He'd have to do something about dinner pretty soon. The doorbell startled him. Who would be out on a night like this?

"God, I'm frozen and wet to my toes." Lena thrust two big bags at him. "Here, grab these and get the door shut!" She went straight for the fire, rubbing her hands and shedding layers. "I know, I know, you've been in a lousy mood—so I brought food and spirit to make you feel better!" She gave him an impish look. "My spirit will have to do—I can't afford the wine you like." She held out her arms. "Well? If you can't think of anything to say, just get over here and warm me up!"

The bag in his hand had delectable smells of garlic and rosemary wafting from the containers. He was suddenly ravenous. "If I refuse to let go of this bag while I hug you, will I get in trouble?"

"Hmmm…pretty man—if you don't hurry, you surely will."

He could smell the clean wet of her hair and her face was stinging cold against his fire-warmed cheek. She buried her face in his shoulder. "Oh… you feel sooo good—so warm and strong." Lena looked up at him, her lids heavy. "Which are you hungry for first?"

He kissed her softly and then loosened his arms so he could smile down at her. "Why don't we hurry through dinner and then take our time over dessert?"

An hour later, they sat back from the table and gave contented sighs. "Can you believe that wind? I think it's howling straight in from the Arctic."

"Nothing to stop it—the snow should be great if the wind doesn't blow it all to Nevada."

He started clearing the table. "Any more wine?"

She held up a palm. "I've had plenty." She watched him clean the dishes and fill the dishwasher. "You're moving slow—those muscles are still hurting, aren't they?" He nodded in agreement. "I know what you need—a good massage. Did I tell you I trained in massage once upon a time?"

"Hey, you've done enough—surprising me with a great dinner. I'm a happy man."

"Not half as happy as you're going to be." She jumped up and clapped her hands. "You wait by the fire while I prepare the 'parlor' properly."

She had better hurry up. After that dinner, this fire was going to put him to sleep. Then he shook his head ruefully. Not much chance of that with this changeable woman in the next room. One day she'd be strident and working her way through her checklist, the next she shows up sweet and loving, like tonight. The fact that nothing was predictable about her was one of the things that kept bringing him back. In reality, he was damn lucky she cared for him.

"All is ready, my man."

She took his hand and led him to the bedroom. The only light in the room was produced by several candles. She had opened mirrored doors strategically and even placed a wall mirror on a chair so the candles were multiplied everywhere. The bed was reflected from all angles in the flickering light. Soft classical guitar murmured from the speakers. She had undressed and slipped his robe on. She started taking his clothes off—slowly, and he started helping. "No—no…I'll do it. Just relax and leave it all to me."

As she took each garment off, she lightly stroked his shoulders and arms and kissed him slowly and lovingly. She positioned him on the bed on his stomach, slipped her robe off and straddled his body. The sensation of her body sitting on his buttocks was profoundly exciting. Patiently and firmly, she worked on his head and scalp, his ears, his neck, shoulders, and back, working oil into his skin and lingering expertly over tight, knotted areas.

Then Lena moved to his feet and, as she kneaded them slowly and gently, he felt the last of his tension slip away. While part of him had been enjoying the sensation, another part had remained distant, observing the process. As she worked on his feet, the watchful part of him finally capitulated. Now he was completely under her control. He wasn't used to feeling this way, but he could become a believer.

Now she moved up, working the heavy muscles of the calf and then the hamstrings. Moving his legs apart, she alternated on the outer and then the inner thigh. Working the oil higher, she massaged his buttocks, first hard then soft, then scratching and following with thumb and finger pressure, rolling and squeezing the heavy muscles then probing gently between them. Her knees pushed his farther apart and he lifted himself as she also stroked below—the sensation was exquisite. He could feel the blood of his body singing through his arteries, then rushing to fill the areas she touched.

Softly, she rolled him over, oiling and rubbing his chest, his legs and then his thighs. He did not think he could stand it any longer. He reached for her but she pushed him down and continued to stroke him deliberately, only gradually coming closer to the part of him that was aching for the stroke of her hand. Finally she touched him there ever so gently and then oiled him lightly as his body leaped in her hand with a mind of its own.

Fixing him with smoky eyes, she moved gently up and then slowly enveloped him with the liquid heat of her body. She whispered. "Look at us."

Every direction he turned, their joining was reflected. With each rise and fall of her body, the sensations seemed to be multiplied by the glowing images surrounding them. She reached behind and gently massaged him as she moved. Gradually she tightened her muscles and increased the tempo of her motion. He gripped and spread her thighs as he felt their passion start to build. Her breath flowed over him and a keening sound escaped her lips. She shuddered and her mouth loosened. When he felt her spasm and saw her eyes glaze, he began to lose control. Suddenly she moved her hand below and quickly squeezed him. His eyes widened in shock as the sensation retreated, but she just smiled and resumed her movements, gently and then insistently milking pleasure from their bodies.

She shuddered again and again. Each time he would build and with a quick movement, she would drag him back from the brink. His body was at the edge three more times. Each time she managed to control him again. He had never had such intense pleasure for so long, but the suspense was agony.

Lena looked deep into his eyes, her hands propped on either side of his head. She began moving again, slowly at first, then gradually altering the tempo. She lowered her face over his, rocking and rotating, then finally kissing him as she pressed him deeply into her. Then gradually, involuntarily, their tempo increased, her hands now cradling his head as she watched him. He saw her face begin to loosen. Her eyes lost focus and finally closed. Her movements became more desperate and concentrated. He guided and pulled at her and arched to meet her thrusts. Finally she collapsed forward against him and rolled to the side, pulling him on top of her and deep within her body. She locked her legs around him and opened herself completely to the power of his body. Clinging ever tighter, they moved together, harder and faster, gasping for air, their steaming bodies molded as one. Free of restraint, he drove himself powerfully and then desperately into her welcoming body. Lost in this frantic search, they finally threw themselves heedlessly over the edge into a blinding mutual release.

He was utterly exhausted—his body limp and useless. He was sure nothing would ever function normally again. As he lay in a sated stupor, he felt Lena rise and head for the bathroom. It was hard to believe she could even move.

Through a haze of lassitude, a few minutes later, he heard her voice from the doorway. "I love you, Matt. I will miss you more than you can imagine." He raised his head in confusion. She was standing in the door completely dressed and pulling her coat on. Her hair was tousled and her cheeks still flushed from lovemaking. "Think of tonight as a present—a goodbye present. Don't call me. I won't be coming back. It's all over."

"Lena? What are you talking about? Where are you going?" His answer was the sound of the front door closing quietly. The sound echoed in the empty house, now eerily quiet in the wake of the passing storm.

25

"Objection. Don't answer that question until it's properly phrased." Conti's heavy lids didn't even flicker; they just continued their bored examination of the wall behind Matt. Matt never should have agreed to have his second deposition session in Conti's office. The defendant and his lawyer were just too comfortable on their own turf. All around them were old trial exhibits—photos of Conti and famous people and myriad other eclectic items. The place looked more like a monument to Conti's huge ego than a legal office.

Murphy had been particularly obstreperous today and Matt had to exercise all his self-control to keep from losing his temper. Their strategy was obvious; if he got angry and off-balance then he would not be as effective. They had also insisted that when Matt finished, Conti would immediately start taking Matt's testimony in the Olsen case they had recently filed against him. They were probably also hoping that if he was upset, he might not do well in his own testimony.

Matt forced himself not to react. He just kept looking at Conti and calmly rephrased the question. "Did you personally ever read the medical records of Todd Gleason?" The soft clacking of the stenographer's keys calmed him and kept him on track.

The elderly lawyer flicked at one of the numerous crumbs on his ever-present black wool vest. Matt could almost tell what he had for breakfast. "I may have, and then I may not have. I've no recollection."

"Was it your custom and practice to read the medical records?"

"Objection. You mean in every case in the office? That's hopelessly vague."

Matt patiently re-worded the question. "Mr. Conti, in the cases that you are personally responsible for, do you usually read the medical records your office has ordered?"

Murphy was silent. Dew-lapped cheeks quivered and puffed in and out slightly as his client perused a sheaf of papers in front of him.

"Can't answer a question as silly as that—depends entirely on the circumstances."

"What circumstances would it depend on?"

"If you had handled as many cases as I have over the years, you would know not to ask such a question." The man's voice had a riveting quality, even though it was high and nasal. "There are just too many varying circumstances to enumerate."

Murphy made a modest effort to hide a smirk. Matt sighed inwardly. "Perhaps you would be good enough to tell us just one example of one of your cases where it was *not* necessary for you to read the medical records you felt were important enough to have ordered, and we're going to want to know why, of course."

The folds over Conti's eyes finally rose slightly and he stabbed a steely gaze at Matt. Ahh, Matt thought, got his attention.

"Objection. He's already said there are too many variables. That's ambiguous. Don't answer it."

"Before the Gleason case, did you have any cases you were personally responsible for where you did not review the medical records—ever?"

The craggy face squinted in thought. "There must have been. For example, I often have a paralegal or young lawyer assigned to do that for me."

Murphy elbowed him. "Don't volunteer any information. You had already answered the question with your first sentence." The defense lawyer got a nasty look from his client for his efforts.

"Mr. Conti, in this case, did you ask anyone to review the records?"

He looked back toward Matt. "Don't remember."

"Would it be your custom and practice to either review them yourself or assign that task to someone else?"

Conti looked toward Murphy for help. The defense attorney, obviously irritated by the previous nasty look, had gotten interested in The Bridge outside the window.

"I don't know." The nasal voice had developed more of an edge. "It would depend on the case."

"I mean in a case like this, where your client is completely paralyzed and is relying on you to do everything you can to provide funds for his future. Then would you be sure that someone, you or someone else, carefully reviewed the medical records you had seen fit to order?"

He contemplated the pen he was playing with and he gestured carelessly. "I suppose someone would probably look them over."

Matt was watching Murphy and caught his eyes move toward Matt. They quickly shifted elsewhere. Good, he thought. I made a point. Now to change the subject before I give them a chance to fix it. I can always come back to this later.

"Mr. Conti, is it customary when your office orders medical records for a case such as this that you also order the x-rays?"

The corpulent advocate relaxed visibly as the subject changed. "That's highly variable also. You can't get x-rays on every case in the office. The clients end up with nothing if you spend money indiscriminately."

"What kind of cases do you order x-rays on?"

He shrugged indifferently. "Ones where there's a good reason to have them."

"Did you order them in this case?"

Murphy sat up. "I see you finally decided to ask something that has something to do with the case. Objectionable though—file speaks for itself."

Matt nodded agreeably. "Yeah, speaks volumes. No x-rays ordered that I can see. My question stands though. I want to know if he knows something that's not in the file." Matt looked back at Conti. "To your knowledge, were there any x-rays ordered on this file?" Conti's pulled his features disdainfully. "Haven't the slightest idea—but I certainly doubt it."

"Why?"

He flicked a crumb off his vest and jerked its ripples temporarily straight. "The case was a simple auto case, a single car rollover. The boy broke his neck. The issue in the case was whether our kid was driving the car or the other kid—not what happened at the hospital."

"Are you saying that you were only hired for the auto case and had no obligation to advise him if you found he had other rights?"

"Objection—compound question."

The witness held up an imperious palm. "I'll answer them both and the implied third question as well." His voice came on strong. "We were hired only for the auto crash—yes. As to the second question—of course we had an obligation to advise if we happened to find other rights. But we didn't. Most important, we had absolutely no obligation to go on a witch hunt in this or any other case to see if we could trump up another lawsuit."

The tough old fox was no dummy. Once again, Matt had hit a brick wall thrown up by the cagy warrior. At the trial, in front of a jury, Conti would be even better. Matt had seen him try cases. He was a master. The only thing Matt could do was keep plugging, searching for everything Conti knew and get him to take positions on every issue possible. That was what the deposition process was all about. *Be patient, keep your cool, the fireworks can come later.*

After five hours of Conti ignoring objections and rephrasing questions, Matt had finally finished. He had gathered enough factual information to be sure he would not be surprised at trial. He had given up trying to gain any concessions. The rest of the tough questions he would leave for court.

* * *

Howell was supposed to be here a half an hour early for Matt's deposition. Instead, he had just rushed into a room of impatient lawyers. Conti wasted no time taking charge. He ignored Howell's efforts to sit and get organized and just looked to the court reporter. "We've wasted enough time sitting on our hands. Swear the witness, Ms. Reporter."

The legal stenographer had been chosen by Conti and nodded to him deferentially. She was in her late sixties, as thin as Conti was stout, and exuded a certain grim efficiency. Her eyes were huge behind heavy lenses and the skin of her face had the texture of a prune. She raised her hand and administered the oath to Matt.

Conti came out swinging. "You're under oath, Mr. Taylor, so think very carefully about how you answer these questions. Your license to practice law may be at stake here. Did you get an offer of two hundred fifty thousand dollars to settle the case you were handling for the Olsens?"

Matt was angered by the patronizing tone, but he knew that it had been phrased that way on purpose. He forced himself to remain calm. "Yes, I did."

His mobile brows lowered portentously. "Did you tell Jim or Mary Olsen anything about the offer before the verdict was rendered?"

Matt wished Jim Olsen were here so he could eyeball him when he gave his testimony. The fact he wasn't spoke volumes as far as Matt was concerned. "I certainly did."

Conti leaned back, shaking his head in feigned approbation. The tone of his next question was faintly sarcastic. "Perhaps you would be kind enough to describe that conversation for us—*if* you remember it?"

Matt found himself leaning forward slightly, in spite of his intention to remain low-key during the process. "Yes, of course. The offer came at the end of our first day of jury selection. They had left for the day so I drove to Marin and met with both of them. I explained the proposal to them. I strongly recommended that it be accepted."

The heavy features of the questioner lengthened in obvious disbelief. "So you told them to take it?"

"Yes."

"Urged them even? You felt strongly about this?"

"Yes, to both."

The questions came faster. "You thought it was in their best interest to take the offer? That it would be a serious mistake for any lawyer to try the case against a good offer like that?"

"Yes to both again." Matt knew Conti was using his testimony to build his case against him, but the fact was he had thought just that and therefore that was the way he had to testify.

Sniffing slightly, he angled his head. "I suppose you were unhappy you had to try the case for a week with an offer that good on the table?"

"Not exactly unhappy. That's my job if they refuse to take the offer… but I was concerned that they were making a mistake."

Conti's features narrowed and intensified. "You were *concerned*. In reality, any lawyer should be *extremely concerned* if his clients turn down an offer that good on a case that was that difficult, shouldn't they?"

Matt could feel his heart thudding under his ribs. Conti was making him an expert against himself, and Matt's attorney seemed to be mesmerized by his own navel. "I thought they should take the offer."

"And, Mr. Taylor, you knew that if they lost this case it would be financially devastating to them, didn't you?"

"I was concerned it would be very hard on them. That's one of the reasons I recommended that they settle."

Conti's face turned stern, his eyes wintery pools. "You knew they owed tens of thousands of dollars for their son's care. If they didn't take the money, and if they lost, they would be *bankrupt*—true?

"That is one of the reasons I pleaded with them to take the money—on more than one occasion."

Conti's heavy head lowered to contemplate the black vest where the buttons strained to contain his girth. The nasal voice softened. "You *pleaded* with them. Was anyone else present when you did this 'pleading'?"

Matt stiffened. "No. Usually confidential client conferences are private."

"I suppose none of your office personnel heard these conversations?"

"None."

"So, you've told us you were very concerned about them and wished them to accept the offer." The tone became smooth. "I presume therefore that you wrote them a letter explaining all this and requesting they sign an acknowledgement of the offer and their rejection of your recommendation?"

"You know I didn't. You have a copy of my whole file."

"You didn't?" The protuberant eyes blinked in feigned shock. "Wouldn't you agree that it is common for attorneys to put important recommendations in writing for the clients to review?"

"Objection. That's much too overbroad."

Conti swiveled toward Howell and snarled. "You wouldn't know a good question if it bit you on the ass. Keep your mouth shut and learn something." He turned back to Matt. "You may answer the question now."

Matt looked at Howell. His attorney was focused on his notepad and he wouldn't meet Matt's eye. Matt looked back to his adversary. "Sometimes lawyers do and sometimes they don't. It depends a lot on the nature of the relationship the lawyer has with the clients."

Conti smirked. "Would you say this is an example of a good relationship?"

"Not anymore. Anyway, a letter is to protect the lawyer, not the client. I didn't think I needed protecting from the Olsens until you came along."

"Really." The voice had gone soft again. "I suppose you didn't write a memo to your file about this offer and their response either?"

"You know I didn't."

"You ever take a Continuing Legal Education course on client relations?"

"Probably. I think, in fact, I've taken several."

The questions were coming faster now, in that soft, menacing tone. "How about the one chaired by my good friend Justice Appleby in December two years ago?"

Matt paused to think back and slow the pace. Where was he going with this? "I have taken a few courses from him over the years. I don't really remember whether I took the one you have made reference to."

The old litigator groaned and huffed as he leaned over and rummaged in his briefcase. "Does this affidavit of education hours look familiar to you?"

Howell finally woke up. "Let me see that document...where did you get this anyway? This looks like it would have to be from confidential bar records."

Conti had a smug look on his grizzled features. "Oh, I don't know that these things are all that confidential. Besides, that is Mr. Taylor's signature, isn't it?" Howell shut up. The questioner looked at Matt. "How 'bout it, Mr. Taylor? Do you deny this is your statement of hours for the continuing education requirement?"

Howell said nothing else and handed Matt the document. His lawyer seemed entirely intimidated by the old warrior. Matt wondered what this was leading to. "Yes, it looks as if it is one of the forms I turn in every three years indicating I've attended the required CLE courses."

He looked through the stack. "It's here somewhere. Ah, here it is. Would you like to look at this one too?" He tossed a pamphlet over the table to Howell, who thumbed through it helplessly and with a shrug handed it back to Conti. The booklet was obviously a handout for a bar seminar. The court reporter's magnified eyes centered on Matt, a prim, disapproving expression on her face. They waited in silence for the other shoe to fall.

Conti searched through it theatrically and then stopped at a page. "Let's see…yes here it is:

'Any practitioner who receives an offer is, of course, duty bound to promptly transmit this information to the client. However, our obligation does not stop there. It is important to put such offers in writing for the client's signature, especially if the client does not wish to accept. This accomplishes the goal of assuring that the client fully understands the terms and risks of refusal and also has the added benefit of protecting the attorney.'"

He looked up at Matt expectantly. "Does that refresh your recollection that one of the requirements of basic ethical conduct is that an offer of settlement be put in writing to the client?"

Matt stared back at the advocate. There was no such canon of ethics. This was just the opinion of the teacher of a bar course on ethics. "I don't have any particular recollection of that, but it is certainly a reasonable idea in principle."

The questioner rose up and bristled. "Pshaw! Reasonable *idea*…in *principle*? The fact is, this is a standard described by a Justice of the Supreme Court in a course you went to. Isn't that true?"

Matt looked at Howell. His lawyer was reading the booklet. "Can we take a break please?"

Conti lounged back in his chair with a self-satisfied expression. "Afraid to answer that one? Have to run to your lawyer? Just remember, you can't take time out in front of a jury!"

In the hall, the two of them faced each other. Howell looked down. "He's right, you know. You have to answer them someday."

Matt pinned him with angry eyes. "What the hell do you mean? I should *never* have to answer questions as argumentative and objectionable as that. When he gets done with me, there won't *be* any reason to ask for a jury. I'll be cooked—finito. Thanks to my lawyer sitting on his hands and kissing that old man's ass." Matt planted his hands on his hips. "Are you just afraid of him, or choosing to throw the fight?"

Howell's face jerked up and tightened in shock and fury. "If you don't want me to represent you, then just say the word."

Matt just looked at him and then saw the hurt behind the angry eyes. Good grief. What was he doing? He had known this guy for over a decade. Howell had never been a great lawyer, but he meant well and tried hard. The problem here wasn't Howell; it was Conti and what he could do to distort the facts. Matt had to find a way to solve this himself.

He let his pent-up breath out slowly and then patted his lawyer on the shoulder. "I'm sorry. I guess things are just getting to me. Let's go back in there and get this thing over with."

As they walked back into the deposition room, Conti and the court reporter abruptly stopped their conversation. The lawyer turned slowly and deliberately to face Matt.

"By the way, Mr. Taylor, I heard you had an accident of some kind not too long ago…ended up in the hospital. So sorry to hear about that. If this is too difficult for you, with your injuries and all, we can always continue this some other day. Might not take much to have you end up in the hospital again."

Matt stared at him. There was the slightest hint of a smile on Conti's face and his eyes were two icy flecks of coal.

26

The coffee house was jammed with patrons in animated conversation. The din wrapped Matt and MJ in a pleasant cocoon of privacy. The heat of many bodies had etched the windows with condensation, softening the outside light and surrounding the customers with a warm glow. Ancient brass coffee dispensers were scattered about between stacks of fragrant bags of beans being used as seats by customers. As they talked, it turned out MJ had strong feelings about Conti also.

"Over at my office, this guy is a known quantity. He's totally bad news." Her face was set in anger. "When he tries a criminal case, as far as he's concerned there're no rules. The judges hate him. My associates won't even talk to him. The rule with that guy is 'get it in writing.'" She gave a short, humorless laugh. "And then don't count on it. He doesn't care who he has to hurt to get what he wants." Her eyes narrowed in thought. "I think you have to take this guy seriously when he makes these comments. He doesn't seem to be restrained by the same sort of social considerations the rest of us are guided by."

Matt rubbed at the bridge of his nose in frustration. "I know he should be taken seriously, but I can't hide in some closet the rest of my life." His face hardened. "And there's no way I'm going to dump a client because Conti's threatening me."

"I can understand the fact you don't want to be pushed around, but are you sure you aren't just being bullheaded?" She contemplated him. "The case still has to be worth the risk…to the body and the pocketbook." She cocked her head. "Is it? Where do things stand financially?"

"We have enough pending to almost keep things going, but the experts and the trial…that's about another one hundred fifty thousand dollars—at least. Not to mention the bank's getting anxious for a payment."

Her gaze shifted sideways, into neutral space, as she thought. "I don't know—I think it's the nature of the beast. You civil trial lawyer types live on the edge, and spend your life balancing between success and disaster." She pinched her lip between her fingers. "You are like buccaneers—especially on the plaintiff's side. I suspect most of you aren't even capable of thoughtfully budgeting your life, much less your finances."

She put her elbows on the counter and opened her palms. "Anyway, all that being said, I still don't see how you're going to pull this one out of the hat, Matt…"

"I've got an idea or two."

She looked askance at him as she sipped her coffee.

In reality, Matt did not feel quite so confident. He had only been able to come up with one possible solution to this looming cash shortfall. In the past, his line of credit had usually gotten him through cash valleys, paid off when the good times hit. This case, coming on the heels of his loss in the Olsen trial, had taken his two hundred fifty thousand dollar line to the hilt. Now the bank wanted it paid down. Then, he wouldn't be able to use the line for at least thirty days. A "rest," they called it.

The only thing he could think of was to convince the bank to extend his line and temporarily increase it. He would have to convince them to do this without any asset to pledge as security. Since the divorce, he didn't have any assets. In order to satisfy the community property laws, he had been required to "buy" his law business from Susan.

"So back to the question—is the case worth the risk?"

He held both hands out. "Who the heck knows? There are parts of it that are held together with bubblegum and baling wire. Other aspects look okay." He slumped back in his chair. "You know any damn thing can happen in a courtroom. Bottom line? I like my clients and I don't think it should've happened."

"The other thing is you *really* don't like Conti. Are you sure your reaction to his bullying isn't impairing your judgment?" She slowly tapped her nails on the table. "Not wanting to be shoved around is one thing. Taking financial and personal risks to prove a point is quite another." He gave her an uncertain smile.

"Also, is it just because you like your clients or because they remind you of someone else?" Concern was written on her features. "What old battles might you really be fighting here?"

He frowned at her. "I'm not sure what you're talking about." He noticed his tone was defensive.

"I think you know what I mean." Her expression challenged him. "You've been a different person ever since your brother died. That horrible accident and your mom having to care for him night and day for years before his death…" She softened. "I think you're looking for some resolution. Somehow, this case has gotten tied into all that."

He took a deep breath, letting it out slowly. "You think I'm just on a guilt trip."

"I think it's something you ought to think about."

She set her cup down and smiled at him. "Such a look! You don't have to do all the thinking right now. Your little brain will never survive the challenge." She reached over and patted his knee. "Enough serious stuff. Let's talk about something amusing. How's your sex life?"

"Non-existent—I've been quite thoroughly dumped."

She clapped her hands in excitement. "Finally, a woman makes an intelligent decision. Tell me every horrible detail."

As he sketched a moderately censored version of the scenario, he found himself relaxing. Whatever the subject matter, MJ's irreverent attitude usually lightened him up and helped to give him a new perspective. Tonight was no exception.

"You know where she's going with this, don't you?"

"I would say that's obvious." His expression was wry. "Out of my life."

"Not even close." Her eyes circled in mock despair at his naïveté. "She just wants a decision. She's holding her breath waiting for a phone call."

"It didn't seem that way to me—seemed pretty darn final. I'd be afraid to call her."

"Sure. If you're not ready to flat out commit—you should be."

His forehead wrinkled in confusion. "If she wanted me to make a choice, why didn't she tell me? Just make an ultimatum?"

"What would you have done?"

He squinted. "Probably wishy-washed around for a while and then eventually wished her well."

"Exactly. So, this way she controls the situation and feels less rejected. Plus she knows you'll never call her—unless her absence actually manages to convince you she was really the one."

Now that he thought about it, MJ seemed to have come up with a reasonable analysis. Matt had a twinge of remorse visualizing Lena hoping for a phone call, but there was also a certain relief. There was no need to do anything to finalize things. His inaction constituted a decision.

* * *

The bank lobby was ornate with old brass fixtures and polished marble. The ceilings were vaulted up to at least thirty feet, with beautifully molded gold-leaf decoration. A uniformed guard asked Matt his business, then directed him to the elevator and told him to get off on the tenth floor. He gave his name to an efficient brunette who didn't return his smile. He took a seat in the reception area. The couch was like the bank; it looked good but wasn't made for comfort.

"Mr. Taylor, if you'll follow me, I'll show you to Mr. Hutchinson's office." The loan officer's assistant guided him through a maze of small offices. It wasn't anything she actually said or did, but both his present guide and the receptionist seemed to be treating him as if they knew he already owed the bank too much money. Probably because everyone who came in here owed it too much money. Heck, if people like him didn't borrow money, these folks wouldn't have jobs. Matt wondered what his new banker would be like. The one he'd known for years had disappeared into bank purgatory.

He was ushered into a medium-sized office with a view of the building across the street. The furniture was like the view—utilitarian. Matt could see few items that evidenced a personal life other than an 8-by-10 photo on the occupant's credenza. It depicted a raw-boned man, his pinched face cracked into a reluctant smile. He had a rifle in one arm and the other arm draped over the rack of a huge, very dead elk.

In a few minutes, the rifleman sauntered in, a steaming cup of coffee in hand. He was about six-four, all angles and elbows, thinning reddish-blond hair and ruddy complexion. His face was thin, long-jawed, and the bridge of his nose appeared as if a powerful hand had pinched it together, narrowing the man's flat, suspicious features. He sat behind the desk without shaking Matt's hand or offering him coffee. He opened a file.

"I've reviewed your loan portfolio with us. In the last year, your line of credit has stayed near the limit most of the time. When can we expect it to be rested?"

Matt's agreement with them allowed him to use the line at will, but required him to "rest" it once a year, which meant to pay it off and not use it for at least a month. He had usually managed to comply in the ten years he had banked with them, but there had been a few exceptions.

"Cash flow has been tight this year. We've done all right, mind you." Matt smiled at him. "Income's about where it usually is, but I did lose one case in trial and there have been major expenses because of a large, complicated case we've spent a lot of time on lately. I'm going to need some time and some extra on the line to get that case ready."

He actually could watch the man's eyes turn cold. Now Matt knew what they meant when they talked about bankers' eyes. His relationship with the previous loan officer had always been friendly and helpful. One time, when he had missed "resting" the loan, the bank had suggested increasing the line to help him out. They said they realized his business was hard to predict and that he needed flexibility. He had paid the bank off five months later and then didn't use the line of credit for a year. Finally, the loan officer called him and offered to lower the interest rate and increase the limit. The bank actually encouraged him to make greater use of the line. Since then, he had used it more often and the amount he owed had gradually risen.

Matt had assumed that the bank wanted him to use it so they could make more interest. This new loan officer, Mr. Hutchinson, had not been quite so accommodating.

"Mr. Taylor, this loan is not secured. It should have been paid off last month. As you know, we've a right to call it right now. We can also increase the interest rate by four percent as a penalty." He sipped at his coffee and stared at Matt with pale, watery eyes. "What assurances can you give us that this will be paid in the near future?"

Matt pulled a sheaf of papers from his briefcase and handed them to Hutchinson. "I have prepared a list of cases that are likely to wrap up in the near future. I included a spreadsheet showing overhead and likely case expenses. As you can see, I need an increase in the line of about two hundred and fifty thousand." Hutchinson's head began shaking back and forth and Matt involuntarily found himself talking faster. "If I win the Gleason case we have listed, which is set for April, it will all be taken care of within six months."

The lanky frame leaned back in the chair and casually flipped the papers onto his desk. "And if you lose the case?"

"I don't expect to lose the case, but I have accounted for that scenario as well on page three."

The long arms crossed on the loan officer's chest and his eyes dropped to the papers he had thrown on the desk. "Yeah, and *if* you then win those other cases you have listed, and *if* the expenses are accurate, and *if* there is no appeal, then you would have us paid back in a little over sixteen months from now." The narrow mouth expanded into a disapproving seam. "I don't think the bank would be interested in that sort of an arrangement. Let's talk about how soon you can retire the present line of credit."

Matt could feel a flush of anger and anxiety creeping up his features. Hutchinson was watching him closely and Matt thought he could see a hint of satisfaction in the man's expression. "You have my financial statements. You get them every quarter. You know I have no funds to pay off the note at this time."

The man's lower lip pushed up in the middle. "Perhaps you could curtail your lifestyle a bit and find the funds to start making payments?"

"What would you have me curtail? Perhaps my alimony or support payments—which I'm up to date on—or maybe you're suggesting I should leave work earlier so I don't have to pay a babysitter or lay off one of my employees?" Matt again looked around the office for evidence this cold fish had a family and could relate to anything other than the thrill of the kill. "You guys pushed me pretty hard to use this line of credit, and have always known the way my business works. It's feast or famine. Even though it's unpredictable in the short run, I've always earned about the same and always eventually paid the bank—with its interest profit."

Hutchinson just stared at him. Matt had heard that the bank recently had some problems and that they had examiners looking over their shoulder. The bank had wanted his business when things were good. Heck, they had practically trained him to rely on the line of credit. Now that they had made some mistakes, he suspected they wanted to solve their problems at his expense. "Look, you know full well I can't pay you. I can't force somebody to settle a case with me just because it would be handy to have the money right now. Calling the loan would just force me into bankruptcy." Matt forced himself to lower his voice and speak reasonably. "On the other hand, if you support me while I work on this big case, we will both probably do fine. My track record has proven that many times."

"*Probably* doesn't cut it in this business, Mr. Taylor." Hutchinson sighed heavily and dropped his gaze from Matt's. "Your line of credit has gotten stiff as a board. We can give you some time to get it paid down, but we can't extend any more credit."

Matt lost his patience and his temper. "You're pulling the damn rug right out from under me. I've always paid you guys. I got into this position because the bank encouraged it—so you could make money. Now, just when I have a big case that could make all the difference for the family that I represent, not to mention me, you flat cut me off." Matt stood and looked down at the banker. "I can't just tell these people to find a new lawyer a couple of months before the trial, and I can't represent them without funds!"

"Guess you should have thought of that before you accepted their representation." Hutchinson was unfazed, his reply laconic. It was apparent that he enjoyed exercising his position of power. Matt wouldn't have been surprised to see him stand up and lay precious parts of his anatomy on the desk. This interaction was definitely at the level of "whose is bigger?" The thought amused Matt and calmed him. He sat back down. Hutchinson seemed irritated by the return of Matt's composure.

"We seem to be at an impasse. What would you suggest, Mr. Hutchinson?"

The loan officer tapped on the closed file. "The only thing I can think of to solve your problem, and ours, would be for you to offer some proper form of security for your performance."

Matt could practically feel his bones creaking with resentment. Now they were down to it. "You have my financials. You know I don't have any assets to speak of. My wife got the house; I'm buying my firm from her. I'm the only asset. You want to have a mortgage on me?"

"Well, I see you own a cabin in the mountains. How about that?"

"Wait just a damn minute." Matt felt a hole yawn open in his belly. "This bank has known for as long as I've been a customer that the cabin is off-limits. That was built by my grandfather. It's meant for my son. It's the only thing I've got left to give him after my divorce."

"The way I see it, it's up to you. Pay us back, in full, in sixty days and everybody's happy." The close-set eyes flitted up to Matt's and then looked back down. "Put up the cabin as security and we can arrange the extra credit and some reasonable time. It's your choice." The gaze came back to Matt full force. "You borrowed the money—you spent it. You figure out what you want to do."

Matt saw it clearly now. Wait for a time when he has no choice and needs help. Then, change the whole deal into a secured transaction. They look good. Matt's got all the risk. Trouble was, they also had all the cards.

"Thanks for your time." Matt stood up and gathered his dignity about him. "I'll think about it." The loan officer was still engrossed with his hands. Matt added ironically, "Don't bother to get up. I'm sure I can find my way out."

As he rode back down the opulent elevator, it occurred to him that they were better at business than he was. The external trappings were impressive, but the guts of the organization were lean and mean. It struck him that he was like one of those animals with an attractive rack of horns. It had taken years to develop them, but suddenly they were in someone's crosshairs.

27

They were getting out of the city later than Matt had planned. The cold, blustery harbingers of a big winter storm started pelting the car just as they hit the Golden Gate and headed north. He was finally relaxing, the start of a three-day weekend stretching ahead of them. The Blazer ran tight and quiet, so the weather seemed far away as they exited on the Black Point cutoff and turned east toward 80 and the Sierra.

"What's that tape? It's wonderful."

He turned and glanced toward Adrianne. She had the seat canted back and her eyes closed. Her profile looked serene contrasted with the rain driving against her window. "John Williams and Julian Bream. Glad you like it. I've got everything from classic and pop to country. Anytime you want a change, let me know."

Her voice was soft and dreamy. "No, this is great for now." She turned her face toward him, but kept her eyes closed. "I thought you were bringing Lena. Why didn't she come?"

"That's all over. She decided to call it quits."

Adrianne's eyes opened and she watched him closely. "So how do you feel about that?"

"I don't know." He opened his hands against the wheel. "I guess it was inevitable." He hitched his shoulders. "She wanted a lot more out of the relationship than I did. I do miss her though."

Adrianne sat up. "I should hope so. She's a very interesting and special woman. It must have been a difficult decision for you."

"It should have been, but she basically made it for me."

"Oh." She said. "Good for her." She stretched like a cat and straightened her legs before curling up again. "Guess it's the time for that kind of assessment—probably the moon or something."

"What do you mean?"

She looked at him for a moment with an expression that was hard to read, and then closed her eyes again. "Oh, never mind, nothing really."

As she tried to sleep, he drove on through the darkening storm, his thoughts wandering as he fought the increasingly violent cross wind. The north wind threw the icy rain against the car like lead pellets. This storm was serious! Jake was to meet them at the cabin after his flight to Reno. It would have been better to have been able to bring Lena to make it a foursome. There was a part of him that dreaded the long weekend with just the three of them in the cabin.

He looked over at Adrianne's relaxed form, and then forced his eyes back to the road. Jake's relationship with Adrianne had been volatile from the start, but they always seemed to work their way through the tough times.

When Matt pulled into Ikeda's, Adrianne woke up. "What's this place?"

"A handy place to stop and eat before you start the climb. As you can see, it's very popular."

"Popular?" She rubbed her face and looked through the streaming rain. "I'd say it's more like totally overrun. There have to be a couple of hundred people here."

Matt rolled his window down and peered through the rain. "This doesn't look good. Stay with the car and I'll check it out."

A few minutes later, he jumped back in and slammed the car door, his hooded parka streaming water. "I was afraid of that. They're metering traffic at Applegate."

"What does that mean?"

"The highway department's only letting fifty cars through at a time— to lower traffic and allow the plows to keep up with the snow. That's why everybody's hanging out here." He pursed his lips thoughtfully and looked at her. "The snow level is between two and three thousand feet. It's already snowed quite a bit and now it's letting up a bit." He paused. "I've got an idea…if you're game."

She gave him a questioning look and he explained. "There's a way around the Applegate checkpoint. I've used it often before when the weather held up traffic. In this lull, we could be at the top before half these people even start up the hill."

"Is it dangerous to head up when they are holding traffic?"

He wondered if he should take her around the stopped traffic. They could always go back to his Mom's place in Sacramento. The trouble was Jake. His plane should get into Reno soon and he would be heading up for the cabin. There was also the matter of three or four feet of virgin powder tomorrow morning. This storm was cold. The powder should be light, dry, and awesome. He wondered if Adrianne understood that part. Powder lovers were a crazy breed.

"It shouldn't be that dangerous as long as they're metering and not holding traffic entirely. That means there's no avalanche danger and the roads are passable. What do you think?"

"I say that powder is calling!" Her expression sparkled as she sat up with excitement. "Let's not waste any time getting to it."

Matt had asked a friend he saw in the line to order them hamburgers. He ran in and brought them out to the car. There were too many people standing around to eat inside. They drove up a side road and cut over to the old winding road that led up to Colfax. There was only one vehicle that accompanied them, a big black Suburban that pulled out of Ikeda's about the same time they did. The rain turned into snow just below Colfax and then stopped. Thirty minutes later they came out on a clear highway that had only a few cars heading east.

"Wow! That was certainly worth it. This is great." She looked over at him. "Do you think we've gotten ahead of the storm?"

He looked out at the empty road and thought about the heavy black clouds that had been hanging over the foothills before it got dark. "I don't think so—I think we're just in a lull."

Sure enough, about ten miles up the road, huge flakes began floating in the headlights and plastering themselves to the windshield. Gradually the wind picked up and eventually the road began to turn white in the glow of their lights. They stared ahead, mesmerized by the swirling flakes dancing in and out of their vision. Matt lowered his headlights and turned on the yellow driving lights.

"That helps a lot. I was beginning to wonder how you were going to see." She sat forward and peered intently out the window. "Wouldn't you think there would be more traffic? Maybe a chain-control stop to be sure people don't try to go up the mountains without chains?"

"Usually it's at Applegate and we went around that." Matt glanced at her. She covered her apprehension well. "But, it might be ahead—the snow level could have dropped on them suddenly. Then they would be moving down the mountain to set up the control." He leaned forward, trying to pierce the swirling curtain. "We can stop at one of the little towns ahead and check out things if you want."

"Don't worry about me." She flashed him a smile. "This is a great adventure. When do you have to put on your chains?"

"I don't have to." There were a few inches on the road already, so Matt pulled over to the side. "I already turned the locks on the four-wheel drive at Auburn and all I have to do is slow down and kick it into gear like this. Maybe this guy behind us will pass and we can follow him for a while."

Adrianne turned and looked out the back. "No such luck. He's slowing too. His lights are sure bright."

"He's probably doing the same thing we're doing, kicking into four-wheel—the lights are bright because his truck's body's even higher than ours is and he has his lights up." He grimaced. "Pretty stupid in this snow to drive with high beams."

They started back out onto the empty white expanse. A heavy gust suddenly rocked the car, swirling snow around and in front of them. For a long, dizzying moment they were locked in a blank white world. They could see nothing forward or back, no roadway, not even the heavy, brightly lit SUV behind them. Just as suddenly, the vision cleared and the thirty feet of highway to which they had become accustomed, reappeared, along with the blinding lights of their friend.

"Whoa! That was rather exciting." Adrianne tightened her seat belt.

Matt gave her a grin. She actually seemed to be enjoying the whole thing. For his part, he was getting mildly concerned. They had not seen a snow plow yet and the weather was obviously getting worse. The snow was falling more heavily and there were now about six inches on the roadway. He had decided to take the next exit but had missed it because of the visibility and the fact the black Suburban was right on his butt. The guy obviously didn't know how to drive in heavy snow.

"Look…there are some lights ahead. Maybe that's the chain control."

"I don't think it would be this far up…yeah, just a couple of plows." He had tried to keep the relief out of his voice, but the look Adrianne flashed him indicated he had failed. They followed the plows for a couple of miles, but had to pass them when they pulled off the road. As soon as they passed, the snow seemed much heavier and the unplowed road had at least eight to ten inches of coverage.

They were in a full-blown blizzard now. Matt could barely pick out the snow walls and plowing guide rods. He and Adrianne were working together to pick out the route through the eddying white mass of blowing snow.

"Matt—if we have to stop somewhere, will we have enough gas and food?"

Matt thought her voice sounded remarkably calm, given the import of the question. "I have an extra-large gas tank, and always bring food and lots of blankets into the mountains." He gave her a reassuring look. "I also have an emergency kit with first aid, flashlights and so on." A look of relief came over her face. "Don't worry. I've waited out more than one storm until the plows came along."

Adrianne returned to her job as co-navigator with a bit more enthusiasm. "Matt—it looks like you finally got your wish—the truck behind us is going to pass."

Sure enough, the idiot had finally tired of tailgating and was coming up fast on the left. Though he had sure picked a terrible time and place to make his move. Matt figured they were near Emigrant Gap and there would be drop-offs into the canyon to the right; also the visibility was worse than ever. As the big black vehicle pulled alongside they looked over in curiosity. The windows were heavily tinted so the occupants were not visible. The Suburban had an oversized lift package installed, so its monolithic black side towered over the Blazer.

"*Matt*! Watch out! He's getting awfully close."

Matt looked back over and barely resisted his immediate impulse to jerk the wheel to the right. The other vehicle was within inches and moving inexorably toward them. He blared the horn at him and eased as much to the right as he dared. Still, the monster moved to the right. Didn't he see them at all? Was he dozing…or maybe ill? Matt could feel the change in the roadway as his tire hit the shoulder and the less packed snow grabbed at his right-side tires.

He pumped the brakes and fought the desire of his car to drift sideways by turning back into the slide. Suddenly his correction threw them to the left and they struck the black truck a glancing blow. The Blazer and Matt reacted by turning away. They then bounced off the snow wall and they were suddenly in a 360. Matt wrestled the wheel and finally they stopped. They were still facing downhill—in the middle of the highway—and the black Suburban had vanished in the swirling snow.

He turned to Adrianne and she stared at him, her eyes dark with fear. He could see her involuntary trembling. Her voice was harsh with adrenalin. "What the hell was wrong with that guy? He just about killed us!" She sat back in her seat, her eyes questioning his.

"I don't know. Maybe he dozed off. I don't have any idea what the heck he was doing, but we've to get moving before someone hits us from behind."

"Are you sure you don't have any idea?" Her body was rigid.

He thought about the steep canyon to the right and he wondered. Matt put the car in gear. "Whatever it was, we can't sit here in the middle of the highway." Matt cautiously started forward and picked up speed. A few minutes up the road, they went behind the lee of a hill. The wind and snowfall abruptly lessened and the visibility increased. They could see a bridge down the steep hill a mile ahead, darkness falling away on each side.

She suddenly clutched at him in startled apprehension. He heard a roar and saw a large black shape charge at them out of the storm from an escape road to his left. Instead of jamming his brakes, as the driver had obviously expected, Matt instantly hit the gas, accelerating down the hill. Rather than t-boning them, as had been intended, the Suburban's bumper glanced off the left rear of the Blazer, momentarily throwing them to the side. The acceleration straightened Matt's Blazer and then the huge rack of lights behind them burst through the night. In the illuminated interior, Matt saw Adrianne's features bloom with anger.

"We know what the hell this is, Matt." She turned back. "You drive and I'll tell you what he's doing." Matt's mind raced furiously. He knew there was little time and the canyon under the bridge just before the turn below was undoubtedly the goal. He had an idea, but the black monster had the edge.

"Matt, he's making his move!" With a huge growl of power, the truck was beside them. Matt immediately turned directly into the side of the other vehicle. The Blazer reeled from the impact and Matt then steered right into the rebound, turning the Blazer into a 360. He straightened the careening car and he and Adrianne found themselves immediately behind the other vehicle. The black SUV instinctively braked and the Suburban abruptly turned sideways into a slide. Matt didn't hesitate. He hit the gas and smashed into the truck directly broadside, adding his momentum to that of the truck. The other driver made the mistake of turning away from his slide and he started sliding backward, straight down the hill toward the bridge. Matt fought the urge to brake hard as the turn leading to the bridge rushed toward them. Instead, he pumped gently to control his own speed and slow the Blazer without locking up.

The truck driver was not as smart. He jammed on the brakes in a panic and slid backward down the icy hill at an unchecked fifty miles per hour. Instead of letting up and regaining control of his locked wheels, the man's foot must have been trying to push the brake pedal through the floor of the big SUV. The heavy black vehicle hit the snow bank about one hundred feet uphill from the bridge right where the road turned to the left. It burst through the plow pack in a cloud of flying snow and then quietly tumbled out of sight into the canyon below, its headlights throwing barely seen flashes as it rolled into the darkness.

Matt and Adrianne came to a rest at the bottom of the hill with the lights of the Blazer illuminating the gaping black hole in the dirty white wall.. The two of them sat in the hush of the falling snow, staring in stunned silence at the place where the black truck had intended for them to disappear. They both unbuckled and moved together in shock. Matt held her trembling body close, burying his face in her hair. The massive rush of adrenaline was firing every nerve in his body. The gradual release of tension and keen awareness of survival made him feel exquisitely alive. They clung together, drawing strength and confirmation from each other.

Finally she looked up at him. "What are we going to do about...." She looked toward the silent emptiness of the huge hole blasted in the wall of snow. The skid tracks were already filling in. Matt's face hardened. "I'm not going to risk either one of us attempting to see what's down there." She shuddered. "I know just about where we are and I'll send the highway patrol back as soon as I can call."

* * *

The storm closed in around them as they worked their way up the mountain. Whiteout after whiteout slowed them and obscured the highway. Finally they made out the yellow lights of a plow pulling out from a dark side road. Gratefully, they followed close behind until it lead them off the highway at the summit.

Matt used a gas station phone to report the accident, Adrianne went to use the facilities and then called the Reno Airport. Back together in the car, they both had news. The highway from Reno to Sacramento had been closed in both directions for over an hour because of avalanches, and the Reno airport was shut down. All flights, including Jake's, had been diverted to San Francisco. The Highway Patrol told Matt they might make it to the cabin if they were lucky and didn't waste any time.

In Truckee, they finally encountered other vehicles and they stopped to stock up on groceries. They followed another plow to Tahoe City and then turned up the west shore toward the cabin. Over a foot of snow on the road along the lake shore and two feet on the side road up the hill to the cabin made the going tough.

"Matt, I've never seen this much snow all at once!"

"This is what can happen in the Sierras. These high coastal ranges can get dumped on with four or even six feet of snow in a matter of hours." He didn't dare look away from the roadway as he talked. "That's what happened to the Donner Party—ten feet of snow suddenly in late October and then more after that. They were stuck like bugs on white flypaper and couldn't move in or out for months."

His shoulders ached from hours of wrestling the wheel. He urged the car up the last few hundred yards through virgin snow.

"I can't believe your car can manage this with the snow so deep."

"The lift package helps. The center of gravity has been raised so it rides over a lot of snow. The fact the snow is very light helps too, which means the skiing could be awesome." They looked at each other. They were each making it a point to concentrate on the next day. "We'd never make it this far through the standard Sierra cement." Somehow, by unspoken agreement, they were avoiding any thought of what had happened.

The car crested the hill and the headlights swept through the heavy snowfall. Just ahead, through the whirlwinds of white, they could see the outline of a dark welcoming mass. Matt felt a wave of emotion, borne of generations of Taylors experiencing this solace from the embrace of the elements. There was his cabin, patiently waiting for them in the heart of the storm.

The road to the cabin had probably been plowed earlier that afternoon. The steps to the house were drifted about four feet deep. Matt broke trail and opened the cabin while Adrianne started carrying in the supplies. Soon a fire was roaring and the cabin was starting to warm. After everything was put away, they opened a bottle of wine and collapsed on the sofa so the fire could chase the chill from their bodies.

After several minutes of exhausted silence, they found themselves looking at each other. Each sensed the other's thoughts. They both sat frozen, in stunned amazement over the events of the last several hours. There was nothing they could say that would do justice to their experience.

Adrianne's fingers pushed her hair behind her ears as she stared into the flames. "One thing I have to say. There was that moment when that black monster slid sideways...only for a second." She spoke slowly, almost as if in a dream. "Before anyone would have had time to think—instantly—you just *rammed* it."

Matt stirred uncomfortably. "It was an instinct...maybe something left from that empty lot months ago—I don't know."

She was still fixed on the fire. Her voice came from a long ways away. "But I *do* know. You see...at that same instant...*my* foot jammed on the floor—searching not for a brake, but for a *gas* pedal." In that instant, there was complete understanding between the two of them.

Matt took a big hit on his wine, feeling the tension slip slowly away. "I can't believe that really happened. Is there any other rational explanation for all that?"

Her eyes were closed, her hands clenched around the glass of wine. "You mean other than Conti just had someone try to kill us?" She let her head fall back on the sofa. "...and, by the way, there is nothing the slightest bit rational about that."

They sat starring at the fire. The only sound was the distant search of the wind and the murmur of the fire.

"Shouldn't we tell the authorities of our suspicions?"

He took another large drink of wine and filled his glass again. "I called Clint on the other line in the kitchen while you were talking to Jake. I told him everything that happened." His thumb rubbed up and down the glass stem. "He told me not to say anything to the cops."

"Why?"

He put down his glass and turned to her. "We got sideswiped by someone who didn't know how to drive in a storm and they lost control. Happens all the time." He caught and held her gaze. "We don't want them looking any harder at this, Adrianne. There are probably two dead people down in that canyon. He said to trust him on this. We don't want the cops to look at why it's them down there and not us."

"Good God, Matt." A gush of air escaped her lips. "This is surreal... and frightening as hell. Someone's after us and we're hiding stuff from the cops..." She sat up. "What can we do to stop this craziness?"

He reached over and put his hand on her knee. "Clint thinks what happened to those guys in the SUV will scare Conti off. He said let him work on it from his end." He squeezed his hand on her leg reassuringly. "Remember—we're in the mountains and all the roads are closed. We're okay—nobody can get at us—nothing's going to happen."

She looked down at his hand and then up at him. "Yeah, but we've got to go home eventually..."

They let the fire warm them and gradually push their anxiety aside as the storm raged.

He finally looked over at her. "Had Jake been home long when you got him?"

"Yeah, his plane got in late, but he was already in bed."

Matt found himself tracing her profile in the firelight. "Too bad he got diverted. He might have been able to catch a shuttle up from Reno."

Adrianne lightly tasted the wine without opening her eyes. "No. He said everything was already shut down even that early. It had been snowing hard up here before we even got to Sacramento and raining up here for days before that. Apparently half the mountain came down several places along US 80 between Reno and the pass. He said the whole highway may be out for days."

He looked back toward the fire. "He must be upset."

"I don't really think so, Matt. I think he may be relieved. I think he knew our relationship was probably not going to make it through the weekend."

Involuntarily, Matt's eyes were drawn back to her. He could see her watching him from under half-closed lids.

"It hasn't worked for a long time, Matt." Her eyes opened wider. She was looking at him directly now. "This weekend I was planning to finish what I've been trying to tell Jake for weeks." She looked sadly toward the fire. "I was going to make it clear the whole thing's not working for me. I just can't keep the relationship going."

Matt didn't know what to say. He had a jumble of conflicting thoughts, but he was too tired to sort them out. She watched the flurry of emotions make their brief appearances on his features. Finally, he just nodded and said nothing. After a few minutes, he showed her to her room and then went to bed.

For what seemed like a long time, he lay there, staring at the moving shadows of the storm outside his window. Finally he fell into an exhausted and fitful sleep filled with angry black machines propelled by drivers that looked strangely like Jake and Lena.

28

Matt woke from his dream in confusion. Where was he? What was that sound? The last elusive wisps of his nightmare beckoned to him and then slipped into his subconscious. He threw back the covers. His body was covered in sweat and he had to make an effort to calm his breathing. The familiar surroundings of the cabin and the reassuring roar of the wind in the pines gradually slowed the frantic thudding of his heart.

He went to the window, wiping condensation from the icy glass. The sky was heavy and grey but, for the moment, the snow had stopped. The room was roasting even though it looked cold outside. He'd left the heat up last night. No wonder he had slept so badly. Matt turned on the shower and let the hot water stream over his head, then turned it icy for a moment and stepped out. That helped. He needed a cup of coffee and then the help of the mountain to blow yesterday and those nightmares out of his head.

The kitchen was cheery with light and the smell of breakfast. "How do you want your eggs?" Adrianne was almost ready for the slopes in her thermal underwear.

Lord, Matt thought, if she had any idea how she looked to him in those tights she would probably have worn a bathrobe. She had coffee made, orange juice poured, and the smell of bacon made him realize how hungry he was. "Wow, it's barely seven fifteen and you've already got breakfast ready?"

She turned and looked at him. "Want some coffee? You look like you were hit by a truck." She saw the sudden change in his face. "Oops, I meant the proverbial type." Her expression was rueful. "Damn poor choice of metaphor, under the circumstances."

"Don't mind me, I just had a few bad dreams—guess the room was too hot." He peeked at her handiwork. "Over easy would be great."

She bit her cheek. "Lot more than a hot room, I'm afraid. I had a rough night too, but I vowed I'd try to ignore the whole thing this morning. Then I come out with that. Sorry." They filled their plates and for the next few minutes they ate by the window in silence, looking up at the peaks that were shrouded under an ominous dark mantle.

"Well, since I already blew it, satisfy my curiosity." She sipped at her coffee. "What exactly did you tell the highway patrol when we stopped last night to call?"

He studied his breakfast for a moment. "I said a guy side-swiped us and then lost control and went over the edge. Luckily, I left it pretty vague." He looked up at her and watched her eyes. "It was easy. I said everything was pretty fast and pretty confused."

Adrianne's attitude was completely supportive. "Well—it was—who the hell knows what was going on." She picked at her bacon. "What about the front of your car?"

He poured a little more orange juice. "I checked that out last night—couldn't find anything at all, but it was pretty dark." Matt looked back at her. "We must have taken the impact on the bumper. I was going to check it again this morning, though."

"Good." She sighed and smiled at him warmly. "Now let's drop that subject and talk about something fun."

He grinned back. She certainly was resilient. "How about four feet of fresh powder. Does that sound fun enough?"

They quickly put the dishes in the sink and went to dress for the elements. A few minutes later, Matt pushed his way through a deep drift of light powdery snow and started cleaning off the car. Just as he finished, he heard the growl of a powerful engine negotiating the hill to the cabin. A big black and white SUV with emergency lights on the roof pulled up next to the Blazer.

The highway patrol officer was tall and burly in his heavy fleece car coat. He had intelligent eyes that were watchful above a business-like smile. "Mr. Taylor? Officer Kemp, following up on that report of an accident last night." He held out a huge paw covered with a soft thick glove.

"Nice to meet you, officer. Did you find anything down in the bottom of that canyon?" They leaned against Matt's Blazer, sheltering from the cold, gusting wind. "We felt bad about leaving the scene, but thought it would be dangerous to try and do much with the weather, except notify you all as soon as possible."

The officer nodded shortly, his expression neutral. "Makes sense. We found the SUV and two occupants—DOA." He watched closely as Matt's face registered shock and dismay. He asked the next question smoothly. "How'd you come to be up there at that hour after the road was closed?"

"We didn't know it was closed. We didn't get back on the highway 'til after five—came on at Colfax—we did think the road was pretty darn empty."

He lit a cigarette. "Imagine so. We stopped traffic about four because of avalanche danger." He squinted against the smoke as his eyes stayed on Matt's. "Did you see anything of that Suburban before he sideswiped you?"

Matt was getting the sense there was more to this than a routine accident follow-up. "Actually we did. He was behind us going up the Colfax cutoff and followed us most of the way up the mountain." Matt looked at him with an open expression. "It was the first time he tried to pass us that he seemed to lose it."

The intense features narrowed. "What makes you think he lost it? Did something happen to cause him to veer?"

"I don't think so—I thought he may have gone to sleep." Matt looked in the direction of the lake, thinking. "Though it seems strange that would happen just as he was going to pass."

The big man nodded slowly. "It does at that." He pulled heavily on the butt and exhaled as he talked. The wind whipped the smoke away, but not the casual words that followed. "Did your vehicles come in contact more than once?"

175

Matt thought furiously. Why was he asking? Was there evidence on the Suburban of the side impact with his car? It was hard to imagine they could tell anything after the truck rolled down into the canyon. "I don't think there was more than one contact. It seemed to throw him into a slide he couldn't control."

The officer field stripped his butt and pocketed the paper. "Yeah, lot of those flatlanders can't drive in the snow worth a damn. Mind if I take a look at your Blazer?"

He was already looking as Matt replied. "Of course not—go right ahead." The sharp eyes seemed to miss little as they looked over the scraped side and then moved around to the front of the car. "While you look, I'll go see if my friend's ready."

The officer looked up at Matt from under the bill of his hat with eyes that were crinkled against the blowing snow. "I'd appreciate it if you'd let me have a word with her first—cold turkey, as they say." Matt agreed and watched closely as the officer finished his inspection of the front of the car. "Hit anything with the front end recently?"

"Not that I know of." Matt kicked himself inside. He must have seen something. If Matt should have just said that his car had unavoidably broadsided the Suburban during the incident. If they think he was lying it would look bad. Wonder what Adrianne would say. The officer stood and sauntered over toward the house, leaving Matt shivering in the icy blast. He got in the Blazer and warmed it up while he waited.

They walked out together; the officer had his hand on Adrianne's elbow as they went through the drift. She leaned on him a bit for support. Funny, Matt hadn't noticed her having that much difficulty negotiating in the snowy walkway on the way in. The officer spoke mostly to Adrianne when they got to the car; she had obviously made a friend.

"Thank you both for your help. Sorry to keep you from that powder." He walked around toward his door. He stopped with the door half open and looked back toward them. "By the way, I think you were both very lucky the other night. It's possible the driver of the other vehicle meant you harm."

Matt stared at him out of his rolled down window. "What in the world makes you say that?"

"Those occupants of the Suburban? We ran a check on them—just routine." There was finally a trickle of warmth in his expression. "Turns out you had run across them before, Mr. Taylor—in a vacant lot in San Francisco. Ran with a bad crowd, those two—nasty people. Quite a coincidence they'd happen to side-swipe you two in the mountains, don't you think?" He tipped his hat to them—mostly to Adrianne, Matt thought. "Y'all have a good day of skiing—that is, if they open the mountain." The two of them sat there looking at each other in numbed silence as the patrol vehicle turned around and made its way down the hill.

Matt started down the hill and finally broke the silence. "Did he ask you if we hit them with the front of our car?"

"Yes, I said I thought we just hit once—when he came at us from the side." She turned toward him. "I just couldn't tell him about the...other time."

Matt expelled pent-up breath and looked at her with a surge of relief. "Thank God—that's what I told him too."

She rubbed the bridge of her nose pensively. "We seem to be on the same wavelength often, don't we?" He nodded slowly and stole a quick look at her.

"It was those same guys?" She was watching him, a searching expression on her face.

"My guess is it became personal with those two...because of how it went down in the vacant lot?" He drove slowly through the heavy snow. "Maybe Conti had nothing to do with what happened yesterday?"

"Huh. Possibly—but either way, Matt, that evil man started everything that ended up happening on that highway last night."

They turned off the highway and started climbing toward the Alpine Meadows ski area. He wheeled into the parking lot and was able to park right near the lodge. He turned off the Blazer and they sat looking at each other for a moment. "You're right about Conti, Adrianne—but let's try to put it out our minds for a while and enjoy this day. I can't think of a better way to clear our heads of all this shit than four feet of virgin powder."

As they walked to the lodge he explained. "I thought we would try Alpine Meadows. It's one of my favorites—here and Squaw Valley. It's a little more sheltered over here, more trees and less exposure to the wind. I'm hoping they'll be more likely to open the lifts."

They went in and found out the mountain was still closed. The groomers were digging out the lifts and shooting the slopes with explosive charges to clear any impending avalanches. Matt knew the supervisor of the ski instructors and they got an update from her. She told them management was hoping to open in a few hours for the hundred or so local powder-hounds who were hanging around. It would be like a late Christmas bonus for the idle ski instructors who would get the day off to ski. The weather reports indicated it was to snow heavily again tonight, so they could have virgin powder in the morning again. Everyone but the operations people were hoping the weekenders wouldn't be able to make it up tomorrow either.

They sat in the bar with cappuccinos, Adrianne looked out at the half full parking lot. "Wow, it's amazing how many cars there are up here with it storming like this!"

"These are all the locals. They wait all winter for days like this. Of course, some skiers are scared of the storms or don't know how to ski powder. All those people we went around down in Auburn didn't make it up here, or that parking lot would be full!"

"I'm not a great powder skier, but I love it." Adrianne shivered in anticipation. "And I *love* the bad weather."

"So do I."

She leaned toward him in excitement. "There's something about being out in a storm; it's cold and windy, snow blowing like crazy. You're all bundled up, hood, mask and goggles—it's you against the elements."

"You feel like that too?" He felt a powerful surge of affinity. "Geez, I've never known anyone else that felt that way. There are only a couple of things in life that can match a thrill like that."

She flashed a secret smile. "I see we agree on that as well." He flushed, and she laughed spontaneously. "I *love* the way you blush. I'm so glad you aren't one of those people who hide your feelings so thoroughly they eventually don't even exist."

"*Skiers, Roundhouse will open in ten minutes; start your engines!*"

They leaped up, threw a few bucks down and, with a rush of adrenaline, they joined the throng of powder-hounds that were grabbing their equipment. They got on the tenth chair and swung gracefully toward the mountain. As they rose through the cloud, the cliffs and heavily laden trees gradually revealed themselves in the swirling gusts of white powder sweeping the mountain. At the top of the lift, they looked up toward the summit. Heavy dark clouds hung sullenly over the heights, obscuring the upper runs.

Matt tightened his boots and led her along a new set of tracks that were already wending their way along the contour of the ridge. At the crest, they poised, enjoying the stormy view, savoring the moment before the plunge. Then, in unspoken unity, they shifted their weight forward and skimmed down the north face in tandem, weighting and unweighting like porpoises playing in a bow wave. All around them they could hear the howls as the pack plundered the untouched mantle of the mountain.

Matt led her to a lonely knob and they laid brand new snaking tracks down another silky face and then cruised to join the small group waiting for the opening of Scott's Lift. It turned out to be their day. The lift opened within a few minutes and they soon were swaying their way up over a long, steep, double-black that was begging for attention from the ravening skiers spreading over the mountain. Matt pointed out the best route down the chute, far to the left as they looked down. He showed her how it funneled to a tight bottleneck at the lower third.

They were the first to touch the far side and bounded in symmetrical glee down the steep face of the mountain. Matt was thrilled. She was one heck of a skier. They attacked the slope like they were tied to each other.

Several hours later, totally exhausted, they stood at the base and looked up at the mountain they had experienced. With a hundred anonymous companions, they had executed plunging kick turns down the rivers of powder in rock-choked chutes, explored the trees, soared in open fields, and combed through little known gullies and crevices. The secrets of the mountain had now been laid open by innumerable exploring blades. Just as fast as they and their fellow powder aficionados had violated the virgin snow, the advancing storm had begun to fill in the furrows and smooth out the man-made wrinkles in the mountain's white cover.

Matt leaned on his poles and peered at her though fogged lenses. "There's enough time for just one more ride before they close the lift. Are you game?"

He could see just the barest hint of her eyes crinkling through the barely visible yellow lens "Ha! Just see if you can keep up!"

Just as they got on the chairlift to the top, the operator closed it behind them. There was no one in the chairs ahead or behind them. It looked as if they were going to be the last two skiers on the mountain. They huddled next to each other in their own little world. Except for the humming of the cable over the rollers at each tower, it was completely quiet on the way up. The wind had stopped and the snow was falling heavily in huge dry flakes. They rode the lift to the top without saying a word, floating upward in a cocoon of Gore-Tex, mesmerized by the opaque beauty of a mountain world curtained in a filmy glaze of cotton.

Skating off the lift, Matt waved for her to follow him to a new run. He had noticed on the last ride up that the signs limiting access to the huge expansive bowl over the ridge to the right of the lift had been removed. If they went into the untouched bowl, they would be the only skiers on that side of the summit. No one had been there all day, and no one would pass this way again until the ski patrol did its final sweep. Cutting around a rocky point and traversing across to the face, Adrianne and Matt converged at a point just under the hovering cornices lining the upper edge of the bowl.

As they coasted to a stop, they were awed by the majesty of their surroundings. They were utterly alone in a soaring natural cathedral blanketed in white. All around them, barely visible through a mist of drifting crystals, were thrusting arches of granite and drifts of icy foam. The silence was so immense that they imagined they could hear the muffled impact of the falling snow. For long minutes, they stared around, mesmerized by the unparalleled sense of spirituality.

Matt's companion was a dark form, only dimly outlined in the waning light. It seemed to him that she was also watching him. She belonged in a place such as this in a way that few others could. Nothing needed to be spoken. He felt a deep connection, as if a part of them were touching.

Reluctantly, they said goodbye to their darkening temple and turned to glide toward the lights they couldn't yet see at the base of the mountain.

29

They got back to the cabin just before ten, both feeling the glow born of exercise fatigue followed by good food and drink. Matt built a fire and they relaxed with the storm providing the background music as the wind searched the trees and the eves of the old cabin. Adrianne spoke toward the blazing logs. "An incredible day—I can't believe we still have two more before we have to head home."

He poked at the fire. "Heck, I may never go back."

"Make it all go away, huh? Would I get to stay in your cocoon?"

"Oh, yeah—for sure. That's part of the magic. The head in the sand trick doesn't work without the perfect companion."

She watched him stare into space. Finally he looked at her sheepishly. "Well…things press in a bit now and again. Lots coming together in the next few months."

"That's an understatement. You going to be able to keep it together?"

"I sure as hell hope so—there's a lot on the line."

"Why have you taken so much on?" Adrianne said reflectively. "You had choices along the way. I mean, you seem driven on this case—not completely objective sometimes." She knotted her face into a query. "I can't help but wonder if it's tied to a personal need…you know…something unresolved?"

He sat up, his back stiff from the day's exercise. "Funny you should mention that. I've been thinking about that recently." He looked out the window and watched the shadows of the storm moving on the glass. "Actually, my friend MJ said something similar the other day." He turned toward her. "I honestly don't know, but if you are thinking that too, it may be worth some thought."

She gave him a quick smile of support before she turned back to watch the blazing fire. He was drawn to her eyes, always compelling, but now glowing in the reflected firelight. As his eyes wandered over her planes and languid curves, he realized he wasn't very objective about this woman. Something about her drew him powerfully, centered him in a way he had never experienced.

She broke into his reverie. "You know, Matt, it's not necessarily *bad* for there to be an emotional element that's playing a role in your decision-making. If it's honest but controlled, passion can be a powerful force to accomplish a lot that's good."

Matt thought about what she had said. Why did he have the feeling what she just said may have had more than one meaning? The silence between them lengthened and solidified, developing a dimension of its own, as their gazes held. With a sudden sense of panic, Matt realized he was about to take her in his arms. He even had the crazy feeling that she may actually *want* him to. Thoughts of his friend waiting for her in San Francisco crowded into his mind. Dragging himself back from the brink, he suddenly stood and stretched, pulling his confused thoughts together. Yeah, it was late.

"That fresh powder will not be denied. If I'm going to be up to it, I think I'd better call it a night."

She mirrored his nod and with an enigmatic smile, said: "See you in the morning, Matt."

* * *

In his room, he stripped off his clothes. Throwing back the covers, he stretched out and waited for sleep's oblivion. The fury of the storm surged outside, stirring and driving his thoughts, whirling them through his mind. Sleep would not come. A half an hour later, he gave up. Matt pulled on his robe and padded through the dark house, drawn by the glowing embers of the living room fire.

As he lay on the couch, he could think of nothing but her eyes, the fullness of her lips, the lithe curves of her body. Images of her carving a turn in the virgin powder or lounging on the couch crowded into his mind. She must be unaware of the effect she had on him. The weekend suddenly seemed long. Perhaps it would be better to try to head back tomorrow. There was no way the roads would be clear though.

Usually, when he couldn't sleep, a few minutes out here by the fire would cure the problem. He began to suspect it wasn't going to work. Tonight he was infused with a surfeit of energy. Thoughts were coursing through him like the storm through the mountains. His mind was so full of her, he thought could sense her presence. Then he saw her standing at the foot of the couch.

Her hair was down, shimmering around her face in the embers' glow. Her eyes were shining, angled cheekbones barely etched by a trace of light. She moved closer, her nightgown swaying as she glided near to where he lay. He was afraid to breathe for fear the spell would be broken.

She stood above him, her eyes smoky. There was a feathery touch in his hair, lingering fingers traced the line of his jaw. His eyes explored her face and caressed the length of her body. He inhaled deeply as the fresh scent of her filled his senses. His heart pumped molten energy through his body. He had fantasized this moment since the first time he saw her striding effortlessly toward The Bridge.

His hand gently lifted the folds at the front of the silken gown. She quivered under his gentle touch. He slid his hand up the skin of her thigh, his fingers lightly caressing the lithe muscles. As he stroked her, her fingers gently touched his lips. The skin of her inner thigh was as smooth as oil. He touched her gently and watched her eyes hood with desire. Her finger circled his lips and parted them, lightly stroking his tongue. With a small cry, she lowered her face to his. They hesitated with their lips almost touching, her sweet breath caressing his face. Her eyes smoldered through heavy dark lashes. His fingers shivered as they discovered her mouth with a feathery touch. With a sigh, their lips finally melted together.

His tongue searching, he molded every part of himself to her sinuous form. Where his robe had fallen open, he could feel the warm curves of her body against the heat of his skin. Slowly, savoring the desire in her eyes, he removed her gown and let it fall to the floor with his robe.

Now on his side, he leaned on his elbow, his eyes admiring the curves and valleys of her body. His dreams did not do justice to the reality of her. He gently stroked her breasts, cupping and molding them with a heated palm. He lightly brushed her lips with his as his fingers caressed her. His tongue explored her lips, then moved slowly down her neck and to the firm breasts below. She moaned deep in her throat and arched her body to him, the gentle stimulation heating and hardening her.

His head moved ever lower, stroking and teasing, but never rushing the search for his goal. Finally, his touch became feather light. As his tongue caressed her, he felt the muscles of her thighs tighten in response. His eyes travelled up her body and saw her bow her neck as his pressure became more insistent. Her head began turning from side to side, a metronome for her increasing desire. A sound rose from deep in her throat. Her rising ardor finally gave birth to a primeval cry as her body shuddered in spasms of unfettered pleasure.

Tears flowing, she pulled him to her, whispering her urgent need in his ear. Matt cradled her in his arms and gently eased his weight upon her, allowing their bodies to fit together from belly to toe. He looked at her for a long searching moment and then covered her mouth with his. Their bodies found each other as if molded only for that purpose. He pressed, gently at first and then powerfully into her. Her limbs gathered him to her as they lost themselves in the pleasure of joining. Her hands caressed and then dug into him as breathless urging gave way to pleas and moans deep in her throat as her passion mounted. He felt her body tighten and then his own rushed to join her as their souls intertwined.

They lay sculpted together, breathless and drenched, neither willing to loosen their grasp on the other. He gazed at her, his heart full, seeing his own powerful feelings reflected. Gently, Matt kissed each of her features. His fingers followed the exquisite contours of her face with feathered brush strokes, touching with wonder the tears of joy flowing from her. Words were not necessary.

Finally, she stood with an inviting smile and held out her hand. They rose and walked to his room, hip nestled to hip. In his bed, they fit together as if they had always been one. Whispering lazily, they drifted off into a deep sleep of contented exhaustion.

* * *

They were trying to have a conversation, but Matt found it hard to concentrate. All he wanted to do this morning was look at her. She was tousled from sleep and her thick hair framed her face in a wild dark mane. He loved the fact she seldom wore makeup. She certainly didn't need it. Her eyes were just as beautiful this morning as they had been last night by firelight. Her features were vivid against rich olive skin. He compared how he must look, unshaven, his blond hair matted by their lovemaking.

She took a bite of the French toast Matt had made. She caught some syrup dribbling down her chin with her finger and licked it clean. Matt loved to watch her revel in her food.

He thought about how they had awakened this morning. They had slept cupped together like two spoons. Still half asleep, the feel of her silken body against his was so exciting that he found himself in a state of profound arousal. Afraid he would wake her, he moved to lessen an insistent pressure. She growled like a big sleepy cat and captured him with her hand. With a subtle move, she slipped her body over him and began rocking him awake. They made love slowly, savoring the feel and texture of their intimacy, exploring and discovering each other with childlike delight.

"Matthew, darling, you aren't listening to anything I say. You're just sitting there with that silly grin on your face." She leaned across the table and gave him an open, lingering kiss, smearing syrup all over his face in the process. He licked his lips and broadened his grin. "You taste so much better this morning. Must be my cooking." He pulled her close. "Let me taste some more of that stuff."

She reached under his robe. "My, my, you do like breakfast, don't you?" She slipped out of her chair and straddled him, their robes falling apart.

He looked down and watched as she slowly engulfed his body. Adrianne reached for her plate and took a piece of the French toast, dripping with syrup, into her hand.

"Maybe it will taste even better this way." She bit half of the piece and gradually pushed the other half in his mouth, rocking on him, keeping time with her lazy chewing. She kissed him deeply, their sweet juices intermingling. She moved on his lap, milking his body with hers. The sensations drove Matt wild. He crushed her to his chest and joined her movements, thrusting deeper and deeper. Her breaths came shorter as she moved harder against him. Finally Matt stood, lifting her with him, their movements becoming frantic. He pressed her against the wall and searched the depths of her. They gasped desperately for air as she bucked and grasped him to her. Her moans converted into a drawn-out wail and he erupted into her welcoming body.

The long weekend went that way. The weather stayed cold and the snow fell off and on, the wind and new snow filling in the old tracks. They enjoyed champagne powder every day and lovemaking all night, until every part of their bodies became deliciously sore. Wrapped in a world of love, life on the other side of the mountains seemed far away. Monday night finally came and with it a call from Jake wondering when they would be home. The roads were clear. They closed the cabin and packed the car. Thoroughly exhausted, they turned toward home and reality.

30

Adrianne watched out the window as they curved out of the wetlands onto the 101 freeway just below Novato. The city was only twenty miles away now. Matt merged into the heavy holiday weekend traffic.

The closer they got to the City, the more thoughts of Jake crowded unbidden into his head. The phone conversation this afternoon with his friend had turned him inside out. Matt thought the relationship between Jake and Adrianne was supposed to be over and that Jake had become resigned to its demise. But all Jake had done was ask Matt about Adrianne. He asked how the weekend had gone, what was her attitude, and how did she seem to Matt? Matt hadn't known what to say. He had stumbled on about the snow and what a great skier Adrianne was. It had felt inane. The conversation had been awful. Overwhelming feelings of guilt had immediately blossomed, and they had been gnawing at him more and more with each mile of the return trip. How could he ever tell Jake now? He wanted to talk to Adrianne about it, but hadn't been able to broach the subject. He had never felt so out of control of his emotions.

He felt like everything was folding in on him, pushing him steadily toward disaster. Maybe it was time to reassess—everything. If there was just a way he could go back a year. If he could have talked the Olsens into settling their case. If he had just said no to Stadahl about the Gleason case and, instead, spent some real time on the cases he had been ignoring this year. Now, he had people trying to kill him, had managed to endanger Adrianne, and was sleeping with the woman his best friend loved. He badly needed to find a reset button.

Adrianne leaned her back against her door with her arm up on the seat back. "I'm so excited about the Gleason case. I've never had the chance to be in the middle of a big case heading into trial."

Matt felt his innards compress as she vented her enthusiasm. It was time to get his tongue unstuck from the roof of his mouth. "I can't stop thinking about that monster truck, and how close it was, Adrianne—all the stuff that's happened. I think we need to rethink this whole situation."

"What do you mean—rethink it, how, what?"

"The case. I was crazy to take it—I'm going broke trying to fund it, they're after my license, I've almost been killed twice now…" He glanced over; her cheeks were turning red as though windburned. "And you could have died. I put you in danger by just being near me—by having you work on the case." He felt like his insides were turning to water. "I mean, I worry about you, about me, about what the hell's next."

"Clint thinks he will back off, though. We have them on the ropes, Matt. The trial's next month, for God's sake." She sat toward him and put her hand on his shoulder. "We can't back out now. What would that family do if we abandon them?"

"I'm being completely unrealistic about this case. We've got second string experts, evidence and witnesses are missing, and there's no way I can pay for the trial." Matt crouched over the wheel, his knuckles tightening. "I worry about you—and I worry about the rest of the crew, too."

"So, you're going to protect me by dropping the case a month before trial? I'll take care of myself, thank you." She fixed him with two wintery pools. "Everyone in town has advised you to stay away from the case and now, on the eve of trial, you're going to bail out and leave that young man hanging?" Her hand dropped from his shoulder. "I don't buy this. The time for a reasonable assessment of your obsession about this case has long passed and you know we'll be with you all the way." Her voice steeled. "What's going on, Matt. What's really the matter with you?"

"Well," His gaze shifted sideways. "That's the other thing—I'm being eaten up by guilt. I just spent the weekend making love to my best friend's girl." His fingers locked on the wheel. "When he called this afternoon, all he could ask about was you. I didn't know what to say. I can't handle this—it's just not right."

Her face paled and she gave him a disbelieving look. "I think you need to figure out what the hell you're doing. I assumed you had given some thought to what was happening between us, but I was obviously wrong."

They burst out of the Waldo Tunnel and the city spread out before them in the crystal clear night air. The lights glinted and sparkled in the distance, the home-covered hills giving way to the brightly-lit financial district. The breathtaking sight was bracketed by the soaring lights of the two bridges. Tonight, the dramatic view just accented his need to face reality tomorrow, and everything that meant.

"Why don't you just drop me at Jake's place, Matt?"

"What?" He flashed a look over at her. "What are you going over there for?"

"Matthew, since you 'can't handle this,' I'm not sure it matters, but I'm going to pick up my car. As you may recall, that's where you picked me up Friday afternoon."

"Are you going in?" He glanced at her quickly. "Are you going to talk to him tonight?"

"Yes, I probably will, Matt." She watched as the city lights flitted brightly between the railing struts of The Bridge. "He obviously needs to know where he stands."

"Sure, you need to make it clear that you two are done." He drove in silence for a while. "What I meant is about us. You aren't going to tell him about that, are you?"

"What did you intend, Matthew—to keep it a secret?" She glanced at his white knuckles. "Just what did you have in mind—hiding and sneaking around?"

His guilt boiled over. "So, you're just going to throw it in his face?" He swung toward her. "That's great. Just dump him and say, 'by the way, I'm sleeping with your best friend.' Sort of ease him into the idea?"

She reeled as if he had struck her. "Actually, I had no intention of telling him about us tonight. I planned to let him get used to the fact of the new reality first." Her eyes were glinting with tears. "Given your attitude," Adrianne's expression was grim. "I guess there's no point in telling him about something that will end up meaning nothing in the long run."

"Just what is that supposed to mean?" His head jerked toward her.

There were bright spots of color on her cheeks.

She shook her head in disappointment. "Just drop me up there, Matt."

He pulled the car over and turned toward her. "Look…" There was an abyss opening in his gut. He couldn't believe how badly he had messed this up. "I'm sorry. We need to talk this out. I'm just feeling really horrible about Jake and what's happened with us. It's messing with my head. Why don't you come over to my place?"

"No, Matt, I'll get out here." Her expression had become remote. "You need to do some serious introspection before any more talking would be appropriate." She got out of the car and pulled her stuff from the rear without accepting any help. Looking back as he pulled away, he saw anger projected in her posture, but also a profound sadness.

Sitting quietly in his car, thoughts churned in his head. He had just had the most dangerous, exciting, and emotionally significant three days of his life and, at the end, had managed to turn the whole thing into a complete disaster. He pounded his fist on the steering wheel. What in the world? Obviously, he was stricken with a heavy dose of guilt. But why had he acted that way with Adrianne? He couldn't have second thoughts about the case at this stage. There was no choice but to forge ahead. It didn't make sense to blame her. Besides, there had been a certain inevitability for a long time. Why hadn't he just talked to her about his concerns, his feelings? He wouldn't blame her if she bailed on him, the case, everything.

The irony was profound. Other than Grant, Adrianne and Jake were two of the most important people in his life, but he could not continue the relationship he wanted with either one of them unless he hurt one of them. On the other hand, hurting one might negatively impact his relationship with the other anyway. He just didn't know what to do. Maybe he should concentrate on trial preparation for now. Maybe he could deal with all this when the trial was over.

31

After the early morning meeting broke up, Matt went into his office and looked at his desk with dismay. Everybody on the team had their assignments on the Gleason trial preparation and his was the longest list. First though, he had to get through all these stacks of paper and return the phone calls.

"Boss, Jake stuck his head in earlier and asked if you would drop by his office sometime today. It sounded important."

"Okay—I'll call and see when he wants to meet." Great, he thought. Conversation with Jake the first day back from the mountains. It was likely he would want to talk about Adrianne if she went over there last night. She had been very quiet during the meeting this morning, businesslike, helpful, and very distant. She hadn't been unfriendly; she just seemed distracted. She hadn't met his gaze directly.

Matt lost himself as best he could in work for the next few hours and then went upstairs to Jake's office. Jake was at his desk and had an open bottle of wine in front of him. It was already half empty.

"Here, have a glass of wine."

"No thanks, I've got way too much to do this afternoon."

Jake's smile didn't reach his eyes. "Adrianne told me the skiing was incredible."

"Hate to tell you, but it was the best snow of the decade as far as I'm concerned. And nobody there."

Jake looked down at his glass of wine. "She's a hell of a skier, isn't she?" Matt agreed. "She had some boyfriend she knew in Colorado that was a ski instructor—used to get free lessons. Some kind of a mogul champion, too. You think she's good in powder, you ought to see her do the bumps."

"She's a hell of a woman."

Jake was pensive. "What kind of a mood was she in this weekend, anyway?"

"Well, great as far as I could tell." Matt kicked himself. Now was the time to tell Jake, but he couldn't bring himself to say anything. "Hard for anyone not to be with all that snow. Why?"

Jake made a visible effort to shake off his morose affect. "Oh, nothing much, we just had a bit of a spat last night. She seemed out of sorts and I thought you might know why." He forced a grin. "Well, at least I'm glad you had a great weekend. I was damn lonely down here!"

Matt tried to look at his friend, but found himself monitoring the black clouds scudding over the bay.

"You alright?" Jake scrutinized his friend for a moment. "You look a little off your feed." Jake hit his desk with his hand. "Hey! What about those assholes trying to do you in on the way up? My God! *You guys* could have ended up down in that canyon." His expression widened in amazement. "Adrianne was very impressed with the way you handled the driving. Said you saved the day."

Matt was relieved the subject had changed. "I didn't have time to think—just reacted. I think it was really just a matter of them being a bit dumber."

"Not the way I heard it."

Matt could feel the heat building in his face. Just what he needed was to have Adrianne bragging about his feats. Jake was a very perceptive man, and already had a watchful look about his eyes. Matt made an off hand gesture. "Grade B movie stuff in real life. Hard to believe it really even happened."

"What are you trying to prove, anyway?" Jake poured some more wine. "Why don't you just give up on this case and get back to a reasonable life?" He sucked pensively at his teeth. "You don't have any money left, do you?"

"You'll get your rent soon." A flash of irritation struck Matt. "I've made some arrangements for funds."

"Never mind the damn rent." Jake waved carelessly. "The bank gave you more? I'm surprised they would without some security." His features froze. "Oh. They finally went after the cabin." The manner became disgusted. "I can't believe you'd take a chance of losing something that important to finance that piece of shit case. It's bad enough it almost got you and Adrianne killed. Now you're gambling the cabin." His mouth curled. "Hell, if it was just money, I'd lend you some—except I'm broke myself." He finished his glass. "Actually, even if I had some, I wouldn't lend any for that case."

Matt threw up his hands in defense. "Hey, you and I have disagreed on cases before. You've sure never been this strident about it. Even if I wanted to get out, it's sure too late now. It's like you take it personally that I'm committed." Matt hooked his hands behind his head. "You got a bet going on it?"

Jake looked startled, but his reply was vehement. "No damned way! I just think it's crazy to take on one of the town's best loved powers and risk Adrianne's life over a case that's not worth a God-damned thing."

"Just a joke. Calm down." He watched his friend pour another heavy glass of wine. Jake's appearance was vacant, and he was drinking even more than usual. Adrianne had probably let him know she wanted to break it off last night. Matt hoped he wouldn't raise the subject. He was the last person Jake should seek solace from for that problem.

They sat in silence for a while. Finally, Jake pushed his empty glass back. His sigh was not one of contentment. "So when do you have to sign the place over to the blood-suckers?"

It took Matt a second to pick up on his meaning. "Actually, this afternoon I'm supposed to sign the papers."

There was an awkward silence. "Adrianne's dumped me, old man." His friend had pasted on a crooked grin. Matt opened his mouth. "No, no. Don't say anything. There's nothing to say." Jake appeared suddenly haggard. "I've really been trying, you know. It's just like there is something standing between us. Something unsolvable." He turned away. His voice lowered and became brusque. "I usually don't give a shit, you know."

His attitude became sardonic. "Anyway, you ought to go for it. Oh, don't give me that look of innocence. I've watched you look at her, untouchable merchandise and all that." The muscles of his jaw bunched. "Well—she's fair game now." He smiled to himself. "Actually, old buddy, I think she likes you. In fact, if I didn't know you better, I'd think you were my problem." He sniggered at his own joke.

Jake stood up unsteadily and grabbed his keys. "Well, this day is shot. I think I'll go drink some lunch."

Matt looked at his friend's condition. "I hope you're just going across the street?"

"Don't think I'm in any shape to drive, huh? Old goody-two-shoes Matt, going to take care of his friend." He waggled a finger at Matt. "Think about what I said, now."

Matt watched him go out the main door and then headed into his own office. There never would be another opportunity like that to tell him. He just couldn't do it, though. There was no way he could have said anything during that conversation. The problem was, if he decided to tell him later, it would seem like he had purposely hidden it from him. It would make it even worse, if that was possible.

The whole parting conversation was bizarre. Did Jake actually know? No, there was no way. He would never have acted that way if he did. Jake was out but, ironically, he still stood between them like a shadow.

The soulful brown eyes stared out at Matt from the framed picture as if trying to warn him not to do what he was planning. "That's a hell of a rack on that elk, isn't it?"

The thin, ruddy face split into the first big smile Matt had ever seen on the man. "Got him in big sky country—Montana." The washed-out eyes shifted from the photo and came to rest on Matt with a certain proprietary air. "There anything else you need explained about those papers?"

Matt had thumbed through the stack of documents twice. He had lots of questions, but they had more to do with what the heck he was doing and why they were forcing him to do it. He knew only too well what the papers meant: pay us back in six months or we foreclose. They meant: screw up this case and you lose everything. Matt looked at the stack of papers. So that's what all the eggs in one basket looked like.

"Something funny, Mr. Taylor?" Matt guessed the guy wasn't used to seeing people smile to themselves at the idea of signing away a birthright. Matt suddenly wondered what Grant would say if he was old enough to ask about this decision. Grant had told Matt that he thought his dad was a brave man. Wonder if he would someday decide he was also a stupid one. Oh well. This decision was made almost a year ago when he met that family down in El Cajon. It was best to get the details over with and get on with the business of a trial.

"Got a pen, Mr. Hutchinson?"

32

The team looked at him expectantly, coffee and rolls in hand. The tension of what tomorrow would bring was palpable. It was half past eight on Sunday morning. The strain of late hours for weeks, restrained tempers, frayed nerves, and too much yet to do, was etched in their posture and in their weary expressions. Matt looked back sympathetically. He knew they were exhausted and yet the real battle was only beginning. Tomorrow they may get a courtroom or they may trail along for days or a week, waiting for a judge to open up. Even then, there was no guarantee the case would start. It might ultimately be bumped by criminal cases having preference, meaning he and his team might have to go through the whole process again, six months later. The preparation money spent once again. And where would that leave him with the loan payment? What about the cabin as security? If they did get a judge, the case would take at least six weeks to try, so they had better pace themselves.

Matt took a deep breath and started the final prep meeting. "So, summarize where things are with you, Emily."

She referred to her notes. "Todd and Debbie are in town and reading their depositions so they will be ready to testify. They expect you to spend a couple of hours with them this afternoon and then again tomorrow night." She checked off a couple of items. "Eight of the briefs are in final form for you to check. Four more are 'getting there.' It'll be a late one tonight. Jury instructions are ready for you and you need to revise the special ones." She grabbed another piece of paper. "I just remembered that the photo enlarge-ment service needed the extra pages of hospital records by this morning. I'll run those over right away."

"We divided scheduling the witnesses between Mary Beth, myself and Adrianne." Emily tapped her pencil. "Most of mine are the experts. I've assumed expert testimony starts on Wednesday and left blanks to be filled in with lay people. Most of the doctors say they'll be flexible about their schedules. Adrianne has a few problems she'll tell you about."

As she went on through her list, Matt thought about how lucky he was to have a pro like Emily heading his team. The logistics of bringing a large case like this together for trial were comparable to launching a small military campaign. Just the process of witness calendaring could drive inex-perienced people crazy.

The trouble was, it was virtually impossible to predict the court sched-ule. The case might start right away or it might wait days for another trial to finish. The judge might move to jury selection immediately or might take a few lazy days talking about the law or settlement. Some judges work long days with little sympathy for exhausted lawyers. Some have trial five days a week and some have "dark days" when they take care of other mat-ters. Some have "banker's hours," taking long lunches and quitting early, even when another half-hour would finish a busy surgeon expert so he or she didn't have to come back the next day at great expense to them and the party that called them.

It sounded like Emily had everything well-organized, but Matt knew it would immediately fall apart whenever they managed to get started in the trial. Every case had at least one important witness that suddenly had to leave town just when they were badly needed. As Emily wrapped up, Matt looked at Mary Beth.

"Okay, I've pulled the whole file apart and organized it like you sug-gested, key items segregated and copies in each witness folder. All our witness depos have been summarized and the testimony cross-referenced." She pulled at her tight curls nervously as she talked. "All the relevant medical articles any witness referred to or authored are copied and number-indexed for quick reference." She looked up at Matt. "I know you'll want to have read them all, but I put in a second copy that I read, and highlighted what I found interesting."

The list went on and on and Matt tried to curb his impatience. If he didn't give his input at this point, the final product might be unusable. The problem was he had at least two days work to cram into the next few precious hours before tomorrow morning's calendar call.

The lanky investigator drifted into the conference room unobtrusively, sipping on a battered old coffee mug. He hadn't been seen or heard from for a couple of weeks. All they knew was that he had some leads he was checking out. They all quieted and several pairs of eyes drifted to his craggy face as he swirled the steaming cup to cool the brew. Long moments stretched out as he ignored the silence his entrance had created. Finally satisfied with the temperature of his coffee, he glanced up at the ring of faces and nodded his greeting.

He drank noisily from the cup. "Some good news, most not." His eyes crinkled as the steam rose from the cup. "I think I found one of the supervising nurses on duty that day. Been to her house. The x-rays are definitely going to stay missing. Turns out they were all destroyed about three years ago in a fire at the storage facility." Matt sighed in exasperation. "Also it looks like the main nurse is going to stay missing too." His broad shoulders hunched up. "Dropped off the face of the earth about four years ago."

"Isn't there any other way to find her?"

The reply was laconic. "Got one more friend to try. Not so sure you'll like what she says if we do find her, though."

Matt's expression turned puzzled.

The PI took another gulp and continued. "The nurse super I found, Sue Anne, she remembers the case some. Says Marie, the nurse on duty, always used to talk about how bad off the kid was when he came in—how lucky he was to have lived."

Matt shuddered inwardly. The whole case rested on the proposition that Todd got worse while in the hospital. Sounded like the witness they were trying so hard to find might kill them, even if they did find her. "So what the heck was *good* about what you've found?"

"Well, I talked to one of the x-ray techs who used to work with the deceased radiologist." Clint chose this time to pull out his plug and pack a pinch of tobacco in his cheek, happily mixing it with his coffee. They all waited impatiently.

"Seems he was a pretty finicky guy—always afraid he was going to get sued for something and not have the film to back up his diagnosis." He looked cryptically at the circle of expectant faces. "So anyway, he made extra copies of many of his films. I haven't found them yet, but somewhere there is a stack of about a zillion old x-rays and just *maybe* ours will be one of them."

Matt looked toward Adrianne for an update. "I'm just about done with my projects. I've been finalizing my suggestions for your opening statement and working on the outline of testimony by the family." She appeared a bit uncertain.

"Anything you're wondering about?"

"Yeah, if you had to make a list, what is the most important rule of the open?"

"Opening statement's absolutely critical. Do it right and the defense starts out the case on the ropes. But it has to be *totally* accurate, or they'll eat you alive when they stand up. Also you have to deal with everything in the case that's bad before they get up to take their shot." He pointed to the stack of materials on his desk. "That's why I'm going through everything and why I want you to give me an exhaustive list of every damn thing they are going to hit us with—it's extremely important."

After they broke up the meeting, Matt went back to his office and sat back down in the middle of a stack of documents. He was working on his first draft opening statement and was combing the transcripts and file materials to check for accuracy on each point. A soft knock on his door broke into his concentration.

He looked up and saw Adrianne. "Hey there." Matt inclined his head toward the couch. He was painfully aware that he would probably have kicked anyone else out. They had both been working so hard there hadn't been an opportunity to confront the looming pink elephant issue. Since that weekend, their relationship had been professional, but reserved. He realized that, busy or not, he welcomed the opportunity to chat with her. "So what's on your mind?"

"We haven't really had a chance to deal with things…between us… both so busy and all. Originally, we planned that I'd sit in with you—in court, I mean." She looked up awkwardly.

"…and you want to be sure that's still okay?"

"I thought I'd better ask. If it would be awkward…if it might bother you, then maybe I shouldn't."

"If I thought it would be a distraction, I'd say so." He watched her closely. "Do you want to be in there? We'll have to work very closely, night and day. Total concentration. How do *you* feel about that?"

Her face lit up. "I can't think about anything else but helping try this case." Determination flooded from her. "I'd die if you said no." She suddenly stopped. "But I thought I'd better give you a chance to duck out on your invite."

"I really need your help; this case is going to be a killer—even with both of us working our tails off." He looked at her seriously. "I need you to help me prepare witnesses, meet people, coordinate schedule changes. In court, you can make phone calls, take notes, kick me if I miss something or get too cute with a witness." He tapped his fingers on his desk thoughtfully. "You can research points of law and might even put on a witness or two." Her eyes widened. "I never considered that you wouldn't be there with me." He pointed his index finger toward her. "We're going to try this thing together. You know the case as well as I do and I don't think I could do it without you."

After she left, Matt took a deep breath. When was he going to deal with this pink elephant in the room? When Adrianne was around there was a subliminal communication, both emotionally and intellectually, that could not be ignored. She made him feel charged. Just her presence invigorated him, gave him a sense of renewal.

Right now, though, he had to get his mind back on the trial that he hoped would start tomorrow morning. Consciously, he made himself think of the points Murphy would make in his opening statement and what he could say to anticipate and defuse the impact. Immediately a chill of adrenaline began to chase the last vestige of passion from his mind. His mantle of concentration dropped seamlessly into place.

33

As Matt mounted the steps to the huge old City Hall and courthouse, his thoughts slipped back to the case he had tried in this building just a year ago. He certainly hoped that the Gleasons would be more pleased with the result of this effort than the Olsens were with his last verdict.

He looked up at the silent gray stone and tried to visualize the cross-section of humanity that had probably already responded to the random jury summons issued by the county bureaucrats. Some angry, others impatient, certainly all of them apprehensive they would be chosen to serve. These plumbers, accountants, housewives, and messengers were gathering to participate in a process that had its inception over a thousand years ago. Inside these somber walls, they would be asked to set aside their own personal concerns and take their turn serving on a jury of their peers. Laypeople dispensing justice for the acts and omissions of their fellow man.

Matt shuddered when he thought about the negative attitude he would face when selecting the twelve person panel. Matt knew the public kept hearing complaints about the jury system. People said it didn't work and made up examples of juries gone wild. Most of these negative claims came from big corporations and insurance companies, or their paid lobbyists, entities that stood to lose big-time if shoddy business practices hurt someone and a jury got angry. Advertisements about "run-away" verdicts, and "crazy claims" were subtle propaganda designed to create a bias in the defendant's favor among the people who would eventually sit on juries.

These special interests were doing quite an effective job of poisoning the jury pool.

Matt noted, ruefully, that these same companies, when confronted with a lawsuit against them, almost invariably refused to waive a jury. They didn't want to have the decision made by a judge. Most people knowledgeable about the legal system knew that, while juries occasionally made mistakes, these were usually easily fixed by the judge. They knew the present system was much better than any others that had been proposed. In other parts of the world, decisions were made by autocratic rulers, professional judges, or paid bureaucrats. In America, Matt reflected as the elevator took him to the fourth floor, both sides were happy to pray they would get the right decision from their local butcher.

Chill tendrils of apprehension and excitement played with the lining of his gut as he pushed through the heavy brass-studded doors of the presiding judge. Even twenty minutes before the master calendar session was to begin, the big room was crammed with the animated bodies of a hundred lawyers, the remainder spilling into the marbled corridor. The acrid odor of tension assailed his senses. By the end of the day, half these lawyers would have to send their suits out for cleaning. It was trial call on Monday morning in San Francisco Superior Court.

"I see you got your trial haircut. I guess you think we're going to actually get a courtroom?" Murphy grinned at Matt. He had also obviously had his hair trimmed in anticipation of facing a jury today.

"You heard something I haven't? There are several judges available and only about fifteen cases ahead of us. Sounds good to me."

The defense attorney looked around the room. "Yeah, but most of the judges available don't want long cases. My bet is we'll get bumped."

"Sure hope you're wrong."

A senior partner of one of the biggest plaintiff's firms in town sidled by on his way to a seat up front. He put his hand on Murphy's arm. "Hi, Lew, hear you're starting battle for 'The Prince' today." His cold eyes flicked toward Matt and then back to Murphy. "Hope you kick the shit out of them. Not even animals go after their own kind."

Murphy smiled as if to soften the words, but Matt noticed his eyes stayed cold. After the guy moved on he spoke under his breath. "I told you how it would be if you pushed this one, Matthew. Can't say I didn't warn you."

Matt moved toward the seats as the clerk and bailiff came into court from chambers. "Man's gotta do what a man's gotta do, Lew." He inclined his head to where Conti was holding court in a corner of the room. "Watch your ass with that one; he's not exactly the docile client type." Murphy just reached down for his briefcase.

The judge took the bench and quickly began winnowing the list of cases set for trial that week. Shorter cases were sent out for trial. A few announced they had settled or asked for a continuance. All but one of the judges had been assigned when they got to Matt's case. A friend leaned over to Matt just before the call and told him the one judge left, Denise Lynch, had a vacation coming the next week. If that were true, there was no way they would start today.

"*Gleason v. Conti et. al.,*" the clerk intoned.

A stir of comments rippled quickly through the watching lawyers and then, as the judge looked up, a heavy silence fell over the room. "Ready for the plaintiff, Your Honor, Matthew Taylor appearing." The two defense attorneys made their appearances as well.

The judge shuffled some papers and then looked at Matt. "Have there been any settlement discussions, Mr. Taylor?"

"No, Your Honor."

"This is a long case, estimated by you at six, and by them, at eight weeks."

Matt was silent. He knew the judge was considering a settlement conference, and Matt was hoping they would be sent to Judge Lynch. A conference would keep the chance of assignment for trial alive because another judge might become available in the next few days. Also, Lynch was a respected settlement judge and might even be able to help them reach a resolution.

"Take this file to Judge Lynch, counsel; you're assigned to her for settlement conference." He looked hard at the three of them. "Be diligent, gentlemen. The court would not be happy to have a courtroom tied up for that length of time."

"Yes, Your Honor."

They trooped dutifully around the corner to the assigned department. Lynch had been a good defense attorney before she took the bench and was considered tough but fair. She ran a tight courtroom, but was user-friendly for experienced trial attorneys. She had shock of grey hair pulled back in a business-like bun and a handsome face weathered by a lifetime of resolving conflict. An unusually small nose was closely bracketed by piercing eyes that could throw fire across a courtroom if provoked. She had supple artist's hands, which she used to great advantage in communication. Her abundant intelligence and common sense made her one of the most effective settlement judges on the bench.

They spent a half an hour educating the judge and then Matt was sent out while she talked to the defense. Todd and Debbie looked lost in the cavernous courtroom when Matt and Adrianne came out of the chambers.

"What happened in there with the judge?" Todd's voice sounded high and querulous in the silence of the empty room.

"We each explained our positions and the key facts of the case from each perspective. Now the judge is feeling them out privately and then will do the same with us." Matt sat next to them and Adrianne sat across to listen. "Eventually, she will push them to offer money and then push us to accept."

Debbie was puzzled. "But doesn't she want to make sure the amount that is offered is fair?"

"The judge's job is to get the case settled—to twist arms and shove everybody 'til she gets the case to stop plugging up the court's calendar." He gave them a rueful look. "They get brownie points for getting rid of cases. They leave the question of fairness to the attorneys."

Todd's young face wrinkled in thought. "So what they say isn't really sincere? You mean they can't be trusted, even though they're judges?"

"No. It's not that simple. Some are pretty straight—this one certainly is…but you have to remember everyone has their own agenda, even me."

He looked steadily at Todd. "You need to make your own mind up. You have to decide what's right for you."

Todd turned his mom. Debbie then turned her big brown eyes back to Matt. "What agenda do you have, Mr. Taylor?"

Matt held her gaze. "I'd like to think it is yours and Todd's, Debbie, but don't forget I have a business to run and I have to make business-like decisions."

"Yes, of course, Matt, but it seems we are rather completely tied together in this. We wouldn't be where we are if not for you." She put her head to the side, the smile spreading. "A good result for you is a good result for us. Right?"

Matt noticed Adrianne was watching intently. He nodded sheepishly at Todd and Debbie. "Of course you're right. But remember, my goals may be more easily satisfied than yours."

The defense lawyers told Matt that the judge was ready to see them. Matt and Adrianne left the Gleasons out in the courtroom and sat in front of Lynch's battered old desk in chambers as she signed some documents. The room was paneled with golden oak and the yellowing varnish was in bad need of work. A large family grinned from photos of ski and beach trips, with grandchildren interspersed among snaps of toothy politicians. The judge had a reputation as an empathetic person with sensible instincts. She finished the last of the papers and handed them to her law clerk, then leaned back in her chair.

"So what would you say your chances of success are in this one—realistically?"

Matt thought for a moment. "Well, it's a long and complicated case to predict, but I'd say six out of ten."

The judge blew out a long breath of air. "Big difference of opinion—they say one or two out of ten."

"Ha! They're blowing smoke, judge. I wouldn't have taken a case that was that much of a long shot." Matt leaned forward. "I've told you the facts. Remember though, I've got a lawyer as a defendant and a great family with a serious injury."

The judge responded thoughtfully. "Normally that might work in your favor, but Conti's a hero in this city. He's a darling of the press and has a national reputation. The other thing is that this injury was from an accident. Conti didn't cause it—he just didn't figure out how it happened." The judge leaned back and contemplated. "We're talking about an act of *omission* here, not *commission*. There's nothing here a jury's likely to get mad at."

"With all due respect, I disagree. He promised to do this case himself and then gave it to a kid."

"Happens all the time in the law, Matt. No one can do everything themselves, not even you."

"It shouldn't happen. Not when somebody this young's so badly injured and needs a great lawyer."

The judge watched Matt as she gathered her thoughts. "Well, there are lots of serious questions about the medical case as well." She stroked her throat. "You say it's worth several million. We've only had a couple of verdicts of any kind that've gone over five million. A little rich, aren't you?" Matt just looked at her. The judge moved her gaze over to Adrianne and rolled her eyes, elaborately. "Don't forget what happened to you last year in Judge Huston's department, counselor."

Matt knew the judge was softening him up and he was suddenly anxious to get to the bottom line. The judge fluttered both hands. "I know, I know. Look, I think they may be thinking in the million range. They haven't said, but that's my read at this point."

"No way, Judge." Matt stood up and Adrianne followed his lead. "It's not worth discussing."

"Now sit down, you two." She gestured at the chairs. "I didn't say I agreed with them." Matt turned back from the door and looked at the judge. The artful hands engaged them. "Come on. I can work on them, but I have to know where you're coming from."

Matt came back and sat, but Adrianne sat over on the couch near the door. The judge looked at her, gave a small smile of appreciation for the message expressed by her staying near the exit, and then looked at Matt expectantly.

"If I win this thing," Matt stated firmly, "I'm going to get between seven and nine big ones. I know there's risk, but it's a good case they should be very worried about. I'm willing to recommend about five and a half. That's a good buy."

The judge covered a small smile, but her expression said: *Okay—here we go, horse-trading time.* Matt would actually recommend less to the clients, but he knew the judge would cut whatever number Matt gave. The fact was, he had to negotiate with the judge as well as the defendant. The woman behind the desk allowed her face to frown elaborately.

"That's way too much, Matt. I can't even tell them that figure or they'll do the same thing you started to do—walk out."

Matt gave a "so what" gesture. The judge stuck her lower lip out pensively. "Okay, so let me work on them a bit and I'll see where we can go. Why don't you send them back in?"

Matt and Adrianne went back to the courtroom and huddled with the Gleasons. Matt explained what had been said and tried to help them understand the process. He warned them that the judge would not be able to get five and a half, but they should soon get a reading of what the defense would be willing to pay.

Todd listened and then cleared his throat tentatively. "What amount do you suggest we take, if they offer it, Matt?"

Matt sat thinking for a moment, aware from the look on her face that Adrianne was as curious as the others for his answer. He hated to be pinned down on that question until he saw how things went, but clients always wanted to know and they had a right to an answer. He had found it was best to talk in ranges. "I think a good figure would be four to four and a half million. It's not enough to do everything you'll need, but it'll help and it's a lot better than losing." He looked at Todd and Debbie's faces and saw that they thought that was a lot of money. "Two things, though. First, that's not really near enough. Second, don't plan on them offering that much." Their faces fell. "Better to be realistic, you guys." He looked at Adrianne and saw her unobtrusively release a quiet sigh.

The rest of the day, the judge spent a lot of time with the defense and only occasionally called them in. About half past three, she sent the defense home and called Matt and Adrianne in. She cut out the niceties and came straight to the point.

"Here's the deal. They have authority for two million, two hundred thousand dollars." She paused to gauge the reaction and didn't seem surprised by the fact the number failed to elicit even a flicker of response from either one of them. Nodding to herself, she continued. "I've told them that's not enough, but they say they've run out of authority and inclination." Matt opened his mouth to speak, but the judge hurried on. "Hold it. I said they have to get more, and we argued for a long time. They finally said they would recommend two and a half million, but not a penny more." She frowned at Matt's stony expression. "They won't go try to get authority from the insurance company to offer that amount unless they know you'll take it."

The judge played with the letter opener in her hand, sliding it absently between her fingers. She finally looked up at Matt with a stern expression on her face. "I want you to listen to me carefully, Matt. This is a damn tough case. I know you've been through a lot getting it up to this point, and I admire the guts you've shown taking it this far."

The judge eased her chair back. "This is a hell of an offer. You can be proud of what you've accomplished for your client and you can put a lot of problems behind you." She raised her eyebrows. "Forever." She looked back and forth between the two of them and then looked at Adrianne. "I don't know what influence you have over this hard-headed guy, Miss, but this is a lot of money to turn down. That nice young man out there can do a lot with that much money." She looked back at Matt and her face tightened with determination. "Matt, I wouldn't want you to have to look this kid in the eye if you left that kind of money on the table. This is an easy one to lose."

The judge stood and came around the desk and steerer them both toward the door. "I don't want to hear any response right now. Talk to those nice folks out there, and then go home and think about it. Come back in the morning and let me know." The judge opened the door. "I know you'll do the right thing, Matt."

They rode in silence most of the way back to the office where they had told the Gleasons to meet them. Matt could feel Adrianne's occasional glance. Finally he looked over at her. "So, what do you think?" He smiled at her. "Exercise your influence!"

"Little does she know, my thoughts and a couple of bucks will get you a cup of coffee."

"No, the judge is pretty sharp. She doesn't miss much. She can see that I do value your opinion and she was pitching you as much as me."

Her face turned serious. "I don't know what I think at the moment. I'd rather hear your thoughts and think about it, then let you know."

"Chicken."

When they reached the office they went in and, over some coffee, explained to their anxious clients what the judge had said. Debbie and Todd sat thinking for a while and then looked at Matt. Debbie spoke for them both. "We know it's less than what you had said, but it seems like a lot of money. What do you recommend?"

"It's a tough number. It's well placed." Matt looked at them helplessly. "It's not anywhere near enough to take care of you properly, but it's high enough to make us sweat. That's the idea, of course."

"You've said that before: 'it's not enough.'" Debbie put her hand on Matt's arm. "But to us, it seems like so much more than we have. Can you explain why it wouldn't be adequate to care for Todd?"

Out of the corner of his eye, he could see Adrianne nodding her agreement with the question. He marshaled his thoughts. "Debbie, you do everything for Todd now, and Todd's brother, Bob, helps out some. You're going to be sixty years old soon and your back is a mess. I give you only a few years before Bob will have to give up his work and his future marriage to keep things going."

"Todd can't survive without full-time care. If—no—*when* your back goes out for good, Debbie, he won't even be able to get out of bed in the morning, much less deal with the rest of the day. That's every day, every night." Matt looked back and forth between them. "You guys need twenty-four-hour care, three hundred and sixty-five days a year. That, and the other needs, comes close to three hundred thousand a year." He scratched his beard, searching for words. "With this offer, *if* they come up with it, you net, after costs so far and the third fee, maybe one million six hundred thousand dollars. That'll be gone in less than seven or eight years, even with good investments."

He sought for the right phrases among the heavy beams overhead. "If Todd doesn't have help, he'll have to go into an institutional type situation or get by in very marginal circumstances on his own. It'll be a poor life and it'll be dangerous to his health, both physically and emotionally." Matt looked at Debbie and his eyes softened. "You can't kill yourself doing this caretaking much longer. Bob will help when you can't anymore, but it will be at the expense of his life also."

There was silence for a while and then Todd spoke up. "So…what do you think we should do?"

"They've offered enough to help out part-time for maybe eight years, and if you do it minimally, for fourteen to sixteen years. Todd, you are barely twenty. With good care, you should live another forty plus years, many of those years without your mom. That's why, if we win, we should get a lot more." He looked at Adrianne; she was looking down. "On the other side is the risk. *One million six hundred thousand* net will sound awfully good if we lose this case. I think that our chances of winning are a little better than fifty percent, but not a lot better. I'd hate to see you get nothing." He was quiet for a moment. "Remember, predicting a trial or a jury is a lot like going to Vegas and throwing the dice."

They sat there and looked at him, waiting for the answer he was finding hard to articulate. He pinched his nose between his eyes to ease the pounding in his head. "The bottom line is this. I don't feel comfortable telling you what to do with this offer. I think I could live with a decision either way from you two." He sat back in the couch. "Basically, it's hard to call. I think you should decide. At this point it really should be up to you."

Debbie looked at Todd and then looked back at Matt. "Why don't you two get some dinner and let us talk a bit. Let us know where you are and we'll call you."

Matt and Adrianne didn't need to think about it. They ran across the street. Even on Monday night, the Fog City Diner was crowded. They ordered oysters and a salad quickly. Matt wanted to eat and get back to reworking the outline of his opening statement.

"What do you think they ought to do?"

He put sauce on an oyster while he thought about her question. "Obviously I have mixed thoughts. I can think of good reasons to go either way."

A tiny frown appeared between her eyes. "This ambivalence sounds like the trip down from the mountains, Matt." He looked at her steady green eyes. "Set aside all that lawyer-like weighing and balancing for a moment and tell me what you really *feel* about this 'almost offer.'"

Matt thought back on his feelings this afternoon when the judge was telling them about the figure. The first thoughts he'd had were pretty selfish. With the fee he would clear close to eight hundred thousand dollars and also get his costs of one hundred thousand dollars back if the case settled for that amount. The loan would be paid off and he would actually be ahead of the game financially for a while. Of utmost personal importance, he could keep the cabin. Most people in his business would consider it a win.

He could see in Adrianne's expression that she had already figured it out. She had sensed how he felt even before he had confronted his feelings. The truth was, he'd had a sick feeling in his gut ever since he heard what the judge said. Why? Because he was afraid the Gleasons would want to settle. The fact was, in his head he felt two and a half million was way too cheap, even though the conservative part of him felt that they should take the sure thing. In his heart, he thought they should go for it, even if he lost the cabin.

"You want to tell Conti and his crew to go to hell, don't you?"

"How come you got me so figured out?"

She slowly let out her breath. "You're not all that hard to see through, Matthew Taylor. I know how you really feel about this case, setting aside that moment of self-doubt. You want to do more for those folks than that. You believe in this case."

"All true—but so what?" A wan smile. "It's their life, not mine. I can't put my feelings ahead of their immediate needs. Besides, what's my motive really?" His face appeared drawn with stress. "At this point, the whole thing has become personal with Conti. Have I also lost my objectivity? Am I thinking less like a lawyer and more like a kid in a playground shoving match?"

She covered his hand with hers. "I think I can help you on that point. I've watched you through this whole thing, even worried that you were doing just that, and voiced it a few times." Her hand squeezed his firmly. "I watched you when you had a serious moment of weakness, at a bad time." She picked up her fork to eat and brandished it at him. "I know this case now, and I know you. You're thinking like a lawyer, a damn good lawyer, but one with a heart." She took a bite of her salad. "It's in their lap right now, but I say, if they'll give you the chance—go for it."

Matt stared at his plate. He had been hungry, but now the salad looked like cardboard. "Matt." The hostess was at the table. "Call for you. You can take it in the back."

A few minutes later, he came back and sat down. He played absently with his food for a moment. Just as she opened her mouth to voice her impatience, he looked back up and his expression was serious.

"That was Debbie. They decided they would leave it to me. She said they have gone this far depending on me and they're really comfortable with either decision."

His expression became one of wonder. "You know what else she said? Todd told her he thinks I really want to turn the offer down." Adrianne's eyes widened. "He said 'tell Matt I can live with losing.' Debbie then told me that he went to the State Championship for JV basketball the year before he was hurt. He loved it. They lost, but I guess they played a heck of a game." Matt had a difficult time seeing Adrianne for a moment. When he could, he saw her eyes were shining with moisture too.

34

When Matt came out of the judge's chambers, he sat next to Todd. "I told them we rejected the offer. The judge said it was a mistake. Murphy said they wouldn't be offering any more money." Matt put his hand on Todd's thin shoulder and gave him a crooked grin. "Her actual words were: 'You bought yourself a trial—hope you made it clear to that kid how much money that is to lose.'"

Matt gave Debbie a reassuring look. "The money is there for now. If things don't go well, we can always revisit the issue of settlement."

Todd hooked his arm over the back of the wheelchair and shifted himself so he could see Matt straight on. "Can they withdraw the money they've offered?"

"Anytime." Matt said. "It's traditional they give you notice before they do that, but they don't have to." He watched them both closely. "Are you alright with this decision. *Really* alright with it?"

Debbie gave her son a sweet smile. Still looking at Todd, she replied for them both. "You're our lawyer, Matthew. We trust you to do the right thing for us."

Todd reached awkwardly and grabbed at Matt's hand. "To heck with them, Matt. Let's give 'em hell!"

Just then Adrianne walked up with the court file. "We've been assigned to Department Six, Judge Marvin Rigoletti. He wants us there right away to start picking a jury." Department Six was on the opposite end of the building so, as they talked, they started pushing Todd and walking down the long marble corridor.

Matt thought quickly about Rigoletti and what he knew of the man. He had not been on the bench that long and Matt had never tried a case in front of him. He had done labor law in private practice and had a reputation as a smart lawyer. On the bench, the scuttlebutt was that he had trouble making decisions. That would be bad in a case as complicated as this one. He was Italian. Matt wondered how that would cut in a case where Conti was the defendant. Well, all would become known with time.

Pushing through the heavy swinging doors, Matt and his small entourage were confronted with a sea of curious faces. The room was crammed with prospective jurors. White, black, and brown faces watched as they made their way to the front and sat in the row the clerk had kept free for the parties. Conti was not in sight.

Matt shoved the swinging gate aside and approached Sandra Anderson, the judge's clerk. Frizzy grey hair framed thick lenses that magnified knowing, black eyes. She acted prim, but could surprise you with her sudden nasty sense of humor. Matt had always gotten along well with her because he had learned to follow her unique rules.

She looked up at him and swung her eyes dramatically. "Got a humdinger by the tail here, don'tcha?" She waved her hand at him. "Don't answer. Just go on in to see the man. They're all in there already."

Matt and Adrianne knocked and then opened the door to the chambers in response to the booming voice of the judge. In front of his desk were the two defense attorneys, Murphy and Anderson, and, on the sofa, Conti, looking like he owned the place. Matt took in the scene and decided that he had better deal with this immediately. "Hello, Your Honor, Matt Taylor representing the plaintiff, and this is my associate, Adrianne Gardner. Sandra didn't tell me you wanted clients in chambers. Give me a moment and I'll get them."

Conti was sprawled across the couch, acting imperial. He looked dismissively at Matt, and then cleared his throat to get the judge's attention. His nasal voice sounded chummy and casual. "That's all right, Marv. The plaintiffs aren't attorneys, so there's no reason for them to be in here with us."

The man in the black robe glanced sharply at Conti and then over to Matt, still standing at the door. "That won't be necessary, Mr. Taylor. Actually, I prefer discussions in chambers to be with counsel only and I like parties to remain in court or the hallway." Matt looked at Conti and noticed that the old bull just shrugged. He was settled in for the duration. Matt looked back to the judge, but found him looking pointedly at Murphy. The defense attorney got the message and addressed his client.

"Sal, I think the judge wants you to wait outside with the other parties. Would you mind?"

The heavy features knotted in irritation as he harrumphed his way to his feet. As he brushed by Matt he spoke *sotto voce*. "Hope you're wearing your iron pants, kid. We're going to kick your smart ass all over this courtroom."

When the door closed, the judge waved them to seats in front of him and addressed Matt. "Now that you've been properly warned about your immediate future, perhaps we can go over a few ground rules and then start picking a jury." They talked about court trial days, and he told them his hours. They agreed on the approach to jury selection and then he told them to be ready to start in a few minutes.

* * *

The judge took the bench and the courtroom listened in rapt silence as he explained the selection process and gave a brief summary of the case. A buzz rippled across the jury pool as they heard Conti's name and realized the famous white-headed litigator sitting in the front row was actually the defendant. Sandra picked twelve names at random and the first group took the box. The room full of prospective jurors stood and swore to answer the selection questions honestly.

Matt looked at them with intense curiosity, but knew it was unlikely that many of the first twelve would actually sit on the eventual jury. As the judge asked preliminary questions, Matt wrote down information and thumbed through the packet of information he had paid the jury service firm to put together for him. For a fee, they would tell him information seldom gleaned from the questioning process and, most importantly, give him voting information from prior jury service. Finally it was time for the parties to question the impaneled twelve. Matt was first.

He stood and smiled at the blank faces in front of him. He reminded himself that many of them were at least as nervous as he was. Six plus weeks of trial and this was the start. Mao's comment about the thousand-mile march needing a first step was comforting.

Juror number one, Mr. Madison, was overweight and had a pugnacious look. His narrow gaze was impaling Matt with unbridled cynicism. He had told the judge he was a cabinet shop foreman, and Matt's book said he had no previous jury experience. "Mr. Madison, you've heard my client, Todd Gleason, has a very serious injury and has brought this action against Mr. Conti for compensation." The pig eyes stared at him without a flicker of compassion. "How do you feel about the fact that Todd is seeking justice from a jury of people like yourself in a court of law?"

The voice was more a growl than anything else. "Damn fool if he picks a jury that thinks like me."

The guy didn't want to sit on the panel. Maybe Matt could just get him off before he made any speeches. "Thank you for your candor, Mr. Madison. I take it that you feel you have a frame of mind that would make it difficult to treat my client the same as Mr. Conti?"

The man's face puckered like he had eaten something sour. Uh oh, Matt thought, here we go. "I don't care what you take. I don't like people suing for getting themselves hurt and I don't like the fact that stupid people sit on juries like this and give away crazy amounts of money." His eyes got even smaller, if that was possible. "I'll bet you're asking for millions. That's ridiculous for an injury." The last was spit out, like the words had left a bad taste in his mouth.

Matt cringed inside. There was usually one like this guy, and others who may think it but didn't say it. Usually you didn't get hit with it right out of the blocks by the first juror. Matt could feel Anderson snickering to himself and could see the judge looking at him out of the corner of his eye. Matt knew that the court would excuse the juror for obvious bias if Matt asked, but maybe he could try to counter this a bit.

"I see, Mr. Madison. Tell me, do you believe it is important to have a court system to deal with disputes in this country?" A grudging *yes* followed.

"But if I understand correctly, you don't think you could give millions of dollars for this serious injury to Mr. Gleason even if we proved that it was needed to care for him. Do I have that right?" This time, the *yes* was clear and ringing.

"Are you a person who could be fair-minded if you were called upon to judge a dispute you thought was reasonable?" Matt knew that most people wanted to think of themselves as fair. Madison nodded. Apparently, he was no exception. Matt turned and caught a glimpse of Murphy's smirk. They thought Matt was digging a hole for himself. Matt hoped they didn't turn out to be right.

"So Mr. Madison, suppose that IBM built a very special computer for a large furniture manufacturer here in San Francisco." The scowling face showed a twinge of interest when he mentioned furniture manufacturing. He had him hooked, but Murphy was getting restless. He had better hurry this before the defense objected.

"Now suppose while they were unloading the computer, it fell off the ramp and was smashed beyond repair." The porcine features looked interested at last. "You're on the jury and the company proves the cost of the computer was ten million dollars. Ten big ones. That was the evidence."

Matt walked around the podium and stood near the rail. "Tell me, under those circumstances, would you have any difficulty bringing in a verdict for ten million dollars?"

"No. It sounds like the cost of the computer was clear."

Matt leaned his hands on the jury railing and looked around the room at the silent prospective jurors. "So, Mr. Madison, you have no difficulty at all assessing value in a case involving an expensive piece of machinery, but you are opposed to placing such a value on a human life." Matt turned back and looked directly at the shop foreman. "Even if it is proven that it would take such a sum to care for my client."

The room was dead quiet. "Tell me, Mr. Madison, do you think a person who thinks as you do should sit as a juror on a case of this nature?"

The corpulent man glared at Matt and then cleared his throat. "No I don't. I already told you that."

Matt nodded solemnly. "Thank you very much for your candor. Plaintiff would ask that Mr. Madison be excused for cause, Your Honor."

"The juror will be excused. Thank you, Mr. Madison. Will the clerk please call another juror." Matt snuck a glance at Murphy and was pleased to see the smug look had disappeared.

The next juror was a grandmotherly woman with a sweet face. She smiled at Matt when she took her seat. He smiled back with relief, but he knew better than to trust that smile without a few questions. It was going to be a long day.

* * *

Adrianne and Matt drove back to the office after they told the Gleasons they would meet them later. "Good Lord, that was so intense today. How do you do it?"

"I wish I could say you get used to it. This was an extra tough day, though."

"So many people have negative attitudes about lawsuits." She thought back on what happened. "But what gets me is most of them claim they could be fair anyway." She clicked her tongue. "It was the nice ones who felt sorry for Todd that excused themselves."

"Yeah, you get worried it's going to end up a defense-oriented jury when it's like that. I hate it when the sweet, caring people leave and the ones without a sympathetic bone in their bodies stick." He gave a short humorless laugh. "How 'bout when the judge keeps asking the ones who hate lawsuits if they can forget all that and be fair anyway?"

"Right. He never does that to the nice ones. Then you get to use up your peremptory challenges on the meanies tomorrow!"

When they got to the office, they each attacked a list of problems and shared a delivered pizza. The Gleasons arrived and they spent an hour poring over the jury list, trying to decide who to keep and who to bump off.

Debbie asked, "How do these challenges work? I'm confused."

"The lawyers can challenge any juror for 'cause.' That means anyone who acts biased during the questions. Like that guy, Madison. He had an axe to grind, so the judge felt it was appropriate to dismiss him." Matt grabbed a last slice of the cold pizza. "The judge has the call on challenges for cause. After challenges for cause, each side gets to use their 'peremptory' challenges. We each have six peremptory challenges. We can use those without giving any reasons." He added, "When we exercise the peremptory challenges, then new jurors are seated and they are also questioned for 'cause.'"

Todd broke in with a question. "Matt, how do you really tell which ones make the best jurors?"

Matt smiled without any humor. "The reality is, there's no good way to tell. We guess and ask questions and rely on instinct and questionable information. Basically, picking a jury or predicting them is like Russian roulette."

Adrianne took them away to work on their testimony and Matt hid out to polish his opening statement. After that, he went over the testimony he needed from the first few witnesses; then he drove home to get some sleep. He had to meet an expert witness for preparation early in the morning.

35

The courtroom clock said half past two, and Murphy had already spent well over ten minutes on Mrs. Simonsen. Murphy obviously didn't want her as a juror and was hoping to get her to admit to sympathy for Todd so he could get her off for cause and didn't have to use one of his peremptory challenges. Unobtrusively, Matt looked over the present jury panel. There were two people he was afraid of, an accountant and a bank manager, but the rest of the ones in the box looked reasonable.

Each side had used four of their six peremptory challenges. Jury selection would be done if they both ran out of challenges or if both sides "passed" the peremptory challenge. Matt thought the defense might be more worried than Matt was about some of the jurors. There was a chance Matt could get ahead in this chess game if he passed the challenge and the defense decided to bump a couple more. It was risky though. If they passed the challenge also, then the jury was set and he would be stuck with the accountant and the banker.

Murphy finished his questions, smiled, and thanked her, hiding his irritation that the prospective juror steadfastly claimed she could be fair. "We pass the juror for cause your honor."

The judge spoke to Matt, "Your turn, Mr. Taylor."

Matt looked at the panel with a pleased expression. "Todd Gleason is happy with the panel as constituted, Your Honor."

The judge addressed the defense table. "Defense challenge?"

While Murphy and Anderson huddled, Adrianne leaned over and whispered. "I'm surprised you're willing to accept the accountant and that banker, the guy with the brother who's a doctor."

"I'm playing poker with our friends at the other table. Watch."

Murphy rose and smiled at the last juror. "The defense will thank and excuse Mrs. Simonsen."

Matt smiled to himself. Now he was one challenge ahead. Sandra called a new name and the seat was filled by an African-American airline mechanic. His juror history said he had voted for the plaintiff in three prior cases. Matt asked a few questions and then shut up. Anderson tried to develop something to get rid of him for cause and failed. Both sides passed for cause and the judge moved his gaze toward Matt.

"We are happy with this jury, Your Honor."

Murphy shot him a suspicious glance, but Matt kept smiling at the panel. The defense huddled again and there was a touch of agitation in their whispered tones. Murphy rose and Matt held his breath. "Mr. Conti will excuse Mr. Thompson with a thank you for your time, sir." The United Airlines' mechanic gave the defense lawyer a dirty look; the juror knew why he was being dismissed.

Now Matt had two challenges left and the other side was fresh out. The judge called for another juror. This one was a grandmotherly type who had smiled at Debbie during the lunch break. Anderson tried to develop a cause challenge with his questions, but to no avail. With his back to the jury, he rolled his eyes at Matt, and they both passed the juror for cause.

The judge sat back. "Shall we pick two alternate jurors, gentlemen?"

Matt cleared his throat. It was time to dump the accountant and the banker. All but one of the jurors left of the pool in the back of the room looked pretty good to him. "Your Honor, the plaintiff has reconsidered and will thank and excuse Mr. Steele." The accountant jumped to his feet. He was just as happy to get back to his office.

The next juror called was a whip-thin Asian gentlemen dressed conservatively in a coat and tie. Matt's heart sank. With twenty people still out there, the odds had seemed good he would get one of the plaintiff-type jurors. Mr. Lee was an engineer and according to Matt's cheat sheet, had been a foreman on two previous juries. Each had returned verdicts for the defense after lengthy battles, each successfully led by Mr. Lee. He was intelligent, defense-oriented and clearly a leader, very likely to be a disaster for any plaintiff. Matt questioned him at length. The man was pleasant and firm. He could be fair to both sides. Murphy smiled at Matt and asked no questions at all.

The judge referred to his notes and then said to Matt. "You have one challenge left, Mr. Taylor."

Matt observed the sitting jury. Looking back at him were several reasonably neutral-looking people and two obvious ringers. He had only one challenge and two strong defense types left, either of which would be his pick to ultimately end up the foreman. It was a Hobson's choice at best.

"Could I have a minute with my client, Your Honor?"

The judge glanced at the clock. "Perhaps it would be a good time to take our afternoon break." He addressed at the jury: "Be back in fifteen minutes and don't discuss the case."

In the witness room, Matt addressed the issue directly. "We now have Mr. Steele off, and he was a defense juror all the way. We got ahead, but the dice came up against us. We have to choose between Mr. Addison, the banker whose brother is a physician and Mr. Lee who has a history of leading juries down the defense path. Let's each give an opinion."

Todd was obviously uncertain. The frail shoulders finally lifted. "I think we should let the banker go. He's got to like doctors and, while he said he makes loans to lawyers all the time, he bothers me for some reason."

Matt understood completely. Clients could usually tell, and he happened to have the same reaction to the man. Lee, on the other hand, was quite urbane and Matt responded well to him on a personal level. He looked at Debbie.

"I'm afraid I'm not going to make this any easier. I like the bank manager better than Mr. Lee. I felt I could relate to him better as a person."

The break was nearly over. Adrianne raised her hand tentatively, "Do I have a vote?"

"Of course you do."

"I think you two men are unconsciously reacting to the fact the banker is gay, at least I think he is."

Matt and Todd were startled, but Debbie nodded in agreement. "I think she may be right. Maybe that's why I liked him."

Matt thought furiously. They had to decide. The court would resume in two minutes. "Todd, I'm going to overrule the two of us. Adrianne may be right and that is a possible plus. Gays know what it is like to face adversity. They can be very empathetic with people who have a difficult life, like you." Matt regarded his nervous little group. "Also, most gay folks I know at least have open minds. That's all we need."

The rest of the selection went fast. When Matt challenged Mr. Lee, the next juror turned out to be a pleasant Russian deli-owner with a wife and three children. His oldest boy was only a few years younger than Todd. Matt liked him immediately. They picked two alternate jurors in case one of the sitting jurors got sick, and the judge dismissed the remaining jurors.

* * *

Matt studied the panel. A familiar feeling of relief and affection for the jurors swept over him. The selection process, with all its blind choices, was over. Now Todd had his jury. For better or worse, they were wedded to these people for the next several weeks. For an instant, Matt caught the gray eyes of Mr. Addison, the banker. His look was neutral, reserved, and perhaps even a bit cold. The power of his personality, and intellect, was clearly evident in his gaze and the way he carried himself. Matt felt a chill trickle along his spine. Addison definitely looked like a foreman. He hoped they hadn't made a bad mistake.

The judge looked at the jury and they quieted in response. "Mr. Taylor, you may proceed with your opening statement."

Matt walked up to the podium and put his notes down. "Thank you, Your Honor." He looked at each juror in turn, savoring this quiet moment of beginning.

"Ladies and gentlemen, by giving your oath, and answering the questions as you did, you have consecrated yourselves to be part of one of the most ancient and venerated methods of dispute resolution in the world.

We, all of us, thank you for agreeing to lend your time and energy, and your considered judgment, to combine with this group of fellow human beings to decide the facts of this case."

"And just what are they, the facts of this case? You've heard many questions, and vague hints, but you still know very little except that the defendant is a famous man and the plaintiff is very seriously injured. Now I have the opportunity to tell you those facts, first in general, then in specific detail."

He walked out from behind the podium and stood directly in front of the panel. "Todd Gleason was sixteen at the time of the accident, and riding in the family car, which was being driven by a friend. They had each had a few beers, but were not seriously intoxicated. Todd's young friend lost control on a curve and rolled the car. The driver was uninjured, but Todd's injuries appeared serious and he was transported to the hospital by ambulance.

"The paramedics had taken spinal cord precautions because Todd had trauma to the head. This is standard procedure. They told the physicians at the hospital that they had seen Todd move his arms and legs while being transported. In the E.R., Todd was evaluated by the attending doctor and then by a consulting neurosurgeon. Both of them noted he had signs of neurologic problems in his arms and legs, but was able to move them when they stimulated them. Yet, he was generally otherwise unresponsive. Thinking he may have a head injury, they took head and spine films."

Matt noted the jury seemed interested despite the late hour of the day. Most of them watched Matt but some of them, Addison among them, looked at Todd from time to time. The clock said three p.m., so when he was done the judge would probably take the afternoon recess, and the defense would give their statements tomorrow. Too bad, they would have the night to prepare their response.

"The skull films were read as normal. We've seen them and we agree. The spine films were also read as normal. However, we do not have those films to see if that was an accurate reading. They've been lost. Despite the abnormal neurological signs, no further efforts were made to stabilize his neck. Todd was then transferred to the intensive care unit to be watched closely for a possible head injury.

"In reality, Todd Gleason had a broken neck and that's why he had abnormal neurologic signs. He had an unstable fracture of the pedicles, the parts of the neck vertebra between number six and number seven, that connect each to the other and hold the spine rigid to provide a protective bony canal for the spinal cord.

"As many of you know, the spinal cord arises from the brain stem and is the bundle of nerves that communicates with the rest of the body. Many of you have been in Boy or Girl Scouts and learned about how to protect the spine if there is a head injury or if the victim has any tingling or numbness of their feet or hands. Others may have seen football players, hurt on the field, checked for feeling and abnormal signs in their arms and legs. If they have these neurological signs, medical personnel stabilize the neck and rule out a fracture before the injured are allowed to move.

Matt paused for a long moment. "The evidence will be that despite the abnormal neurologic signs Todd had, these medical people didn't take any of these precautions. After their initial evaluation, they simply put Todd in ICU and waited for him to wake up. Todd didn't even get the care you would expect from a Boy Scout."

The jury stared back at Matt. Some of them watched Todd. A few frowned, but most of them had that unreadable "sphinx" look Matt had never gotten used to. Matt stepped close to the railing so he could emphasize the next point. "Three hours after he was put in the ICU, the nurses decided to change his linen. To do that, they 'log-rolled' him from side to side."

Matt paused again and this time he spoke directly to Mr. Addison. "Immediately after he was log-rolled, there is an entry in the record that he was not able to feel or move his legs." Matt scanned up and down the attentive rows of faces. "The evidence will be that the medical personnel in charge of the care of this young man severed his spinal cord at that moment. They severed it by moving him without protection. Severed it by causing those bones in his neck to grind and then slip and then slice through that delicate bundle of nerves like the action of a French guillotine.

"Ladies and gentlemen, the evidence will be that this was medical malpractice, pure and simple. Todd Gleason was injured in that accident but he was not *paralyzed* until they neglected him at the hospital and then damaged his spinal cord as surely as though they had dropped him through the trap door of a gallows."

"Objection!" Murphy was on his feet with a red face. "I have tried to be patient through this argumentative opening statement, but this is too much. Opening statement is for presentation of the facts, not for argument of the case."

The judge responded sternly. "The objection will be sustained. Stick to the facts, counsel. Save the drama for your closing argument."

Matt nodded mildly. "Thank you, Your Honor." He looked back to the jury. "We will have experts who will explain that is *exactly* what happened to Todd Gleason's spinal cord. That is the reason he is today, and forever will be, unable to walk, or to urinate or defecate without help. It is why he is unable to feel *anything* below his mid-chest and is required to depend on others for *all* of his basic activities of daily living, night and day."

Matt then stepped back from the railing and walked over to the defense table where Conti sat with his attorneys. The man was staring with elaborate boredom out the high courtroom windows. "We will prove that this man, sitting right here, took Todd's case and agreed to handle it personally for a fee of forty percent. He gave it to the youngest attorney in the office and then had little else to do with it from that point forward. That is, until he convinced Todd and his mother to settle with the driver's insurance company for six hundred fifty thousand dollars of a one-million-dollar policy, inexplicably leaving three hundred fifty thousand dollars on the table."

"Objection. He's arguing again."

"Sustained."

Matt didn't skip a beat. "No one in that office ever read the medical records they ordered and Todd paid for, and no one ever figured out that Todd had not become a quadriplegic until several hours after his admission." The jury was mostly looking at Conti now.

"The evidence will be that this law firm's failure to properly evaluate this case and discover the medical malpractice was a clear breach of the standard of legal care that applies in a case of this nature. We will prove that this serious omission on Mr. Conti's part caused Todd Gleason to lose his ability to pursue his case against the medical defendants. Unfortunately, when the medical malpractice was finally discovered, the statute of limitations had run and they could no longer be sued."

Matt watched the jury as he talked. They showed little obvious reaction, but he felt he was connecting. They were definitely listening. Matt now began to go back over the detailed facts and wove important details into the fabric of the case, here and there anticipating what the defense would say and giving them facts to consider in rebuttal. At four-twenty he finished. The judge recessed the case until the next morning.

As Matt walked back toward the counsel table, he saw an apparition in the back of the courtroom giving him the thumbs-up sign. It was Hairy Harry, a well-known courtroom denizen who wandered the halls looking for interesting trials where he could spend the day away from the elements outside. He was homeless and had apparently adopted the courthouse as his personal shelter. He was incredibly hirsute and his hygiene left much to be desired. You didn't want to get closer than three or four feet if you could help it. Deeply set inside that wild mane of hair and uncontrolled beard, were clear blue eyes that occasionally sparkled with interest and intellect. While his clothes were old and ragged, you could tell they had been high quality at some time in the past and he wore them like he had just gotten them new from his personal tailor. No one knew his true story, but the courthouse scuttlebutt was that he had once been a trial lawyer who had fallen on hard times. Everyone treated him with respect, in unspoken recognition of the vagaries of life in the practice of law. Matt gave him a smile of recognition. The interesting old character often sat in on his trials.

* * *

He gathered his team to debrief before attacking the night's work. Matt felt exhausted, but high on the day's left-over adrenaline. Todd smiled at Matt and held his mother's hand. "That was fantastic! I think we've got them." He looked at his mom. "Did you see them watching me and Conti? I think they're on our side."

Adrianne said, "They say a jury often starts making up its mind during opening statement. I can see why today. That was great, Matt."

Matt felt good too, but there was a long way to go yet. "Juries do get swayed by the opening, but this is a long case and lots will be forgotten unless it keeps confirming what we told them." His mouth set in a somber seam. "Also, see how you feel tomorrow when they get their say."

They talked a bit more and then broke up, the Gleasons to review their depositions and Adrianne to outline their testimony for direct exam. Matt planned to work on the first few experts' examinations and make a list of areas to prepare them on for cross-examination. Later he was meeting the first witness to prepare for tomorrow.

36

Murphy stood in front of the jury without notes, relaxed and smiling at them warmly. Matt had seen him do this before. He was like a teacher who had done the first day of school for decades. He had the process down to a science.

"Good morning, ladies and gentlemen, Your Honor, and my esteemed colleagues. As I listened to my talented adversary yesterday, I was impressed, as I'm sure you all were. He speaks well and his presentation was compelling. If I hadn't known the facts of this case, I would have been ready to vote for him myself. However, I, like him, believe in the jury system. I believe that intelligent and well-intentioned people like yourselves will keep an *open mind* until they hear *both* sides of the case, whether it is in opening statement or in the evidence itself," He turned to look at Matt, "…which I can assure you will be much different than represented to you by my very *clever* colleague." Matt had never heard the adjective sound quite as much like an expletive before.

He walked over to the defense table and around to stand behind Conti. He put his hand on his shoulder. The leonine-maned litigator looked steadily at the jury as Murphy spoke. "I do agree with counsel in one respect. My colleague and I do have the honor to represent one of the most famous lawyers in the history of this great country, a man who has been compared to Clarence Darrow and many of the other lions of the Bar. This man has devoted his life to representing the injured, the poor, and people accused of crimes they did not commit. Many times, he has done this without any recompense."

Yeah, Matt thought, when Conti's clients turned out to be guilty and they couldn't pay him. Murphy was arguing his case shamelessly, but Matt couldn't really object since he had also argued quite a bit in his own opening. Matt looked at the fleshy features of the defendant and felt ill. The man certainly was one of the best. But this jury would never be able to figure out what an evil person he really was. There was no way to let them know about his attacks on Matt or his false claims in the Olsen case. Matt had to concentrate on how badly he had treated the Gleasons.

"There are many things Mr. Taylor did *not* tell you about this case. For example, he did not explain that when a teenager has been drinking it makes it much more difficult for an E.R. doctor to evaluate him. Is he hurt? Or, if he's *stinking with alcohol,* is he just a drunk? Many of the so-called neurologic signs were typical abnormalities for someone who had been drinking. The x-rays were read as normal."

"Mr. Taylor made it seem as though it is a foregone conclusion that the spinal cord was all right when the patient came to the hospital and was then, he claimed, *severed* by the nurses. Very dramatic rhetoric, but the evidence from our extraordinarily well-qualified experts will be that the cord was probably damaged in the car wreck. Just ask yourselves, what would be more likely to damage a spine—a *car wreck*, a *rollover of a vehicle*, or two nurses gently turning a patient over in the *intensive care* unit?" He paused and nodded like he was agreeing with them as they thought about what he said.

The jurors were very attentive and a couple of them eyeballed Matt from time to time. Addison was listening very carefully. "There are lots of things that Mr. Taylor *neglected* to tell you. Our experts will explain that a spinal cord can be damaged by impact in an accident and the function can then lessen over time. The cord is irretrievably damaged at the moment of impact, mind you, but it may take a while to have that damage cause the nerves to stop functioning.

"They will also explain that a cord can be damaged in a car accident, so there is no feeling or ability to voluntarily move, but the *legs will still move* in response to local pain stimuli, like when a doctor pinches them. They move from local *reflexes,* arcs that do not involve the cord itself.

"It was perfectly reasonable for the doctors to think this kid, who appeared to be *drunk,* had no spinal injury and might have a head injury, so they put him in *ICU* to be watched closely. As he woke up, and could be more accurately examined, it became apparent that he had also suffered a spinal injury *in the car accident.*"

Matt returned the jury's gaze calmly when they looked over at him. He had told them many of these things during his discussion of the details, but Murphy was putting his own spin on each point in hope that the jury would see it as new information. He had to hope they remembered what he told them yesterday. Matt let no hint of the anger that suffused him show in his expression. He knew that juries often keyed their own reaction from the emotional responses they saw in the parties and in the attorneys. He had carefully prepared the Gleasons on this long ago.

Murphy walked up to the jury and put his hands in his pockets. He regarded them with his thin jaw jutting aggressively. "Now let's talk about the Law Firm of Conti and Associates, the most famous law firm in this city and maybe the whole darn country. These people over there, the Gleasons, came to my client because this firm was the best. They came to them because of Conti's name and reputation. They knew full well that there was a young lawyer working on the case. Did they leave the office because of that? Did they complain to Mr. Conti? The answer, ladies and gentlemen, is *no.*

"They hired the Conti firm to represent Todd Gleason in an automobile accident. That is exactly what the firm did, and *did it well.* There is no requirement in the law that lawyers go beyond what the firm is hired to do. There is no requirement that they beat the bushes to create new cases against innocent physicians, busy doing their best to deal with a drunken teenager who had gotten into an accident. There is no requirement of the law that they be clairvoyant. How are they supposed to know to look for something in medical records if they were never put on notice?

"Even if, somehow, they became aware there was an issue about the medical care Todd Gleason received, what they would have discovered had they investigated was that there was nothing of any medical significance. Todd had been injured in the rollover, pure and simple. The doctors treated him appropriately at all times."

Murphy was good, Matt thought, no question about it. His job was to handle the legal malpractice case. Todd had to prove the underlying case first. Todd had to prove that the medical people had been negligent and that this negligence had caused his quadriplegia. Then he had to prove that Conti and his firm were negligent. Murphy was defending the law firm, but, wisely, had spent much time on the medicine. Anderson was defending the medical case and he planned to take another bite of that medical apple.

When Kevin Anderson stood up and did the detailed defense medical case opening, Matt was again impressed with how difficult the battle ahead was going to be. Matt felt that old surge charge through him. Competition generated energy in Matt, luckily, because it was going to take a lot to sustain him through the war ahead. Surreptitiously, he scanned the jury. They looked very interested in the two defense lawyers' presentations, but still relatively neutral. This case was going to be won or lost in the presentation of the evidence over the next several weeks. Just then, he realized Addison was watching him watch them. The man's eyes were unreadable.

* * *

Matt put Doctor Harvey Goldbaum on the stand first, to take advantage of his professorial style while educating the jury on the medical issues. The direct exam by Matt went well and, after the lunch break, as the doctor warmed to his subject, the jury seemed to be fascinated with his testimony and the large, colored illustrations showing the bones of the neck and the spinal cord encased within them. When Matt finished, Kevin Andersen started his cross. He was halfway through when the judge recessed for the day. He asked the lawyers to stay afterward and meet in his chambers.

"Well, we have this beast underway finally. The secret now is to keep it moving and not get bogged down in problems." The judge had a serious look on his face as he looked at the small group of attorneys. "That means witnesses ready to go, no gaps and no excuses. Got my meaning?"

Matt and the defense attorneys exchanged worried glances. Matt looked back at the judge. "Your Honor, this is a malpractice case with multiple experts in medicine and the law. It will be a minor miracle if both sides don't have some scheduling problems."

The judge's expression hardened. "I'm not going to waste this jury's time. Have a witness ready or expect to rest your case. No witness and you're done with your part of this lawsuit."

Matt was stunned at the judge's comment. Occasionally, a federal judge would enjoy making such autocratic pronouncements, but it was unusual in state court where judges eventually had to stand for re-election. This would be hard on both sides. It would be a particular disaster for Matt because he would be required to have expensive witnesses standing by at three or four hundred dollars an hour during the whole case. One screw up and the whole case would be out the window.

The judge looked at the sheaf of papers in front of him. "There are several motions we should deal with. The first is this defense contention that the measure of damages should be the subject of expert opinion. Mr. Murphy, do you want to address this?"

"Yes, Your Honor, we would like to offer expert testimony concerning the reasonable jury verdict range in San Diego County in 1982 when this case would probably have been tried. This is a San Francisco jury and they need to know what San Diego juries do with similar cases. The measure of damages should be what would happen down there. To let a jury in this town set the damages without evidence on that issue would be quite unfair."

The judge nodded thoughtfully and looked toward Matt.

"We are very much opposed to such evidence Your Honor. This would open Pandora's Box. They would love to have so-called 'experts' opining about how the case would have been tried, what a jury would have done, and so on. It is up to *this* jury to decide the value of this case based on the evidence presented to it in *this* courtroom. It should *not* be up to some lawyer they bring in, who claims to be an 'expert' on what some jury might do. What they really want is to prejudice this jury on damages by claiming that San Diego is a cheap jury area."

The judge drummed his fingers on his desk. "I see your point, Mr. Taylor, but isn't the real loss to your clients the missed opportunity to present the case in San Diego? I assume the defense just wants to point out what the case was worth in that area. We all know cases go for less money down there. If the jury wants to give more, they can."

Murphy smiled triumphantly. "Exactly, Your Honor, a San Francisco jury verdict would not reflect what would have happened in San Diego."

Matt bristled in anger at the sloppy thinking. Between the judge's comment on this issue and the "no gaps" admonition, things weren't looking so good. "With all due respect, Your Honor, the defense position on this issue is ridiculous. They get somebody to opine that juries are cheap in San Diego and we get somebody to do the opposite. That doesn't prove a darn thing that's relevant to the issues in this courtroom. If this case degenerates into a battle of incompetent opinions about what some hypothetical jury would have done in some hypothetical trial before some hypothetical judge, we are going to have to resolve the case in the appellant courts."

Matt's voice had risen toward the end of his statement and the judge's eyes had hardened in response. He sat back and stared at Matt, conflicting thoughts reflected in his face. Abruptly he picked up the papers and stood. "I'll take this under submission and let you know soon what my ruling will be. We'll discuss the other points tomorrow." He looked at Matt. "Would you stay a moment, Mr. Taylor?"

After the others left, the judge still stood near the door. He looked at the floor and then his eyes came back to Matt. "I received a notice from the State Bar that there is a hearing on some matter called the "Olsen" complaint. I called the hearing officer and he said it's pretty serious stuff. They say it will take the whole day and have asked for us to take a day off to hear it." The judge took off his robe and took down his suit coat, which was hanging on a hook behind his door. "I told him that I didn't want anything to affect the trial of this case. If they take action against you, I want it to be after the trial." He shrugged into his coat and gave Matt a cool look. "So, anyway, expect it to happen immediately after this case goes to the jury. And don't forget, have a witness ready at all times or your hearing may come faster than you expect."

The judge strode away, leaving Matt standing in the ornate hall staring after him. Adrianne came up beside him. "You look kind of pale. What was that all about?"

He turned, relieved to see her warm, friendly expression. "That damn Willistin has gotten to the judge and probably Conti has, too. I think that's why his rulings are going sideways on us."

She frowned. "What can we do?"

"Not a damn thing but keep our heads down and try the heck out of this case. Let's get out of here."

37

Kevin Andersen was a pacer. He prowled the courtroom like a restless animal during cross-examination. His massive shoulders hunched toward the witness aggressively, like he was going to charge him at any moment. The effect was quite intimidating. Doctor Harvey Goldbaum was handling the probing cross-examination well, but the stress was beginning to produce hairline fractures in the appearance of his testimony. He smiled back at the bull facing him with a show of cool aplomb.

"No, no, Mr. Andersen. You persist in this failure to grasp the medical issue in this instance."

Matt winced. Come on, Harvey, calm down and speak English. The jury was beginning to frown and a couple of them had just crossed their arms.

Andersen put on a show of innocent bewilderment. "I'm sorry Doctor Goldbaum, but I'm just a bit thick in the head, I guess. Let me try to ask it another way." He scratched absently at his heavy mane of brown hair. "If a patient is drunk, can his reflexes be depressed?" He spread his big arms out. "You know, like, can the reflexes be abnormal at all?"

"Well, yes, but this boy wasn't actually drunk and it would be dangerous for the doctor to assume he was."

Andersen's heavy head swung abruptly toward the witness. "He reeked of liquor, didn't he?"

"Yes, so the record says."

"He was unconscious and flailing about like a drunk, wasn't he?"

"Yes, the record describes that, but that is a classic finding in a patient with a head injury. This child had blood on his head and was in an accident."

Andersen looked at the jury with a smirk. "Now, Doctor, I know you are real anxious to tell us your opinions in this case, over and over again. But I'd like you to try to just answer my questions for a change." He stopped moving as if a thought had just occurred to him. "Speaking of giving opinions, you've given opinions for Mr. Taylor several times before, haven't you?"

Goldbaum sat up straighter. "Yes."

"You usually charge six hundred fifty dollars an hour, like you are now?"

"Yes."

"Now I asked you about that in your depo and I took the liberty of adding up the cases and hours you work for lawyers, remember? You made about one hundred fifty thousand dollars last year on legal work. All that money, just saying things lawyers like Mr. Taylor want to have juries hear in their cases, didn't you?"

"Something like that. But that is a small part of my yearly salary, and I resent the way you put that, by the way."

Andersen's head jerked up and his face broke into an evil smile. "So you make a lot more than that, do you, and you resent my inference?"

"Objection, compound and argumentative."

"Sustained."

"Well, Doctor, can you tell me about *one* time that you can remember coming into court to testify as a witness for a doctor in the last two years?"

Matt tightened inwardly. The question was worded neatly. It didn't include cases that didn't go to court and was casually limited to two years, because in former years he had quite often served as a witness for doctors. Goldbaum was getting off balance.

"The way you ask that creates a false impression. I've given depos for other doctors often, and testified for them many times over the years."

Andersen smiled. "Did I ask you about other years or depos?" He shook his head sadly and looked toward the jury. "I didn't think you could just answer a simple question, Doctor Goldbaum."

"Objection, that's just argumentative editorial."

"Sustained."

Andersen gave the jury a "we-both-know-the-other-lawyer-is-just-try-ing-to-get-in-the-way-of-the-truth" look. "Well, Doctor, in this lucrative *side business* of testifying, you have, most of the time—actually, over eighty percent of the cases, you testify for some lawyer like Mr. Taylor who is rep-resenting a patient. Isn't that right? You spend eighty percent of your time in a courtroom claiming some poor doctor messed up." He stabbed his finger at Goldbaum. "Isn't that true?"

Just say yes, Matt thought. He's already got you to say that in your deposition anyway.

The doctor flinched at the tone and set his jaw. "I don't think that's true at all."

The defense lawyer sighed theatrically and walked over to his table. He made a show of rummaging for the deposition, even though Matt was sure he knew exactly where it was. Slowly he thumbed through the pages and then read a passage. "Yes, here it is. You remember giving me your testi-mony under oath at the deposition, don't you, Doctor?"

The witness shifted his eyes to Matt. Matt smiled calmly toward the jury. *Don't look at me Harvey, it looks bad. Look at the jury, look at Andersen, look away damn it!* Matt could feel a trickle of sweat run from under his arm.

Harvey Goldbaum looked back at the waiting attorney and swallowed. "Yes."

"I'll read it for the jury: 'Question: So, Doctor, you have testified in court about twenty times in the last five years? Answer: Yes. Question: And in only four of those instances you were testifying for the doctor, correct?'" Andersen looked over at the jury. "Your answer was *yes.*"

"And, Doctor Goldbaum…four out of twenty…that equals eighty per-cent—doesn't it?" He grinned patronizingly at him.

Harvey stared at him balefully. "Yes."

The big man moved his head up and down at the jury, his manner saying *"See, I told you he can't be trusted."*

Then he wheeled on the witness and drilled the next question at him in a staccato fashion. "And the fact is, that if a teenager is stinking of alcohol, and comes into a busy E.R., and has a difficult time talking, and has depressed reflexes, it is *perfectly reasonable* for a doctor to think he may simply be suffering from the effects of drink and that he will be okay as soon as he sleeps it off, isn't it, Doctor Goldbaum?"

Matt sat calmly, but cringed inside. Soften him up with a body blow and then follow up quickly with a question that appeared, at least on the surface, to go to the heart of things. Effective technique, if the witness was off-balance. He held his breath. Now was the time to fight back. Don't make me do it with redirect questions. The jury will think it's coming from the lawyer rather than the witness. He held his breath.

The doctor sighed. "Yes, that's true."

Andersen's look was triumphant. "No further questions."

Matt smiled at the jury, as if to say "That's just what we planned all along." Never let them know how you really feel. Inside, he was in knots. Great, he thought. Now we have to spend time trying to fix this and the jury may never accept the result of our efforts. Andersen was good and Goldbaum was a bust. He looked up just in time to see Hairy Harry vanishing through the big swinging doors.

38

"Your Honor, may we approach the bench?" The judge inclined his head and they all trooped to the sidebar. Murphy leaned away so the jury couldn't see him and whispered. "The court has not ruled on the motion about evidence from experts on what a jury in San Diego probably would have done with this case. Mr. Taylor is winding down and I wanted to know if I can cross this witness on that subject."

The judge rubbed his jaw. "I haven't decided that point and so I'm going to let you cross on it. Whatever I decide later, we can fix it with an instruction."

Apprehension flooded through Matt. "Judge! Allowing testimony on this point is a huge mistake. I haven't gone into this whole issue during my direct because I'm opposed to the introduction of this evidence. This would obviously be out of the scope of my direct exam."

"I've ruled, counsel." The judge gave him a cold look. "They can go into it."

"Isn't that the whole point, Judge? You haven't ruled." He strode back to the counsel table.

"Why would he do that?" Adrianne whispered in his ear. "Henkle won't be ready for those questions."

Ted Henkle was the lean, hard-eyed defense attorney who was on the stand. The slate gray eyes bored confidently right back at Matt, just as they had done in so many trials from the other side of the counsel table.

The two of them had fought enough battles over the years that they had finally developed a grudging—and finally warm—mutual respect. When Matt had talked to Henkle outside of the courtroom many months ago, he had decided a defense attorney who had done battle with Conti might be perfect. So far, Henkle had been great, but direct exam was easy. Matt whispered back to her. "Murphy might be in for a surprise."

Matt stood back up to finish the direct. He knew he couldn't go into the San Diego jury evidence, because Matt was objecting to the whole line of questions. He had to let the defense raise the subject. "By way of summary, Mr. Henkle, let me revisit a few of the points we have discussed: do you feel that Mr. Conti's office breached the standard of care for attorneys in this field of practice and would you tell us why?"

"Yes. The Conti office is expert in personal injury. They take cases from clients and attorneys from all over because they are supposed to know what to do with a case." Henkle leaned forward and looked directly at the jury for emphasis like any good trial lawyer. "When you have a serious injury case and inadequate insurance coverage, the first thing the good ones do is look for another way to help the client." He glanced toward Murphy. "You get the medical records and you *read* them. I've defended malpractice cases for twenty-five years. If I saw what was in these records, the first thing I'd think would be, 'we're in trouble.' The doctors and the nurses messed up, big-time."

Matt's steely-eyed expert turned his attention back to the jury and his focus narrowed with the strength of his feelings. "What went wrong here? You want to know what I really think? There is no way that Sal Conti would have missed this if he'd seen this record." He scanned around the courtroom, as if to emphasis the absence of the man to whom he was referring. "He got too busy. He handed this one off to an inexperienced attorney and never supervised him. Simple as that."

Matt was pleased to see a few answering nods. "That's all the questions we have at this time."

Murphy was on his feet in an instant, striding to his favorite area, triangulating the jury and the witness. "Mr. Henkle, you are a defense attorney. You make your living defending doctors."

"Yes, I do."

"You have defended doctors who were accused of missing fractures on x-rays and causing injury?"

"Yes."

"Even handled a case involving a neck fracture once didn't you? One that the plaintiff claimed, like here, caused him to become paralyzed when the doctors didn't diagnose it?"

"Yes." Matt knew about this case, but it was actually quite different than Todd's case. Murphy was clever, though. His questions were short and well-phrased to leave little wiggle room.

"And in those cases, you took the position that the person who lost their movement while under medical management had no case against the doctors or hospital, right?"

Hinkle frowned at Murphy and sat forward. "Yes, but those cases were quite different from this one."

Murphy put his hands on his hips and his jaw jutted toward the witness stand. "Just answer the question. You've *always* said the docs weren't at fault in these cases, haven't you?"

"Well sure, that's my job."

Matt tightened up inside, *wrong way to put it, Ted.* Murphy's brows tried to reach for the ornate ceiling. "Oh, so you tell juries things you don't really believe?" While Henkle's mouth was still forming an answer, Murphy bulled forward with another question. "Or, is it that you just say whatever the people paying you want to hear?" Murphy looked around toward Matt then back at the jury, a knowing smirk on his face.

Hinkle's face reddened and he half stood. "I resent that implication. I'll bet you don't believe what your client's saying right here in this courtroom."

The defense attorney spun on his heel, then spoke in a clear, ringing voice. "I believe in *my* client and, unlike you, I don't take cases to say things I don't believe in." He turned slowly back to Henkle. "For money."

Matt stood. "Your Honor…"

"Objection sustained." The judge's face registered stern disapproval. "Mr. Henkle and Mr. Murphy, you both know better. Kindly save your speeches for the street corner. Next question please."

Matt sat down and concentrated on looking unconcerned. Henkle was letting Murphy bait him. Conti's defense lawyer smoothly changed his line of questions.

"Mr. Henkle, have you reviewed all this material thoroughly?"

The man's gray eyes widened. "I certainly have." He reached down and pulled a storage box full of paper up and dropped it on the witness stand with a crash. "Every darn piece of this stack of paper, I might add." He pulled thick sheaves out and plopped them down on the witness table. The jury could see there were tabs all over the volumes.

Matt was surprised Murphy would raise that subject. Henkle was famous for his thorough preparation and workaholic methods. He kept three secretaries busy full-time and still managed to swim and run several hours a day. If he said he had read it all, then you could bet he knew it backwards and forwards. Matt hoped Murphy would test his knowledge. That would be a mistake. But, no such luck.

"You've told us the medical case is a clear one, that the medical defendants were in trouble. Am I right?" Hinkle moved his head down, warily. "You're famous for your preparation. Indeed, I think you've often said, 'You can't evaluate a case until you have all the evidence.' Am I right?"

The two defense attorneys stared at each other. Finally, Henkle answered. "That's a general rule of mine."

"Tell me, Mr. Henkle, what did you think of the testimony of the charge nurse in the ICU that evening, or the radiologist?"

Henkle rattled his head back and forth, impatiently. "You are fully aware the nurse is missing and the radiologist deceased."

"Yes, and what did you think of those all-important films of the neck?"

Henkle just sat and looked at him. Murphy rubbed his jaw. "You would agree with me these are very important elements of the case against the doctors, wouldn't you?"

Henkle still was quiet. "So you, who spend your life *defending* docs, decided that the medical people here screwed up without *several of the key bits of evidence* you would normally rely on to defend them. That is, if you were being paid to do that in this case instead of this. Right?"

Matt stood to object. "Argumentative." The judge opened his mouth to rule and Henkle suddenly interrupted. "That is ridiculous. There is plenty of evidence here to see what happened."

Murphy, watching the judge turn red when interrupted by Henkle, smoothly interjected. "Move to strike that answer as unresponsive, Your Honor."

"Sustained. Just answer the question that was asked, sir. And you can answer it with a yes or no."

"My answer is yes." Henkle's complexion had darkened. "But I would like to explain my answer, Your Honor."

"Next question please, Mr. Murphy."

Matt's pent-up breath expelled slowly as the cross-examination wound down. He was sure the judge had been about to rule the question argumentative. Now the jury was left with the impression Murphy had wanted. It was not like Henkle to lose his cool that way. Murphy sauntered back to the lectern.

Murphy casually thumbed through some notes. When the jury's attention had been recaptured, he tapped deliberately on the slanted wooden platform. He smiled at Henkle warmly. "Ted, you and I devote a large part of our time valuing cases and advising our clients what a jury is likely to do and how much different types of injuries are worth. Isn't that correct?"

The expert witness watched Murphy warily. "That is one of the things we do."

Adrianne nudged Matt, a small wrinkle of concern bridging her eyes. Matt gave her a slight warning shake of his head. Trust Murphy to start treating his competitor as an old buddy now.

"Tell me, Ted, have you ever settled a case involving a quadriplegic injury similar to Todd Gleason's?"

"I have settled a few over the years."

"Tell us, Ted," Murphy walked out from behind the rostrum. "What's the most you've ever paid for one of these?"

"Your Honor," Matt stood. "We have registered our objection to this line of questions. It's just a transparent attempt to invade the power of this jury to hear this evidence and determine its own value for this case."

"Your objection has been made a part of the record, counsel. Please proceed, Mr. Murphy."

"I think we paid about three million dollars for one case of quadriplegia at this level." The witness looked askance at the judge. "But…"

Murphy raised his hand. "No 'buts,' Mr. Henkle. Just answer the questions. Tell me, do you read *Jury Verdicts*, the publication that lists all the jury awards in California?"

"All trial lawyers do."

"I had the damages portion of Mr. Taylor's opening statement written up by the court reporter." Murphy pulled out a sheet of paper and looked at it for a moment. "Yes, here it is. He told the jury he would show them that this case was worth many millions of dollars, well over *fifteen million* he claimed." Murphy wheeled from the notes and looked over the jury. "Have you ever paid anything like that for any quadriplegic case, verdict or settlement?"

Henkle crossed his leg and looked over at Matt for a moment. "No, I haven't, but I do know of…"

"Just the question I asked, Ted, old buddy. You know how it works. Anxious as you may be to help out your side here. Tell me, Ted, have you ever heard of a verdict in San Diego County, *where this case would have been tried*, or any county that touches on San Diego County, coming in for anything anywhere even close to fifteen million, or let's say even *half* that? Ever even heard of anything even close?"

"Never have." Henkle eyeballed the judge again.

"Make you a bet, Ted." Conti's attorney moved two quick steps toward the witness stand. "Defense lawyer to defense lawyer. I'll bet you've never told a client one of these would come in at such a ridiculous figure or ever even thought a judge would let such a verdict stand if it did. Am I right?"

"Well," the witness shifted in his chair. "I've often worried that…"

Murphy spun toward Henkle, his mouth a tight line. His finger stabbed though the air at the expert. "*Ted Henkle—I said—am—I—right?*"

The witness jerked his head up as Matt stood to object, but the answer had been startled out of him. "Yes. You're right." Henkle looked over to Matt helplessly.

The cross was soon over and Matt was standing to do re-direct just as Adrianne came in the courtroom and sat down next to him. Her hand caught his sleeve and she whispered in his ear. "Our E.R. expert had an emergency. He can't be here until late today or maybe even tomorrow."

Matt had no other witness planned until the next day. He stared at her in consternation. He could feel a prickly heat of apprehension sweep through him and a thin trickle of moisture trailed down his body under his shirt. He whispered back to her. "See if you can find anyone else and I'll finish this witness." Matt stood and walked over to the podium and looked around the courtroom slowly, forcing his racing heart to calm. As he scanned the room, he saw Hairy Harry slouched in the back. From deep in his grizzled visage, Matt could have sworn that a clear blue eye gave him a wink.

Matt walked to the lectern in front of the jury. "Mr. Henkle, counsel asked you about the cases you've handled that involved spinal injuries that were undiagnosed—where you felt the doctors should be defended. Were those cases the same as this one?"

"In no way were they similar." Henkle addressed his answer directly to the jury. "In one case, the fracture was not even unstable and the paralysis was evident immediately on admission. In the other, a girl lost her function later because of a clot that formed in the cord. The doctors ruled that out here."

Matt looked at the jury. "If you had a case like this, would you defend it?" Matt turned back to the witness, before asking. "Would you stand up here and tell a jury that the doctors and the lawyers did no wrong?"

"If I had a choice, absolutely not." Henkle looked over at Murphy and then to the jury. "The sensible thing to do with a case like this is settle it out of court for lots of money. As fast as possible."

"Objection, Your Honor."

The judge had a pained look on his face. "Overruled. You did raise this subject, Mr. Murphy."

Matt let his gaze rest for a moment on the man in the black robe. Go ahead and squirm, Judge, Matt's look said. I warned you where this would lead. "About this issue of the case's value. Does the value of any given case depend on the facts of each situation?"

"Absolutely. Each case is different. That means it's hard to compare what a jury may do with different circumstances. For example, many of my spinal cases involved older people, or plaintiffs with serious health problems that affected their life expectancy." He tried to catch the eyes of each of the jurors. "Those problems would significantly lower the value of a case. That's a very different situation from this case. "

"Now, Mr. Murphy asked his questions very carefully about your settlements and then about verdicts in San Diego. He cut you off when you tried to complete your answer." Matt paused for emphasis and then walked up nearer to Henkle. "Tell us if there have been any bigger verdicts in other counties in this state please."

"Sure, that's easy. There have been…"

"Objection, Your Honor. May we approach the bench?"

The judge waved them up and they huddled at the oak barrier, the court reporter leaning in to hear. Murphy whispered intently up to the face hovering over them. "They are about to bring up evidence of a verdict a few years ago in San Francisco. It was very high and set a record in the state. It is our position that such evidence is completely irrelevant because it involves a San Francisco County jury. Our case would have been in San Diego, where there would never be such a maverick award. It would be highly prejudicial for them to mention what some San Francisco jury did years ago. Never to be repeated since in California I might add."

The judge looked over to Matt. "They raised this issue, Your Honor. They want to talk about what other juries do. Well, this is an example. Our jury *is* a San Francisco jury. They want it all their way. We just want some fairness in the evidence that goes to this jury."

The judge regarded both parties in silence. It was clear from the expression on his face he was beginning to regret his decision. "The fact is, Mr. Taylor, this is a case that would have been based in San Diego, which we all know is a more conservative area for jury verdicts. It seems to me that a San Francisco jury award is just not all that helpful."

"Your Honor, there is no established basis for the so-called 'conventional wisdom' that one area is more conservative in verdicts than another. No one has gone out and tried the same case, the same way, in several different counties to test such a hypothesis. Many lawyers think a big case is a big case in any county. This decision should be left to this jury."

The judge sighed. "You may be right, but I've started down this path and I have to limit it to the damages in a San Diego case. The objection will be sustained." Over the judge's shoulder Matt could see Henkle widen his eyes at him in dismay as the witness peered over the witness rail to hear the sidebar conference.

Matt tamped down his frustration. Perhaps he could try it another way.

"Mr. Henkle, in evaluating a case for a client, do you use only the verdicts in a particular area or do you consider verdicts all over the state?"

"We definitely consider the entire state."

"In evaluating this case for your client, would you consider verdicts in San Francisco in similar injuries?"

"Yes, definitely."

"Have there been verdicts in San Francisco that you would consider relevant to such an analysis?"

Murphy leaped to his feet. "Objection, Your Honor. He is trying to do by the back door what the court told him he couldn't do at the front door."

"I can do without the salesman metaphors, Mr. Murphy. We have been over this, Mr. Taylor. The objection will be sustained."

Matt chanced a sidelong glance at the jury. They looked intrigued at the drama. Juror Addison watched Matt with curiosity in his expression. Matt decided it might not be all bad just to leave a question in the jury's mind. Let them wonder what the defense didn't want them to know about San Francisco jury verdicts.

"One more thing, Mr. Henkle. Since it seems we are restrained from discussing this last subject, Mr. Murphy asked you about all those bits of evidence that were missing from your file. I presume that bothered you?"

"Sure, that bothered me, but there was plenty other information we did have." Henkle sat back and crossed his legs. "I could tell that the doctors blew it badly." He addressed the jury. "Please understand, I'm not a doctor, but that's just my opinion as a specialist in defending medical malpractice cases."

"But would you like to have that information, Mr. Henkle?" Matt moved to the side rail near the jury. "That is, if you could?"

Matt could see the light dawn in the defense specialist's eyes. "Of course I'd like to have it, but Conti's firm never ordered the x-rays. And, the fact is, none of us have this vital information because the defendant lawyer's office *missed the malpractice case.* So much time went by that afterward the nurse was gone, the x-rays were gone, and the radiologist was dead." He looked over at Murphy, then back to the jury. "Bottom line is Conti's responsible for that too."

He had to quit with Henkle, but Adrianne hadn't returned and there was no other witness to put on the stand. Reluctantly, he passed the witness and so did Murphy. The judge excused Henkle and looked at Matt.

"Next witness, Mr. Taylor?"

"Your Honor, may we approach?"

They gathered close to the reporter on the other side from the jury. The judge had an ominous look on his face. Just then, Matt saw Adrianne hurry through the door. She shook her head with a grim look on her face. Matt cleared his throat.

"Sorry, Your Honor, but a medical emergency has kept our next witness from the stand. Unfortunately, Todd is home in San Diego with his brother seeing his doctor and, as you know, Debbie's already been on the stand." As Matt's voice trailed off, he was dismayed to see the judge's face darken with anger.

"Mr. Taylor, I don't really care what your problems are. I made the rule clear at the start. No witness—no more trial." He stared at Matt. "I declare a fifteen-minute break and then we will resume. Either with your next witness or the defense case."

Matt met Adrianne in the hall. "I'm sorry, Matt, but there is no one I could find to fill in for the rest of the afternoon. What are we going to do?"

"I don't know. If we stop now, the case is lost. We might get him reversed on appeal for this ridiculous ruling, but who wants an appeal?" They stared at each other helplessly. There was not any solution at hand.

39

When the jury sat back down, the bailiff called the court to order and Matt walked through the swing gate into the counsel area. The judge looked at him impatiently. Matt scanned the courtroom desperately. Just then the florid face of Salvatore Conti appeared in the doorway to the courtroom. Murphy saw the change of Matt's expression and jumped up, heading quickly to the back of the courtroom to warn Conti away. It was too late though. Matt grabbed at this fortuitous solution like a man heading under water for the third time.

"Your Honor, Todd Gleason calls the defendant, Mr. Salvatore Conti, to the stand."

It was a calculated risk, but there was really little choice. Since he had the right to put the defendant on as a hostile witness and cross-examine him in his own part of the case, Matt had prepared the skeleton of a cross-examination over the weekend. He had the rough outline in his briefcase. He was not nearly as ready for Conti as he would have liked to be, but maybe Conti wasn't quite as prepared for his testimony as they would have preferred either. In the back of the courtroom, he could swear he saw a smile deep in Hairy Harry's gnarly beard.

The portly trial attorney settled comfortably into his seat in the witness box and smiled warmly at the jury, murmuring a friendly good afternoon to the expectant faces. Many of them smiled and nodded back at the famous man they had so often seen on TV and in the newspaper and whose fame was so inextricably interwoven with the fabric of the city's reputation. This was a guy who was in the paper virtually every day. His likeness was painted on local buildings. He was discussed in books and movies. He was more than a famous lawyer; he was a big-time national celebrity. A few of the jurors didn't even try to hide the excitement they felt to be so close to the man who was known far and wide as the "Prince of Personal Injury" and who had represented famous and infamous people all over the country.

Matt could sense the man's confidence grow. He was thriving in the familiar atmosphere of the courtroom like a plant responding to the humidity of a hothouse. Matt was hoping a chill of factual reality would wilt some of his foliage. After the witness was given the oath, Matt stood quietly until the attention of the jury left Conti and began to concentrate on the questions to come.

Matt decided to swing from the floor. "Mr. Conti, while you were representing Todd Gleason, the time limit within which he had to file a malpractice suit against the hospital and the doctors expired, didn't it?"

His features compressed reflexively. He tossed his head in dismissal. "Time can't expire on something that doesn't exist, young man."

"His right to sue for medical malpractice existed until the statute ran out while you were representing him, didn't it?"

"No."

"The statute gave him an outside limit of three years to file, didn't it?"

"Not if he didn't have a case."

"Let's set aside the issue of the merits of his case for the moment. The statute of limitations for any case that might have existed expired while you were representing him, didn't it?"

"Can't set that aside. Statute doesn't run on a case that doesn't exist."

Out of the corner of his eye he could see the jury swiveling its collective head back and forth like tennis spectators during a volley. Come to think of it, they had the look of a group watching a blood sport, maybe hoping to see some. Matt could either argue with the man or go on and let the jury ponder his refusal to admit the obvious. Matt looked at his notes and moved on.

"Mr. Conti, was there any lawyer in your office who had less time practicing law than Mr. Youngstone, the inexperienced lawyer you assigned to the Gleason case?"

"He was one of the youngest and one of the smartest."

"But in terms of actual years of experience, didn't all the other attorneys have considerably more?"

"There were older lawyers who I wouldn't have let anywhere near a case like that. He was a good man, wish I had him back."

"Then why did you fire him not too long after it was discovered the statute had expired in this case?"

He swiveled his head from the jury to stab a baleful look at Matt. "I told you that a statute can't run on a non-existent case."

Matt returned his glare calmly, still waiting for the question to be answered. Finally he looked to the judge. "Your Honor, if the witness could be instructed to answer the question, we could proceed."

The judge leaned back. "Ask your next question, counsel."

Conti's mouth turned up in amusement. Matt restrained himself from frowning and reframed the question.

"If he was so smart, why'd you fire the man?"

"I didn't want to, but my partners did, so I went along with them." He moved his head back and forth sadly. "Much to my regret."

Two hours and an afternoon break later, Matt was beginning to feel an enlarging flow of blood from an assortment of wounds inflicted by the veteran barrister. Conti looked like he was enjoying himself and the jury seemed entertained. Things were not going as well as Matt had hoped. He suddenly decided to throw his rough draft script away for the last few questions and let it rip.

"So, you agreed to represent Todd for a percentage of what you got him, correct?"

"Just like you."

"Yes, but my fee only goes to forty percent when I go to trial. You charged him forty percent for collecting six hundred fifty thousand of a one million dollar policy in a settlement, right?"

He changed positions in the chair. "Well…"

"You left him with less than three hundred and sixty thousand net and left another three hundred fifty on the table, didn't you? Isn't that what some people in this business call 'skimming the easy money'?"

"This wasn't an easy case." He peered at his knuckles and crossed his legs. "There was a serious question whether he was actually driving."

"Oh." Matt stepped forward. "Then you didn't believe your own client when he said he was a passenger?"

Conti sat in silence, his eyes darkening with anger.

Matt bore in quickly. "Tell me, before you took the two hundred forty thousand dollar fee for representing someone you were worried was *the driver*, did you spend any money on an expert to see if you could prove where in the car he was actually sitting? No? How about to have the medical records reviewed, or to obtain the x-ray films—no to that, also?" No response.

"While you were supposed to be doing something to earn that two hundred forty thousand dollars, Mr. Conti, did you take any steps at all to investigate whether there was any way to recover more money to help this badly injured boy?"

The thick mane of white hair flopped characteristically over his forehead as he sat forward in his chair. "I wasn't hired to try to create cases and find new people to sue, Mr. Taylor. You may do that in your business, but that's not my style."

Matt looked at the flushed face, projecting feigned indignation, and felt revulsion well up.

"Oh really? Then what were you doing in Atlanta after the Pan Caribbean Airline crash a few years ago when you set up a desk in the lobby of the victims' families' hotel and signed up a hundred of the families?"

"Objection. That's irrelevant and entirely inappropriate." Murphy had leaped to his feet, his face flushed.

"That's what I thought. Entirely inappropriate." Matt nodded agreeably. "They hadn't even had a chance to identify the bodies yet."

Murphy's mouth opened and closed like a hooked salmon, but no sound emerged. The judge straightened the amusement from his features and cleared his throat. "Gentlemen, calm down, please. The objection will be sustained."

Matt didn't care. He had seen the jury's reaction as they were reminded of the wave of negative coverage and public revulsion that had accompanied Conti's shameless solicitation efforts. There was also reward in the stunned look that hadn't yet been erased from the heavy features of the witness.

"Mr. Conti, we were discussing your obligation to do your best to provide an adequate recovery for the sixteen-year-old client you had undertaken to represent. Tell us, did you ever read those medical records yourself?"

"I can't remember."

Matt leaned on the jury rail. "Now, don't you think, with all your experience in this business, you would remember if you had seen that set of records? You know, with the notation about 'legs thrashing about and respond to painful stimulus' and all given that he was now a *quadriplegic*?"

"No, actually that would probably not have impressed me. In my years of experience I have seen many cases of paralysis that developed over a period of time. That's pretty meaningless."

"*Meaningless!*" Matt's voice lashed through the quiet courtroom. "Are you saying that you would know more than a doctor about the importance of such notations?"

"No, I just..."

"Sir, my question is, if you had gone through those records yourself, early on, and you had seen he could move his legs. If you had then seen the comment by the nurses where he complained he couldn't move *right after he was rolled over for a linen change*, wouldn't you have had these records reviewed by an expert neurologist?"

The heavy head oscillated back and forth contemptuously. "I have no idea what I would have done under circumstances that never even happened."

"Never happened because you never even bothered to look at those records, isn't that right, sir?"

"I certainly didn't look at them. Why should I, when we were just hired to represent this youngster in a car accident. That's what I've been trying to explain here all afternoon." His thick mouth curved challengingly, his expression encouraging Matt to use his head against that brick wall again. Matt started to frame another question.

The judge cleared his throat and swiveled his heavy chair away from the witness toward Matt. "Is this a good time for our afternoon recess, Mr. Taylor? Good. Let's reconvene at nine o'clock tomorrow, ladies and gentlemen, and remember the admonition—no discussing the case at all."

* * *

Matt felt the tension of the day drain from his muscles as they walked out the main doors of the courthouse. The hiss of an involuntary sigh caused Adrianne to inquire. "So how do you think it went?"

"Not so well as I might have hoped. Oh, we made a point or two and caught him napping a few times, but no knockout blows, that's for sure." He slumped wearily. "I just have this feeling they're a jump ahead of us all the time. It's scaring me. What else are they going to pull out of the hat?"

"Yeah, he seemed awful sure of himself, didn't he? There's something happening that's not kosher." Her face shrunk. "They seem to know a lot about what we're doing."

He glanced askance at her as they headed down the stairs to the garage. "You've got conspiracy on the brain. You really think they have some sort of spy in our midst?"

"It's not all that far-fetched Matt. There's a lot they seem to know. I wouldn't put anything past that egomaniacal old man." She stared thoughtfully out the window.

40

Matt stretched and closed his eyes in exhaustion. He had just talked to the neurosurgeon back in Atlanta. He was due on the stand Friday. The elderly doctor had been very friendly and accommodating. The only problem was, he tended to wander a bit when he answered questions. Matt hoped he had all his marbles. Probably it was just the late hour. Matt looked at his watch—half past ten—time for home and bed. He could get up early and finish the rest in the morning before court.

He lugged the heavy briefcases through the quiet office. At the door, he hit the master switch to close off the remaining lights. He was startled by a yelp from the direction of Adrianne's office. "Hey! Hard to work with no light."

He flicked the switch again and ducked his head around her door. "Sorry. Thought you left a long time ago. This place has been quiet as a tomb for an hour."

She was sitting with stocking feet propped up on her desk, a book balanced on her lap. "Probably should have, but I got interested in this 'how to do it' book and lost track—obviously." She grinned at him.

He leaned against the doorframe. The golden light from the loading pier across the street was filtering through the fog-dampened window behind her and framed her dark hair with lustrous highlights. Her eyes sparkled out of the shadows created by her overhead reading light. Her features were softened by the incandescent glow. He felt a stab of longing flash through him and realized he was staring.

Stupid damn fool anyway, he thought. Embarrassed, he turned to leave. "Don't stay too late. I'll leave the door locked."

"Hey! So what's going on with you anyway?"

He turned back into the doorway. "What do you mean?"

She gave him an encouraging smile. "You're usually more articulate."

"Like I said, I feel so totally guilty. Jake's my really good friend. Every time I see him, I feel like I betrayed him." A sigh of chagrin escaped him. "I see him every night at the office. Yesterday, I could hardly talk to him. And I know he's dying over the whole situation with you. I should be there for him now, and instead I feel like I caused the problem."

"Wait a minute. What am I—a potted plant?" She sat up and leaned her elbows forward, a frown dragging at her forehead. "I think I'm capable of making up my own mind about my relationship with Jake. Sorry to bruise your ego, my dear. And he bears a modicum of responsibility for the problems that led to my calling it quits."

"Well, sure, but you hadn't officially called it off yet when we were together in the mountains. In fact, he was supposed to meet us there. I feel like I sort of helped shove him out the door, so to speak." Matt folded his arms across his chest. "You know, like maybe things would have worked out between you two if I hadn't been poaching on his territory?"

"Look here." Air punched out of her in disgust. "I told you I had already made up my mind about Jake well before that trip. I hate to burst your bubble, but if I were still in any way involved with Jake when we went up there, we would *not* have ended up in the sack. Period." He held up his hands in embarrassment. She waved at him impatiently. "Matt, what we're talking about is timing, pure and simple. The relationship had ended. All that was left was to tell him, not that he didn't already know. Heck, we hadn't had much of a relationship for months. There's no reason for you to beat yourself up over something that was already dead, but just hadn't been buried."

"I know, I know. Intellectually, it's easy—putting a bullet in a dead man is not murder in the eyes of the law, and all that." He looked at her with

259

anguish in his eyes. "The problem is, he's my friend. And, he didn't even know he was dead when I put a bullet in his head. And he doesn't know, even now, that I pulled that trigger." He came into her office and sat down. "I just feel like I've got to tell him about it. Too much unsaid, you know? But I just can't. I haven't even been able to talk with you about it. It just hangs there between us—me and Jake—you and me—just hanging there."

"Well, I sure know how to get everyone upset, huh? And you were probably just hoping to get a good night's sleep." She set aside her book and then looked at him resolutely. "There's something else we've got to talk about."

He waved her off. "I don't have the energy, not with that look you have in your eye. Got to be up early and go over some testimony. We got a case to try you know."

Adrianne reached over and grabbed his arm. "Listen to me, Matt. It's about the case." He gently extracted his arm and sat back with his arms tight again across his chest. She paused a moment, then plunged in. "Matt, I really do think there's a spy…" Matt started a negative gesture. She stopped him. "And so does Clint." A heavy breath of air escaped his lungs, but his eyes remained on hers. She swallowed and continued. "There've been too many strange things. Our experts that jumped ship, their papers that anticipated our motion on the x-rays, and how did they know that we were going to change our liability theory on the hospital and nurses? They had the cross all set up and even had prepared a diagram to go with it!"

He rotated his head negatively. "They get paid to anticipate. They're smart lawyers."

"No way. No one's that smart. And how could they have anticipated Archie, the friend that saw Todd in the E.R. that *nobody* but us knew about. But know they did. Matt you *know* they knew about it. How *could* they have known?"

He stared at her thoughtfully. "It definitely explains some things."

"You're damn right it would."

"Just for argument's sake, suppose someone was letting some things slip. Who could it be? I can't imagine anyone on our team would ever be that careless with their mouth."

Adrianne blew her breath out impatiently. "You still don't get it. Nobody's being *careless*. They've sold us out. Someone's telling the other side things *on purpose*, big-time."

"Then I *really* don't believe one of our team would do that."

She inclined her head slowly. "I agree, I don't think it's one of our team."

"Then who?"

She watched him think about it. She could see the light dawning. "That's right. You don't office alone. There are others who are not on your team around all the time."

"I suppose it could be one of Jake's people." He frowned at her. "It's hard to imagine—but I guess it's possible."

"Yeah, but when we talk about most of that stuff it's after court, or on the weekends. They're all gone."

Matt stood to leave. "Right. So that blows your theory."

She gave another, bigger, sigh. "Nope, I'm afraid it doesn't." She looked at him sadly.

His eyes widened suddenly and then his face darkened in anger. He moved abruptly out her door. "That's ridiculous. No way in hell would he ever do anything like that."

She followed him out the door, jogging to catch up with him. "Matt, there's no other logical explanation. Think about it. He's the only one who's there late all the time. Both of us talk to him a lot about our theories, too much maybe." She put her hand on his shoulder, pulling him around to face her. "Clint thinks it has to be him. He has some proof too. You should talk to him."

His face was set in fury. "I'll never believe it of him. You've no idea. We go back to law school for God's sake. He's saved my butt a dozen times. I owe him big-time. Stuff you wouldn't believe, things only the two of us know about."

"And you for him as well. He's told me some of those things, too. Matt," She squeezed his arm gently. "I know Jake's important to you, but I still think it's him."

"What is it with you?" He thrust her arm off, pulling abruptly away from her. "Is it payback time or something? What did he do to you to make you so angry at him? This is one of the best friendships I've ever had and now you're trying to sabotage it." She hurried after him into the garage, quivering with frustration. She caught up with him just as he threw open his car door and jammed his briefcase over the seat.

"Matt listen. This isn't about Jake and me. This isn't even about your friendship or us. You're forgetting something important." He stood rigid in the car doorway staring angrily over the car at her. "This is about Todd Gleason, Matt. Your client's case is getting trashed. Something stinks here. This is just a theory—one potential explanation." Gauging his reaction, she carefully chose her next words. "It needs to be tested. Clint and I have an idea how we can tell." She raised her shoulders. "If it proves you're right, no one will be happier than me. Don't you see?"

He stared at her a moment longer, then abruptly got in his car and gunned it down the dark ramp. As the angry shrieks of his tires faded into echoes, the burgeoning silence provided his response.

41

The narrow eyes and pinched features of the first alternate juror bothered Matt every time he looked at the man. The juror had his arms tightly crossed and his head lowered, so that he watched the witness from under graying brows. Matt was asking his questions from the back rail so he could sneak a quick look at the jury while they listened to Doctor Hanlon emphasize the importance of ruling out spinal injuries in cases of severe trauma. The first alternate juror always looked stern and disapproving, but at the moment he did not seem to like anything Matt's emergency room expert was saying. Thank God the man was not one of the first twelve who would actually get to vote when the jury deliberated—at the moment.

Matt summarized a few of the main points with follow-up questions and then turned the witness over to the defense for cross-examination. Walking back to his seat, he glanced quickly at Adrianne and was the recipient of a small, neutral smile.

Matt allowed himself to feel a temporary sense of satisfaction. The morning had gone well with one of Todd's physical therapists giving moving testimony and, except for the expression on the alternate's face, the direct of Hanlon had been smooth and seemed to interest the jury. They had worked very carefully on the direct exam questions so that there would be no reference to the E.R. specialist's first opinion to Matt, which had been quite negative about Todd's case. It turned out that Matt's office had left out an important part of the records when they were first copied and sent to the doctor. That caused his initial negative opinion. Explaining that in front of the jury would have been awkward at best. Accordingly, Matt's questions had been worded carefully so that the answers could be completely honest without that information being revealed. The testimony had gone better than Matt had hoped. Matt sat back and watched as Andersen rehashed the direct ineffectually. Matt allowed himself to relax a bit. Another twenty minutes and the judge would recess for the day.

"So you firmly believe that the emergency room physician in this case breached the standard of care?" Anderson was fumbling with some papers as he questioned. He seemed to be throwing lob shots up for Doctor Hanlon to hit without any clear goal in mind. Guess even big shot defense lawyers had bad days, Matt thought.

"Yes, I certainly do. This was an admission involving a history of high impact with severe potential trauma to the patient." Hanlon looked at ease, his legs crossed, gesturing casually, talking more to the jury than to Anderson. "Whenever a qualified E.R. specialist is confronted with this situation, it is incumbent on them to rule out head and spinal injuries."

"So just with that information alone," Anderson did not even look up from his fumbling, "Any knowledgeable physician would rule out such injuries, and if they didn't, they would be guilty of malpractice. That's your opinion?"

Uh-oh. A little bell started ringing in the back of Matt's mind. His instincts told him this didn't smell right. Matt straightened slightly in his chair and felt prickles of apprehension work up his spine. Hanlon nodded confidently. "Yes, sir, this is textbook kind of stuff."

Anderson looked up now. His features tightened and his gaze focused on the witness. Unfortunately, he wasn't bumbling anymore. "This was so obvious to you that you knew immediately that the doctors treating Todd Gleason had blown it badly when you first saw these records?"

Matt rose to his feet. Maybe if he said something Hanlon would see the pit yawning in front of him. "Objection, Your Honor. Counsel is just plowing the same ground here over and over or else *he is suggesting something else entirely* and therefore the question is ambiguous."

The judge raised sleepy eyes at him and hesitated for a moment. "Well, that will be overruled, counsel. Answer the question please, doctor." The doctor obediently answered in a relaxed, confident manner. "Yes, I certainly saw that right away, as any competent practitioner would." Matt kicked himself mentally. The jury had probably been asleep like the judge. All Matt had succeeded in doing was waking everyone up so they would catch Anderson's point, which Matt knew was soon to be forcibly imprinted on the anatomy of his case and that of Doctor John Hanlon.

Anderson moved out from behind the table in front of the jury. "Tell me, Doctor Hanlon, has it *always* been your opinion that the E.R. doctor here breached the standard of care?" Hanlon's face stiffened slightly and his eyes flickered involuntarily toward Matt. "You don't have to look to Mr. Taylor for help in answering this, do you, Doctor?"

"No, of course not. I just wasn't quite sure what you meant."

"And you thought Mr. Taylor could help you? Actually let me rephrase the question to make it very clear. The very first time you looked at the records and talked to Mr. Taylor—that time, Doctor—did you tell him you thought the E.R. doctor made a mistake?"

Hanlon looked at Matt again involuntarily. This time the jury followed his gaze and looked at Matt too. He tried to look nonchalant, even though he could feel the back of his shirt becoming damp. "Well, our first conversation was actually before I had received all of the records."

Anderson edged closer to the witness. His eyes narrowed to slits. "Doctor, listen to my question. I'll try to make it even clearer yet. When you first talked to Mr. Taylor, after you reviewed the records he sent to you, did you tell Mr. Taylor that you did not see any evidence of malpractice by the E.R. physicians during the care of Mr. Gleason?" The jury seemed to sit up and lean forward to wait for the answer. Now they were definitely awake. The alternate juror's cold eyes were riveted on Matt.

The doctor looked down and flicked at his pants while he considered his answer. Finally, after much too much time had gone by he looked back up. "Yes, that was my first opinion…that is, before I had seen all the records."

265

Anderson moved back behind his chair and pretended to look at his notes. "But, Doctor, I wrote down a few minutes ago that you said '…all a physician had to know was that there was a history of high impact and the potential of severe trauma to the patient and *anyone* would know it would be malpractice not to rule out head and spinal injuries,' remember that statement?"

"Yes, but…"

"No buts, Doctor. When you saw what Mr. Taylor sent you, it certainly contained information that the patient had been in a high impact rollover and that he may have suffered severe injuries, didn't it? Indeed, that information was contained on the admission sheet alone, wasn't it?"

"Yes."

"And then, after reading that, you called him up and told him there was no case, didn't you?'

"Yes, I did."

How in the hell did they know about all this stuff? This was obviously more than an educated guess. No experienced trial attorney would go fishing with such questions without concrete, reliable information.

"So, after you said there was no case," Anderson came back out in front of the jury to emphasize his point, "then you talked to Mr. Taylor, right, Doctor?"

"Yes."

"…and then he was upset and said, well let me send you more records to try to change your mind, right, Doctor?"

"Well, yes."

"…and then you read some more. Oh, and by the way, you are paid by Mr. Taylor for this opinion, right?"

"Yes, of course."

"…*of course*, and after spending more time, for which you were paid quite *handsomely* by Mr. Taylor," Anderson gifted the jury with a cynical smile, "then you changed your mind and decided that these doctors *had* committed malpractice—right?"

Hansen shifted nervously in his chair. "Well, not handsomely…"

"Oh really? Well six hundred fifty dollars an hour, that sounds pretty *handsome* to me." He looked at the jury. "Over four times what I charge an hour. Oh, Doctor, by the way, do you get paid six hundred fifty dollars an hour for doing E.R. work at the hospital?"

"Well, no, but for legal work I…"

"Excuse me, Doctor, you mean for legal work where you *accuse other doctors of committing malpractice*, for that you want to be paid extra?"

Matt stood and cleared his throat to get the judge's attention. "Your Honor, counsel is getting *quite* argumentative."

"Sustained."

Matt sank back in his chair. He could break this up now and again, but nothing was going to stop Anderson from having his fun. He would run his course with Doctor Hanlon and it was not going to be a pleasant afternoon. Nor would Matt be able to do much to help things on re-direct. Another witness would definitely have to be put in the minus column. Matt looked for Hairy Harry, but he had left.

* * *

The team looked at each other glumly. The day had not ended well. To top everything off, Murphy had stopped Matt in the hall on his way out of the courthouse and informed him that the defense was reducing their outstanding offer to one and a half million dollars on instructions from Conti's insurance company. More and more, it seemed the only way out of this mess was to forge ahead.

Adrianne brightened and looked at Matt. "Well, tomorrow's another day and our best expert's getting off the plane in an hour. I hand-picked this one and he's as good as it gets."

Matt appreciated her enthusiasm. It was too bad her experience was only a few rather questionable witnesses, and most of them in this case. He decided not to point that out. "Well, I hope you're right. We don't need any more disasters." He looked around the deserted office as Clint joined the group. "The one thing that bothers me a bit about him is his age. Sometimes when I talk to him, I'm just not sure he's on the same page."

"Well, he's getting on a bit, but he still does surgery. I think he'll take the time to be extra well-prepared." Adrianne lifted her chin optimistically. "After all, he was the head of the department there at Emory University and is still there in an emeritus status." She looked at Matt defensively. "Apparently they still think he's with it."

"Hey, I was just commenting on that one occasion." Matt made a calming gesture. "We tried all over. He was it, the best we could come up with." He gave her reassuring look. "Beggars can't be choosers."

"Beggars is right." Clint eased back on the couch and stretched his long legs out. He pulled a thin file from his briefcase. Glancing quickly around the dark office, he spoke softly. "I turned up a problem on this big shot neurosurgeon when I did a double-check this morning." He gave Adrianne an apologetic glance. "Seems your guy has a skeleton or two in his closet. If I can find out about it so can they. These guys always do their homework."

"Shit!" Matt felt a worm of fear start gnawing at his gut. "What the hell problem have we got now?" Everybody looked startled at his uncharacteristic loss of control.

"Seems that the old bird got caught in a lie in a case up in northern Mississippi." Clint tipped his hat back and lowered his heavy growl even more, his eyes again checked the darkened corners of the reception area. "He just barely avoided a perjury conviction. He got hauled in front of a Governor's commission of some type and was barred from ever testifying in Mississippi again." He waved the file in the air. "Ironically, it was the only plaintiff's case he ever testified in. If this comes out, they'll trash the old man—big-time."

There was a lengthy silence as the group absorbed this latest blow to the case. Finally Adrianne broke the silence. "Well shit indeed! What the hell do we do about this?" She swallowed hard. "Can we even use him tomorrow?"

"We have no choice now." Matt looked around at the grim faces. "Without a neurosurgeon, the case is dead. And you know this judge will never let us substitute in the middle of the trial." He grated his hands over his beard in frustration. "Well, we'll just talk to the guy and see if we can fix it. And pray they don't get on to it. Remember, when things seem blackest, there is always one good thing to think about."

Emily gave him a weak smile. "Okay, I'll bite. What could that be?"

"Things can't get any worse, so maybe they'll get better!"

They all quietly contemplated that thought. Suddenly the sodden silence was shattered by a hearty voice.

"Hey y'all, why so glum? Things couldn't be that bad." Jake came around the corner from his end of the office and stood looking down at them. Matt and Adrianne stared at each other for a second and then looked up at Jake. Matt broke the silence first. "We thought you'd gone home, Jake. Hope our moping around in here wasn't bothering you." Clint was staring at Jake. A clump was twitching in his jaw.

"Oh no, not at all, I was just in the small conference room trying to put things together for my case next Monday. Things going okay?"

"Some good, some not so good." Matt's insides were on fire. "We got trashed a bit today."

"Sounds like a trial to me. Never fear. It'll get better tomorrow and today won't seem important. You know what it's like." Jake picked up his briefcase and waved casually. "Break a leg, guys. See ya."

As he walked out the door, Adrianne, Clint and Matt eyed each other helplessly. Adrianne bared her teeth in disgust. "He didn't even ask what went wrong today."

"What do you mean?" Mary Beth looked at them with a quizzical look. "What's wrong?"

Matt looked away from the other two. "Nothing, MB. We're just tired, I guess."

The pit of Matt's stomach burned with uncertainty and apprehension. The little conference room was right next to the reception area. He was sure the light in Jake's office and that conference room had been off when he checked around the office earlier.

42

It was almost midnight and Matt was desperate. Everything they talked about, the elderly neurosurgeon seemed to screw up. Two hours of effort and the man still couldn't even remember the records. Every time Matt asked a question, he gave an answer the defense would love. Matt shivered involuntarily. Snakes of adrenaline were nibbling at his entrails. It would be hours before the expert would be ready for testimony, and they hadn't even touched on the Mississippi situation. The surgeon stretched and yawned.

"Well, young man, I guess I'm a bit tired—jet lag and all. Maybe we all better call it a night or I won't be worth a thing in the morning."

Lord, thought Matt. You certainly won't be worth a thing if I can't spend a few more hours with you. Sleep be damned. "Maybe we should go over this a few more times and then I'd like to talk a little about that situation in Mississippi. It might come up."

"Don't worry, I'll get up early and go over this a bit in the morning." The tired eyes crinkled. "Things will be all right after I've had a few hours' sleep."

Matt winced. This witness would need a week of sleep to do even as well as the E.R. guy today, and that had been a catastrophe! "I'm really worried about a few of these points, and that other situation definitely needs discussing."

The doctor just smiled indulgently and started packing things up. "Well, maybe so, but I'm going to be asleep while you do that." He patted

Matt on the shoulder. "You don't look so good yourself, Mr. Taylor. A good night's sleep wouldn't do you any harm either."

He guided Matt to his hotel room door and opened it for him. "I wouldn't lose any sleep over that Mississippi thing. I doubt they know anything about it or care if they do. It's come up before. I can handle it. Good night." A bony finger waggled at him. "Get to bed now."

Easy for him to say, Matt thought. The case was falling apart around him and his witness thought Matt needed a good night's sleep. That wasn't very likely. He thought of Todd and Debbie Gleason, the stricken look on their faces after Hanlon's testimony. He had apologized to them, but they would hear none of it. They were sure that tomorrow would be a good day. Their faith in him was unshakable. Unfortunately, it may have been misplaced. He was failing them, his family, and himself, and he couldn't even toss in the towel and take the settlement offer. A big piece of it had gone down the drain, just like Todd's case was doing.

* * *

The atmosphere in the old courtroom was thick and oppressive already at half past nine in the morning, or was that Matt's imagination? He had tried to meet the neurosurgeon early, but the doctor said he had to make some phone calls. The judge was about to take the bench and his witness hadn't even arrived yet. It was early to break through his deodorant, but Matt had managed.

"All rise, Superior Court of the City and County of San Francisco, Honorable Marvin Rigoletti presiding. Be seated." The old chairs creaked and sighed as spectators and jury sat. The judge looked at Matt. "Mr. Taylor, call your next witness please."

Matt pretended to finish scribbling some notes to buy time and then slowly stood. The court reporter's fingers hovered over his machine; the heavy air was laced with the sickly, sweet smell of the oil polish layered onto the tired oak paneling. He cleared his throat reluctantly. "Good morning, Your Honor, we…" He felt an urgent kick on his ankle and looked down at Adrianne who was thumbing toward the back of the room. The neurosurgeon actually looked quite spiffy, a bright bow tie, sharp blue suit, white hair swept back from intense eyes and a friendly grin. He was poised expectantly at the rail, a neat file of notes in his hand.

"...call Doctor Henry Roberson as our next witness." Too bad his testimony probably would not match up to his appearance.

A good deal of time was spent emphasizing the doctor's extensive qualifications and experience. He encouraged the witness to expand on points whenever possible to let them glimpse his southern charm and genuine humility. His hope, of course, was to perhaps make them more kindly disposed to what he had to say. Matt was pleased to observe that the doctor was relaxed and the jury seemed to respond favorably to him.

They worked their way into the substantive material gradually. Doctor Roberson missed a few points here and there, but Matt was able to work back around and patch up the shaky areas. Obviously, the doctor had done some studying early this morning or else sleep had made a difference, or both. Nonetheless, the physician still came across as very nice, but not exactly overwhelming. Matt wanted to emphasize a few points before he handed the neurosurgeon over to Anderson, but he was afraid if he asked the questions a different way, the house of cards would begin to fall apart. It was maddening. The man was doing much better than Matt had expected last night but, at this point, the case needed a star. His mouth went dry. If Doctor Roberson wasn't a star during a friendly direct examination, he could be a disaster on cross. Finally, his points made and unable to postpone the inevitable any longer, Matt conceded the witness to his impatient adversary.

Anderson started slow and probed around the corners a bit at first, warming up to the task at hand, getting to know the witness. Roberson was friendly and forthright, clear on his opinions, giving ground when appropriate. Matt stayed out of the action and felt himself relaxing a few millimeters at a time. This fellow wasn't a star yet, but he was holding his own. Thank God there had been no hint of that Mississippi thing. Maybe Matt had at least ducked that particular bullet.

The defense attorney's voice deepened a notch and he moved out to the jury rail. The time for sniffing around the edges appeared to be over. "Doctor, you have testified that the neurosurgeon in this case, Doctor

Escobar, breached the standard of care in the treatment of Todd Gleason. Is that right?"

The witness sat up a bit straighter and looked Anderson in the eye. "Yes sir, that is my opinion."

Adrianne nudged him. Jake had just taken a seat in the back of the courtroom. Matt lifted his head in greeting. That was interesting; he hadn't been in to see the trial since the first few days.

Anderson's tone had changed. There was more insistence, more growl in the tenor of his voice. "Doctor, you have told us that the neurosurgeon should have recognized that this young man could have had an injury to the spinal cord because of the changes evident on examination."

"Yes."

"Isn't it true that alcohol can depress the reflexes?"

"Yes, it can."

The big frame of the questioner moved forward, encroaching on neutral territory again. "You have said that the withdrawal to painful stimulus— the movement of his arms and legs in the E.R.—could indicate that Mr. Gleason had retained normal function in his legs?"

"Yes, it certainly does."

"…and these are the main findings in the E.R., aren't they? That is, depressed reflexes and movement to pain of the arms and legs in a kid that smelled strongly of alcohol?"

The doctor inclined his head slowly. "Yes…"

"And, if you had a kid who had been drinking, had been in an accident and wasn't in fact injured at all." Anderson paused and looked the jury up and down to emphasize his question, "Doctors carefully examining such a fellow would have just such findings, wouldn't they?"

"Yes, I suppose they would."

The cross-examiner spun and pointed triumphantly to the witness on the stand. "So, with such findings, a reasonable physician could easily and *correctly* come to the conclusion that there was nothing wrong with such a patient and just put him in for observation such as was done here?"

Here's what it's all about doc, this is what we pay you for. Don't screw it up.

"Well, yes…"

Anderson broke in forcefully. "…and that's why…"

The doctor continued speaking quietly, but firmly, "…and no."

"Objection, Your Honor; counsel is interrupting the witness."

The judge looked at Anderson. "I do think he was still answering your question when you started your next one."

Anderson bowed with ironic grace and gestured for the doctor to continue.

"…as I was saying, the answer is yes *and* no." Matt was happy to see him look toward the jury and held his breath for the answer. "It would certainly be reasonable for the doctor to decide that the patient may well be affected by drink and otherwise be perfectly okay." Matt's insides began to shrivel in dread. "However, and this is the heart of the matter, with history of trauma in a major rollover accident, *other possible causes of these findings must be ruled out immediately.*" He paused to take a sip of water. Anderson quickly started a question, but the doctor held up a hand. The room hushed expectantly. "Under these circumstances, it is very common for us to see head or spinal injuries masked by the presence of alcohol or unconsciousness. We teach our residents from the first day to *presume* a more serious injury for the welfare of the patient. Films of the head and neck must be taken immediately. Once serious, treatable, life-threatening conditions are ruled out, *then* the patient can safely be admitted for observation."

Atta-way, Doc. Finally the man was taking charge of his own testimony. But they were not out of the woods yet.

Conti's attorney moved his bulk back against the rail behind Matt. "All right, Doctor, but that's exactly what they did in this case, isn't it? They took films of the head and they were normal?"

"Yes."

"And took spine films and they were read as normal?"

"And you certainly think that the plaintiff's expert, Doctor Hanlon, was testifying reasonably when he said that it was perfectly all right to not take more films, don't you?" His face split in an encouraging smile and he looked again toward the jury.

The expert's brow hourglassed in concern. "Well, I'm here to talk about the care of Doctor Escobar, and…"

Anderson's encouraging expression disappeared as he wheeled abruptly toward the witness box, his voice knifing through the humid atmosphere. "Doctor Roberson, you're not suggesting that the neurosurgeon should be held to a higher standard than the radiologist in dealing with when and when not to do films, are you?"

"Uhh...no, no, certainly not." He looked at Matt apologetically. He was leaning forward in his chair, lines of tension evident in his posture.

Anderson quickly moved closer to Roberson, intending to intimidate. Matt rose to his feet.

"Excuse me, Your Honor, can we request that counsel not crowd the witness podium. It does make it difficult for the jury to see."

Startled, the judge looked at where Anderson was and then pointed to the back of the court with his chin. "You know better than to get that close to a witness, counsel. Back to neutral territory." It came out like a command to the judge's dog. The jury snickered and Matt smiled innocently during Anderson's retreat to the back rail. Matt was also pleased to see Doctor Roberson relax and sit back. Perhaps the brief respite and change in tempo would let him regroup.

"So, Doctor Roberson, where were we? Oh yes, the neurosurgeon is not required to request additional films if the radiologist is not requesting them. Correct?"

"I don't think so, no..."

Anderson broke in and Matt's heart sank again. "Exactly, so..."

The neurosurgeon cleared his throat abruptly. "Just a minute. I'm not quite done with my answer. While he may not be required to do more films, he certainly cannot assume that the young man has no injury to the spine if he hasn't visualized the entire cervical spine. He should look at the films himself and he should certainly stabilize the neck until a spinal injury is ruled out. That was not done here."

"Well." The defense attorney stared at him for a minute in frustration. "If he should look at the films, then they are rather critical in your mind?"

"Yes."

"Because if they are entirely benign, that may lead away from thought of a neck injury?"

"Yes…"

"And you have not seen those films yourself?" Anderson said, tapping his pen against his mouth.

"No. I understand they are missing."

The pen pointed at the witness. "And you have no reason to suspect that Doctor Escobar did not review the films?"

"Well, yes. I guess that's correct."

"So if the doctors who were treating Todd Gleason saw these films themselves…" The gesturing pen was timing the cadence of the question. "…if they saw that they were completely normal, just as the report done at the time indicates, then they would be in a better position than you are, years later, to decide if more films were necessary?"

"Objection, Your Honor. That is quite ambiguous." Classic, Matt thought. Artfully worded to sound like it meant more than it did. All he was asking was if they were in a better position, not if that would make any difference to the doctor's opinion.

"Overruled, answer the question please, Doctor."

"Well, I would have to say yes, they were in a better position having had a chance to actually see the films themselves."

Anderson would be content with that minor victory in this area. He smiled broadly at the jury to make them think he had won the match and went back to his notes.

"Changing the subject a bit here. Doctor…"

Matt felt some relief. For the moment, they were a bit ahead on points. Happily they had apparently not tumbled to the Mississippi thing. The doctor should be good on causation, which just established that the negligence here caused the paralysis. Anderson was working on that at the moment. Matt listened with one ear and went over the afternoon in his mind. His rehabilitation doctor would be on and that should be pretty straightforward. Then the weekend would be here and he could catch his breath. It was too bad about Roberson. He was close to being a good witness, but his testimony needed something special to make him a witness the jury would remember. Adrianne bumped his elbow.

Anderson was working his way up that rail in front of the jury again. "…so about twenty cases in your career?"

"Something like that, but it's spread over forty years or so." Roberson looked relaxed and in control. "I haven't really done that much testifying—more interested in opening heads." He smiled at the jury, but didn't get much response. Matt shifted uneasily in his chair. Careful, Doc—don't get cute. The jury doesn't think brain surgery's funny.

"Do you enjoy testifying?"

"Not that much. But sometimes it needs to be done. Help out doctors in trouble and to keep our profession honest, you know."

"Honesty. Yes, that's important isn't it? You think that's important, Doctor?" Uh-oh, Matt felt that worm of nervous anticipation start gnawing at his internal organs again. The blood had drained from Adrianne's face.

The doctor responded vigorously. "Yes, of course."

"You do this for the money also, don't you, Doctor?" Anderson's gaze wandered casually out the window.

"Actually not," A small knot grew between his eyes. "I prefer to do surgery and stay home with my wife and my golf game. The money is not that attractive."

"Well, you charge five hundred fifty dollars per hour, right? That's a lot more than you make in the operating room isn't it?"

"I do, and actually, no, I make about that much doing surgery." There was an expression of mild distaste. "Frankly, I prefer to be the one doing the surgery. In the courtroom, I sometimes feel like the patient." He got a smile out of the jury on that one. Anderson didn't smile.

"What you are doing to Doctor Escobar in this courtroom is like surgery, isn't it? Don't you think he's feeling the knife?"

"Actually," Roberson feigned confusion, "I thought the defendant here was Mr. Conti."

Anderson's hands went to his hips. "You think Doctor Escobar doesn't care what you have to say about him?"

It was time to slow things down. Matt could feel a set-up coming, big-time. "Objection, argumentative."

"Sustained."

The defense attorney didn't miss a beat. "You know the doctors you testify against care very much what you have to say about them, don't you?"

"Yes." The body language was only modestly acquiescent. "Although, I have only rarely testified in a case against another physician. Usually I am called to defend the doctor."

"You were called to testify against doctors in Mississippi on more than one occasion, weren't you?

"Yes." A simple nod.

The lawyer's head rotated toward the jury. "So you often go out of state to say other doctors have done something wrong?"

"Once in a while, not often."

The questions were coming faster now. "You've never been back to Mississippi since then, have you?" The jury was moving its collective head as if at a tennis match.

"No, I haven't."

"Is there a reason for that?" The two were separated from the spectators by the increasing cadence of their interaction.

"Not really." The witness seemed slightly bemused. "I haven't thought it appropriate."

"You haven't thought it *appropriate*?" Anderson's head pivoted toward the witness. "Is that the only reason?"

Matt leaped to his feet. It was time to at least deflate and perhaps derail the tension. "Your Honor, may we approach the bench?"

The massive shoulders of the defense attorney plowed across the room toward the bench, muttering darkly as he advanced. They gathered on the side away from the jury and the witness. Matt's voice was soft but urgent. "This is an entirely inappropriate line of questions, Your Honor. Counsel obviously thinks he has something about Mississippi and intends to forge ahead. I suspect he may make unsubstantiated allegations of some sort in front of the jury. We object strenuously to that."

An impatient snort was the reply. "Your Honor, this is legitimate cross. I don't have to show my hand to him. Besides, I suspect he knows full well where I'm going with my questions."

"I think he has a right to a full cross of this witness, counsel."

"Yes, but at least there should be an offer of proof outside the hearing of the jury." Matt leaned closer, his voice becoming insistent. "We have no idea where he is going with this." Another sound of derision from the defense lawyer punctuated Matt's plea to the judge.

The judge flashed a disapproving glance at Anderson's courtroom decorum, but obviously wasn't going to put a leash on him at this point. "That will be denied."

Anderson swaggered back to his place in front of the jury like a successful matador. "You may answer the pending question, Doctor Roberson."

The physician seemed to have been revived slightly by the break. "Thank you. The answer is 'yes', that is the only reason."

"In that last case in Mississippi, you testified against a doctor, didn't you?" His questioner hadn't wasted any time getting right back into it. "You testified, like here, that a doctor had committed malpractice, right?"

"Yes, I did."

"And after that case you stopped testifying in Mississippi, didn't you?" His chin thrust forward. "And that was because you were not allowed back in the state to testify again against any more doctors, isn't that true?"

"Well, sort of…I…" A tiny frown and quizzical pull of his mouth.

Anderson's hands went to his sides, elbows jutting truculently. "After that case, there was a hearing, wasn't there, a separate proceeding?"

The neurosurgeon turned with obvious concern to the judge. "I'm not sure I should go into all of this, Your Honor."

"You will need to answer the questions, Doctor Roberson." The judge projected a certain degree of sympathy, or was it pity?

"Well, then…" The doctor pondered his response. "Yes, there was a proceeding after the trial."

"And that proceeding was all about someone committing *perjury*, wasn't it?" Anderson's voice had deepened as he leaned closer to the small figure on the stand.

"I don't understand, Your Honor." Roberson had turned to the judge again. "I thought all this had been sealed by the court and couldn't be gone into anymore." He was pale and looked confused. "Do I have to answer these questions?"

Matt stood quickly. "Perhaps this would be a good time for a recess, Your Honor?"

"I think not, counsel." The judge's eyes mirrored the disgust with which Anderson had laced his questions. He looked at the doctor. There was no sympathy in his eyes anymore. "Yes, Doctor, you do have to answer the question. Please proceed, counsel."

The neurosurgeon suddenly looked older and unfocused as he turned away from the judge and back to Anderson. The burly defense lawyer moved closer again, his features quivering with anticipation. "Do you need the question restated?"

The old man answered as if in a fog. "I'm not sure what it was you asked?"

Anderson's face turned crimson as flecks of moisture sprayed toward the shrinking figure on the stand. "*Perjury,* Doctor, we were talking about *perjury.* Isn't it true that you went back to Mississippi because of a charge of perjury?"

The elderly neurosurgeon looked around the courtroom, then to the judge and back to Anderson. He shook his head slowly.

"Are you *denying* it?" Hands raised to the ceiling, incredulously.

"No—no—no." Roberson sat there quietly for a minute, wrestling with himself over something while the courtroom held its collective breath. Matt's emotions were churning violently. He knew the next few minutes could potentially make or break Todd's case. What was the man going to say?

Finally, the witness seemed to make a decision. He sighed and lifted his head resolutely. "Yes, that's true. It was a perjury hearing I went back for—and a licensure hearing."

"And the result of that hearing was a conviction for perjury!" Anderson bobbed his head triumphantly. "You lost your license to practice in the State of Mississippi—isn't that true?"

"Yes, perjury and loss of…" The expert's features contorted in dismay. "What? What are you saying?"

Anderson strode right up to the witness box, no longer worried about the niceties of courtroom decorum. His voice was strident, his tone accusatory. He pointed his finger at the white-haired man sitting before him. "You lied and got caught! You lost your license in that state. That's why you've never been back isn't it! They banned you, didn't they?"

The ringing indictment echoed in the sultry courtroom. The witness and everyone else sat stunned.

Doctor Roberson's features suddenly hardened with realization and his eyes turned icy. "Absolutely not. I can't imagine where you got such a ridiculous idea."

Anderson stiffened and stepped back, supporting his weight with the sagging rail.

"...but you said..."

Roberson was half out of his chair in anger. "It wasn't *me* who was accused. You, sir, have it all *wrong*. Yes, I did testify against another doctor in Mississippi who was accused of perjury. The defendant altered records and testified falsely at trial. I had been involved in the original case on behalf of the plaintiff. Because the doctor was politically powerful in the state medical society, the Governor himself asked me to come in and give testimony against him, because no other doctor in the state would. On the basis of that testimony, they convicted him and he lost his license."

Anderson was reeling. He retreated to the back rail. "...but, you haven't testified there since?"

"True. I angered the local medical establishment very much by speaking out against one of their own. The Governor gave me a Distinguished Citizen's Award, but the doctors there hated me. Still do, I suppose. I felt I should let the wounds heal and decided not to appear in that state's courts anymore."

The lack of sound was palpable. The jurors were staring at the actors, their faces reflecting an amalgam of revulsion and admiration. The judge seemed content to allow the silence to provide its own form of testimony. Anderson was slumped against the railing, his victory turning to ashes in his mouth. He looked as if he had been blindsided by a truck. Indeed, Matt reflected, the man had been blindsided. It had actually gone much better than Matt had dared to hope. The defense had fallen for their ruse completely. In one searing moment, the psychological axis of the trial had been essentially reversed. Why then did Matt feel sick to the very depths of his soul?

Matt watched Anderson's face as his mind worked through the devastation of the last few seconds. The defense attorney's eyes suddenly focused on Matt and the realization struck home. Involuntarily, the defense attorney's gaze then searched to the rear of the courtroom, to the source of this disaster. Matt followed the accusatory look to its inevitable target. There, still sitting alone in the rear, pale and shrinking from the reality of discovery, Matt met the anguished gaze of the man who had been his best friend.

43

"You may cross examine the witness, counsel."

Matt stared at the witness and then at Murphy, who was trying not to let the jury see his smug smile as he sauntered back to his seat next to Anderson. The old saw was that for a successful trial, you should always start your case with a powerful witness. Conti's defense lawyers had certainly followed the rule book this morning with their first expert, Morton Crenshaw. The defense attorney expert exuded barely restrained aggression from the witness chair, his body hunched forward in anticipation of the cross-examination. Matt had handled many cases against Crenshaw over the years and knew him well. He only defended physicians and knew no tactic but scorched earth. He always attacked, never gave ground. The man was about six-five, two hundred and fifty pounds, and growled like a bear when he talked. He was a force of nature.

Months ago, Matt had gone to the Crenshaw's office to take his testimony under oath. For hours, he had carefully tried to question the man. The goal was to establish everything the defense witness was going to say at trial and also to try and gain concessions on important issues. Most honest experts would provide a skilled examiner with several points for later use in trial. The exercise had been a complete waste of several exhausting hours. Murphy had barely been able to restrain his amusement as he watched Crenshaw toy with Matt like a bull playing with an extra small and unarmed matador. The big man wasn't actually dishonest in his testimony;

he just argued, criticized, and rephrased everything he was asked. Matt left late in the afternoon discouraged and with a splitting headache.

Last night he had reread the worthless deposition transcript with dismay. The next morning he knew Crenshaw would be sitting in the witness chair and the jury would be looking at Matt with anticipation, wondering what he could possibly ask this powerful and impressive man. Usually, there were at least a few points that could be established in a deposition. Crenshaw had been unshakeable. Over and over, he testified that everything the Conti office had done was perfectly reasonable. Matt knew the nine in the morning court call would be here in a flash. Somehow, before he went to bed, he had to come up with an approach to derail this freight train bearing down on Todd's case.

In the wee hours of the morning, Matt finally realized that Crenshaw's ego had taken over. His testimony in the deposition wasn't really about Conti, the facts of the case, or the law. It was all about winning, and about taking Matt down. The old courtroom was going to become an arena. A beast was planning to stalk the weary gladiator while the crowd held its breath, knowing they would soon see blood in the sand. Matt had realized his only chance was to harness the force that would emanate from this warrior and turn it to his advantage. It was kill or be killed.

* * *

Dark orbs stared out of the round face, following Matt closely as he bought time thumbing through his worthless notes and walked to the podium. He knew well that Crenshaw was astute, well-read, and very cunning. This expert was both physically intimidating and a master at communicating with juries. During the direct examination, Murphy had seemed to simply throw out a subject and the expert trial lawyer had been off and running with it, warming to his thesis, and mesmerizing the jurors in the process. Crenshaw had turned to the panel during his testimony, pulling them in with his riveting manner, and involving each one of them with his logic and his passion. It was very hard not to be sold by this kind of a true believer.

"Mr. Crenshaw." The witness' head dipped slightly, a tiny smile of anticipation. "I listened to your testimony with Mr. Murphy for the last two hours. You seem to have very strong feelings on the subject of Mr. Conti's conduct of Todd's case."

"At least there's nothing wrong with your hearing, counsel. Like I said, the file was handled perfectly. Your client got good lawyering from one of the best in the business."

"Well, the Conti firm had this file for almost three years and several different lawyers did work on it." Matt nervously shuffled his papers. "Have you reviewed everything that was done?" The witness inclined his head affirmatively. "You looked at the depositions taken? The memos to the file? All of the records of his care? Everything? Even read my depositions of Sal Conti and Youngstone and the others?"

"I told Murphy I reviewed everything. Maybe your hearing isn't as good as I thought." There were a few amused sounds from the direction of the jury.

"Well, yes, I did hear you say that you couldn't find any problems with anything they had done—that it was 'excellent work' I wrote down." Matt turned a few more pages of his notes. "I think you used the words 'handled perfectly' with me a few minutes ago. Are you sure that you really feel that strongly about it?"

"What is it about this that you don't understand?" The litigator jiggled his head in feigned frustration. "I told Murphy and I told you over and over again when you took my deposition several months ago. This was work of the highest quality. They did a great job. Your client doesn't have a case. He never had a case. You are grasping…at…straws! Give it up, counsel." His thick lower lip thrust out truculently.

"Mr. Crenshaw, some of these attorneys were new at lawyering, weren't they? They were just learning the business." Matt stared at the floor. "Are you saying Mr. Youngstone always did everything right—completely right?" He looked up at the witness hopefully. "I mean some of this stuff was actually in the low average or barely passing category, wasn't it?"

"I'm not going to say it again, Mr. Taylor." The witness rotated his head wearily. "I've stated my opinion. Repeating the question ad nauseam is not going to change a thing." The expert settled in with a smug and content look. He had enjoyed seeing Matt flutter futilely for hours at his deposition, like a moth frying its tiny brain as it repeatedly battered a light bulb.

Matt took a last look and then dropped his notes on the stand. He stepped out in front of the jury and surveyed each of them thoughtfully.

"So Mr. Crenshaw, you read everything in the file to prepare for this case, even all of the records of Todd's care?"

"I've said yes to that."

"And you read the depositions where all of the lawyers in Conti's office said they never even read those same records, never even knew he could move his arms and legs when he came into the E.R., right?"

"Look." Crenshaw's big arms crossed. "No one reads every record on a regular auto case. I…"

Matt took a step forward. "But *you* told us that *you* read these records and you didn't even represent Todd."

The big head shook back and forth. "Yes, I've made it clear that…"

"Oh, okay, I understand. There isn't anything wrong with a lawyer not *ever* looking at the records they have ordered. Indeed, in your mind that's *great lawyering*, right?

"It certainly is."

"How about those X-rays we would all like to see? No one in the Conti office ever ordered them, did they?" Matt looked at the members of the jury. "That's another example of 'top-notch' lawyer work, right?"

His head thrust forward. "Nobody orders the x-rays in a simple auto case…"

"*Simple!*" Matt looked at juror Addison. "This is a sixteen-year-old kid who became a *quadriplegic*. This case might have to be tried, right? Wouldn't it be helpful to have x-rays of the neck to show the jury where the fracture occurred and the cord was damaged?"

"Mr. Taylor, there was only a million dollar policy of insurance." Crenshaw shifted one leg over the other to get comfortable. "The case is probably going to settle. You don't want to unnecessarily spend the client's money."

"Yes." Matt's eyes roved the jury box. "So this is another example of the highest standard of care, right?"

Crenshaw's mouth spread in a smile. "Yes, it is."

Matt turned slowly and looked at the witness. "By the way, you mentioned the one million dollar policy. That reminds me, in this case that was sure to settle, did Conti get the million when he settled the case?"

The big guy waived his thick hand casually. "No, I don't think they offered any more than six hundred fifty thousand dollars."

"So the policy limits are one million and Conti takes six-fifty? Why did he give up three-fifty?"

"That's a judgment call. You can't second-guess the lawyer handling the case. There might have been problems with winning. Maybe he didn't think he could get more."

"So where in the file did you read about evidence of these problems? What did you see to explain that judgment call?"

"Not everything is written in the file, Mr. Taylor." The witness spread his hands. "Maybe the insurance company just wanted to roll the dice."

"Gee, isn't that the perfect situation? The insurance company low-balls the plaintiff and then you get to collect whatever the jury gives you against the insurance company if you try the case and win?"

"Counsel, you know it isn't that simple." The defense expert sighed elaborately. "The insurance company has to be set up and then, if you win, you have another lawsuit on your hands to try and collect. The man did the right thing for this kid; he got him some money to help him and his family out. You saw how grateful they were—the letters they wrote."

Matt looked at Todd and Debbie sitting in the front row. "Yes, they were very grateful to their very famous lawyer, weren't they?" Matt turned back to the expert. "Conti had collected a quick fee, right?"

"I don't know how quick it was. It took a few years!"

"Yeah, that long to get three hundred and fifty thousand less than the insurance available." Matt stood near Todd. "But Todd and Debbie didn't even know there's a whole law field called 'bad faith' litigation that scares the heck out of insurance companies, did they?"

"I don't know what they knew."

"Exactly." Matt said as he took a couple of steps toward the witness stand. "Because in that whole file you read, there wasn't one letter to them about this, was there? No memo saying it was explained to them that they should consider holding out for the one million and try the case if the insurance company wouldn't pay it, right?" Crenshaw's expression pulled tight. "Nothing in that file at all about that, is there?" Crenshaw stared at him. "Can we have an answer, Mr. Crenshaw?"

"I've heard that you don't put everything in your client files either, Mr. Taylor." The big defense lawyer snickered and sat back with a knowing look. "Isn't that what you told the Bar investigator?"

Matt could feel the flush of anger flood his face. "Move to strike, Your Honor. That comment was gratuitous and completely unresponsive."

Murphy jumped to his feet. "You raised the subject of what should and shouldn't be in a client's file. That's just fair comment."

The judge eyeballed Murphy. "Address your comments to the court, counsel. The motion will be granted. The comment is stricken and the jury admonished to ignore what was said." He looked down at Crenshaw. "The witness is well-versed in the law and knows better. He is instructed to address himself to the question he is asked and *only* what he is asked."

Matt consciously tried to calm down. Damn, all these years of doing this and his face still got red. "Mr. Crenshaw, there is *nothing* in that file indicating this family knew there was an option to turn down that offer and maybe collect everything Todd was owed, is there?"

The thick muscles under his sideburns bunched. "Not that I can remember."

"You've heard of huge verdicts against insurance companies that failed to protect their insureds and refused to pay out their policy limits in cases that were clearly worth more money, right? Companies that were then punished, by juries like this, because they had tried to save a few bucks at the expense of their policyholders, haven't you?" The man's mouth was clamped shut. "Haven't you, Mr. Crenshaw?"

"There have been some verdicts of that type."

"But, here again," Matt drilled the man with his eyes. "This is another example of *perfect lawyering*, I think you called it? The highest standard of legal practice, right? This decision to take the easy money and leave three hundred fifty thousand dollars, the rest of this policy, on the table?"

"Yes, it is. This is within the standard."

Matt canted his head. "Just, *within* the standard? Actually, you said this is *perfect* law practice, isn't it?"

"Yes, it is." There was that lower lip again.

"Let's look at some other details in this prime example of great legal practice." Matt moved back to the podium with his notes on it. "Todd came to the Conti office as a quadriplegic, didn't he?" The witness agreed. "Isn't that one of the most devastating and debilitating injuries a person can suffer?"

The expert looked at Matt cautiously. "There are worse injuries. But yes, it is a serious condition."

"Well, on the scale of things that can happen to you, it is right near the top, isn't it? I mean paralyzed, dependent on others for everything for the rest of your life. Pretty bad, right?"

Crenshaw looked at Todd and Debbie and then at the jury waiting for his answer. "I wouldn't want it to happen to me or to my loved ones."

"Yes, nor would I, Mr. Crenshaw." Matt regarded his notes for a moment. "If it did happen to you, and you went to a famous lawyer for help, for your loved one, for yourself, tell me, Mr. Crenshaw..." Matt eyed the witness again. "Would you want the experienced, famous lawyer to help you or would you want to be assigned to the youngest person in the office?" Matt turned and watched the jurors, looking briefly in each one of their eyes as the silence grew.

After a long moment, Matt broke the silence. "Tell me, how many quadriplegic cases had Mr. Youngstone handled in the six months since he took the bar exam? How many medical records had he read? How many x-rays had he ordered?"

Murphy didn't even look up as he objected. "Which question does he want answered?" Matt spun around toward the judge. "Any or all, Your Honor. The witness can pick one!"

Crenshaw glared from under beetled brows. "Good lawyers have to work on their first case. Many great results come from baby lawyers with no experience."

"Really? So you are telling this jury that you personally would chose to have your loved one's case handled by someone who just took the bar exam rather than his well-known, famous lawyer boss?"

"I think the case was handled fine—within the standard."

"So this is another example of *perfect* legal practice—the best of the best—right?" In the ensuing silence, Matt watched the expert's knuckles whiten as he gripped the railing next to him.

Matt continued to question the defense expert. Sometimes you could smell the psychology of the courtroom changing. The jury was watching closely. Matt noticed that more than one of them had crossed their arms and leaned back as though to distance them from the testimony.

"You used the term 'baby lawyer' when you referred to Mr. Youngstone a few minutes ago. One of the built-in potential benefits for this 'baby lawyer' was access to a famous boss with lots of experience, right?"

"I suppose, if he needed it."

"Are you suggesting a brand-new lawyer, one who has never represented a quadriplegic, wouldn't benefit from Mr. Conti's help or advice?" Matt waited a few beats. "I mean, you said he was one of the best in the whole country. That's what you think, right?"

"Right."

Matt was starting to enjoy himself. He had managed to string three questions together with one affirmative answer and no objection. Crenshaw was getting disoriented.

"You remember I asked Mr. Youngstone in his deposition what Mr. Contihad taught him during the case?"

"Vaguely."

"Do I need to read it?" Matt turned to Adrianne and opened the transcript. "Here it is. Youngstone testified, 'The only thing I remember is that Conti read the deposition I took of the driver and said it was lousy and a waste of time and money.' Does that sound familiar?"

"It sounds familiar." His meaty hands scrubbed his pant legs.

Matt picked up the deposition and held it up to Crenshaw. "He also said he couldn't ever even talk to the famous boss, right? Never could ask him what to do on the case or how to do it. He wanted to learn. He was frustrated, right?"

The expert's hands crossed his chest and looked over toward Murphy, who was studiously writing notes with his head down.

Into the hush of the huge ancient courtroom, Matt quietly said. "Top-notch, the best, *perfect...*" Matt walked over near Todd and Debbie and held his hand out toward them. "Nothing but perfection for this family, right?"

As Matt paced back toward his table, he caught Adrianne looking at him intensely. Suddenly he got her message. Don't over-do it. Quit while you're ahead.

"No further questions of this witness, Your Honor."

The massive head pulled up and his mouth opened. You could almost see him saying *"No! I have more to say—I'm not done!* Crenshaw stabbed a pleading look at Murphy.

The judge cleared his throat. "Redirect, counsel?" Murphy never looked up from his studious writing. "No questions, Your Honor."

44

It was a late spring Friday in San Francisco and there was no court today. The forecasters were promising a great weekend ahead. The five of them sat in Matt's office trying to ignore the weather and concentrate on the last weeks of the trial.

Matt looked at their expectant faces. He could see hope and even anger, but mostly resolve—not a quitter in the bunch. He felt full of emotion. They had been working their hearts out. None of them had had a day off for six weeks and they were ready to devote the next few weeks to doing the same—night and day. His team was amazing. Most people had no idea the amount of work that went into the preparation of a complex trial. The courtroom was the tip of the iceberg. Roberson had been Todd's last witness, and yesterday Crenshaw had started the defense case. Matt looked around at his little team. It was time to deal with the pink elephant in the room.

"We have to talk about Jake and what happened this week. As you know, thanks to some detective work by Clint and Adrianne, we were able to discover he was providing the defense with key inside information. They've been using it to destroy our case." The group sat in dejected silence. "We set a trap for them with Roberson and they fell for it. Doesn't undo all the damage, but it's a start."

"How much do you think he gave them?" Mary Beth finally asked. "I know it was all our experts they burned back in October. Do you

292

think it was also the records problem with the radiologist that came out in his cross?"

"We think it was all of that and much more." Matt looked at Adrianne and Clint. "They've had all our strategy from the get go and knew all of our potential problems."

"What the hell could be the reason he would do such a thing to you?" Emily asked Matt. "He's like family here and been your best friend for decades!"

"Nobody has the slightest idea."

"So, have you seen him at all?" Emily was asking Matt and Adrianne.

"Not since in the courtroom at the end of Roberson's testimony. I don't think he's even been to the office since then—at all."

"I talked to Mary, his assistant. She's frantic—hasn't heard from him." Adrianne slowly expelled a breath. "He can't just drop out, can he? He has a practice, clients…" She looked at them all, searchingly. "Where could he have gone?"

"I should probably look for him, go to his place or something. I have a key." Matt looked at Adrianne. "For that matter, you do too, I guess."

She looked back at him and her features narrowed. "What the heck could either of us say to him? What could have possessed him?"

Clint broke into their thoughts. "I don't think anyone should go near him or his place. We've got a case to try. He and all his people are the enemy." He pulled out his chew. "I 'spect we'll find out soon enough why— not that I give a damn."

Matt watched them as he pondered. Had Jake betrayed him because he felt betrayed by Matt and Adrianne, or did he even know about that? Was this something else entirely? Even if Jake had suspected Matt's feelings about Adrianne, the spying had started long before the weekend in the mountains. Moreover, sabotaging the trial was far beyond what a betrayal of friendship might reasonably be expected to generate. The ethical and moral breach involved, for a lawyer to feed confidentially-obtained information to the other side, was beyond unforgivable.

Jake was more than a spy. He was a double agent, a traitor to his own side. Armed with key data they never could otherwise have obtained, the defense attorneys had eviscerated many of Matt's witnesses. Jake hadn't just hurt Matt; he had hurt an innocent young man and his family. The damage done to Todd's case might be irreparable.

Obviously, Jake had never liked the case, but something must have happened to convince him to actually sabotage the trial. Matt didn't see how it could be his relationship with Adrianne. Matt felt sick inside. He had no energy and his heart was empty. Over the last few months, he not only had managed to lose his lover and his best friend, but he was well on his way to tanking the most important case of his career. At least he owed it to Todd to try and find the strength to solve that particular problem.

Matt decided to change the subject. "Well, they're ahead on points, but it's still a horserace." He smiled at them encouragingly. "As you well know, in the end it's the clients who make the difference. We have a huge edge with Todd and Debbie." He gestured toward Adrianne. "The job Adrianne did with their testimony was truly amazing." Happy to have something to cheer, they all turned to her and clapped. She took a little bow.

"On the other end of the spectrum, we are stuck with the famous Mr. Conti." Matt's eyes turned over. "I called him as a filler in our case with mixed results. I mostly left him for them, hoping to do well with him on cross during the defense case. We'll see." He looked around at their thoughtful faces. "I have to score with my attack on the nurses and doctors they call from Todd's original hospitalization and then hopefully nail their experts. We've a long way to go."

"There are still things that would really help at this point." He addressed Clint. "Have you made any headway on finding those missing x-rays?"

"I've chased that widow-lady all over, but she's out of the country." The big investigator didn't look happy. "I've no idea when she'll be back. I'm working on it, got a couple of contacts who may know something soon."

"I've got to get something on their experts. I know they've testified in other cases." Matt directed his attention to Mary Beth and Emily. "Find me every deposition or transcript of trial testimony you can get your hands on." He stood and paced intently. "Get me the lawyers on the phone, if you have to, so I can call in some favors. Another trial lawyer knows what it's like to face an expert with nothing but bare knuckles." His tone was emphatic. "Most of them'll bust their asses to help if they've got something."

Adrianne looked at him questioningly. "What're you hoping to find in other depositions?"

"You never know what you might find. Sometimes there's some great stuff in previous testimony."

"It can be worth the effort." Mary Beth smiled in recollection. "I've seen Matt spend a whole weekend reading a hundred depositions just trying to find one question and answer to use in trial."

Matt was back to the issues at hand. "The other thing's that nurse, guys. Where's she gone to? She's listed on their witness list, but we couldn't get her deposition before trial." He kneaded his knuckles. "Are they hiding her? Is she going to come out of the woodwork?"

"I think she is." Adrianne pulled out a file. "I searched for her on the registry and found her in Arizona, but she's been ducking my calls."

"Damn!" Matt slammed his hand on the desk. "Clint, can you do some good here? I know you're jammed, but she's the one who wrote the key notes in the record."

The investigator calmly held up a palm. "We're ahead of you here, boss. We talked and I got a guy with the force there checkin' on things." He broke a confident grin. "I 'spect we'll have the inside track on her deal right soon."

They broke out to get to work. Matt sat for a quiet moment looking out the window and wished he could take a long run. Maybe later, before dinner, he thought and turned to his stack of deposition testimony. He had to get this done because he knew the others would be bringing him more to work on throughout the long weekend.

At half past four, he looked up to find Emily and Adrianne standing in his doorway. He smiled at them. "Are you guys packing it in already?"

They didn't smile back. "We just got served with this Notice to Appear."

He stretched his shoulders and rolled his stiff neck. "Someone they plan to call next week in their case?"

They both shook their heads. "No such luck." Adrianne came over and handed him the papers while Emily took a seat. "This is from the Bar

Association. You're ordered to appear a week from Monday at nine in the morning for an Order to Show Cause regarding suspension of your license to practice law." They looked at each other in silence.

* * *

Matt ran panting up the hill from Crissy Field. He finally stopped, breathing heavily. He hadn't been running regularly because of the trial and the hill was killing him. Even a few weeks off changed everything. He walked on toward his place. The sounds of San Francisco enjoying the evening surrounded him in the balmy air. He could hear people out on seldom-used decks and he could smell the barbecues being fired up after months of disuse. It would be his luck this weather would probably last the whole weekend, just when he was immersed in a trial for the duration. He wasn't sure he had the energy to get back to work right away. Maybe he would see if he had any gas and charcoal for his grill.

He headed through the living room, ignoring his two heavily loaded briefcases. As he looked in the pantry closet for the charcoal, the phone rang.

"Hey! You're home!" Matt heard MJ's voice on the phone. "Want some company for dinner? I'm in the city."

"I'd love it. How 'bout cooking on the deck?"

Matt pulled some steaks out of the freezer and jumped in the shower. Two hours later, they sat back in contentment, enjoying their beer.

"That was a damn good steak. 'Course, anything would taste good on a night like this."

Matt was amused at his friend's comment. Spring could often be quite nice, but everyone had to comment when you could sit outside in San Francisco.

"Okay, enough beating around the bush. You got to tell me what's bothering you." MJ pulled her short hair behind her ears.

"Come on—I can see you're totally uptight. My job is to get your head straight so you can attack the weekend trial prep fresh tomorrow, fair enough?"

Matt thought about her question. MJ might be the perfect person to talk to about all this. He took a deep breath and started from the beginning.

During dessert, he told her how he and Adrianne had met, and about the snowbound weekend in the mountains—and his guilt and the unpleasant parting when they got back into town. He also told her what had been happening in the trial, about Jake's betrayal and how they caught him.

"So you're thinking Jake did this because you slept with his girl?" She waved impatiently. "There's no way. Jake wouldn't risk his law-ticket over a woman, even if he was crazy about her. There's something else going on, definitely." She pulled at her hair. "What's Conti's insurance carrier?"

Matt thought for a moment. "Greater Pacific, I think." He sat forward. "Why?"

"I've heard some stuff from the guys at the office who know Jake well. Vague stuff, but..." Her mouth pulled to the side. "Like Jake's got big money trouble..."

Matt leaned forward. "And...so what?"

"So who's Jake's biggest client?" MJ sat back, threading her long fingers delicately around her glass of beer. "Where could the pressure come from? Who's he need for the overhead every month?"

Matt arched his back. He didn't have a clue what his friend was implying.

MJ said, "Homestead Assurance, right?" MJ pointed one of the fingers on her beer glass at him. "My friend told me Homestead Assurance is his big client...and I happen to know that Homestead owns Greater Pacific—lock, stock, and bad case results."

Matt felt realization course through him. That certainly could explain a lot. Was Jake's biggest client really the insurance company that had the exposure to a verdict on Todd's case? If Matt hit big, Conti's insurance company could look to its parent company to make good on the verdict. Homestead's bottom line would be at risk. Maybe they had gone to the fox they knew was living square in the middle of the chicken coop for help.

Matt stared at his melting ice cream. "I suppose it could explain things."

"You're damn right." MJ nodded slowly. "This Adrianne thing might've just helped shove his conscience farther into a place where the sun doesn't shine." MJ paused and contemplated her friend. "Sounds like Adrianne was fed up anyway. Y'know, women like that don't just change horses on a whim." She poured herself another beer. "Why are you having such a hard time with this—especially after what he did—and why haven't you patched things up with her?

"I was feeling I had to deal with this whole 'poaching on Jake's territory' thing."

MJ's finger traced the rim of her glass absently. "I think this guilt thing is a cop-out." She raised her hand at the look of protest. "I know, I know, you feel bad about the fact you slept with the woman your *ex-friend, by the way*, was hot for, sure…" She fortified herself with a sip of beer. "…But she was planning to dump him anyway. That's all a matter of bad timing." She gave Matt an appraising look. "I've not got a handle on it yet, but it sounds like you're scared of something. That's why you're holding her off like this."

Matt held up his hands in protest. "I'm not holding her off at all. She's…"

MJ's expression was decisively negative. "She's not doing anything any smart woman wouldn't do. She knows you've got issues and she's giving you room to work it out." She snickered knowingly. "Don't plan on her waiting forever, though."

Matt stared at her thoughtfully. "I dunno, can't imagine what I could be afraid of. She's just about everything I could ever want in a woman."

The dark eyes widened in wonder at her dense friend. "That's as good a place as any to start your analysis. Here's a woman who's your intellectual equal. She's independent and obviously not ready to kiss your ass or anybody else's."

45

Anderson was having fun tossing soft ball questions at the emergency room doctor who had treated Todd after the accident and the doctor was swinging for the fences with every pitch. Occasionally the doctor, a bullet-headed ex-marine, would give Matt a quick self-satisfied glance and then zero back in on the jury. He sported a blond buzz cut and had a sculpted jaw. Fashionable wire-rim lenses softened his appearance and gave him an intellectual air. The jurors were wide awake and taking it all in.

"So, Doctor Allen, how did you know the patient was drunk when you were evaluating him?"

The doctor let his expression appear amused, but the eyes were cold. "He smelled strongly of alcohol, was thrashing about and mumbling incoherently. Of course, we also did lab work and determined he had a high blood alcohol level."

Anderson had positioned himself where the jury could see him and the witness at the same time. "Did the fact the patient was drunk make it more difficult to evaluate his possible injuries?"

The defense attorney was leading the doctor, but Matt chose to remain silent. Even though more testimony was coming from Anderson than the witness, it would all come out anyway. Objections usually irritated jurors who wanted to hear what the witness had to say.

"Yes, it certainly did. We weren't able to take a good history from the boy and our physical exam was not as effective because alcohol depresses the central nervous system." The E.R. doctor addressed the jury directly. "If we can't ask the patient where they hurt or do an adequate neurological exam for possible changes in sensation, or in their reflexes, it's hard to figure out what his injuries may be."

"So the boy's previous drinking was interfering with your ability to tell whether the boy already had an injury to the spinal cord from the accident?"

"Yes, it was."

"Were there any findings that could have been suggestive of an injury to the spinal cord?"

"In hindsight, it seems clear to me that this kid already had a cord injury when I first saw him. I think that is why he really only moved when I stimulated him with pain and why his reflexes were so depressed. His blood alcohol level really wasn't high enough to affect the reflexes to that extent."

Anderson pretended to be puzzled. "But Todd could move his arms and legs, Doctor Allen. How could that be if he already had a cord injury?"

The E.R. doctor swiveled to address the riveted jury. "Reflexive response to pain can cause movement of the extremities independent of the spinal cord." He sat forward, warming to his subject. "I might even be able to get his arms and legs to move right now based on a local reflex response, even though the cord is no longer functioning at all." Easy for him to claim, Matt thought ruefully, since the doctor could hardly do a neurological exam in the middle of the courtroom. "Also, a traumatized spinal cord can lose function as swelling develops and over time, the ability to move can be gradually lost."

"So, you mean that he could have had a cord injury that was going to make him a quadriplegic, even though his arms and legs moved when you saw him?" The defense attorney acted like that testimony was news to him.

Matt saw the judge looking at him as if in anticipation of an objection. He resisted the temptation. Anderson was an experienced trial lawyer and would just ask it another way; the whole point would become highlighted. Matt felt like asking the judge to make the defense lawyer raise his hand and swear to tell the truth, since Anderson was doing most of the testifying.

"That's right, Mr. Anderson." Doctor Allen looked over at Matt triumphantly. "It's too bad the kid was so drunk that I couldn't do a proper neurological exam."

The lawyer pretended to look over some notes and let the testimony sink in. Matt looked up and caught juror Addison looking right at him as the silence wore on. Finally, Anderson straightened up and addressed the witness. "Let's move on a bit, Doctor. When you first saw the patient, you ordered x-rays, didn't you?"

"Yes, the boy had been in a rollover accident and we had to assume a variety of injuries might be present." He ticked off points with powerful-looking fingers. "We ordered head and neck films, a chest x-ray, and pictures of his legs and pelvis." Anderson inclined his head encouragingly. "He had no skull fracture and a fracture of part of the pelvic bone and of the femur. No other fractures were described." The witness shot a quick glance at Matt, who made a point to write a note. It was important the doctor remember the cross that was yet to come.

Anderson moved out away from the counsel table. "Doctor, what about the neck films? What was the radiologist's report on that study?"

There was another nervous glance from the E.R. doctor over Matt's way. "They were entirely normal. There was no evidence of a fracture in the boy's neck."

The lawyer was now in the middle of the open space in front of the jury. "Have you had a chance to see the films recently, Doctor Allen?"

"They are missing, I was told. No one has seen them for years." He looked toward the jury helplessly. "They are usually kept in the radiology department at the hospital. Somebody must have checked them out and not returned them."

"Well, tell me, Doctor, did you ever look at them yourself back then when you were treating Todd?" There was a slight pause, just a heartbeat. Matt noticed the witness wipe his hands down his thighs. Anderson was looking down at his notes and didn't seem aware of the hesitation.

"No, no, I didn't. I'm not a radiologist and I usually rely on what they tell me. They were read by the radiologist as perfectly normal."

Interesting, Matt thought, wondering what to make of that. Matt scanned the jury quickly, not wanting to obviously scrutinize them. They looked involved and thoughtful, with open body language—unfortunately. The judge had his head propped on his hand and was watching the fog billow against the windows, rattling the old oak frames. The man in the robe could daydream, Matt thought. He didn't have to cross-examine this guy.

Matt could sense the jury liked the doctor and was impressed with his testimony. Matt had a choice. He could hold the witness tight to a few answers he would have to concede because of his deposition testimony and then get rid of him fast, or he could take a chance and go for it. Despite the rattle of the old courtroom steam pipes, Matt imagined he could feel the foggy wind wrapping around his spine. He suppressed a shiver of apprehension.

"So, Doctor, what was the patient's condition when you last saw him?"

"He was still unconscious but seemed to be more responsive. He had not shown any signs of a central nervous system injury, like a change in his pupillary response or posturing. His arm and leg fracture had been temporarily splinted, his pelvis stabilized. His vital signs and lab values were essentially in the normal range." The physician looked from the jury back to Anderson. "We were relieved that there didn't seem to be any evidence of a more serious problem."

Anderson then walked over and stood in front of the jury. "Doctor Allen, had you done everything reasonable and required in standard practice to determine if there was a neck injury or any other serious injury to this boy?"

"Absolutely everything and more." The doctor had straightened his spine and was speaking directly to the jurors. "This young man was handled like a textbook case."

"No further questions at this time, Your Honor."

Anderson had to sidestep quickly as Matt propelled himself out of his chair and squared up in front of the witness with his arms jutting from his sides and his notes left behind. "Did *absolutely everything*, did you? *Nothing* more you could have done, you tell this jury!" The witness seemed to rear back as Matt threw his arm toward the twelve. He gave the stunned doctor a beat and then his furious, controlled voice filled the huge room. "So, tell me, Doctor, why is Todd a quadriplegic today? Why did the broken bones in his neck crush his spinal cord? Why did this young man who was able to 'thrash about' lose his ability to move his arms and legs forever a few hours after you sent him upstairs?"

The questions were still echoing when Anderson jumped to his feet. "Objection, Your Honor! "Which of these argumentative questions is the witness supposed to answer?"

The startled judge cleared his throat. "Sustained. You do have to give the witness time to answer your questions, counsel."

"Are you trying to tell this jury that there was *nothing* you could have done to find out Todd's neck was so badly broken that it was about to chop his spinal cord in half?"

The doctor gathered himself and his visage knotted in anger. "He got the whole menu of E.R. tests—all negative!" He exuded disgust. "Hindsight is pretty easy, you know. When I'm in the real world and a patient comes through the door, I don't have the benefit of knowing what's going to happen like your bought-and-paid-for experts!" His features constricted. "We can't assume every drunken kid who comes through the door has a broken neck!"

"Yeah, let's talk about that. You keep throwing 'drunk' out there like he was in a coma from drinking. His blood alcohol was point-oh-nine, wasn't it?" Matt moved a step closer. "That's about two or three beers, isn't it?" The angry doctor just glared back at him. "So are you telling us that if one of us…" Matt looked back at the spectator benches and then scanned his gaze through the rapt jurors before he came back to the fuming witness. "…has a couple of beers after work and then ends up in your E.R.—are you saying that you can't do an adequate exam to see if we hurt ourselves in a fall?"

"No, I just say…"

Matt cut in. "Exactly—*no*!" He quickly moved on as Anderson opened his mouth to object. "You just said you can't assume every kid who comes in has a broken neck." He paused for a beat. "Well, let's not count the kids who have a bump on their knee from a skateboard crash, okay? Let's not count the folks who slip and have a back that hurts." He walked back toward where Todd was sitting. "Let's just count the few that have just been in a high speed rollover accident when they come through the door—the ones who can't tell you what hurts because you think they might have a head injury, okay?" The doctor crossed his arms over his chest. "Doctor, is there a possibility that you may have serious injuries if you have a high speed rollover in a car? Is there?"

"Yes, there could be."

"Yeah. That's sort of a classic dangerous situation for an E.R. doc, isn't it? Big time rollover, possible head injury? You start worrying about brain injury, internal injuries, bleeding somewhere, all of that, right?"

"Yes those are all in your differential."

"Yes, *differential diagnosis*. That's where you make a list of the things you are required to consider as possible injuries and rule them out, right? That's basic standard procedure for an E.R., isn't it?" Anderson stood and slowly objected to change the developing rhythm of the interchange. Matt waited impatiently as the judge sustained. "Well, that's what a differential is, isn't it?"

"Yes, you normally consider the potential conditions and try to determine whether they are present." The muscles in the side of his face leaped into definition. "Within reason."

"Well, how about when the victim of a car crash has the car roll over violently and his head gets smashed so hard he's unconscious, okay? The head is like a bowling ball whipping around on the thin stem of a neck when the car is rolling, isn't it? The body can be thrown up and the roof crush down toward the head and neck at the same time, can't it?" Matt paused his pacing and zeroed his gaze in on Doctor Allen.

"There can be a variety of forces exerted in that kind of an accident."

Matt looked askance. "A 'variety of forces exerted?' Doctor Allen, it's well-recognized you can have a brain injury from this, right?" Matt paused. "You can have severe pelvic injuries and internal bleeding, right?" The witness reluctantly nodded. "And, Doctor Allen, when your head is whipping around in a rollover and getting mashed down by the roof of the car, that can put that slim little neck we have holding up this big old bowling ball of a head at risk, can't it? That's why this kid was put on a backboard by the paramedics and had a neck collar on when he arrived, right?"

Anderson sighed audibly, but kept quiet. "Yes, the neck can be injured." The witness was exasperated. "And that's why we took the standard steps to rule out a fracture to the cervical spine or the spinal cord. All of which was completely negative." He sat back in satisfaction.

"That's right. You knew you had to 'rule out' a spinal fracture, didn't you? You actually wrote that in your initial plan, right?" The bullet head inclined. "The only way to do that is to get x-rays of the neck, correct?" Another inclination. "Tell me, how many vertebra are there in the neck—seven?"

"Yes"

"So you got two sets of films of the neck, right? A set shot front to back, and a set shot from the side, correct?"

"Yes, and they were read by the radiologist as normal—no fractures."

"Let's look at the radiologist's report." Matt went to the table. "Do you have it there, Doctor?" The witness looked through his records.

"The front to back view," Matt held up the document. "Says that there's no evidence of a fracture or misalignment of cervical one through cervical seven right?"

"Yes"

"By the way, you can have all the bones of the neck in line after a neck is broken, can't you? That is why a broken neck might not yet have caused any damage to the spinal cord right?"

"That's rare, but it's been known to happen."

"Well, it's so well-known that even Boy Scouts and paramedics know to stabilize the neck after a possible injury even though the patient can move their arms and legs, true?"

"That's a standard emergency procedure if there's the possibility of a neck injury."

"Doctor Allen," Matt walked out into the middle of the arena. "One of the main things you and every E.R. doc are worried about when there is a big-time, high speed rollover, is that the patient might have an unstable fracture of the neck—true?"

The witness grunted dismissively. "We worry about everything."

"You wrote down 'rule out cervical fracture.' That's because if he has one, it might be unstable and the spinal cord might be at risk—true?"

"That's one of many things we consider."

Matt shook his head slowly. "Why is it I feel like a dentist…you know, pulling teeth?"

"Objection, Your Honor."

The judge tightened his lips, like he was suppressing a smile. "Sustained. Keep on track here, counsel."

"Thank you, Your Honor. I will *certainly* do that."

"Doctor Allen, you take two angles of the neck because some fractures will show up in only one of the views, right?"

"I'm not a radiologist, Mr. Taylor." The witness looked at his watch.

"I'm sorry, are we keeping you, Doctor; do you have somewhere else you need to be?" Anderson started to rise, but Matt forged on quickly. "Radiologist or not, you order neck films on patients several times a day, don't you?"

"Yes."

"You know the radiologists always take two views to be sure whether fractures not seen in one view might be seen in the other, right?" The judge seemed to sit forward, interested in where this was going.

"That's pretty standard."

Matt looked back toward his client who was watching intently. "Todd's fracture was at the lower level of the sixth cervical vertebrae, wasn't it?"

"I think that is correct."

"So on the lateral here, the film taken from the side," Matt waved the radiology report. "It says here that cervical one through five are visualized. You see that?"

"Yes"

"So where does it say that they can see vertebral bodies six and seven?"

The E.R. doctor looked at the report for a long moment. "I don't see that mentioned here."

"So, Doctor Allen," Matt tossed the report on the counsel table, "how do you '*rule out*' an unstable cervical fracture if you can't *see* those two vertebra in Todd's neck?"

Allen's short hair seemed to bristle. "I can't be responsible for the reading by the radiologist. This report doesn't even get typed up for hours or even until the next day. I was told the films were negative."

"Ahhh, so you *did* have a conversation with the radiologist about the films?"

His hands tightened on his biceps. "I usually would."

"Actually, this was a portable x-ray done at the bedside, right?" Matt leaned back against the counsel table. "Usually there's what's called a 'wet read' right on the spot, correct?

"That can happen."

"Well, it certainly does happen if the patient's in the E.R. and there is an immediate need to 'rule out' an unstable fracture of the neck for their safety, right?"

The E.R. doctor licked his lips nervously. "That is one of the standard procedures."

"Well, you can be right there and look at the films with the radiologist, can't you? Weren't you interested in seeing these films?"

Anderson stirred to life. "Objection."

Matt waved his hand, not waiting for a ruling. "In this dangerous situation, you had the option of looking at the films yourself, didn't you, right there with the radiology expert? That way you could find out if these x-rays were adequate to 'rule out' an unstable fracture of his neck, couldn't you?"

The ex-marine's head swiveled toward Anderson who was writing studiously. "I don't remember."

"Wait a minute. This kid is unconscious, was in a big-time rollover." Matt stalked the witness stand. "Are you telling this jury that you may not have even looked at the films of his neck with the radiologist?"

"I'm not sure. I might have..."

Matt stood away from the table abruptly. "Usually you would, right?" Matt looked at him hard and counted a beat. "In this dangerous situation, true?"

Doctor Allen's cut features slackened and he looked down at the record in his hands. "Probably"

"Doctor Allen, what's a 'swimmer's view'?"

The doctor's head jerked up. "I…think it's a certain kind of film of the neck. That's really not my expertise."

"Isn't one of the big problems with the side-shot of the neck—that the shoulders can get in the way—keep you from seeing vertebral bodies six and seven?"

The E.R. doc seemed to be looking around for help. "Something like that."

Matt walked back in front of the jury and put his hand on the rail. "Sir, isn't the swimmer's view the angle that's typically used to see the lower vertebrae of the neck if the shoulders are in the way?"

"Yes." His body slumped.

Matt leaned both hands on the rail and looked slowly around at the faces staring back at him. "And did you order swimmer's views to see if vertebral bodies six and seven were okay?" There was a long silence. "Doctor Allen, did anyone order those views of the side of those two vertebrae?"

"No."

Matt needed to give the man an exit path. "Actually, you couldn't see the last two vertebral bodies. That's why you knew you really hadn't ruled out an unstable fracture when you sent him to the floor?"

Allen's face was set in stone as he stared at his tormentor. Matt made his tone sound encouraging. "That's why you never documented in the record that a broken neck was 'ruled out,' correct? You were worried about that— and you expected those nurses on the floor would keep his neck stable until it actually could be ruled out later, right?"

"That's true." The doctor grabbed the lifeline with both hands. "I didn't think he had a neck fracture, but I wasn't positive…so I made sure it was still in the record as a possibility. That's why I never said it was ruled out."

Matt nodded thoughtfully and pretended to review his notes as he let the testimony sink in thoroughly with the jury. Finally he looked up and addressed the court. "No further questions, Your Honor." He turned toward the counsel table and was saddened to see tears flowing uncontrollably down Todd and Debbie's faces.

46

The next morning, as they entered the City Hall, Matt felt buoyed by the successful cross of Doctor Allen the day before. His elation was somewhat tempered, however, by the testimony of the intensive care charge nurse Anderson had put on the stand later in the afternoon. She had been firm and untouchable on cross, so Matt got her out of there quickly. He still had his fingers crossed that Clint could come up with the nurse actually on duty when Todd woke up. She was still being elusive.

No matter how well the cross had gone with Allen, they had to prove the hospital was responsible or even a good verdict might not be collectible. He thought back to his conversation with Adrianne many months before. Under the law, Conti was only responsible for what his firm could have collected against the potential medical defendants if Conti had done everything right. Todd could win big against Conti's firm and only collect from them the amount of a doctor's small insurance policy. The only way for a big verdict to be collectible was to have the jury also say the hospital had been negligent, because it had a large insurance policy. Even winning big on this tough case could end up being a loss if the jury didn't say the hospital would have been liable in the underlying case.

They carried their boxes through the heavy double doors of the courtroom and pushed through the swinging barrier into the lawyers' inner sanctum. Murphy was at the defense table. "The judge wanted to see us when you got here."

"What about?"

Murphy exchanged a quick glance with Anderson. "Dunno."

They traipsed together in single file through the back door and looked for the clerk. She stuck her head into the outer office and pointed mutely toward the chambers. The door was open.

They found chairs and waited expectantly for the judge to speak. He seemed smaller without his robes. He addressed Murphy and Anderson. "So what's your estimate for the rest of the case?"

"Hard to be sure. Depends a lot on cross, but our guess is the end of the week."

The judge turned to Matt. "Any new evidence or rebuttal testimony, Mr. Taylor?"

"It's possible. It depends on what we hear the rest of the week, Your Honor. We are still trying to chase down a couple of witnesses who have been eluding us; that's possible too. Wouldn't be more than a day or two extra."

"We got word this morning that they do want to go ahead with that Bar hearing on Monday, Mr. Taylor. I tried to get it continued until after the trial, but this Willistin guy is insistent." He looked at Murphy. "Can't you do something about that, counsel?"

"I don't have any pull with the Bar, Your Honor." The defense attorney feigned surprise. "That has nothing to do with us."

"Your client represents the complainants in the Bar matter, counsel. Obviously he is pushing to have this heard in the middle of this trial for his own purposes." He heaved a sigh. "He is messing with our trial schedule and the lives of this jury for a tactical advantage. Your client's clearly trying to distract Mr. Taylor from the work at hand at a critical stage of the case." He shook his head in disgust.

"We're going to have to take the day off Monday for you to deal with this, Mr. Taylor. We'll finish up the evidence on Tuesday and Wednesday, if necessary, deal with instructions and motions on Thursday, and plan to argue the case on Friday." He stood up and pulled his robe from the hook near his desk. "I'll see you, gentlemen..." He paused and smiled at Adrianne. "...that is, gentle*persons,* in the courtroom in a few minutes."

Sitting in the courtroom, Adrianne leaned over. "I thought they were going to be able to get this moved to well after the trial." She had a stricken look on her face. "How are we going to be ready for that and do the trial too?"

"That's the whole idea."

The gavel rapped. "All rise, the Superior Court of the City and County of San Francisco is in session, the Honorable Marvin Rigoletti presiding."

As the defense called their rehabilitation expert to the stand, Matt tried to focus on the testimony, but his mind kept wandering to the Monday hearing. If Jim Olsen actually testified under oath that Matt never told them about the two-hundred-fifty-thousand-dollar offer, that could be devastating. Even though Matt could give his own version of what happened, it was well-known that hearing officers in Bar proceedings usually believed the clients rather than the lawyers. Rumor had it that Mary and Jim were estranged. She had disappeared into thin air. The devastating loss of their only child was just compounded by the jury decision and then the big bill from the defense costs the Olsens now owed for the lost trial. Matt was sure that he could have at least gotten the costs waived in return for dropping an appeal, but Conti was representing them now, and he probably thought the costs would just make Matt look worse. After the Bar hearing, he was sure a legal malpractice suit would follow in short order. He was at a loss how to defend himself from Monday's expected onslaught.

He dragged his thoughts back to the matter at hand. The doctor on the stand was the head of the biggest brain and spinal cord rehabilitation facility in Northern California. Matt had been dismayed to see his defense report on Todd and then hear his testimony during deposition. The guy had done a hatchet job on Matt's damages claim. Matt's experts had said Todd needed twenty-four-hour care for the rest of his life. This guy had cut that way down and also said Todd was going to die soon. The less care needed and the fewer years of it, the lower the damages number the jury needed to award for the future. Matt's guess was that Conti had a relationship or a hold over this expert. The rehabilitation doctor and Murphy were systematically dismantling the expert damages testimony Matt had supplied to the jury in the first part of the case.

311

"It is my opinion that Mr. Gleason will do fine in the future with about four to six hours of attendant care a day and eight to sixteen hours a day of respite on the weekends. The family should have someone to come in for the morning process, getting him up, bathing, dressing and helping with toiletries. The same would be necessary in reverse for the evening hours. On the weekend, we provide for more hours so the family gets a respite and can have time to themselves and for shopping, cleaning, and so forth."

Murphy picked up the report of Matt's rehab expert. "But Doctor Matson, the plaintiff's expert, said twenty-four hours of care was necessary every day for the rest of Mr. Gleason's life." Murphy paused for effect. "Isn't that a reasonable position given the fact that Mr. Gleason is paralyzed and can't do very much for himself?"

"Actually, that is very unreasonable and unrealistic in the extreme." The gray-haired doctor looked down at the attentive jury panel. "I have taken care of hundreds of spinal cord patients in my career and virtually none of them have attendants hanging around them every hour of every day. In modern rehab medicine, the goal is for self-reliance. Too much care encourages dependence rather than independence. That can be psychologically crippling." A well-defined nose rose in disdain at the report the defense lawyer was waiving about. "Mr. Gleason needs to be self-reliant. What few needs he has, in between the attendant hours I have provided for, can be supplied by his family. They are very loving and attentive to his condition."

"Are you saying you have many patients who are doing well on four to six hours of help a day?"

"Absolutely. Many of them on much less. I have proposed a generous life care plan."

"Doctor Appleby, you have a cost of care of nineteen dollars per hour on what you term a 'self-hire' plan. Can you explain the reason you have chosen that figure and contrast it with the plaintiff's life care plan which calls for thirty-five dollars per hour and uses a home health care agency?"

"Of course. Mr. Gleason's care is being provided by his mother and his brother now." The narrow, handsome features zeroed in on the jury. "They are lay-caregivers and do a great job for him. He doesn't need a licensed care provider—just a competent layperson who can take instruction." His head moved back to Murphy. "Virtually all of my spinal cord patients use such people as helpers."

Matt kept his face stony as he listened to them. The doctor was carefully referring to his "spinal cord patients." Many of the doctor's spinal patients had injuries at different levels. A person with a cord injury just one-vertebral body level lower could almost live independently. A great rehab physician had once told Matt it was the "silly millimeter of difference" at C6 versus C7. At Todd's level and above, a patient had no triceps and little biceps function. Therefore they were unable to push or pull their body up and independently transfer from bed to chair, chair to car. They couldn't shower and drive and needed constant help for most activities of daily living. Just below that level, cord damage was still a terrible injury, but the patients could do most things for themselves except walk. For example, wheelchair Olympics involved people injured at lower levels of their spine than Todd. Matt knew this expert was just clumping many levels of spinal injury together to leave a false impression with the jury.

"One other thing, Doctor Appleby. Do you have an opinion concerning Mr. Gleason's life expectancy?"

Matt hated for Todd to hear this, but the young man had opted to be present for all of the testimony—good and bad. At least Matt's expert had said his life expectancy was only 10 percent less than normal because of his condition, but this would be hard for Todd to hear.

"This is a subject I prefer not to discuss with a patient present, Mr. Murphy. Your Honor, perhaps Mr. Gleason would like to take a break during this portion of the examination?"

"Mr. Taylor," The judge inquired. "would your client like to leave the courtroom during this testimony?"

Matt tried to keep the revulsion at the doctor's grandstanding out of his voice. "Your Honor, my client is definitely *not* this defense witness's patient and I can assure the court that he does not give *any* weight to his opinion."

"Very well." The judge was repressing a small smile. "You may proceed."

"Unfortunately, despite lots of efforts, our experience with this injury hasn't improved life expectancy much over the years." Appleby stabbed

Matt with a cutting look. "There are well-known complications including pulmonary and bladder infections, skin breakdowns, and metabolic disorders that occur. These conditions inevitably result in an early death. The medical evidence indicates that he has a life expectancy that is fifty percent less than normal."

Matt hoped he was not turning as red as his face felt. This guy was heaping it on. He really must owe something to someone. While intuitively a person might think that a lower life expectancy would be a bad thing for the defendant, actually, reducing the years of future expensive care could save the defense millions. The economics of a verdict was a simple matter of multiplying the annual care expenses times the future years of need. They were already hacking at the amount of care needed and the costs. Whatever the annual cost of Todd's future needs, cutting his life expectancy that much would dramatically reduce the number of years the jury would plan on him needing care. As the defense lawyer and the doctor finished their dance, Matt made an effort to tamp his emotions down. He needed to keep his cool. This guy was not going to be easy to undo.

As Matt approached the podium, he watched the urbane doctor lean back and get comfortable. The man did not look apprehensive in the least. Well, Matt thought, let's get right at it. "Doctor, you have taken care of and examined hundreds of spinal cord injuries over the years, correct?"

"Yes."

"Many of them are injuries to the lower back, some in the mid-back and some in the neck, right?"

"That's true."

"Only the ones with a complete cord injury at C6 or above are unable to use their triceps and biceps muscles to transfer themselves, isn't that true?"

"Well, that's a bit of an oversimplification but generally, yes, that is correct."

"So hundreds of those 'below C6' spinal injury cases you have treated or seen can get themselves out of bed, can dress themselves, can move from wheelchair to a chair, get in a car, drive themselves and, with some hours of help, while having a difficult life, can actually live independently?"

"You are trying to compress a lot of rehab medicine into a pretty small box." His head waggled in irritation. "But, yes, some lower cord injuries allow for more independence and they can do some things for themselves."

"Todd Gleason can't do any of those things on his own, can he? He can't transfer his body without the help of an attendant?"

"He needs help for transfers."

"He doesn't just need help. He needs full assistance, right? He can't get out of bed, a chair, or his wheelchair or back in, without being moved by a trained attendant, isn't that true?"

The doctor just sat there. Matt finally cut into the silence. "Doctor Appleby, it's three in the morning. There's a fire. A trained attendant has to get Todd out of bed and away or he burns to death—isn't that true?"

"Counsel, it's just not realistic to have high-priced attendants sitting there watching him sleep all night in case there's a fire." The patrician features hardened. "His family's there; they've been trained, they can get him out of there if this one-in-a-million thing happens."

Matt looked back at the kind, worn face of Debbie Gleason, selflessly wearing herself away day-by-day because of this huge burden thrust upon her. Then he regarded the haughty expression on the expert's face. If this guy had his way, this horrible state of affairs would continue until the day Debbie died.

"That's exactly right, Doctor. All of the other hours of help Todd needs to manage—to have some kind of a reasonable existence—you have his family built into your plan, don't you? You have Debbie and Bob Gleason working all the rest of the twenty-four hours, isn't that true?" Matt leaned forward on the counsel table. "Have you provided any compensation for them from Mr. Conti's firm in your 'life care' plan, Doctor Appleby?" The witness sat there in silence. Matt added, "His brother Bob's put his whole life on hold—no girlfriend, no college, no family. Is that your plan for the rest of his brother's life?"

The rehabilitation expert finally stirred. "Look, there just isn't that much care that's required if the morning and evening hours are taken care of by a paid attendant." He turned to the jury. "I have patients like Todd Gleason who get by just fine on six hours a day of help."

"These patients of yours get by 'just fine,' do they?" Matt's eyes bored in on him. "So, at two in the afternoon, Todd has to pee and needs to be catheterized, or wants to have lunch or, hard to imagine I suppose, this young man actually wants to go out and see friends or even go to a movie. So who's going to help him do it? Huh?"

The expert's gaze narrowed.

"He's got a skin breakdown starting and needs to go to bed for a nap to take the pressure off, right?" The doctor was shaking his head. "What is it you disagree with here, Doctor? It's one in the morning and he can't sleep. He needs to be repositioned. Remember, Debbie gets up and does that three times every night." Matt stared at him for a beat. "What if Todd's mom has a bad back? You know about that. You treat people that can't do this type of work because their back hurts?"

"Look, life just isn't perfect for folks who have these injuries, counsel. Families pull together and do the best they can." The rehab expert's eyes were trying to burn a hole in Matt. "Our society isn't set up to make their world just like it would be if they had never been injured."

"Right, Doctor. Life will certainly never be 'perfect' for Todd or his family again." He walked over and stood in front of the jury. "But what this jury has been tasked to determine is whether Mr. Conti failed to do a proper job for Todd Gleason." He put his hands on the jury rail and looked at each of the riveted faces. "And then, if so, to assess what's reasonably necessary to take care of Todd." He whirled back to the witness. "It's not what's the cheapest, not what the defense would rather have the family sacrifice in order to save Mr. Conti's firm money!"

"Objection, Your Honor—he's making argumentative speeches!"

"Is there a question in there, Mr. Taylor? Sustained. The jury will disregard counsel's comments."

Matt said loud and clear. "Thank you, Your Honor." Matt turned back to the witness. "Doctor Appleby, I certainly do have a question for you. What happens to your master plan if Todd wants a life of his own? Most young men his age haven't been this dependent on their mothers since they were babies. What if, God forbid, he actually wanted to live alone—to feel independent—to have people he chooses bathe him, catheterize him, and

316

help him evacuate his bowels, rather than have this done by his mother or his brother for the rest of his life?"

"Objection. That's another argument to the jury."

"Well it is a bit long, but I think I heard a question in there. Overruled. You may answer, Doctor."

"Well, there are ways to work all that out without paying for someone to sit around for twenty-four hours every day of his life. He could live in a group home with other people who have similar needs and share the cost of an attendant. He could set up an intercom system and call on a neighbor in an emergency. Group home arrangements can work out very well and give people with common problems a chance for socialization."

"Doctor Appleby." Matt walked over and stood behind Todd. "Don't you think that should be *Todd's* choice—how and where he wants to live— not *yours*?"

"Well, yes. But I haven't made that choice for him."

"Well, you haven't exactly provided him with enough hours of help to have any *other* choice, have you?"

The witness's mouth opened and then closed. Matt pressed on. "So *if* he can find a group of people with whom he is compatible—*if* he wants to live with a bunch of other people with serious disabilities—*if* this group arrangement can last his whole life—so, then how does he get to be *independent*?" The doctor looked at him blankly. "I mean, so one afternoon he wants to go to the mall, or to a movie, or to see a friend. All these people are sharing one attendant, right?" Silence.

"Doctor, that's what you're suggesting—a shared attendant, right?"

"Yes, basically."

"So, do they take a vote or what?" Matt fixed him with his gaze. "See Doctor, in your group home proposal, his life is tied to all these other people—every hour of every day—forever, right?" Matt walked to the jury rail. "So, doctor, you think this is a 'reasonable' life care plan designed to make him 'independent'?"

Breath gusted from the rehabilitation doctor. "It's a reasonable plan, counsel, and it's realistic. It's how most of my patients manage—every day of their lives."

317

"Yes, Doctor, I'm sure it is." Matt walked up close to the witness. "But tell me, how many of them are *forced* to 'manage' because they just don't have enough money to have any other reasonable choice?"

Murphy half stood and then seemed to think better of it. The witness sat there in silence.

"This opinion on a fifty percent reduced life expectancy—you said that was based on the risk of complications he could have?"

The expert sat back and seemed to relax a little. "Yes, those are the most common complications."

Matt tapped his notes with his index finger. "So it's important to have the best care possible to try and avoid these complications? Someone really good and careful to check his skin, to use sterile technique in inserting the catheter to drain his urine?"

"Yes, it is always good to have the best care possible." The slim body shifted in the witness chair. "We have provided for that in the plan."

"Doctor, many of those patients that die young may not have gotten good care?"

"It's possible."

"Well, the better and more caring the daily attention a patient receives, the better chance they have to beat your odds and live a long life, correct?"

The aquiline features firmed. "Mr. Taylor, I have assumed and provided for good care in this plan and it is my opinion that his life will still be *at least* fifty percent less than normal because of this terrible injury he has suffered."

"You feel strongly about that, Doctor Appleby?" The witness nodded. "Are these statistics getting worse in injuries like Todd's or have they always been this dismal in your opinion?"

"Been the same for decades. We are working to improve them but, unfortunately, to no avail."

"So any C6 quad has always had a fifty percent less than normal life expectancy and that has always been your opinion?"

The angular jaw squared. "I said yes to this already."

"How about your analysis on the need for six to eight hours of care only and not the twenty-four hours our experts thought reasonable and necessary. Has that always been your opinion, Doctor Appleby, or is this a new thought more recently arrived at?"

"That is a reasonable plan." The expert's tone was becoming more impatient. "That has always been a reasonable plan in my opinion. Twenty-four hours is ridiculous!"

"Okay, well, that's clear enough." Matt glanced at the banker on the jury and then walked back toward the far end of the jury box. "You've given testimony before in cases like this—haven't you, Doctor—on these issues we've been discussing?" Out of the corner of his eye, he could see Murphy stiffen and lean forward.

There was the briefest pause. "Yes, a few times over the years."

"In the past, Doctor, have you always testified that C6 quads only needed six to eight hours of care and that they have only a fifty percent life expectancy?"

"I'm pretty sure I have." The expert shifted nervously. "That has always been my opinion."

"*Pretty sure*, Doctor? Are you thinking you may have given a longer life expectancy in the past and in fact testified that twenty-four hours of care was appropriate in some other case?"

"Objection." Murphy tried to throw a life line. "He's badgering the witness and arguing with him."

"That will be overruled. You may answer the question, Doctor."

"Certainly not. That's never been my opinion on these injuries." Murphy sat down reluctantly, his eyes flickering apprehensively between the witness and Matt.

Matt opened the booklet that Adrianne handed him. "Ever testified in Hawaii, Doctor?"

"I'm...not sure. Maybe, many years ago." Murphy looked down and started writing studiously.

"Let me refresh your recollection a bit, Doctor." Matt walked slowly toward the rehab expert, a trial transcript in his hand.

"Melissa James, twenty-two years old, a C6 quad. You were the treating doctor called to the stand in her lawsuit filed in Hawaii about twelve years ago. Remember that?" Matt walked slowly toward the rehab expert, a transcript in his hand.

"I'm not sure." The expert's carefully combed hair seemed to be wilting. "Sounds vaguely familiar."

"Well, Doctor Roger Appleby, Chief of Rehabilitation Medicine at North Bay Rehabilitation Institute, does that sound like you?"

"Yes."

"Let me read a couple of your answers, under oath, to the defense cross-examination: Quote: 'Look, this young woman is a C6 quad, she is completely dependent and unable to do anything useful to care for herself. She *absolutely* needs to have attendant care twenty-four hours a day. Anything less will affect her quality of life and will increase her risk of multiple complications.' Does that sound familiar?"

"Now that I recall, I suppose so, yes." Beads of perspiration appeared on his face.

"There's more on page two hundred and thirty-five. You are testifying again: 'This child has a perfectly reasonable life expectancy, close to normal. The only reason she might die early is if she doesn't have the proper medical care, including top-quality daily attendants twenty-four hours a day." Matt held the transcript up. "You are really good in this part right here, Doctor Appleby: 'There is no reason to die early if you get top medical care. Early death is caused by inadequate care. Period.' Do you want to hear more, Doctor Appleby?"

"I don't think that's necessary, no." He looked down at his white knuckles.

"Well, I think you should also be reminded of this bit on page two hundred and thirty-eight, I have it here if you would like to read it to the jury yourself? No? You are testifying again: 'No family should be forced to hire their own help for a quadriplegic. They shouldn't have to screen applicants, find someone on a moment's notice if an attendant fails to show up, perform accounting functions, and so forth. An agency takes responsibility for all of that and it's well worth the extra few dollars an hour in peace of mind for the patient and the family.' You are very articulate, Doctor Appleby." Matt ran his thumb through the pages. "Would you like to hear more? There's lots more, you know. You were very persuasive. The jury certainly thought so, it would appear from the result. Do you remember the verdict?"

Murphy didn't look up. "Objection."

"Sustained."

The physician sat back in the witness chair and crossed his leg in the silence, carefully and laboriously straightening the crease in his pant leg. The lack of sound in the weary old courtroom built in volume as everyone looked away. Matt finally just sat softly down in his seat and folded his hands.

Murphy's terse, "No questions," ended the morning.

47

The depressing drone of the fog-horns seemed to match Matt's mood as he drove to the Bar hearing Monday morning. It had been a tough weekend. This could well be the last week of the trial and he had made a long list of things to accomplish before Monday. He had tried to work, but just couldn't concentrate. He hadn't been able to sleep at all, waking in the middle of the night with wild thoughts tumbling uncontrollably through his mind—the trial, Jake, Adrianne, the bank loan due in a few months, the hearing today. The only thing that had gotten him through the weekend was Grant. His mother had gone away for the weekend and left him with Matt. The simple joy of spending time with his son had centered Matt and kept him sane. The fog whipped through the intersections like his thoughts, heavy and dank. The windshield wipers barely managed to keep the thick mist at bay.

Willistin took a seat across the table, with his back to the glare of the dark gray day. Like a judge, he faced Matt and his lawyer on the left and Olsen and Conti on the right. There was a court reporter to the hearing officer's left. The tension in the room felt a lot like the weather outside the window. Matt turned his chair a bit so he could see the other players. Unfortunately, Conti's heavy form blocked his view of Olsen.

Willistin cleared his throat. "We will follow the rules of court in this hearing. Address any objections to me rather than other participants. I'm the finder of fact, so I may ask questions of my own from time to time. I have written statements from both sides in lieu of opening statements. If you are ready, we'll start with testimony from Mr. Olsen."

Matt listened as Conti took the man through some preliminary questions. Matt had let himself get personally involved with these people. As a father, Matt had identified with Jim Olsen's channeled anger and been particularly impacted by Mary's disconnection and despair. A trial lawyer had to walk a very fine line—allowing empathy and understanding to give soul and credibility to the client's representation, but avoiding the trap of emotional entanglement. Since then, he had constantly revisited the trial and the decisions that led to the result.

He made an effort to pull his thoughts back to the proceedings at hand. Matt felt alone in this sterile and mostly empty environment. He had hoped to have Adrianne accompany him to the hearing, but she had left for Atlanta Friday evening with some kind of family emergency. Conti was starting to build some steam. "Did you and your wife have any discussions with Mr. Taylor about the issue of settlement of the case?"

"Well, yes. We often asked him if this would actually go to trial and he said settlement was always a possibility. I know at one point he spoke of presenting a proposal, or demand of settlement, and discussed that with us."

Conti passed copies of a letter around. "Is this the letter he sent out?"

Olsen took the paper and read it. "Yes, I believe so. Yes, this is the amount we discussed he would ask for—seven hundred fifty thousand dollars. We couldn't believe he set the value of our son so low, but..."

The litigator interrupted smoothly. "Let me ask you this. Did you give him permission to make this demand on your behalf?"

"Well, yes, he said we couldn't make it too high or they wouldn't try to settle with us. So we said yes."

"Were there other discussions about settlement?" Conti's jowls folded down over his white shirt collar as he peered over his glasses at Jim Olsen.

"Well, sure. He said he was talking to them as we got closer to trial." Olsen looked out the window. "He seemed hopeful, but it didn't seem like the drug company really cared about what they had done. They didn't really care about our son's life. They..."

The veined hand closed tightly over Olsen's arm. "Now listen to me. Listen carefully, this is important. This isn't about the drug company, Jim. Did Mr. Taylor ever tell you and Mary that the defendant had made an *actual offer* of two hundred fifty thousand dollars to settle your case?"

Matt leaned forward to look at Jim Olsen. The man was still watching the swirling fog. Conti shook his client's arm abruptly. "Jim, did this lawyer ever get your permission to turn down an offer of two hundred fifty thousand dollars for your case?"

He finally whispered into the silent room, avoiding everyone's eyes. "No."

"Jim, speak up. No one can hear you!"

"*No.* I said, no, he never did."

Howell gave Matt a long look.

Howell's cross was good, but Olsen was somewhere else. His monosyllabic responses stuck to the established party line. They had never discussed it. Never were they told about the offer. Matt couldn't get him to even look in his direction. Soon enough it was Matt's turn. Howell took him quickly through the case and then he zeroed in on the day of the offer.

"Mr. Taylor, how close to the trial were you when the final offer was made?"

"I think it was the Thursday before we were scheduled to start on Monday. We had just finished the last expert's depo and the defense attorney said he had his 'last best offer' to relay. I hadn't really ever come down from the seven hundred fifty thousand dollars because Jim Olsen was so unhappy even with that figure." He looked at Olsen and caught a guilty glance. "The defense lawyer said he had two hundred fifty thousand dollars and that was it. He said he couldn't guarantee it would still be there Monday morning."

"What did you do then, Mr. Taylor? Did you in fact discuss this offer with your clients?"

"I most definitely did." Matt spoke directly to Jim Olsen. "I called them up and asked them to come to the office that Friday morning. I have a copy of my appointment calendar and I can bring in my legal assistant to testify about the appointment if the hearing officer would like." Matt looked at Willistin who was studying his pen. "That next morning at ten, we met and discussed this in some detail. I told the Olsens about the offer and gave them my recommendations." He willed Jim Olsen to look at him, but the man stared fixedly out the window.

"What was your recommendation?"

"Well, I said lots of things, but, basically I said it was not an easy case and juries were hard to predict. I told them that this was not in any way a measure of the value of their son's life. This was just a number against which the potential risks and rewards had to be measured." He saw Olsen's head bowed. "I told them that juries often gave inadequate sums for the death of children, because they couldn't see what good the money would do—since the child was gone." Matt then turned his gaze directly to Willistin. "I told them I wished I could get them more, but that I thought the risks were too high to turn this amount down."

Howell let that sink in for a moment. "What did they say?"

"They were both upset, to say the least, and I couldn't blame them. It really wasn't enough for what had happened to their son. Jim was angry. Mary was uncertain at first and then said she wanted the whole thing over, that she couldn't face a trial." Matt kept his gaze on the man at the other end of the table. "Jim would have none of it. He said they had killed his son and he wouldn't take what he called their 'blood money.' He wanted to go to trial. He insisted…" Matt hesitated. "I must say, I understood his decision."

Matt addressed Willistin directly. "Frankly, I think that's why Mary's not here. I think they've never gotten over this. I wish you could've heard from her on this."

"Objection, Your Honor. That's pure speculation." Conti said, shaking himself into action. "If she disagreed with what's going on here, she'd be at this hearing."

"Actually we aren't sure she's even been told." Howell interjected. "They've been estranged for months and she's supposed to be somewhere back East. I don't think a decision should even be made in this matter until this key witness can be heard from."

"That's ridiculous." Conti snarled. "We know exactly what she would say. We've filed an affidavit and talked to her at length." Matt saw Jim Olsen's head jerk up in obvious surprise.

"Gentlemen, gentlemen. This hearing's been discussed for weeks." Willistin said, holding up his hand. "If Mr. Taylor wanted to call another witness, he could've done so. We'll make the decision based on the evidence that's been produced."

"Mr. Willistin, with all due respect, that makes no sense." Howell blurted. "We can't talk to Mary Olsen. She's represented by Mr. Conti, according to him anyway, and we did demand in our papers to have her present at the hearing. Also this hearing was set just a week ago. This is most improper."

"*Counsel!*" Willistin's face had turned bright red. "I will decide what is proper and what makes sense in my hearing." He pointed a shaking index finger at Howell. "You will quiet down and listen. I am prepared to make my ruling in this matter."

Matt was pleased his lawyer was at last fighting. Not that it would do any good. This had been nothing but a puppet show. There had never been a chance for a fair hearing. His career and his reputation were going to be trashed. Taking on this old bull had been the biggest mistake of his life.

Willistin carefully organized his notes and seemed to draw himself together. He looked around at the participants. Conti was trying to suppress a smug grin, Howell seemed to be shocked into submission, and Olsen just stared out the window at the moist, swirling air. Matt watched the scene from a gathering distance. How had it come to this, after all these years of disasters and triumphs? He knew there were people who cared, but what could they do? He felt so lonely.

"So, is there any more evidence to be proffered by either side? No? All right then, the case is submitted and I am ready to render the judgment of the Bar on the matter of *Olsen v. Taylor*." The court reporter waited for him to continue.

"I have listened to the testimony carefully. It is obvious there is a direct conflict in the evidence between Mr. Taylor and his former client on this critical issue. The Canons of Ethics absolutely requires that any offers be immediately transmitted to the client." His expression became stern. "Decisions as to matters of settlement versus trial fall exclusively in the domain of the client. The lawyer *must* advise and *must* follow the decisions of the client." He tried in vain to firm his receding chin. "The burden in a State Bar proceeding is on the attorneys to prove by a preponderance of the evidence that they acted in accordance with the Canons of Ethics and in the best interest of their client. Given the direct conflict in the evidence, it is my judgment that the essential element of proof is the presence or absence of some form of written confirmation of the claimed communication." He turned his narrow, cold eyes directly on Matt.

"From time immemorial, lawyers have put important interactions with their clients in writing. Attorneys have always sent confirming letters, or at least put self-serving, confirming memos in the file." He paused for maximum effect. "Where is such corroborative evidence?" He spread his arms and looked around the room, enjoying his moment of power. His eyes paused on each person until he came to Matt. "Where is it, Mr. Taylor? I waited to see such evidence in vain. I must assume it does not exist."

The phone in the corner of the room kept ringing as he talked. Obviously irritated, he continued his dissertation. "Accordingly, it is the judgment of this tribunal that…" He paused as a head poked in the door. "We're busy right now. Come back later please."

"Busy or not, we have business in this hearing." Matt looked up in shock as Adrianne pushed through the door, followed closely by Mary Olsen.

Olsen whispered to Conti, who jumped quickly to his feet. "This is entirely out of order, Your Honor. Obviously, these lawyers have been communicating with my client without my knowledge or permission. This is another example of outrageous and unethical misconduct by Mr. Taylor and his employees."

"What is going on here? Who are these people?" Willistin rapped his gavel sharply. "We're engaged in a duly convened hearing of the California State Bar Association." He was practically shouting. "I am an officer of the Supreme Court of California in this proceeding."

"I would like to introduce my former client, Mary Olsen, to the hearing officer." Matt smiled at Mary and then cut a questioning look to Adrianne. "The young lady with her is my associate, Adrianne Gardner."

"This is highly irregular." Willistin was standing as well. "The evidence is over and the case has been submitted. I am just giving my judgment in this matter. We will deal with the allegation of improper contact of Mr. Conti's client by Mr. Taylor's office later." He pointed to the door. "Mrs. Olsen, you may have a seat of course. Ms. Gardner, you may immediately remove yourself and wait to be called when we deal with these additional serious issues."

Adrianne looked at him calmly. "If the hearing officer will just give us a moment, I am sure all of this can be explained. If you could…"

"Not another word. I said get out—now!" Willistin's face turned to stone. "I am a duly sworn officer of the Bar."

In the ensuing silence there was the hesitant clearing of a throat. "Your Honor, sir…"

"Not now, Mrs. Olsen. I am just finishing. Then we will talk about how you were improperly contacted while represented by Mr. Conti." He turned back to his papers.

"But, sir…" Again came the still hesitant voice. "Mr. Taylor is my lawyer, sir. I've never met Mr. Conti and certainly never hired him to represent me."

"This is a circus act." Conti growled his response. "Who's in charge here, Willistin, them or you?" Willistin's mouth hung open. "Kick her out and let's get this over with."

Willistin suddenly seemed to hear the clicking of the stenographer who was dutifully taking all of this down on her reporting machine. He looked at her in shock and then slumped into his chair.

"Perhaps we should give you a moment with your husband and Mr. Conti, Mrs. Olsen?" He gave Mary a shaky smile. "Then we can decide how to proceed."

"I don't need to talk with either one of them, thank you." Mary drew herself up. "I have a very simple thing to say." She looked around the small room and then her eyes came to rest on Matt. "This man, Matthew Taylor, was a wonderful gift to us, sir. He tried his hardest to do what my husband wanted—even against his own judgment." She sadly regarded her husband. "Jim just couldn't stand it. He just couldn't take Mr. Taylor's advice and let that horrible company get away with it. It became more about revenge than us going on with our lives." Willistin's eyes widened as what she was saying dawned on him. "We should have done what Matt told us back then and taken the money." She wiped her eyes. "Maybe if we had just followed his advice, Jim, we'd still be together. Who knows?"

48

Matt dumped his briefcase and dropped into the chair behind his desk. My God. So close. How could disaster come that near and still be avoided? He could feel the pulsing of the windows. It was either the wind or his blood pressure. "What the heck happened? You're back so soon. Are you okay?" Mary Beth and Emily stood at the doorway, concern all over their faces.

"Adrianne will be here in a minute. I'll let her tell you. I gotta say, I really don't even know…"

As they lowered into the couch, Adrianne breezed through the door. "Hey, guys. What's happening?"

"He won't tell us."

"He's still stunned." She moved a chair out to sit. "Clint managed to find Mary Olsen's sister back East and found out Mary'd been hibernating in a cabin they have in the mountains. Clint and I decided I should go back there and see if I could talk her into coming back." She laughed. "It occurred to us that Clint, in person, might be a bit too intimidating." Her head rolled in wonder. "Turns out, she didn't know *anything* about all this Bar stuff at all. We think Conti contacted Jim and put the whole idea in his head."

"Sorry about the surprise, but she was still in the mountains when I got there. I didn't catch up with her until late Sunday and we had to book an early morning plane." Adrianne looked at Matt ruefully. "I was scared

330

to call you before I spent time flying with her and felt really sure what she would say. We came straight from the airport to the hearing."

"You knew where she was and left on Friday without telling me?"

"Our boss wouldn't let anyone contact her." Adrianne pulled her hair off her neck. "So Clint and I had to take things into our own hands." She turned to Emily and Mary Beth. "It was a gamble. We didn't know if we would catch her or what she would say if we did." Her shoulders sagged helplessly. "If I told you, then you might've been distracted or even told us we couldn't talk to her. I just guessed that might be worse than not knowing." She sighed at Matt. "Sorry, you must have had a horrible weekend."

"Hey, wait a minute." Mary Beth suddenly broke in. "Nobody's telling us *what happened.*"

"Oh, well, basically Mary came in and said Matt was her hero and this was all a bunch of bull." Adrianne smiled in memory of the moment. "It would be an understatement to say that Conti and Willistin were stunned."

"Actually, I think Willistin was embarrassed and upset. He mentioned something about a 'further investigation' of the situation. That was *after* the case against Matt was tentatively dismissed, by the way." Adrianne told Matt: "I drove Mary to a hotel and, when I left, she was on the phone with Jim."

Mary Beth frowned at Matt. "What did Willistin mean by 'further investigation'?"

"I'm not sure, but I do know Conti contacted a client I represented and solicited him. It also looks like he filed a forged affidavit from Mary and we know he lied to Willistin's face about having talked to Mary. And it's all on the court reporter's record!"

"So *that's* what Willistin was talking about." Adrianne's eyes widened. "Do tell me all the details while you drive me home and I'll tell you about Clint's latest discoveries."

Matt pulled up in front of Adrianne's apartment and turned off the key. "So what else has Clint found?"

She tucked a leg up on the seat. "I think it might be pretty good." Her eyes sparkled. "First, I think he has dug up those x-rays."

"Wow, that's fantastic!" He paused. "Well, depending on what they show, I guess…"

"There's always that, two-edged sword and all." She gave him an excited look. "Same with the nurse. He found her. I guess it depends on what she says, too."

He jerked back in shock. "Good lord!"

"Yeah, and he says the stuff she says has possibilities. I'm planning on heading to Arizona to talk to her tomorrow, so we'll see."

"I have to think about what we can do with this." His eyes hazed over. "How to use it, if there's something that helps." They spent a moment planning for contingencies and then she reached for the door handle. "Hey, before you go in…"

She picked up her purse and waited.

"Look, I owe you a huge apology for being, well, a complete ass. And more thanks than I can possibly express for all this stuff, you know, saving my tail and all." He sighed painfully. "I just don't know what's wrong with me…"

"Matt, it's okay. Don't beat yourself up." She put her hand on his arm. "You've got way more on your plate than most people could manage." Her gaze caught and held his. "People care for you, you know. Hang in there. Everyone's pulling for you." She pulled her stuff together, opened the door and got out. She hesitated for a second, then put her hand on the window-sill. "Win or lose, Matt. "

He watched her walk toward her stairs. He felt an overwhelming flush of emotion well up. He just wanted to follow her, put his head on her shoulder, and be held. Reluctantly, Matt started the car and drove off. He had to concentrate. There was a lot to get through before he could let him-self try to figure all that out.

49

"The defense calls Doctor Weston." As the tall, rumpled neurologist made his way to the stand, Matt steeled himself. This guy looked like an absent-minded professor, but he was deadly on the stand. The rangy expert's vague demeanor concealed a brilliant intellect. Matt had carefully worked his way through the usual options last night, going through his deposition. He concluded he had little substantive to work with. Attacks on his charges and possible bias accomplished little with Bob Weston. The amiable doctor testified for both sides in cases, charged about the same as Matt's witnesses, and seldom let himself be maneuvered out onto a severable limb. Matt had made a few good points in the man's lengthy deposition and would use what he could and then get the hell out of Dodge before he got his ears shot off. He did have one idea, but was not sure whether he should try it with this guy.

Matt listened carefully. He knew intellectually honest witnesses could telegraph areas of weakness or uncertainty in their words or demeanor. He looked in vain for possible openings. The experienced defense attorney methodically elicited every weakness in Matt's case. The jury seemed to hang on every word. He had to fight to concentrate. Five weeks of intense effort and stress couldn't help but take its toll. He had to find a way to put on a burst of energy to get through this last week. How had he had managed to endure eight-week trials before? Basically, you did what you had to do and then you fell apart.

"So you do not believe the patient had normal function of his spinal cord when he was admitted to the E.R.?"

"I think it is very unlikely, Mr. Anderson. He could not be adequately evaluated, despite the attending physician's best efforts, and the potential mechanism of injury and damage to other parts of his body were certainly suggestive of a major problem. Nothing about his condition on admission was particularly reassuring except the movement of his arms and legs with stimulation." His avuncular style embraced the jury. "I am convinced that was simply a reflex response and that the injury to his cord had already occurred or was evolving when he was admitted."

"But, Doctor Weston, the plaintiff has made much of the fact that it was shortly after he was log-rolled in bed by the nurses to change his linen that he first complained of the inability to move his arms and legs." Anderson was smart enough to play devil's advocate, since he knew Matt would soon be the devil. "Doesn't that indicate his injury might have occurred then?"

The neurologist scratched his sparse hair. "That's an interesting point, counsel, and I looked at the question carefully." He again zeroed in on the jury, his stringy hair now pointing in several directions. "There are no entries by anyone, nurses or doctors, that indicate he's conscious or aware of his condition before that occurrence." He raised his index finger like a teacher making an important point to his class. "I think it is highly likely that the jostling involved in the movement process lightened his level of consciousness. Because of that, he finally became aware of his pre-existing condition."

"Pre-existing condition?"

"Yes, his paralysis, which he almost certainly already had when he was admitted to the E.R.."

As they wound down, Matt made a few notes. There was a small opening, he thought. He might be able to do something with what the doctor had just said. When they finished, Matt rose, hoping to leave a few favorable impressions on the jury before he said goodbye to Doctor Weston. As he positioned himself, he scanned the courtroom briefly and suddenly caught Hairy Harry's eye from way in the back. Was it his imagination or did the old man actually seem to be giving him a nod? What did the codger see or sense that produced that reaction? The unkempt character then sat back as if ready to watch another in a series of beloved theater productions. Matt turned back to concentrate on the doctor, who was gazing kindly down at him like a patient grandfather watching a soon-to-be unruly youngster.

"Doctor Weston, since it is almost lunch time, I will just ask you a few questions and get you on your way."

"Counsel, I'm not really in a hurry. Please feel free to take your time and fully explore my opinions." He gave Matt his most engaging look. "I am quite willing to come back after lunch if that would be helpful to you and the jury." He turned to them and bestowed his "I am so happy to be cooperative" expression on them as well. Great start, Matt thought. I either keep him around to beat up on me some more, or I look like I'm trying to hurry his wonderful self out the door.

"You, of course, remember the deposition I took of you several months ago?"

The man positively beamed. "I certainly do and a very thorough job of it you did, I must say."

The man was starting to irritate Matt. He had to be careful not to be sucked into a lengthy verbal contest that he would probably lose. He laid the transcript on the podium. "Doctor, today Todd Gleason cannot move his arms and legs, correct?"

"Yes, he is a quadriplegic, which I believe happened to him at the time of the rollover collision."

"Did I ask you when it happened?"

"No, of course not, but I was sure you were interested in knowing that as well."

"I would very much appreciate it if you would just answer the question I ask, Doctor Weston."

"Well, certain..."

"Objection, Your Honor. The witness can certainly amplify his answer."

"Overruled." The judge turned toward the witness. "Doctor, this will go much faster if you just limit your answers to the questions you are asked. Proceed, counsel."

"Thank you, Your Honor. Doctor, if he were quadriplegic at the time he was admitted, he would not have been able to move his arms and legs and would have had absent reflexes, correct?"

"Well, not really. As I have stated, he could move by reflex response to painful stimulus and his reflexes would at least be depressed."

Matt opened the deposition. "Doctor, on page one hundred and thirty-two in response to the same question, you simply say 'yes'. Do you remember that?" The doctor opened the deposition and looked.

"Well, yes, but as I have explained…"

"Doctor, all I just asked you is this: when I asked you that question before did you simply say 'yes.' You did, didn't you?"

The friendly smile was fading. "Yes, I did."

Matt turned a few pages in the transcript. "Medically speaking, Doctor, there is a difference between 'depressed reflexes' and 'absent reflexes,' correct?"

"Yes." A barely suppressed sigh emanated from the witness stand.

"Depressed can be caused by drinking and absent suggests damage to the cord, right?"

"That is way too simplistic, counsel. Actually, medically…"

"Doctor Weston, pardon me, but can you look at page ninety-seven please?" Matt held up the deposition. "Do I need to read this to you to refresh your recollection as to what your sworn testimony was?"

"That's what it says." The angular chin tucked down. "Depression of reflexes can be caused by drinking and absence suggests a cord injury."

"In these records, Doctor Weston," Matt held up the medical records, "The initial exam finds '*depressed*' reflexes, doesn't it? There's no mention of '*absent*' reflexes anywhere, is there?"

"That's true."

"The nursing notes comment that the patient is 'thrashing about' upon admission, don't they?"

The expert smiled indulgently and scratched at his hair again. "Yes, but it is difficult to say what they meant by that. It may mean…"

"Doctor Weston." The witness stiffened. "A yes or no will be adequate. Do they say that or not?"

He shook his head reluctantly, his hair pointing wildly about the room. "There is that written comment, yes."

Matt opened to a page marked in the deposition. "Sir, is it true that the term 'thrashing about' indicates that the patient was probably moving his arms and legs when he was admitted to the E.R.?"

"That certainly does not necessarily mean any such thing, counsel. Such a comment is subject to interpretation and may well simply mean movement of the head or upper torso."

"Doctor." Matt opened the deposition again. "If you would refer to page one hundred and forty-eight over to the next page. Do you see that I asked you that precise question and your answer was 'yes'?"

"Your Honor, there is an objection to the question in the deposition."

"Yes, counsel," The judge looked up from his copy of the transcript. "And that objection is overruled. Doctor, you may answer."

"Mr. Taylor, you know full well that we went around and around about this issue. It is unfair to take one question and answer out of context."

Matt moved toward the witness stand, the deposition held up as an exhibit. "The question is simple, Doctor. Yes or no. What was your answer?"

The eyes that looked back at Matt were not quite as kindly as earlier. "The answer to *that* question was 'yes.'"

Looking around the courtroom for a moment, Matt actually saw Hairy Harry giving him a thumbs-up. He quickly looked back at the expert, hoping the jury hadn't noticed. "Doctor Weston, the first time that Todd was noted to be quadriplegic was after the nurses rolled him over in bed to change his linen, correct?"

"Yes."

"We know that Todd had an undiagnosed, unstable fracture of his neck from the accident, correct?"

"Yes, that's true." The medical expert shifted uneasily.

Matt tapped the deposition. "It is also true that, if a patient with an unstable fracture of his neck is log-rolled in bed without his neck being properly stabilized, that could cause dislocation of the fracture and subsequent injury to his cord, correct?"

"Well, he could already have an injury to the cord—like here."

"No, Doctor." Matt raised the written record of the pre-trial questions and answers again. "If you assume there's no injury to the cord yet, the nurses could certainly cause an injury if they move him wrong, isn't that right?"

"Yes, of course." This time the sigh was more audible. "In that *hypothetical* situation."

It was time for the acid test. Matt walked back to the podium. He opened the deposition transcript and looked through a few pages, then stopped and appeared to read the next question. "Doctor, in this case, the observation that he was thrashing about upon admission, the fact that he was only noted to have depressed reflexes and not absent reflexes, and the fact that he was only noted to have lost his ability to move his arms and legs after he was log-rolled in his bed by the nurses, indicates that Todd's cord may well have been damaged at the time the nurses moved him, does it not?"

The neurologist stared at Matt for a long moment and then looked down at his deposition transcript. Matt moved out from behind the podium, looking from the booklet in his hand back up to the witness. "That's correct, isn't it, Doctor?"

"Objection. Counsel is badgering the witness, Judge!"

The judge's chin pulled back. "I didn't know that was a legal objection, counsel. I thought that was only used in the movies. Overruled. Please answer the question, Doctor."

Weston looked uncertainly at the deposition in his lap and then up at Matt, who began lifting the book as if to read. "Yes, yes—that is correct, Mr. Taylor."

"Thank you, Doctor Weston." Matt closed the deposition. "Ms. Reporter, would you mind marking this part of the daily transcript for me for later reference?" He turned to look at the jury box. "We have no further questions of Doctor Weston."

Anderson leaped to his feet. "Doctor Weston, is it your opinion that this young man actually had his injury to his cord upon his admission to the hospital and not when the nurses rolled him over?"

"Objection. Counsel seems to be doing the testifying."

"I assume you are making an objection that the question is leading. It is, counsel; please let the witness give the answers."

Anderson threw his head impatiently. "Well, what is your opinion on this subject, Doctor Weston?"

The physician's face looked around the courtroom uncertainly. "I've testified it is more likely that his cord was already damaged, but it is certainly possible that it was injured later or some more damage occurred to it when they moved him."

Matt watched as Anderson worked to undo the chink Matt had opened in their armor. As he listened, he sneaked a surreptitious glance at the jury. He let himself hope that they might not be quite as taken with this defense expert as they were before his cross-examination began.

* * *

At lunch, over a quick sandwich, Adrianne seemed preoccupied. He asked, "What are you pondering?"

"I'm bothered by something. You know that last question you asked Weston? I went over his pretrial testimony pretty thoroughly I thought, and I don't remember you getting that answer anywhere. In fact, I thought he fought you on that one pretty consistently."

"You're right. I took a chance. Sometimes you can keep impeaching a witness with what you've already got established from their deposition. Finally, they get embarrassed and unsure of what else is in there. Once in a great while, you can throw in a pretty good zinger at the end, and they'll be afraid you've got that answer in there." He grinned at her. "If you get lucky, they'll be afraid to fight you and just say yes."

"You mean you bluffed him and he bit?" Her eyes got huge. "What if he had called *you* on it?"

"Well, I would simply have moved on or acted offended that he failed to agree with me." He sipped at his iced tea. "It doesn't always work, and I always have another interesting question ready to distract the jury if he doesn't bite. I had another topic I was going to try on him, but when he gave me that answer, I decided discretion was the better part of valor and sat down."

"Anderson was never really able to fix that. The guy had agreed with you and wasn't going to go back on it."

"Yeah, he is really a reasonably nice guy and pretty honest. I think the jury liked him."

"I'm not sure I agree." She said reflectively. "I think he was a bit too cute and I suspect the jury was getting bothered by his absent-minded professor act."

Matt half-listened as she went over some of the jury instructions they would be discussing with the judge that afternoon. He wondered if Hairy Harry had reacted positively in the courtroom because he had sensed the same thing Adrianne had just commented on.

* * *

"Hey, Dad?"

"Yeah? Wipe your chin, son. You've got more pizza on your face than on your plate."

The boy dutifully smeared the red sauce around. "Mom says we're going to lose the cabin. Is that right?"

Matt felt his chest constrict in anger. What was he supposed to say to that? "She's just talking about some business stuff, Grant—nothing for you to worry about."

"She says you gave it to a bank or something like that? Is that true?"

He looked into the earnest blue eyes. "Well, it's a bit more complicated than that and nothing's for sure at this point. But that's possible, I suppose, son. We'll see."

"She said you did it for a client." The boy ate another bite. "Was it that nice guy in the wheelchair I met at the office a couple of weeks ago?"

"It did have something to do with him, Grant."

He wiped up the plate with the garlic bread and stuffed it into his mouth, chewing massively. "I liked him, Dad." He looked up at his father. "I'm glad he has you to help him get better."

Matt heard the phone ring. That would probably be Adrianne.

"Hey, it's me. I'm bringing a witness back tomorrow so you can talk to her."

"She'll actually come?" Matt could feel his heart accelerate. "What's she going to say?"

"Well, it's not exactly perfect." There was a pause. "Actually, she's pretty defensive. But I thought it might be worth laying a subpoena on her and paying her way to come in so you could kick the tires."

"She bought the subpoena thing?"

"Sort of. Turns out she's got friends in town she'd like to see."

Matt thought for a moment. "We can lay a real subpoena on her when she gets here. If we want to, that is."

"Yeah. I have some ideas I'll run by you when I get back." She hesitated. "Are you okay?"

"Nothing a week in Hawaii wouldn't solve."

"Ha! Now that sounds pretty tempting, I must say. You'll probably need an associate to help you out with that."

There was a moment of awkward silence and then she broke in. "By the way—Clint's got those x-rays. We better have them looked at."

"Yeah, yeah, can you take care of that while I finish prepping for the 'Prince?'"

"Sure. Well, talk to you tomorrow."

After he hung up, he mentally kicked himself once again. What was his problem anyway? All he had to do was say "Yes, yes, yes, you're invited!" Win, lose, or draw, a chance to spend a week in paradise with her would be worth spending money he didn't have.

"Dad? Was that Adrianne?"

He pulled himself back into the moment. "Yes, son. How'd you know?"

Grant took his plate to the sink. "Because of how you sound when you talk to her."

50

The white-maned walrus was in rare form. It looked like he had finally dry cleaned one of his trademark three-piece black suits. The shirt was soft and creamy against a power-red tie. His jowls flowed over the high collar as he pulled the jury into the powerful orbit of his rich personality. There was something wrong with a person who could be so evil and yet so charming. Actually, the shrinks had a name for it—a sociopath. Murphy and his client had spent an hour mesmerizing the jury with his pedigree. It was pretty damn impressive, Matt had to admit. Now they were detailing the litigator's amazing devotion to detail during the handling of Todd's case. It turns out that he had assigned the case to the youngest lawyer simply as a challenge to his own marvelous ability to teach a talented young man the ropes in an interesting case. Matt wanted to bring his breakfast up and decorate the floor as he listened to the high, nasal voice.

The jury was hanging on every word, the spectator section looked like it was ready to clap, and the judge was dozing. Hairy Harry was nowhere to be seen. Matt missed Adrianne. She was getting the x-rays looked at and chaperoning the nurse from Tucson. Todd and Debbie were hoping for a miracle. He felt pretty damn alone.

It was time.

He went halfway to the witness stand and stood contemplating the defendant warily. He felt a surge of heat rise from his core. This was ridiculous. The man was as phony as Vegas morals and he had ruined the lives of Todd's whole family.

"So what do you have to say to Bob Gleason about what's happened to his life?"

The leonine hairdo reared back in confusion. "What the hell are you talking about?"

"Do you even know who that is?" Matt stalked forward a few feet. "Do you?"

A veined hand waved negligently. "I assume that's the father who took off. Who cares what's happened to him?"

"Todd's father did abandon him." Matt looked back at Debbie and Todd. "Leaving him in the hands of the famous San Francisco lawyer who was going to help his boy out."

"Objection, Your Honor. That isn't a question!"

"I think one is on the way, counsel. Time to ask one, Mr. Taylor."

"You don't even know who I'm talking about, do you? You didn't even know my client's brother has had to give up his life to help Todd?"

"My job was to handle his case and get the boy money, counsel." Conti shrugged dismissively. "It wasn't necessary to know all the details of his family situation."

"Details." Matt looked toward the jury. "Bob Gleason is a 'detail?'"

"Objection."

"Here's a 'detail' question for you. What happened to the rest of the one million dollars? Was the other three hundred fifty thousand just a 'detail?'"

Conti's hooded eyes looked at Matt over heavy black rims. "I relied on the recommendation of the lawyer handling the case as to the chances of a greater recovery."

Matt cocked his head. "The advice of a six-month lawyer? Someone who'd never handled a big case before?"

"He was a brilliant young man."

"Yeah, so that's why, as we discussed, you let him go a year later?" Conti's cold eyes stared at Matt. "We also read his deposition to the jury, you know. He says you fired him."

"We were downsizing." The white hand waved. "It happens all the time in our business. You know, like happened to you at the Wallace firm."

Matt figured the man knew that was wrong, but he wasn't about to let the cagy character provoke him. "Another thing Youngstone testified in his deposition: he said he tried to talk to you about Todd's case, but you were just too busy." Matt pulled out Youngstone's deposition. "When you went down to the settlement conference, you didn't even take your brilliant young lawyer with you, did you?"

"I don't remember." The fleshy face eyed the deposition warily. "I don't need help to handle something like that after all these years."

"Tell me, while getting ready for the settlement meeting, did you review the file at all?"

"I have no idea. Perhaps."

"How about the medical records? Did you look at what your young client had been through?" Conti was carefully examining the back wall of the courtroom. "Did you look for the x-rays of his broken neck and severed spinal cord so you could educate the settlement judge about his terrible injury?"

The broad head tilted to look under his horn rims while he picked at dead flesh on his hand. "I'm sure we had medical reports to describe the nature and extent of the boy's injuries."

"So were the experts sent the medical records and the x-rays so they could do a good job of analyzing what happened to him?"

"You know we didn't order the x-rays." Conti's jowls quivered dismissively. "That would have been a ridiculous waste of the client's money with a limited coverage case."

"So this medical report you got, did you at least read it to prepare for the conference?"

"I suppose so." He pulled a gold-cuffed sleeve back to check the time. "I would usually be given a packet of some sort to take down there."

Matt felt a tingle of excitement. Adrianne had found something while she was poking through the court file while they were down in San Diego that was not in the file they received from Conti's office. He had a few things to try and tie down first, though.

"You mentioned this was a 'limited coverage case.' Did it bother you that there was such inadequate insurance available for such a terrible injury?"

"Not really. The coverage was on their own car, after all. The Gleason family had chosen to set it at that level. It's not unusual to have a serious injury and an underinsured defendant—it happens all the time."

"Didn't it concern you that your client was paralyzed, and this money wouldn't take care of him for very long?"

"They chose the policy limits, counsel." Conti flecked imaginary specks from his recently cleaned vest. "That night he also chose to get drunk with his friend and they went out driving. When you've been around as long as I have, you learn that people have to live with their choices."

"Your firm has done quite a bit of medical malpractice work over the years, hasn't it?"

"We were one of the pioneers in the field." He puffed up a bit and looked at the jury. "I was doing medical work when you were still in diapers."

Matt noted a few chuckles from the panel. "So you've handled E.R. cases before?"

"Too many to count."

"And in those innumerable E.R. cases, I'll bet lots of those clients were admitted after doing something that caused them an injury, right?" The old warrior looked daggers at Matt. "You took lots of those cases where people did something stupid, got injured, and then were made worse by the medical treatment, didn't you?" Matt held up a binder with numerous tabs in it. "I've got many write-ups from your office. You know, the ones to advertise your victories. Do you need to be reminded of them?"

There was another floppy wave of the blue-veined hand. "I suppose there were some like that over the years."

"Yes, and many of them had been drinking—even driving their own cars? You took those cases because, *legally*, it's entirely irrelevant how someone managed to get hurt before they needed to get help in the E.R., isn't it? Everyone in an E.R.'s entitled to proper care; *isn't that true?*"

"That's the law, counsel."

"Mr. Conti, when you represent a badly injured client and the coverage to compensate them is inadequate, an important part of your job is to look for other potential possible cases against other defendants, isn't it?"

"We've gone over this before, Mr. Taylor." The defendant drew himself up indignantly. "I was hired to represent this young man against the driver of his car, not to play ambulance chaser and file frivolous lawsuits against everybody in sight."

Matt looked at him in puzzlement. "Well, I'm not talking about frivolous cases, of course, but isn't it common to start one case and then discover another cause of the injury and then file an action to protect your client's rights?"

"Absolutely not. Unless that is what you were hired to do in the first place." He looked at the jury for emphasis. "We run a class operation. My firm doesn't go looking under rocks for worthless cases like this just because there isn't enough insurance."

"Really?" Matt leaned against the back rail where he could see everyone. "Isn't it common for a law firm to start one case, like an auto accident case, and then, in serious injury cases, also sue the manufacturer of the vehicle on a crashworthy theory, or even sue the state or the county for poor design of the roadway?"

"Very unusual, and then only when that is what the client hires you to do."

Matt shook the black binder. "In many of the cases your office has handled, and reported for advertisement, you have sued more than one defendant, haven't you?"

He crossed his leg and sighed. "Of course, if that was appropriate."

"Well, are you suggesting that a sixteen-year-old client has to be smart enough to figure out who might have hurt him—who to sue—rather than that being the job of the famous lawyer he hires?"

"Todd Gleason had a family, Mr. Taylor."

"Yes, he had a father who had abandoned his family. That's right. And Todd had a brother that stayed home from college so he could help his mother work night and day to care for his brother. Are you telling this jury that this *desperate* family should have figured out who might have hurt him?

Are you suggesting that *they* should have ordered the medical records or x-rays and looked at them?"

Conti stirred restlessly in the witness chair. "That wasn't what we were paid for."

Matt stood up from the rail. "Right. Paid for. You were paid two hundred forty thousand dollars plus costs to get your client about three hundred sixty thousand dollars as I recall. But none of that was to make an effort to be sure nobody else caused his injury?"

"Don't act so righteous. You charge the same in cases all the time."

Matt looked at the jury before turning back to the defendant. "I certainly do, but you can be assured that when my clients aren't being fully compensated, I look at every other reasonable possibility to take care of them."

Murphy snapped stridently: "Objection. Mr. Taylor's not under oath."

"That's true, but he's responding to your client's comment about him. Let's move on, gentlemen."

Matt continued. "Mr. Conti, do you recall the case of *Marlowe v. Good Samaritan Hospital?*"

"Vaguely."

Matt opened the binder Mary Beth had laboriously compiled. "Your publicity write up on that case says that, while investigating an auto injury case, you *discovered* the client's amputation wasn't necessary and sued the E.R. where he was taken. Does that sound familiar?"

The heavy black shoulders shrugged. "I suppose."

"So how did your firm 'discover' that without looking at the medical records Mr. Conti?"

"I don't know." Even through the sagging cheeks, you could see Conti's jaw muscles tighten. "Maybe the client told us about it and hired us to sue them for it."

"So this write-up is false advertising?"

"Argumentative." Murphy interjected.

"Sustained."

Matt moved closer with the binder. "If I told you there are several cases in here where your firm said it had 'discovered' another claim and then sued on it while representing a client, would you be surprised?"

"I suppose it could have happened over the years." The witness loosened his red tie.

Matt tossed the binder onto the counsel table. "A few minutes ago, you told us you 'probably' read the medical report on Todd Gleason to prepare for the settlement conference. Remember that?"

"I may have." Conti looked more comfortable.

"Well, if you paid the client's money to get a medical report," Matt held his hands out to his sides, "certainly somebody in the firm should at least read it, make sense?"

"I suppose that's reasonable."

Matt picked up a sheaf of papers from his materials. "Do you remember what it said?" The witness's body language suggested he didn't know and didn't care. "This is a certified copy of the statement your firm filed in Todd's case for the settlement conference." Matt gave a copy to Murphy, one to the witness, and one to the clerk, saying, "We would like to have this marked as plaintiff's next exhibit."

Then Matt resumed his examination. "Does this look like the statement your firm filed?"

"Yes, it has our letterhead."

Matt turned to the page in question. "There is a report that is attached as Exhibit D to the conference statement. Do you have that in front of you?"

A tingle of anticipation ran up his spine. Matt couldn't believe what Adrianne had found on her exploration of the court file last week. "This is a report of the neurologist you hired to give a report on Todd's condition."

"Yes, yes, I see that."

Matt turned over to the last page. "Can I refer you to the second paragraph in the 'Impressions' section? You see in the third sentence what the neurologist says about his findings on review of Todd Gleason's records?"

"Objection, Your Honor, this is obvious hearsay and inadmissible."

"If I may, Your Honor, this is offered as a classic exception to the hearsay rule. It's offered not for the matters stated in the report. It is simply offered on the issue of notice to Mr. Conti's firm of the possibility of medical malpractice, which is based on the report they requested and which they filed with the court."

A buzz ran around the courtroom. Conti was sitting up now and leaned toward the judge. "That's ridiculous! This…"

The judge held up his hand. "That's quite enough, sir. You are a party. I will hear from the lawyers on this issue. Gentlemen, you may approach the bench."

The lawyers quietly argued the evidentiary point out of the hearing of the jury, with the court reporter taking everything down for the record. It occurred to Matt that Conti's reaction in front of the jury alone was a golden moment. He suspected the judge would have little choice regarding the admissibility of the doctor's comments. It didn't matter whether the doctor was right or wrong in his report. The important thing was that Conti's firm had been sent the letter and the potential significance of its contents had apparently been missed or ignored.

After the discussion, the judge sat back. "I've heard enough, counsel. The comments in the letter can be discussed in front of the jury. I will reserve my ruling as to whether the entire letter itself can be admitted into evidence. You may proceed, Mr. Taylor."

"Mr. Conti, the sentence I am going to read is in this letter addressed to Mr. Youngstone, at your firm, dated more than a year in advance of the statute of limitation expiration date. This report, as you testified, was 'probably' in the package you read to prepare for the settlement conference and states as follows: '*A review of the records reveals that the patient apparently could move his extremities when first admitted to the E.R. and later was noted by the nurses to have become quadriplegic a few hours after his admission to the ICU.*'" There was a louder buzz in the back of the room this time. He looked up at the crimson-faced defendant. "Sir, do you remember reading this sentence when you were preparing for the settlement conference?"

"I certainly do not."

Matt stood with his hands on his hips. "Don't you agree, Mr. Conti, that an experienced and competent trial attorney reading this report would immediately be concerned that Todd Gleason may have been rendered quadriplegic by the acts or omission of the hospital personnel?"

Conti roughly cleared his throat and poured himself some water. "It would be pure speculation to say what a knowledgeable attorney, reading this, might think."

"Well, are you telling us that if you, or one of the other experienced lawyers in one of the most famous law firms in the country, read this sentence, that they might have ignored this opinion—the opinion of a neurologist hired by the firm to evaluate the case?"

Conti's voice was turning into a growl. "I'm telling you I don't have any idea what other people might do."

"Well, sir, why don't you tell this jury what *you* would have done if you had seen this report and read that sentence?"

Conti's florid features hardened. "Well, the question calls for pure speculation, because I never saw it before today."

Matt thought it might be even better that he was refusing to answer the question. Obviously, Murphy didn't want to object. He knew the jury needed to hear a response from his client. Matt turned and looked toward the jury. "Perhaps you didn't see it because the baby lawyer you put in charge of the case didn't recognize the importance of this medical analysis and bring it to your attention?"

Conti brusquely tided his vest. "Why are you perseverating on this? Demanding my psychoanalysis of everyone in sight? I don't have any idea what he was thinking or doing. Why can't you ask an intelligent question?"

Matt suppressed an urge to grandstand with the jury. He just looked down for a moment, shaking his head wryly. "I suppose I do have a tough time with that."

Then, suddenly he raised his head. "Okay. Is this intelligent enough for you?" His eyes bored into the evil man trying to appear so casual in the witness chair. "Mr. Conti, perhaps you can explain why we could find this 'smoking gun' letter in the papers your office filed in the court's file but it is, in fact, nowhere to be seen in the office file we subpoenaed from your office and admitted into evidence at the start of the trial?"

Murphy was on his feet. "Objection! Argumentative!"

The judge leaned forward. "That will be overruled. The Court would be interested in hearing the answer to this question."

51

"So let me get this straight, Adrianne, you think she's tough as nails and against us, but you brought her up here anyway?" Matt immediately regretted his tone, but he was wound pretty tight. What if the defense found out she was here?

She looked at him defensively. "It was just a feeling I got talking to her." She took a deep breath. "I went carefully over the records and thought I saw a way to go. She says she doesn't think they did anything wrong, but I think she's incapable of shading the truth." Her expression was helpless. "The jury's got to decide the hospital is liable in the verdict to make this work, right? It's possible this might be the answer. I've watched you work. I think you might just get some good stuff out of her if you approach it the right way."

"Good lord, I won't even be able to talk to her. She's just showing up in court this afternoon?"

"Yep. She wanted to see her friends, but I can call her and tell her not to show up if you want?"

"After Mary Olsen and the way it just went with Conti, thanks to your discovery?" He gave a deep sigh. "Hell, I gotta trust you. I'll give it a shot."

As they went over the records and he listened to her idea, he thought it was a long shot, but it just might work. The nurse hadn't seen the records and had only a vague recollection of Todd's treatment. As they talked, he warmed to Adrianne's enthusiasm. Suddenly a stab of terror swept over him. What if he undid today's gains with Conti? What made him think he could pull this off? That was the trouble with the advocacy system—after a while you begin to drink your own damn Kool-Aid.

"Matt, where are you? Hello? Does that approach make sense?"

Abruptly he drew himself back to reality. "Yeah, it does. Sorry, just a bit spaced-out, I'm afraid."

"Stay positive." She set her chin. "The end's in sight. Things are gonna work out."

"Well, they will or they won't. That's the thing about a trial—sort of all or nothing…"

* * *

Matt looked around the huge old room that was the judge's chambers. Fancy it was not, but he had lots of pictures of his kids and old buddies that now were mostly all well-known politicos or personalities. In the judge's day, if you were going to be somebody in San Francisco, you either went to Saint Ignatius or to Lowell High. Obviously, the judge had gone to Lowell. There the judge was, in the pictures back in the day with Mayor George Moscone before he and Harvey Milk were gunned down in the famous murder case that gave rise to the "Twinkie Defense." Matt even saw pictures with the two Willies, Willie Mays and Willie Brown. Impressive. The judge was relaxed in shirt-sleeves with his robe hanging on a hook a few feet away. "Okay folks, the defense has rested its case. Mr. Taylor, do you have any rebuttal testimony?"

Matt glanced at Adrianne and thought—*here goes*. "Actually, we have two witnesses who we think will take up the afternoon and then we'll be done as well." Murphy and Anderson were listening with interest. The plaintiff seldom called rebuttal witnesses and didn't have to disclose them in advance because they were just a response to something the defense had put forth in their case. It was rare for the plaintiff not to have anticipated anything the defense might say and already have dealt with it in their main presentation.

"Can we have an offer of proof, Your Honor?"

Matt wasn't surprised. Anderson wanted a preview of what might be coming.

"That seems reasonable, Mr. Taylor. That way, if there are any objections, we can take care of them outside the presence of the jury."

Matt made a show of consulting the tablet in front of him. "We have a radiologist for a short discussion of the x-rays and then we're calling one of the other nurses who treated Todd."

Anderson almost stood, his reaction was so strong. "That's not rebuttal, Your Honor. They are putting on evidence that should have been included in their case in chief. They had a radiologist testify and both sides have discussed the x-ray reports. How do we respond to this? With more rebuttal evidence? This is totally improper!"

"This is not really rebuttal evidence, Mr. Taylor . Are you asking to reopen your case and, if so, why couldn't you have brought this evidence in during your case-in-chief?"

"Actually, they talked a lot in their case about what the x-rays showed or didn't show and their experts also talked about the nursing care and how good it was. So it could certainly be characterized as rebuttal." Matt caught the judge's eye. "Most importantly, however, we found the missing x-rays two days ago and just had them looked at last night. The ICU nurse who cared for Todd has also been missing for a couple of years and we just found her." He opened his palms. "This is potentially critical evidence, Your Honor. The facts, whatever they are, need to be out in front of the jury. We think that's far more important than the typical rules about the order of evidence."

Anderson and Murphy started talking over each other. "But, Your Honor…"

The judge stopped them. "Mr. Taylor has a point. This is new evidence that has just become available. If you need some time to rebut what's said, then I'll consider it after we hear the evidence." He stood up to put on his robe. "If it turns out this evidence finishes the case, we'll talk more jury instructions late this afternoon and start final arguments in the morning."

Matt walked through the outer office of the chambers and into the packed courtroom. The word must be out that the case was close to finishing. Only the jury seats were empty. As he waited for the jury to come in, he felt his apprehension build. He wasn't sure how this last bit of evidence would come out. He hoped he hadn't argued himself into a disaster.

Matt spent some time re-qualifying his radiologist again and then addressed the new subject. "Doctor Matson, you have had a chance to look at the actual x-rays taken of Todd Gleason?"

The radiologist was in his mid-forties and had short, sandy hair and sharp features. He was a born teacher with a lay-friendly approach to medical testimony. "Yes. Note these are not the original films. I understand they're copies the radiologist had made for his own records."

"Are you sure they are the films of Todd Gleason?"

"Oh yes, they have his name on them, the time they were taken, and the date of his admission at the hospital in El Cajon where he was treated."

"Doctor, can you describe the type of films and what the purpose was for taking them?"

"Yes, of course." He looked toward the jury. "Simply speaking, this young man was in a serious motor vehicle accident and the films were done to be sure he had not broken his neck. As we have previously discussed, they also did films of his head and other portions of his body." He gestured to his own anatomy. "The idea is to take a film of the neck from the front, called an 'AP view'—meaning anterior/posterior—to show the seven vertebrae of the neck and then also to take one from the side called a 'lateral view.' Between the two films, you should be able to visualize all of the elements of the individual vertebral bodies and see if there are any fractures."

"What made them want to check that in this case?"

"Ah!" The teacher held up his index finger. "He was in a rollover accident and had evidence of a head injury. Both are red flags for a possible neck injury. That's why the admitting E.R. doctor wrote 'rule out cervical fracture' on his history and physical at the end where it said 'plan.'"

"Doctor Matson, how did the radiologist at the hospital read the original x-rays?"

"Doctor Fulton, now deceased, I understand, basically said the films were normal." The radiologist opened the records and put his finger on the page. "He described the seven vertebral and thoracic bodies in the AP view as unremarkable and said he could see C1 down to C6 in the lateral view and they had normal configuration, with no evidence of fractures."

"Doctor, have you reviewed the recently discovered films of Todd Gleason's neck that we provided you?"

"Yes, I have."

Matt moved back where he could see the jury while he questioned the witness. "Do you agree with Doctor Fulton's reading of the films?"

"Well, I agree with most of what he says." The radiologist pulled out the films. "There are a few findings that need more comment and a finding that was not mentioned."

Matt looked toward the jury and they seemed attentive. "Doctor Matson, can you tell us what your findings were and how they differed from the original reading?"

"First, I found small chip fractures of the outer transverse process on the C6 vertebral body on the AP view." The expert turned to the portable x-ray view-box next to the stand and turned on the light. "These are subtle and not in and of themselves dangerous, but I believe it should be mentioned. Most importantly, on the lateral view, the caudal portion—the lower portion of the vertebral body—of cervical 6 can't be visualized and cervical 7 is not seen at all."

"Why is that important, Doctor Matson?"

"First, the chip fractures are a potential clue of trauma in the area. Think of it as a waving red flag. 'What's here?'" The bright eyes sharpened and he looked at each jury member, including them in the discussion. "Why have I been broken? What else in the area might be broken?'" He held up the two films and put the front view on the viewing screen. "Secondly, these vertebral bodies are round and you can only see the front part of them from the AP view." He pointed to the film. "To see all of C6 and C7, you have to see the side view also." He put the lateral film on the screen and tapped the film. "On the side view, they are missing an important view of the last one and one-half vertebral bodies."

"But why in the world would you not be able to see them from the side if you can see them from the front?"

"Aha!" The eyes sparkled. "Look here where the last portion of C6 is." Matt saw the jury craning to see. "That white round thing in the way here? That's the patient's shoulder." He demonstrated on his own body. "See how my shoulder is in the way of your view of my lower neck? This is actually a common problem, particularly in unconscious patients where you can't get them to drop their shoulders."

"What do you do about this?"

"Well, there are various solutions. You can try to pull down the shoulders while shooting the film, but then you are exposing the technician to radiation. Or you can raise one shoulder and thereby drop the other in what is called a swimmer's view. Visualize a person swimming using the crawl stroke."

"Did they try those maneuvers?"

"We can't tell. There is no record of that." The expert held his arms up, helplessly. "But there is no film showing those hidden vertebral bodies. We do know that if they were done, they should have shown the fractures of his neck."

"Well where does that leave these doctors who are supposed to 'rule out a cervical fracture'?"

"The record is not clear at all from this point forward. After these films, the patient went to the ICU for observation." The radiologist's expression was serious as he looked toward the jurors again. "What the standard of care would be is that the radiologist would talk to the E.R. doctor or the neurologist and say that the films are not adequate to rule out a fracture. They would ordinarily then wait until the patient is awake enough to cooperate and do more films."

"Can you tell what they did here?"

"I believe so." The doctor nodded slowly. "There is nothing written that indicates that the danger of a broken neck has been ruled out. Moreover, there's no note that the collar was ever removed. I suspect he was transferred to the ICU to be observed until he was more conscious and then they planned to finish imaging the part of the neck they couldn't see." He pulled the films off the view-box. "That was the only reasonable way to deal with the situation under the circumstances." He looked somberly at Matt. "The nurses just had to be very careful with the patient until they could be sure he didn't have a broken neck."

Matt held up the written report. "Earlier you said you would have expected more comments than you found in the report by the radiologist?"

"Yes. Do you want me to explain?"

"Yes, please do."

"Perhaps the most important way for the radiologist to communicate with the attending doctors and the nurses is to highlight concerns in the report. This also makes it clear what he has already communicated to them orally." He tapped the report in his hand while looking at the jurors. "What's left out of the report is that C6 and C7 have not been visualized and that a fracture could not be ruled out, especially with this chip fracture. That's a red flag and you need to write a red flag report. Doctor Fulton didn't."

Matt paused to let the jury consider that information. "Doctor Matson, have you looked at the films that were taken later that evening when Todd was found to be quadriplegic?"

"Yes, I have."

"And what do they show?"

"Unfortunately, they show a severe fracture through the lower portion of C6 vertebral body with associated fractures of the pedicles." The doctor sighed audibly. "This was an unstable fracture and, by that time, C6 had massively dislocated posteriorly relative to C7 and was impinging on the spinal canal."

"Can you explain what that means to the jury, please?"

"Simply put, the bones of the neck which are meant to protect the spinal cord had broken completely through and were unstable. When this picture was taken they had shifted and had severed Todd Gleason's spinal cord."

Matt turned to look at his notes in the hush as the listeners absorbed the doctor's testimony. He caught Adrianne's eye and she gave a subtle movement of her head toward the gallery. He saw a middle-aged African-American woman who was watching with a very intense and concerned expression. That had to be Nurse Hays.

"Just so I am clear, Doctor Matson, what was the status of the decision-making process about whether he had a broken neck when he was transferred to the care of the nurses in the ICU?"

"It's pretty straightforward. There is a clear statement that a fracture of the cervical spine has to be ruled out. The x-rays they had could not do so. He is transferred with that serious danger still to be ruled out. The ICU nurses are expected to know and understand that. They must protect the spinal cord until a neck fracture has been ruled out."

Matt listened while Anderson cross-examined. He established that Matson wasn't an expert on neurology and had no opinion on when the damage to the cord had occurred. He emphasized that the radiologist wasn't there at the time, and had no idea what the doctors had actually said to each other or to the nurses in the ICU.

Finally, the defense lawyer was finished and they took the afternoon break. Matt turned toward the back of the courtroom and saw the person he presumed was Nurse Hays moving quickly out of the courtroom through the big swinging doors.

Adrianne stopped him. "It may be best you don't talk to her. I suspect that was hard for her to hear."

"Do you think she'll even come back?"

For the rest of the break, he pondered how to approach her if she returned. Technically, she was supposed to return because they had served a valid subpoena on her when she got into town. She was ex-military, so he expected she would submit to the authority of the court and go on the stand. What little Adrianne had been able to tell him, suggested she was a disciplined and dedicated nurse. While Nurse Hays said she did not feel the nurses had done anything wrong, Adrianne thought she would be intellectually honest. They were going to put her on the stand based on his young associate's instinct about the witness and her confidence in his ability to obtain helpful testimony from a person he had never talked to or met. He wished he could be as sure as Adrianne that this was the right thing to do.

Adrianne put her hand on his shoulder. He turned and saw Nurse Hays moving into a seat in the back just as the clerk returned to the courtroom. It was showtime.

52

"Plaintiff calls nurse Marie Hays to the stand." Matt thumbed through some papers and let the nurse get settled for a moment after she was given the oath. "Can you state your name and occupation for the record, please?" As he took her through her background and established that she had been one of the nurses caring for Todd when he was admitted to the ICU, he watched her demeanor closely. She spoke clearly and, while obviously nervous, exuded an aura of warmth and competence. He felt the jury warm to her immediately. Even the judge seemed to smile down on her. She was a perfect image of the person you wanted to have taking care of you in the ICU. He was going to have to handle her very carefully.

"Have you ever testified in court before?"

"Never before."

"Well, just take your time and do the best you can." He smiled at her. "We won't bite."

Murphy looked at the jury and remarked, *sotto voce*, "Well, the rest of us won't, anyway."

Matt laughed at his own expense along with everyone else and was pleased to see the nurse unclasp the hands she had been desperately clenching. "Let's talk a bit in general about what you are doing in the ICU—your overall job, okay?"

She nodded and seemed visibly to relax. That sounded easy. "One of the things you're there for is to monitor the patients, correct? Their condition, any changes?"

"Yes."

"You also are to notify the doctor if there are any significant changes in the patient's condition." He nodded encouragingly and added, "Basically, to be the eyes and ears of the doctors?"

She nodded. Matt pointed at the stenographer with her hands poised in the air. "You have to answer out loud for the court reporter." She flushed. "Oh, sorry. Yes, that's true."

"Also, an important part of your job is to keep a record of all of this in the chart—so you and the other health care professionals can be aware of the patient's status at any point in time and see if there are any trends one way or the other, correct?"

"Well, that's generally correct." She ducked her chin. "But nobody can keep a *perfect* chart."

"So you do the best job you can to make sure the chart is as accurate as possible, so supervisors, other nurses, and perhaps doctors can come in later and always be able to see what any patient's condition was and what has been happening?"

"That's part of our job." She frowned slightly. "But, of course, treating the patient comes before treating the chart."

"Well, sure, but, at the time, if you can, or later if necessary, the pertinent, significant medical facts such as status, changes in condition of the patient, are supposed to be put in the chart. Is that right?"

"Yes."

"Is another important thing to be sure you know what the doctors' concerns are about the patient's condition and to follow their orders?"

"Well, yes." She inclined her head slightly. "Of course."

"So, hypothetically, if a doctor was worried about blood clots in the leg, it would be important for you to communicate with the doctor, be aware of that, and watch for any signs of that sort of a problem?"

"Sure." Her lower lip jutted out thoughtfully. "That is, if you know they are worried about that."

"Well, how are you to find out what they are thinking—what they want you to watch out for in the patient you are caring for?"

"Certainly the best way is if they tell you." She sat back and smiled. "But good luck on that. They don't always do that, unfortunately. So you have to look at their diagnosis—what they've written and see if you can figure out what they're thinking."

"I suppose if you're not clear, you can always call them and ask?" Matt paused a moment. "It's important to know what you're supposed to be watching for, what they want you to be worried about, right?"

"I suppose." Her head inclined negatively. "But we can usually figure it out without having to call them."

"Nurse Hays, do you actually have a recollection of this patient and his condition separate from the medical records? It *was* about five years ago that you cared for him."

She sat thinking for a moment. "Well, not details, but I do remember this patient. It's not every night you have a patient wake up and find out he's a quadriplegic."

"I expect that is true." Matt walked over to the podium where his records were. "But other than remembering that he was found to be paralyzed at some point, do you have specific recollections of his condition at any given time, or would you have to rely on your records?"

"Not details. I would have to use the records for exact findings and things like that."

"These are the records of his admission." He picked up the records. "You have a set in front of you and we have the same numbering on the pages for your convenience." He saw her turn to what looked like the admitting ICU nursing notes. "On page fifty-seven, there is an initial assessment on his admission to the ICU, correct?"

"That's my admitting evaluation."

A large chart on an easel displayed a copy of the page in question. He took her through some of the entries she had placed in the chart, pointing them out for the jury. Then Matt moved closer to her. "He's not in a coma. He's somewhat responsive actually, correct?"

"I don't think he was in a coma." She looked at the record. "It says here RTC which means 'responds to commands.'"

"Tell me about that. What are the standard ways to give commands and see if the patient does respond?"

"Well, you ask them to do things and see if they do them. RTC means he did."

Matt put his hands casually in his pockets. "Isn't the standard way for an ICU nurse to check for response to command, to ask the patient to move their legs?"

She put her hand in the record to keep her place. "That's one way to do it."

"That's how you do it, isn't it?"

"That or squeeze my hand."

He went to the chart on the easel. "You're doing an initial neurologic assessment here, aren't you?" He looked around the rapt courtroom. "We can tell you're a very thorough nurse. You would do both hands and legs and also check to see if he moved and could feel the leg or body part you touched, wouldn't you?"

"I'm not sure."

Matt pointed to the blow up of the assessment page. "Nurse Hays, you did this full neuro exam and didn't note any problem with movement, sensation or anything else with his extremities except depressed reflexes, correct?"

"Well, he was unconscious…"

"Where in your evaluation does it say he's unconscious? It says 'responses to commands' and that he's not talking, right?"

Her eyes closed momentarily. "That's true."

"So let's review." Matt pointed to the big chart. "We have a patient with reflexes present in all extremities, responding to commands to move his legs, feet and upper extremities, with intact sensation and he's not talking. That's his condition according to this chart you filled out at six that evening, correct?"

"Look." Her hands went up defensively. "I just don't remember him as doing all that well."

"Well, where in your assessment do you say he's doing worse than that?" Matt looked at the jury and then back to her. "Where do you note that you called the doctor and told him he was not moving normally, or had sensation problems?"

Her eyes searched the chart. "I don't say that here."

"According to this record—your record—at nine fifteen, with fifteen-minute checks having occurred for almost three hours, there's been no note of any change." Matt pointed to each of the entries on the chart. "So he's still able to move all extremities to command, has sensation, has only depressed, but intact, reflexes and he's not talking?"

She shook her head violently. "Well, I can't say that."

"Where here in your chart does it say anything else?" He held up the records and pointed to the blown-up chart. "Isn't that what these little boxes, checks, and entries tell us?"

She stared at him for a long time. "I guess so."

"Tell me, you're a good nurse." He willed his eyes to hold hers and spoke quietly. "Isn't that what your own records say to us here?"

She sighed. "Yes it does seem to be what they say."

Moving back toward his counsel table, he then wheeled back to face her as if in afterthought. "By the way, when you do procedures in the ICU, don't you usually document what you do?"

"I suppose." The ICU nurse gave him a puzzled look. "What do you mean?"

"For example, if a patient has a broken leg—like he did—wouldn't you usually describe in the record the precautions you use to move him?"

"Yes, and here we did." She pointed to the record. "We noted when we changed his linen here how we protected his leg when we rolled him."

Matt studied the records to control his elation at the answer. "So what did you understand were the main concerns and worries of the doctor for Todd when he was admitted to the ICU?"

"I'm not sure." She stared at the materials. "I know he was worried about a head injury."

"Yes, you were to watch carefully, and if his consciousness showed any signs of deteriorating, it would be important to tell the doctor at once. You didn't see any evidence of that, did you?"

She responded quickly. "No, that's right."

363

"What else was the doctor worried about?"

She thrust her lower lip out as she worked her way through the record. "Watch for abdominal signs and for clots from the leg fractures for sure."

He nodded encouragingly and then, after a moment of silence, made a show of opening to a specific page of the record and looked back up at her. "What else did he say they were worried about and needed to be ruled out?"

She spent a long time thumbing through different pages of the record as the courtroom seemed to hold its breath. "He did say 'rule out cervical spine fracture,' but they did x-rays on that."

He carefully put the records down and crossed his arms, leaning against the counsel table. "Tell me, did they 'rule out' fractures of the neck with those x-rays before he got to the ICU? Did the E.R. doctor and neurologist actually clear his spine?" She paused, looking through the records. "I don't remember. I don't see any place where they say the c-spine is cleared."

He kept his gaze on her, willing her to look him in the eyes. "Wouldn't it be important to treat him as if he might have a broken neck with him there in the ICU? That is, if the doctors had a standing order to 'rule out cervical fracture,' and then later never actually cleared his c-spine?"

She glanced up at him and then away. "We were very careful with him, Mr. Taylor. Very careful."

"I know, Ms. Hays, I'm sure you were." He remained still and kept watching her, his demeanor kindly, but firm. "But, can you answer my question?"

She sat there looking at the records. "That would be important, and I take your inference." She looked up at him sadly. "I don't see any place where we said we protected his neck when we rolled him for the linen change."

He went from the front of the table and stood behind his chair. He gave her a moment. "Ms. Hays, right after you rolled Todd he said he couldn't move—that he couldn't feel his legs. Isn't that true?"

You could barely hear her answer in the hushed courtroom. "Yes."

He gave her a look filled with compassion. "That's the real reason you agreed to come here and talk to this jury after all these years, isn't it?"

She sat mutely for a moment. Then a tear coursed down her cheek.

53

The fog was howling and eddying around him as he walked from the parking garage. As he walked toward the building, he saw many lawyers he knew glance at him and then turn away. It was like they didn't want to be a part of what they thought was coming. The sound of the marble steps echoed as he climbed slowly toward the finish of Todd Gleason's trial. He couldn't bring himself to use the beautiful old elevators today.

As he turned into the corridor on the third floor, he was abruptly face to face with his old mentor, Steven Wallace. Matt nodded and started to walk on when Wallace grabbed his arm. "Hey, good luck in there today, Matt. Rigoletti says you've done a hell of a job." He gave him an awkward pat on the shoulder. "I'm proud of you, son."

A warm feeling flooded through Matt and he said, "Thank you Steven. That means a lot to me." They smiled at each other with understanding, and then each went on their way.

Matt sat in a cocoon of restrained energy waiting for the judge. If there was a sound in the courtroom, Matt didn't hear it. He knew juries primarily made their decisions based on the evidence they had heard, and usually not on the arguments of the attorneys. On the other hand, this was his chance to solidify the thinking of those in favor of his case and raise questions with those who were somewhere in the middle or leaning the wrong way. Perhaps most importantly, he could give Todd's advocates some structure, some arguing points, as they talked over the evidence and began moving toward a decision. In California, since this wasn't a criminal case, he needed nine of twelve to get a verdict. He had to give Todd's core jurors as much to work with as possible. He looked up and watched dust motes floating in the light streaming in through the big east windows. His thoughts danced and swirled with them as he waited.

"All rise." The judge took his seat, greeted everyone, and then nodded toward Matt who rose and strode to the lectern.

At last, he stood in front of the jury. Finally it all came down to this, a carefully orchestrated summary of six weeks of trial by three lawyers who were totally convinced they, and they alone, were right. Matt had always believed this was the time for calm, thoughtful persuasion and convincing logic, not showmanship or emotion. These twelve people knew the cast of characters, they knew the personalities, and they probably remembered most of the important evidence. He had to weave the best facts into a cohesive, compelling fabric, clearly demonstrating Conti's responsibility. Meanwhile, he needed to shore up and explain any areas of potential weakness. At the end, it had to feel right to them. It had to appeal to the jury's common sense.

He started his argument behind the podium with his notes in front of him, but soon he was out in front of the jurors, connecting with their eyes and hopefully their minds, his notes referenced only occasionally. He started by explaining how the law the judge would give the jurors applied to the facts, and then he developed an outline of the evidence, showing how the pieces of the puzzle fit into a compelling picture.

As he presented the heart of the case, he watched the jurors carefully. Some wrote notes while others just listened carefully. All of them were frustratingly impassive in both look and demeanor. Matt tried not to let their collective blank expressions derail his focus. So many times in the past, he had tried to read jurors and failed miserably. Sometimes they purposely refused to reveal that they were actually applauding inside. Others looked friendly, nodded, and then stabbed you during deliberation. Most conveyed nothing. The banker, Addison, was a pillar of stone. He was listening with his arms crossed in a classic defensive posture.

Matt was feeling good about the flow of his presentation, and his rhythm became more and more insistent as he moved toward the close. When he finally pulled the diverse elements of the case together into what he hoped was a compelling synopsis, he felt the psychology of the room finally coalesce. He would only know for sure if the facts had come together in a compelling fashion if the defense attorneys were off balance when they stood up to make their argument.

Matt was not disappointed. Anderson seemed defensive when he started his summary of the medical case evidence. At first, he spent more time responding to what Matt had just said than delivering a cohesive presentation of his own. Finally, he calmed down and zeroed in on the primary medical points he had prepared. "The plaintiff has cleverly attempted to obscure the facts and the medicine of the underlying case. Let's look at the conduct of the medical personnel. First, the radiologist. There's no evidence he breached the standard of care. He read the x-rays correctly and it was clear he wasn't able to see the lower part of C6 and C7."

His body hunched forward aggressively. "The E.R. doctor appropriately said: 'rule out a cervical fracture.' He then sent the young man to ICU to be carefully handled."

"You have heard from two ICU nurses. The first was the supervisor and she made it clear they did everything they're required to do. Then when he woke up and said he couldn't move his legs, they immediately informed the doctor." Anderson leaned with his hands on the jury rail. "The second nurse was the poster nurse for the best the El Cajon ICU has to offer. She said they were very careful with Todd Gleason. You know in your heart that she never could have done anything but give Todd the best care possible." He threw his arms wide. "Remember, the *plaintiffs* have the burden of proof in the case. Did they have an ICU nurse come in after Nurse Hays was on the stand and say anything she did was improper or a breach of the standard of care? No." He held up a thick finger. "Remember, that's *their* burden of proof. They didn't sustain it—*at*—*all.*"

"Second, let's look at causation." He set his hands on his hips. "Did the plaintiff prove that the conduct of the medical personnel caused his quadriplegia? The clear answer is *no.*" Now he was counting on his fingers. "Yes, this young man was in a terrible accident. We feel sorry for him about that. Let's set aside the fact he'd been drinking and got into that car to start with. It's most important to remember what the judge will instruct you. The case is *not* to be decided based on *sympathy*. It must be determined based on the evidence put forth in the courtroom." His forehead crashed into a knot. "The overwhelming probability is that his spinal cord was irreparably damaged when the car rolled over at high speed. Why do we know that? Because the evidence is that ninety-five percent of the people whose spinal cords are injured in a rollover accidents are paralyzed *immediately*." The big man straightened directly in front of the jury and looked at each of them in turn. "Remember, Todd Gleason's case is about probabilities. The plaintiff has the burden of proving his case by a *probability*. *Ninety-five percent* of the evidence is against them from the get-go."

"What else do we know for sure? He was out of it when he got to the hospital and never woke up until after the linen was changed. Horrible accident occurs—ninety-five percent likelihood of paralysis at the time—unconscious and then when he wakes up, lo and behold, he's paralyzed. What's the most probable cause of that? Clearly, it was the terrible accident he was in when the car rolled over at high speed. All the medical evidence is that it's *extremely* rare to have your neck broken but no injury to the cord until later."

"The jury is entitled to bring its common sense into the courtroom, ladies and gentlemen." He wagged his finger at them. "Ask yourselves, what's the evidence the plaintiff has to weigh against these powerful facts? They say, well, reflexes are only depressed and not absent. Our experts made it clear that injury to the spinal cord can develop over time and that reflexes can be depressed at first and then lost completely. Their only other point is that he could move his extremities when stimulated. Our neurologist was the most highly qualified doctor in the courtroom and he explained that this was simply a localized reflex and can happen long after the cord is irreparably damaged."

"Weigh this evidence, ladies and gentlemen. The facts proven by the defense are overwhelming." Anderson started walking toward the counsel table and then wheeled back toward them. "All the substantive evidence proves that Todd Gleason's spinal cord was already injured in his horrible rollover auto accident."

* * *

They took the lunch break and were now back in the courtroom. Murphy was on his feet. Without preliminaries, he immediately launched into his argument on the legal malpractice part of the case. As Matt made notes, he compared the styles of the defense attorneys. Like their legal expert, Crenshaw, Anderson was physically imposing and the big man used that in his presentation, looming over the jury and letting his voice and size emphasize his positions. Murphy was subtler, using his eyes, expressions and small body movements to convey significance and highlight his points. Where Anderson would pace, glare, hunch and throw his arms about, Murphy quietly centered himself on the podium and let his eyes twinkle with questions and his bushy eyebrows dance like wooly caterpillars on amphetamines. Both attorneys were effective advocates, because they clearly weren't playing a role. Their positions and thoughts were each presented differently but were real and came from the heart.

Murphy had been given time to reflect on Matt's opening during Anderson's argument and during lunch. He started out much calmer and was more organized than Anderson had been. The defense attorney carefully walked the jury through what he thought was important in the evidence, and patiently began undermining each of Matt's major contentions. He obviously was of the "say what you are going to say, say it again, and then say what you said" school. Finally, he was wrapping up.

"This auto case was an extremely difficult case that most lawyers would probably reject. My client took it on to do what he could to obtain some recovery for this young man. The plaintiff was drunk and injured in a solo car accident in his own car that he claimed was being driven by the other drunken boy. The car rolled over and the young man was brought to the hospital unconscious with multiple injuries." The eyebrows rose. "What reasonable professional would think to blame the emergency hospital personnel that swarmed to his rescue for his injuries? What should Mr. Conti have done? Brought a lawsuit against the paramedics and police responders who scraped this drunken teenager up off the road like a squashed squirrel and quickly got him to the best medical care available?"

"This case was assigned to one of the most brilliant young lawyers my client ever had the pleasure to work with." He spread his arms plaintively. "This hardworking young lawyer, now working in a major firm on the East Coast, got the records, took the depositions, and tried to overcome many of the terrible problems they faced." He looked toward Conti sitting at the counsel table. "My client, who was busy representing badly injured people all over the country, took time out of his impossible schedule to attend the court settlement conference personally. You've heard the legal experts we called to the stand. What he accomplished was a remarkable achievement by *any* standard."

"Let's look at the big picture here. When a lawyer's hired to represent a client in an auto case, there's no legal requirement that the lawyer has to look under every rock to find other people to sue. We're already way too 'sue-happy' in our society." He gestured toward Matt. "The standard the plaintiff wants to create would mean that, if a drunk teenager has an intersection collision, the lawyer has to sue the city for the design of the street, sue the manufacturer of the car for not keeping him safe enough in the collision, sue the passenger beside him for not warning of the impending collision, and then sue the doctors who saved his life at the hospital." He threw his hands wide. "Where does it end? Who is going to draw the line?" He brought his hands to his side and then gave the jurors a long, steely gaze. "I suggest that *you* are the conscience of this community. That's what juries are for. Tell the plaintiff, '*Enough*—not in our town, not with a lawyer who's spent his life representing the victims in our community, a lawyer who's become famous all over the country for his innovative and creative representation of people like you and me against the powerful and entrenched institutions of the world.'"

"As to the issue of damages, frankly, my preference would be not to even discuss it." Murphy paused with a regretful expression. "It's obvious to me that you'll never get to this question because the medical personnel weren't guilty of malpractice and the spinal cord was already injured. My client and his firm were certainly not guilty of legal malpractice." He lifted his shoulders in resignation. "However, in an excess of caution, in case there are a few members of the jury who want to hear about this, I've been designated by the defense team to address these issues."

He finally stepped out from behind the podium. "There's a theme in this case and the plaintiff's damages case is a perfect example. The theme is *overreaching*." He leaned one elbow on the lawyer's stand. "We offered highly-qualified witnesses who presented a sensible proposal to help the family take care of Todd Gleason, give them sorely needed respite, and provide for all the medical care he's likely to require in the future." He held his hand up toward the man in charge. "The judge will instruct you on the law; it calls for *reasonable* damages based on proof. There's no requirement for Rolls Royce care with all the chrome options and extra bells and whistles. America has done well for generations on solid Chevrolet thinking."

"What're we talking about here?" Still leaning on the podium, Murphy stuck his other hand on his hip. "They're insisting on a highly-paid nurse to sit there all night long while he sleeps, for goodness sake. They want nurses provided by a professional agency when Debbie Gleason can put an ad in the paper and have people lining up to work for half that hourly rate." Murphy looked at them from under his eyebrows. "If Mr. Taylor has his way, this family won't even be together anymore. Debbie Gleason would be out on her ear and strangers would be taking care of her son. She's done an incredible job of caring for him and their plan calls for that to end." His arm pointed at Matt. "This Rolls Royce plan of Mr. Taylor's says Todd's going to need over a week in the hospital every year for complications. He hasn't averaged that in the past five years because he's had top care from his mom. That will change if they put in twenty-four hours of hired help." He gave Debbie a warm look. "This family's done a brilliant job of caring for Todd Gleason. Yes, they need help and we have generously provided for six to eight hours of well-paid help every day for the rest of his life and also made sure this tight-knit family stays together." His gaze worked its way up and down the jury. "You know that's what is best for this family." He indicated the blow up of the defense team's life plan. "We've created a reasonable, long-term plan for medical and therapeutic care based on the national average of care provided to quadriplegics just like Todd Gleason.

But that's not good enough for Mr. Taylor. Oh no, he wants more, much more." He looked at Matt. "*Overreaching*."

"I'm also required to talk about life expectancy." He sighed delicately. "Everybody agrees that being paralyzed has many likely complications: pulmonary and bladder infections, metabolic disorders, skin breakdowns, and so on. It's unfortunate but true that these conditions are dangerous and likely to cause an early demise. The national statistics are clear. Life expectancy is reduced by fifty percent. Once again, Mr. Taylor is overreaching and claiming almost a normal life expectancy."

"There is a claim for loss of future earnings. This is sheer speculation. When he was injured, he'd never even worked before. There's no evidence of his ability to earn any amount. He's paralyzed, but he's quite intelligent and can do many different kinds of work that involve the use of phones. As our vocational rehabilitation person testified, it would be much healthier for him to be productive. The amount discussed by plaintiff in this area is unreasonably high and should be cut in half and then reduced again for his continuing ability to earn money."

"This whole area of pain and suffering is more of the same." Murphy studied the jury panel. "Of course, there's a place for this and, in the unlikely event that there's discussion of damages, something sensible and reasonable should be considered. That, after all, is the standard set by the law for such damages. For example, I think half a million dollars is extremely reasonable for this area of damages. Or, some people may think a bit more would perhaps be reasonable. Certainly, something in this range would satisfy the strict requirement of the law that such amounts be set fairly, reasonably and dispassionately."

He moved back behind the podium. "I would ask you to do two things in that jury room. First, don't leave your common sense at the door. Bring it in the jury room with you and use it when you evaluate the evidence." Murphy braced his hands on each side of the stand. "Secondly, please remember, all us have a great deal of sympathy with Mr. Gleason; that's natural. But sympathy has *no place* in the deliberations of a jury. Mr. Taylor has founded his whole case on a quest for sympathy, but the law the judge will give you makes it clear. You are not to base your verdict on passion or sympathy. A verdict should only be based on a reasonable, thoughtful, and dispassionate analysis of the evidence." He nodded confidently at them. "If you do, I know you'll return a verdict of not guilty and let my client go back to what he does best—representing downtrodden victims of corporate overreaching and greed."

Murphy looked at each one of the jurors before quietly taking his seat. The judge stretched and cleared his throat. "We'll take the afternoon break now. We'll reconvene at three fifteen for the plaintiff's rebuttal argument. Remember not to discuss the case with anyone."

During the break, Matt read quickly over his notes. Just before court reconvened, he stood up and went over to Todd. "How are you holding up?"

His client had a thin sheen of perspiration on his face and looked pale. "Well, a lot of that was pretty hard to hear."

Debbie looked up at Matt and said, "Whatever happens, we're so happy we've had you representing us, Matt. You've been incredible."

Todd nodded with moisture in his eyes. Then he said, "Give 'em hell for us, Mr. Taylor."

54

Matt stood quietly in front of the panel of jurors. "My worthy colleagues are very skilled. I admire their eloquence. But sometimes as I listened, I wondered if we were sitting in the same courtroom during this trial. First, let's address the evidence of the medical management." Matt picked up the newly discovered x-rays of Todd Gleason's neck and rattled them in front of the jury. "Doctor Matson sat right here and explained that there were chip fractures in these films that weren't even mentioned. He pointed them out to you. He said the radiologist failed to make it clear in his report that more films needed to be done. We have no clear evidence in this record that the E.R. doctor even *talked* to the radiologist, or to the ICU nurses, or what was said if they did." Matt put the films down. "They apparently admitted Todd to the ICU without a clear diagnosis of his dangerous situation." He looked at the jury with disgust. "The only thing the radiologist did right was say he saw only down to C6 in the lateral view. The only thing the E.R. doctor did right was state in his initial workup that a fracture of the cervical spine needed to be 'ruled out.' They then proceeded to transfer the patient to the ICU without ever doing anything to figure out if there was a broken neck." Matt positioned himself up near the jury rail and scanned the panel. "There was terrible communication up to that point. No, there was *no* communication at this critical time between these key medical personnel. We do know the nurses in the ICU were aware that a fracture of the neck *still had to be ruled out*. We are left to guess that perhaps the doctors were waiting to later do the definitive films, which would have shown the fracture."

He held his hands out toward them. "All the evidence in the case— every medical witness who got on that stand—said you can have a broken neck, but the spinal cord still be fine—that can happen." He started pacing in front of the jury box. "Ladies and gentlemen, even *Boy Scouts* are taught to guard the neck in a major trauma. It's *essential* that the ICU nurses guard the patient's neck until they can find out if it's broken. Let's look at the evidence and weigh it. All the evidence is that he can move his arms and legs before he's admitted to the ICU. The ambulance personnel said he was moving, the E.R. record says he's 'thrashing about' and moving to painful stimuli. He still had reflexes—though diminished." Matt walked over to the easel where he had propped a large blowup of the ICU record. "Then he's transferred to the ICU where this initial assessment establishes all these same things. Look at this elaborate record. There's no evidence whatsoever of any weakness, lack of movement, or loss of feeling in his body." He pointed to highlighted entries. "Then, suddenly, at nine fifteen they log-roll him to change his linen. The hospital nurses note right here that they *protected his broken leg,* but say *nothing about his neck.* A few minutes later, there's this note that the patient can't feel or move his legs. And *now* he's a quadriplegic."

"Let's think about this ninety-five percent argument. The defense claim is that if you break your neck in a rollover collision, ninety-five percent of the time, the cord is injured immediately. Remember, I asked the defense doctor what that was based on. Did he show us a book, produce medical evidence, a study, and/or statistics? No, he admitted he didn't have any. He just said that was his 'personal experience,' whatever that means." Matt threw his hands in the air. "We don't know if that's even close to accurate." Matt looked hard toward Anderson. "But, let's consider what counsel is proposing here. If what Mr. Anderson says is true, then one out of every twenty coming into an E.R. with a broken neck *haven't injured their spinal cord yet*—five out of a hundred!" He looked at Todd. "For every one of *those* five E.R. patients, like Todd, still having reflexes and still moving their arms and legs, that means there is a serious risk of injury to the spinal cord if you don't protect their neck. For each one of *those* five patients, *that* risk of paralysis is *one hundred percent.*"

Matt stopped to study the jurors. "Weigh this compelling evidence, ladies and gentlemen. There's a reason that very nice nurse cried during her testimony yesterday." He pointed to the now empty witness stand. "She knew they were supposed to protect Todd's neck when the doctor's order is 'rule out neck fracture,' and she knew they failed to do so. The nurses had the last chance to protect his neck. They didn't protect it. *That* is why he's paralyzed today." He leaned toward the jury. "Remember, those nurses were employees of the hospital." He inclined his head slowly. "So, that's the heart of our medical case. What we call the 'underlying case.' That's what the Conti office could have proved, if they'd simply done their job and recognized there was a case against the doctors and the hospital before the statute of limitations ran out."

Matt let out a long breath of air. "Let's talk about Salvatore Conti. Mr. Murphy spent a lot of time talking about me in his presentation. Maybe that's because he didn't really want to talk about Todd Gleason. But this case isn't about the lawyers presenting the evidence in this courtroom. It's about the priorities of that man right there." Matt turned and looked at Conti. "A lawyer Mr. Murphy calls the most famous attorney in the country." Matt turned back to the jurors. "Our case against Mr. Conti is very simple. Oh yes, we spent time talking about the settlement of the case for less than the one million dollar policy, the failure to order the proper films, and many other details any reasonably experienced lawyer would have managed differently. Frankly, these are side issues that simply give you a flavor of how poorly the case was being handled. The heart of this matter is the commitment that Mr. Conti would handle the case personally, as agreed in that letter sent to the attorney who referred the Gleasons to the famous Salvatore Conti. It's about Salvatore Conti's decision to violate that agreement and assign this catastrophic injury case to the most inexperienced lawyer in his office."

Matt picked up his notes of the defense arguments. "What did Mr. Murphy say? 'Took time out from handling the cases of badly injured people all over the country'—'impossible schedule'…?" Matt's expression darkened. "Let me ask you this. Why did he even agree to take Todd's case if he was too darn busy to give it the time it deserved?" He looked at key jurors and gave them a moment to think about that question. "Overreaching? Who's actually 'overreaching' if Mr. Conti's so busy he doesn't even have time to talk to the youngest lawyer in the office or read the medical report filed by his own office for the settlement conference?" Matt looked again toward the man in the three-piece black suit. "By the way, exactly *why* wasn't that report in the Gleason case file produced by the Conti firm for this trial? No one's ever given this court an answer to that important question." He saw some jurors turn to look at Conti, who was feigning imperial indifference.

"Another thing. They talk about 'sue-happy.' All those ridiculous lawsuits Mr. Murphy created—suing the police, suing the paramedics, and suing the passengers—what's that about? Who has suggested anything even remotely like that in this courtroom? Here's another question for you. Did they bring in even one competent lawyer to tell you that if they *had* read the records, if they *had* discovered that Todd could move his legs when he got to the hospital and then, later, became paralyzed when the nurses rolled him and severed his spinal cord—that any reasonable lawyer *wouldn't* sue for that? Did Sal Conti himself even try to say that? No. Ne wouldn't even answer that question because the answer, of course, is that no attorney would fail to sue for that."

Matt paused for a beat. "No, the fact is that Sal Conti is an accomplished lawyer with a national reputation. He may take too many cases, but I firmly believe that if he or one of the other senior partners were handling this case, the medical records would have been analyzed, the films ordered, and the report of the reviewing neurologist read. There's no way this famous lawyer, or any other experienced trial attorney, would have missed the fact that Todd Gleason could move his arms and legs when he was admitted and then was paralyzed when the nurses rolled him in the ICU." He looked back at Conti. "I don't blame that young lawyer. I blame the man who was just too darn busy to do what he promised—personally handle the case for this horribly injured young man."

Matt went to the easel and uncovered the blow-up of the damages life care plan. "We've discussed the damage issues in detail already, but there are a few thoughts I would like to leave with you, given the defense arguments." He put his hand on the side of the podium. "Todd Gleason was like any other sixteen-year-old boy with his whole life ahead of him. Soon he was going to go away to college and begin the natural separation that leads to a life as an independent adult, ready to find and develop a career, meet someone to love, and have a family. That's never going to happen for Todd." His eyes sought out Todd. "This young man will be dependent on other people for all the most basic functions of daily life forever." Matt gestured toward Todd's mother. "Debbie was soon going to see her son go off and fulfill all of her dreams for him, develop as a productive young member of society she could be proud of, find a wife, give her grandchildren." He looked back to the attentive jury. "Instead, life for both has been totally reversed." Matt sighed. "Now he's as physically dependent on his mother as he was when he was a baby." He held his palms up toward the jury panel. "But, mentally he's still an independent adult, appreciating his mother's devotion, but *deeply* resentful of its necessity." He took a deep breath. "In a close family like this one, the ripple effect of Todd's disability is difficult to overstate. For example, the impact this situation has had on his brother Bob's life has been stunning."

Matt walked over near the defense table where Murphy was writing away. "Rolls Royce care? Overreaching? Tearing the family apart?" Matt stood near Murphy but addressed the jury. "Let's take a look at the defense's 'Chevrolet' care for a moment. With their plan, Todd will never have a normal family relationship again. Most hours of the day, his mother and brother will remain his caregivers for the rest of their lives, working for *nothing*, by the way. Where in their plan is there provision for any compensation for them for working night and day until Todd dies or they do?" Matt felt his face growing hot.

"'Somebody paid to watch him sleep,' Mr. Murphy scoffs. Yes, darn right, so Debbie doesn't have to get up three or four times a night to reposition him, so if he has a problem or wants a drink of water or if, God forbid, there's a fire, someone's there to help him." He was gripping the podium again. "Agency rates—yes, so there is a business responsible to make sure someone competent shows up, so the attendants are trained and screened and get benefits, so Todd doesn't mind living with them and they are paid enough to stay more than a month or two." Matt pointed toward the defense table. "There is certainly nothing wrong with a serviceable Chevrolet, but their plan is a Chevrolet *without any tires*."

Matt took a deep breath. "Ladies and gentlemen, it's critical that this young man has a chance to take control of his own life. He's got to have the means for independent attendant care, twenty-four hours a day, so he can have his own place, and have a normal relationship with his mother and his brother—as a family, not as the people who bathe and toilet him." He frowned toward the defense table again. "They suggest the national average care expenditures for medical care and therapy are what should be awarded? You heard our evidence. Most quadriplegics in this country have totally *inadequate care*. That's why the national life expectancy statistics are just fifty percent of normal. Our expert explained that with reasonably necessary medical care, and competent, caring twenty-four-hour attendant care, Todd's life expectancy won't be cut in half at all. With reasonable medical care, it should be close to normal."

Matt tried to catch the eyes of each of the jurors. "Our life care plan requires a minimum of three hundred thousand dollars per year to take care of him reasonably. Multiply that times his fifty-year additional life expectancy and that totals fifteen million dollars. This amount is to pay for his care—just pay the bills." His hands went to his hips. "Ladies and gentlemen, if he only gets money enough for half of his life expectancy, he will run out of funds." Matt looked directly at Addison. "Not enough money for reasonable care *and* not enough years of future care? That's a Chevrolet *without seats or a steering wheel*." Matt raised his finger and pointed it toward the defense. "Remember. The witness *they* put on the stand to talk about all this agreed with our expert on the need for twenty-four-hour care, medical needs and a near-normal life expectancy—that is, when he testified in Hawaii for his *own* patient."

"Mr. Murphy gave us his thoughts on a reasonable amount for what he called 'pain and suffering.'" Matt scrutinized the high ceiling for a moment.

"The law says this element of a damages assessment should be whatever the jury in its collective wisdom feels is reasonable and proper. It is to assess not only for 'pain and suffering,' and the Lord knows there's certainly been a lot of that, but also for the change in Todd's quality of life, his disfigurement, his humiliation, his anxiety. Basically, the entire impact on Todd to have become a totally dependent person. A person who, physically, can't do a damn thing for himself." Matt stood beside Todd. "This young man can't compete in the job market. They haven't put in evidence that there's a single quadriplegic in the entire country who has a regular job. It would be remarkable if he would ever experience the joy of a wife or children. Just let yourself think about that for a moment. Todd is unable to feel any sensation below his chest and has zero control of his bowel and his bladder. This injury's probably the most tragic and horrific that can be suffered—*and* he's mentally all there. Todd has all the same hopes, desires and needs that any of us have." He zeroed in on the banker, Addison, for a moment, and pointed to the chart of medical needs. "Remember, the economic part of this plan just pays the bills. That's it. This other part is all about assessing damages because he's a different person today than he was as a carefree sixteen-year-old, before all this happened."

Matt paused and looked down at Todd for a moment, then raised his eyes to them. "Some might say, well, how do we assess a monetary value for all that? What good would it do? How can we put a monetary value on the quality of a human life. Should we?" He narrowed his eyes. "Well, in a civilized society, we don't use guns and we don't seek vengeance." He looked at Conti. "No, in a civilized society we seek justice, and we use money to reasonably and sensibly assess for the loss." He looked questioningly at the jury. "Remember when I asked each one of you during jury selection about assessing damages and we talked about *whether you could give substantial damages if we proved them to you?* I submit to you that we have absolutely proven the devastating changes in the quality of Todd Gleason's life, and the reasonable costs to care for him in the future."

Matt wheeled toward the defense attorneys again. "*Sympathy* they say? Todd's not here for that, not for him and not for Sal Conti either, by the way. Todd gets more sympathy every day of his life than anyone could possibly stand. This young man will have to live with the looks he sees in people's eyes for the rest of his life." He directed his attention back toward the panel. "No, sympathy is definitely *not* what he seeks. No. This is Todd's day in court. Todd Gleason wants plain old-fashioned justice, justice in the form of a sensible, reasonable monetary assessment of his needs and his losses."

Matt's elbows rested on the lectern, his hands folded. "Think of it this way. In our society, we make monetary decisions every day about the value of a human life." He held up a finger. "An example. There's a multimillion dollar military jet in trouble. Do we say to the pilot, 'Take a chance, get it down on the ground at all costs'? No. We say 'Head it out over the ocean and then bail out. We'll be there to pick you up.' Every time, we say 'Save the pilot.'" He ticked another finger. "There has been an avalanche or an earthquake. A little kid is missing and may be trapped and scared under hundreds of tons of concrete and debris. You see that horrible situation every once in a while in the newspaper. Do people say, 'Well, too bad, it's just too expensive to get him or her out'? No, we spend *millions* to dig down and rescue that person, often not even knowing if he or she is alive. No one would think to say, 'It's not worth it to spend all that on one person.' Why? Because, as a society, we place a high value on human life. I could go on and on with examples of the huge amounts we spend to save lives or improve people's quality of life every day."

Matt straightened up and moved away from the lectern to stand in front of the panel of jurors. "As a society, with a human life at stake, we don't set the kind of economic limits suggested by Mr. Murphy. To follow through with his car metaphor, using his proposed five hundred thousand dollar figure—remember, this is to assess the totality of the change in Todd Gleason's quality of life—that wouldn't just leave Todd a Chevrolet with no seats, no steering wheel, and no tires; that would also leave Todd a Chevrolet with *no engine*. Let me ask you: how's Todd Gleason going to manage for the rest of his life with a car like that?"

Matt felt a heavy weight slip away as he stood in front of the jury, now at the end of the trial. He felt he had said and done just about everything he could. Now, he could relinquish his burden to these twelve people. "On Todd and Debbie's behalf, and on my own behalf, thank you so very much for your time and your attention. It's been a long trial." He smiled at them. "Now the lawyers can put down their burden. Our job is done. Yours isn't quite yet." A few smiled back. "You have been so involved and listened so carefully, I feel comfortable putting Todd's future in your hands now. We're confident you'll do the right thing—not with sympathy, but with a sensible and caring analysis of the evidence. We believe you'll provide him with a reasonable and just assessment as required under the law."

He sat down. Relinquishment of control was always the hardest part. He spent his life trying to manage everything but, ironically, it rarely seemed to work out that way.

As the judge read the jury instructions on the law and explained the process they were to follow in determining a verdict, Matt watched the jury out of the corner of his eye. Had he reached some of them? Finally, the clerk gave the oath to the bailiff who then escorted the jury out of the room. Three in the afternoon. Just enough time to pick a foreman and go home for the night.

Matt pulled his papers together and put them in his briefcase. He was exhausted. He felt a hand on his arm and turned to see Todd and Debbie right behind him. "We can't tell you how good we feel. Whatever happens, you were amazing." He could see tears in their eyes.

He gave them a crooked grin. "I just hope it was enough, guys. I guess we'll see soon enough."

Adrianne cleared her throat. "Actually, I wouldn't guess it'll be soon. I suspect it'll take a while."

He shivered uncontrollably. "I sure hope so."

"Matt—you got a minute?" Murphy was standing a few feet away.

"Sure, I'll be right with you." Then Matt turned to his clients and said, "I'll see you guys in a few minutes." Matt walked to where Murphy waited in a vacant corner of the courtroom. He wondered if there was going to be an increase in the reduced offer for settlement of the case. Matt looked at the defense attorney and smiled. "Nice job on the argument. Your case was well-tried."

Murphy looked up, he seemed distracted. "Oh, thanks. Your argument was excellent." He looked rueful. "Especially the rebuttal. I felt that in every orifice, I must say." He looked around like he didn't know how to start. "You tried a hell of a case, Matt. No surprise there, frankly." He finally brought his eyes to Matt's. "Look, this isn't me, okay? Our offer, the two and a half million dollars reduced to one and a half? I've been instructed to inform you that it's officially withdrawn." He gave a gesture of helplessness. "I know, you already rejected it and you're just letting things play out. Between you and me, this is a chickenshit move. It's not my style. Who knows how long it's going to take to get a verdict? Not long, I hope, but I guess Conti's insurance company is feeling brave." He stuck out his hand. "I mean it about the nice job, Matt. I like your clients by the way." He glanced around and then said under his breath, "Good luck to them."

As he watched his adversary walk away, Matt felt those familiar tendrils of fear insinuate their way through his gut again. It was one thing to have bravely turned down a big chunk of cash, but, while the jury was out deliberating, there was always that offer on the table as a fallback position if things didn't seem to be going well. What if the jury sent out a note that suggested they were deadlocked or asked questions that sounded bad for Todd? Up to this point, there had always been the option of taking the money still on the table. But, no longer. The clients had already left. He would talk to them later. He was glad he had a letter Todd had signed, explaining all these risks. He packed up his stuff and headed for home. Adrianne could be on phone standby if the jury came back early. He didn't want to be here anyway if that happened. It was time for a long run—a dose of The Bridge.

55

The next morning, Matt was immersed in paperwork and had meetings with an expert witness and two prospective clients for the afternoon. Emily had him jamming for the next few weeks. Matt had an excuse to put everything off when he were in trial, but that luxury was clearly over. His next trial started two weeks from Monday. He looked at his watch. It was half past eleven. The jury had now been out a total of almost four hours. Well, at least it hadn't been one of those thirty-minute wonders. He had experienced that before and it hurt—badly. He and his team were on telephone standby with the court, as was the defense team, and the judge had already started a new trial. He beat down the apprehension nausea in his gut and tried to concentrate on his desk. They would know soon enough.

"Matthew." Matt looked up as adrenaline shot through him. "No, no. No calls from the court!" Emily leaned in the doorway. "Can you stand to talk about finances for a minute?"

Matt waved her in. "Sure, anything to take my mind off what's going on over there."

"Well, this should do the trick." She brought her notes in and sat on the chair in front of his desk. "I haven't wanted to worry you during the trial, but things are getting pretty tight." She tapped the paperwork. "The loan's down to a hundred thousand dollars and that'll be eaten by the remaining charges from the trial experts. I figure we'll be at total expenses of one hundred seventy-five thousand dollars plus in the Gleason case when the final few expert bills come in. We have the fees from the Durey case that came in during the trial, and that will take us to about halfway through next month." Her expression wasn't positive. "There really isn't much on the horizon to keep us going."

"If the Williams case two weeks from now settles, that'll help for a while." He rocked back in his chair. "I've got a couple of other possibilities in mind." He smiled hopefully. "It could be worse."

She didn't smile in return. "Matt, I think you're forgetting that the loan is due in four months—a balloon payment. Where're we going to get half a million dollars by then?"

Matt felt a stab of fear run through him. He couldn't help but think about that two and a half million dollars that had been jerked off the table during the trial. That money would have solved a lot of problems. They talked a bit more and she suggested a few ways to stretch what they had to work with. After she left his office, he looked through his case list and made a few calls to defense attorneys to see if he could get any settlement talks going. Mostly, they just wanted to hear war stories about the trial. He got the impression the odds-makers had him going down two to one. He consoled himself with the thought that they couldn't usually call the Super Bowl either.

Where could he get some money? In years past, Jake had occasionally been good for a short-term bridge loan, but he could hardly ask the guy who had been sabotaging the case for help. Also, nobody had seen him for three weeks now. That end of the office looked pretty frazzled trying to explain his absence. A law practice doesn't usually handle stopping in mid-flow very well. Matt was hurt and very angry with his friend for the stunning betrayal, but lately he was also worried. He couldn't imagine Jake just disappearing like this. Adrianne hadn't heard anything either. Matt had called Jake's sister and she was mystified as well. Matt made himself plow back into the stacks of work.

About half past one, he was in the middle of explaining why he couldn't take a new case to a prospective client when Adrianne put her head through the door. "The court's called." He broke a sweat immediately as he excused himself and went out to talk to her. "The jury wants a read-back, apparently." He looked at her questioningly. "It's the defense neurologist. They want just his direct exam read back, I guess."

He slumped. "That doesn't sound so good." Then he brightened. "Well, on the other hand, it means that someone's fighting for us."

Adrianne watched various expressions vie for control of Matt's features. "Maybe, but they're obviously still on liability, and it's not the part of the case I'd like them to be working on."

The reading was uneventful and Matt couldn't tell a thing by looking at the jury. He and Adrianne went back to the office. As the day wore down toward the magic five p.m. recess time for the jury, they found themselves speculating once again. It was Friday; would the jury come in with a verdict at the end of the day to avoid having to come back on Monday? Would they ask to stay late if they were close to a decision? It turned out Matt and Adrianne had wasted their time guessing what the heck the panel was thinking or doing. The court called at five and said the jury had gone home for the weekend. Matt wondered what to think. Something serious was happening for sure. Taking time off for lunch, it had been eight hours of deliberations now at least. Well, at least they could try to put it out of their minds for the weekend. Adrianne was going to the beach with a friend, and Matt had Grant for the whole weekend. He was looking forward to being distracted by an active little mind.

Matt was just putting dinner on the table Saturday night when the phone rang. It was Jake's sister. He was in the hospital over at California Pacific. They found his car near The Bridge. He had tried to commit suicide.

* * *

Matt called a friend to watch Grant, put the word out for Adrianne, and headed over to the hospital. Outside the intensive care area, he found Jake's sister Kathy. He gradually put together what was known. The police found Jake's car in the parking lot at the north end of the Golden Gate Bridge after it closed. They searched and a security guy said someone had been seen walking toward the city and had then disappeared. They pulled the videos and saw a man go over the railing close to the shore. A search below turned up Jake—washed up on the shore and still breathing. Matt understood it was rare, but occasionally people had actually survived the fall and the impact. Kathy told him there were many broken bones and Jake had been in surgery for hours to repair a badly damaged chest and other injuries. They weren't sure whether he would make it. His folks were on their way up from the valley. Kathy was obviously distraught.

"Matt, I know about what happened between you and Jake." Matt was silent, not sure what she actually knew. "He told me he had betrayed you and you found out. He was devastated, not because you found out, but because he had done it in the first place." She raked her fingers through her hair. "He didn't tell me exactly what happened or why, and I don't know why in the world he did it." Her eyes were haunted. "I don't think that's what this is about, though. Something has messed him up big-time." She wrung her hands. "He wouldn't have done something to hurt you unless something else was really wrong." Her look was searching. "Do you have any idea what it might be?"

Matt's gaze fixed as he thought. It couldn't be Adrianne and jealousy, could it? He really couldn't imagine that situation throwing his friend into another dimension entirely. He shook his head in consternation. Could it have?

Kathy gripped his arm. "We looked at his medicine cabinet. He was taking some pretty powerful medication prescribed by a psychiatrist. Something called lithium?"

Matt's eyes widened. That would explain a lot. "Lithium carbonate?"

"Something like that."

Matt's concern bloomed. "That's a drug used to treat manic depressive disorder, Kathy. Has he told you he has a problem with that?"

"Not really. He hasn't said much to be honest, just little bits here and there, something about 'cycling.'" She collapsed into a nearby chair. "At first, I thought he meant a bicycle, but then I realized he meant ups and downs." Tears ran down her cheeks. "He always hid when he was down. Most of the time, he was just so full of energy, you know? He could do anything."

It was so obvious when Matt put it together like this. Jake had the energy of ten people most of the time, but once in a while, he became morose and sort of dropped out. Had he been cycling through manic depressive disorder all this time? Matt knew a little about it from a few clients with the disease. It was quite variable and many people with it were highly functional. The manic periods could drive you and make you hugely productive, but could also cause you to lose contact with reality. The depressions could be black holes in your life and were known to result in suicidal episodes. Medications could level things out, but had to be taken regularly or disaster would lurk around the corner. Had the disease gotten worse recently or was it possible Jake had gone off his medication?

Matt spent another hour trying to calm Kathy down. Finally, a doctor came out and said Jake was in recovery and holding his own so Matt decided to go home. He listened to a message on his home machine from Adrianne. She had come home and was waiting to hear what was happening. He called her and filled her in. They agreed to go over to the hospital together the next day.

He just couldn't process what was happening. To concentrate on the trial, he had buried his anger and feelings of betrayal under layers of emotional armor. Now, with the trial over and his thoughts able to range free, he found himself deeply conflicted by these new revelations. How could his friend have sold him out like that? What conceivable rationale could excuse such treachery? On the other hand, perhaps a devastating disorder like this was not a matter of rationality? Could it be that the best friend he had known for all these years now had little or no control over his life? Ultimately, though, how could this man he had always cared about have acted with such astounding disloyalty—whatever his mental condition?

* * *

Matt drove Adrianne over to her place. They sat in the living room.

"It's terrible to see Jake like that. He looked so pale and vulnerable." She was distraught. "I don't get it—how could it come to this?"

"I've been thinking about it all day. As I look back, it does seem that he got more and more distant the last year or so. I guess I thought he had something bugging him, but I didn't really ask. In the past, he always would've told me." He sighed. "I should have insisted he tell me. Maybe I've been afraid to ask him."

"You thought he might be bothered about us? Matt, whatever's been going on with him has been there for a long time. It's why Jake and I had so much trouble, I think. I tried to tell you. Jake and I never really had a chance. We were already going in different directions when I met you."

They sat quietly drinking their wine. "I really couldn't keep up with the mood swings." Her expression was pensive. "I think that may have been this disorder he has. I feel kind of bad I wasn't more understanding, though."

"*You* feel bad. I'm supposed to be his best friend and I didn't have a clue." His mouth contorted in disgust. "I was so busy thinking about his girlfriend and whether he was jealous."

"Look, how could you know he had this problem?" She reached out and put her hand on his arm. "*I* didn't know. His *sister* didn't know—*nobody* did. He hid it well. I think that's the nature of this beast that has a hold on his life." Her eyes were steady. "Another thing, no matter how difficult this disease is, I don't think it could ever justify what he did to you." She pulled her hand back. "I think maybe your perseverance on this thing about me is just a way to excuse what he did." His head came up sharply. "No, really," she continued, "there's a part of you that refuses to come to grips with what happened there. I think you're in denial about it and what it means about your relationship in the long run."

"We've been friends for so long. He's done a lot for me. I really can't imagine not having him as a friend."

She gave him a searching look. "I have a few observations about that, but first, tell me more about that. I mean, what has he done for you?"

"He took me in when I left Wallace. He encouraged me—backed me up. He's always been there for me. We do everything together." Furrows appeared in his forehead. "What're you getting at?"

"Hey, I'm not attacking your friendship. I'm just trying to understand more about it. I know you guys had a lot of fun together and all. On the doing things for you part, he's always charged you rent, right? And you guys filled up an empty part of his office?" He shrugged. "I listened to you both over the last year. You taught him to kayak. You always let him stay at your place in the mountains. You suggest things to do together. If he was in a bad mood, you'd cheer him up." She extended her hands out. "Lots of one-way-street kind of stuff, it seems to me. You've even offered to make appearances for his law practice and do research."

"That's all part of a good friendship. That's the kind of stuff good friends do for each other."

Her head dipped in agreement. "Yes, but it's usually mutual. I haven't noticed a lot of reciprocity there."

"I don't keep score." Matt's head shook sharply. "This is B.S. He's in intensive care. I don't want to talk about whether he's done enough for me lately."

Her green eyes hardened. "Set aside for a minute that he did everything he could to tank this case you've bet your whole future on. Another thing has been bothering me. Why has so much gone wrong on your other cases recently? The defense won't offer money; they always manage to come up with some key information at the last minute." She kept her gaze on him and leaned back. "It's like they know something—like somebody's been talking out of school. You know?" He stared at her. "Maybe it didn't start with the Conti case, Matt."

"Jesus." He stared vacantly for a long moment. "What's the matter with me, Adrianne, am I messed up too?"

"No, I don't think you're messed up. Well, some. A little too willing to let things happen to you and not take charge of your own life, maybe. Worrying about clients a lot, but so involved you don't look or listen to the people around you, perhaps." She pulled at her lower lip. "How many really good friendships do you have with any guys, Matt? I mean other than Jake?"

"I know lots of guys…"

"No, I mean really close relationships—like with MJ. I mean guy friends your own age."

He thought about it. "I never really had many, I guess, except for Jake. The truth be known, I've never been very good at it."

"Why is that, do you think?"

"It never really came easy for me." His gaze got distant. "I guess I didn't really know how to have friendships with guys." She looked at him encouragingly. "Maybe because my dad was always so busy. I never got to have that 'hanging with dad thing' when I grew up. You know what I mean?"

"I do. We learn a lot about relationships from our interactions with our parents—or not."

They sat for a while, thinking. Then he regarded her uncertainly. "So what conclusions do you draw from all that?"

She gave a tiny shrug. "I've noticed a pattern here and there." He waited for her to explain. "Well, maybe that's why you've clung to this relationship with Jake. Maybe it's been your fantasy of what you wanted a best friend to be?" He was silent. "Whatever the facts are, all you see is what you want to see. Sometimes I think the vision of that kind of relationship outweighs the reality with you."

"What do you mean 'that kind of relationship'?"

She looked down at her wine glass. "One that's in a special category. Take MJ. You have an easy relationship with MJ. I hear how you talk about her. That is a relaxed friendship. That's different than how I see you with Jake. You don't put her on a pedestal and ignore her issues. She's real to you and you're completely at ease with her. You seem to accept her for who she is."

He watched her scrutinize her wine glass. "What did you mean a 'pattern'?"

She finally raised her eyes again. "I'm not sure that's how you've been with other people who are more than friends—like Lena or even Susan." She blinked. "Well, me also. How well have you gotten to know me—who I am, what makes me tick? Not some ideal, but the everyday reality of me?" She zeroed in on him. "MJ isn't a fantasy; she's just a friend. You enjoy her as a person. She's an old girlfriend—maybe that's why you're so comfortable with her? She doesn't have to fulfill some dreamed-up concept of yours. You're happy with her just being herself."

Matt sat in contemplation, sipping his wine. A bit of what she said resonated some with him. As he thought back, there was an element of desperation in his relationship with Jake, like he had been trying to make it into something it would never be. But, then he thought about Lena. He hadn't been trying to fit her into some fantasy he held about the perfect companion. No, he really couldn't accept this armchair shrink stuff. None of this explained what had gone wrong with Grant's mom, that was for sure. He sat back and folded his arms across his chest. "I really don't get what you're talking about, Adrianne."

Her expression took on a disappointed cast. "I know. Look, I don't want to be somebody's dream of the perfect woman, Matt. I can't manage that for you or anyone else. I'm just a regular person with pluses and minuses." Her gaze darkened. "I care about you and I wanted to be with you, even though you're my boss and I'd been dating your friend. Not perfect timing or judgment, but very real." She drank the last of her glass with a look of resignation. "Unfortunately, it would seem that two fantasies met head-on when that happened."

"I sort of see what you're saying about Jake." Then his eyes hooded. "But I don't think I need to defend myself when it comes to what I think about you."

Her expression was one of undisguised sadness. He didn't like that look. After a pause, she said, "It's not a matter of defending—it may be your reality. That's what I'm concerned about. There are some things people just can't change."

As he walked with her to his car, the wind was back and the fog scudded fitfully overhead, fitting his mood. He turned to say goodbye and she seemed to hesitate. She looked up and her eyes seemed to flash with pinpoints of fire in the fading evening light. He felt like he could almost swim into their depths.

"Matt…"

He found himself holding his breath.

She suddenly let the air escape from her lungs. "I think I have to go back home."

"Well, sure. There's time now; the trial's over."

"No, I don't mean just a trip. I mean I'll get my desk in order and all, but I can't stay—not anymore." She had that look again. "I just can't."

He didn't like that look at all.

56

Monday was proving to be a lot like Friday as Matt tried to concentrate on work and talk to clients and witnesses. Emily appeared at his door. "Hey, boss; you want a little good news?" She held her hand up. "I said 'a little,' you know. The official Bar ruling has come in dismissing the complaint against you entirely." He smiled. "I also heard from a friend that Willistin was transferred to the Sacramento office. That certainly may even qualify as more than a 'little' good news."

"What the heck was the deal with that guy?" Matt tried unsuccessfully to keep from showing his satisfaction. "He was sure a true believer."

"Less believing and more Conti I think. There was obviously some kind of serious connection there."

Matt buried himself back in work, setting depositions and talking to experts on cases soon to be up for trial. He signed up two new cases and wondered how he would get everything done. He went to find Adrianne, but her office was empty. In fact, it looked pretty clean. Too clean.

"Hey Emily, where's Adrianne?"

"She's vacated the premises, boss. She was here early this morning and cleaned everything up. She dictated on her cases and outstanding work. I'm just typing it up right now." Her eyes looked at him accusingly. "She said she'd hang around for the verdict before she left town."

"What'd you do to make her upset?" Mary Beth had come up behind him. "She said something like 'once a decision's made, it's better to cut the cord.' Said she was going back to her old life. She didn't look very happy about it, though."

The two of them just sat there. What the hell was he supposed to say? It wasn't like he could go into the details with them. Anger flooded through him. What the hell—why the hurry, anyway? You would think she could stick around long enough to say goodbye. It didn't seem very damn responsible of her to just quit with barely twenty-four hours' notice. "You'd think she could give some reasonable notice to the firm."

"Hardly seems required when she's practically been working free." Emily made another unpleasant sound. "She's been more of a volunteer than an employee. Not sure you need to give two weeks' notice if you're just a lowly paid assistant."

"Well—maybe it's for the best." He spun on his heel to go back to his office. "We got along just fine before she got here." He didn't like their attitude.

"Did we?" He heard another rude sound behind him. "I don't seem to remember that."

Damn, he wanted to talk to someone about how long this jury was taking. Maybe he would give MJ a call.

* * *

The next morning, he got a call from the court. The jury had another request for some testimony to be read back. This time they wanted to hear the defense neurosurgeon. Matt was discouraged. This sounded like the jury was hung up on whether he had proved the underlying medical negligence.

He was the first lawyer to arrive and said hi to Sandra, the clerk. "Hi, counsel—this is taking a while to get done, it would seem." Sandra mumbled something under her breath.

"What, Sandra? Did you say something?"

She exchanged a look with the bailiff. "I dunno. Some juries…just don't get it is all." She studiously went back to her work.

He felt a stab of fear. That was pretty cryptic, but it sounded like it could be some kind of a warning. Sometimes the bailiff hears things. Had he told her something? Was she trying to tell him to settle the case? Problem was, she probably wouldn't know that was no longer an option. He heard the other two lawyers come in and then saw Todd roll through the door with his mom. He went to say hi and tell them what was happening—not that he knew.

"Hi, Mr. Taylor. Where's Adrianne?" Oh, great. He had to start by explaining her whereabouts. He was saved by the judge.

"Good morning, gentlemen, Mrs. Gleason. Let's talk about this request a bit before we get the jury in here."

Matt tried to watch the jurors as they came in without being too obvious. He saw a few jurors glance toward the Gleasons, but couldn't read their expressions. He noticed that none of them looked at him. He wasn't sure what that meant at this stage. They all looked tired and serious.

* * *

He tried to work but couldn't concentrate. Mid-afternoon, he started to get up and go talk to Adrianne, but then remembered she was gone. He wondered if she was home. He resisted the impulse to pick up the phone and call her. He decided to go over to Fog City and get a cappuccino.

He sat at the bar and Roger gave him the coffee. "So where's Adrianne?"

Matt stirred in some raw sugar. "She's busy, Roger."

"Right after the trial?" The bartender swabbed the counter lazily. "What's she doing?"

Great, Matt thought, can't even get a cup of coffee without being subjected to cross examination. "Working from home right now." Maybe he'll leave it alone.

Roger leaned on the counter casually. "Is she coming in later today?" He was obviously not busy enough.

"What's with the twenty questions about Adrianne?" Matt tried his coffee. "You haven't even asked me about the trial."

"Are you kidding?" Roger pulled his head back incredulously. "I'm in love with that woman. Who cares about what you're doing?" He headed down the bar to pour a drink for a customer. "Besides, Emily and Mary Beth were in at lunch and told me the jury was still out."

Yeah, Matt thought wryly, and bent his ear about Adrianne, too. He stared morosely at the coffee. He would rather have some wine, but he had better not drink or a call would come from the court for sure. If the jury couldn't reach a verdict and the judge declared a mistrial, that would be bad. All this work and money would be down the drain and he would have to do it again. Actually, there was no way he could afford to do it again. How had he managed to get himself in such bad financial shape, anyway? He had a family that depended on him, not to mention Emily and Mary Beth. Susan might have to sell the house to make ends meet. Why had Matt been so contrary? Why had he been so compulsive about this case?

"That was a big sigh. You all right?" Roger was wiping the clean bar again.

"Oh, yeah. It's hard to wait for a jury. Can't really get much work done and can't do anything about whatever's happening." He gave a crooked grin. "Nervous time, you know?"

"I suppose, but I've watched you sweat out a lot of juries before. You look a bit more wrung out than usual." He swiped at some imaginary spots and gave Matt a sideways glance. "You look kinda like you lost your best friend or something." They were both quiet for a few moments. The bartender stopped wiping and looked up. "Speaking of that, what's the latest on Jake anyway? I heard he was doing better."

"I actually think he must be." Emily had appeared at Matt's elbow. "Jake's sister just called and says he's asking for you. He wants you to go over there tonight before visiting hours are over." She didn't look like she approved of that idea. "Oh, and the court called. The jury went home for the night—again. Sandra said they looked pretty tired and unhappy."

57

Matt got to the hospital about half after six and went to the room where reception directed him. As he went through the door, Jake's doctor was just leaving, but he stopped and said, "Don't be too long, okay? He's pretty weak."

Matt was shocked at Jake's appearance. He was very pale with a sheen of perspiration on his skin and dark brown and yellowish bruises everywhere. His eyes were sunken and looked distant and feverish. His leg was in traction and his head and neck were braced in a rigid position. He looked like hell. His eyes did brighten and focus a bit when Matt walked in. "I must look great, huh? I heard you were here Saturday night. Thanks for coming—I was sort of out of it."

"You were in surgery most of the time."

"I know you were just giving my sister support. I appreciate that." He tried to move a little and winced. "It's hard to get comfortable. Where's Adrianne?"

Geez, Matt thought, did everyone have to ask that?

"She's packed up and vacated the premises—going to head home after the verdict, I guess."

Jake grimaced, either from the pain or the news, and sighed. "I guess we fucked that up, didn't we?" Matt said nothing as Jake continued, "Well, me anyway. Hey, I knew you were crazy about her from the first time I saw you together." Jake tried unsuccessfully to smile. "Adrianne and I were already not going anywhere, but I just couldn't let you two happen. I had to keep trying to get in the way." His mouth worked awkwardly. "It was all part of the same stuff that was going on." Matt thought that if Jake could shrug, he would. "I'm pretty messed up, man—been that way for a long time." The side of his face pulled up in a wretched smile. "Oh, I was good at hiding it most of the time—from you anyway—not from Adrianne, though."

"What the hell are you talking about?"

The mashed-up features stared at him. "I suspect you've an idea at this point, Matt. " His head moved weakly. "The last few months I've been seeing a new shrink—a good one—I've been getting an idea how really fucked up I am." He took a shaky breath. "I guess I've been jealous of you for years. I've done little things here and there to mess you up—for a long time. Of course, recently it hasn't been so little." Matt's mouth opened, but he kept quiet. "I know." Jake managed something akin to his old smile. "Why would *I* be jealous of *you?*" His face tightened in pain. "Well, I have been and I've done some terrible things—unforgivable things."

Matt started to talk again but Jake stopped him. "Don't say anything. I've got some stuff to say. Oh, my firm's been going in the tank financially for a couple of years now and I was desperate, but that's not the real reason I sold you down the river. Yeah, I got business from it and all, but that wasn't the reason I betrayed our friendship." His eyes filled and a tear streaked down a bruised cheek.

"Jake, you don't have to do this. You just need to rest and get better."

"But I *do* have to do this. Maybe this is the *only* thing that'll get me any better. Look at me. I'm like this because I hate myself." His lids closed tight. "If I don't spew this out, I'll just do it again—and I'll make sure it works the next time." His lids flew open suddenly. "That's not a threat, Matt. This is something I need to do." The bruised features were pleading. "I really don't deserve for you to spend the time listening to this shit, but it would help me a lot."

Matt pulled up a chair and quietly listened to the man who had been his best friend for years spill his guts. Somehow this guy, who always seemed to have the world by the tail, had been jealous of Matt, his background, his family, his friends, and his successes—for years. It was a combination of

Jake's hardscrabble, immigrant roots and his own negative image of himself. Matt found that pretty ironic, given his own issues. Jake had wanted and needed the friendship, but more and more he found himself working to undermine Matt's success. This was all massively compounded by his manic depressive condition, which he had kept hidden from everyone.

In the last year or so, Jake had thought he was better and had gone off his medicine without telling his psychiatrist. The manic and depressive cycles accentuated dramatically shortly after he started seeing Adrianne. Jake confessed that he knew pretty soon they would never work out as a couple. He wasn't even bothered about that until he had seen the attraction between her and Matt. Then he had intentionally put himself in the way to make Matt feel guilty. He purposely went to San Diego and surprised them when they were there together on depositions. He and Adrianne were going in different directions long before the planned trip to Tahoe. He probably could have made it up there on that long, stormy weekend, but stayed away and called up there toward the end of the trip and told Matt how much he missed Adrianne just to play with Matt's head.

The most wrenching thing for Matt was Jake's description of his orchestrated effort to sabotage Matt's cases, even the Olsen case, culminating in the Conti case treachery. He was promised the business of the company that insured Conti for years in return for his duplicity. He had sold his friend out on the other cases without any promise of compensation. Jake tearfully confessed he had even given Jim Olsen's phone number to Sal Conti.

The nurse spoke sternly through the open door. "Visiting time has been over for a while. This patient needs his rest." Matt and Jake contemplated each other in silence for a few minutes. Then Jake cleared his throat. "Don't say anything, Matt. This was something I needed to do—to try and regain my sanity." He swallowed hard. "I know this is all beyond understanding and not forgivable." Matt started to say something again. Jake cut in. "No, I was crazy in the head, yes, but that's no excuse. There are some things that are just beyond the pale. Sometimes you just can't go back." He had a sad, lost expression. "I would never be comfortable and you never should be. You deserved to know all this and I needed to do this to start the road back to some sort of humanity." His face closed. "That is, if I ever really had any."

As Matt walked out of the hospital, he felt empty inside. He wanted something badly but couldn't for the life of him figure what would fill the void. When he let himself into his empty flat, he immediately missed Grant. He really needed to hold that happy, uncomplicated little person.

58

Matt figured he was at his desk about the same time the jury resumed deliberations. It had become impossible to accomplish anything. He would look at a document and then couldn't remember what he had read. People called and then asked if he was ill, but he couldn't figure out what to do with himself except perhaps to wander the hallways of City Hall in a daze of evolving tension. He refused to give in to that impulse. It felt like weakness.

Emily buzzed him. "There is a Mr. Contreau on the line for you."

"Who is he?"

"I think he is with the district attorney's office."

A buzz shot through him as he picked up the phone. "This is Matt Taylor."

"Hello, Mr. Taylor, I'm Deputy District Attorney Les Contreau. I'd like to arrange an appointment to discuss some matters with you involving Mr. Salvatore Conti. Is there a convenient time for us to talk?"

"Of course, but I have a jury out right now and need to be on standby. I'm hoping to get a verdict at any moment."

"I understand this is their fourth day out; is that right?"

"Yep. We're getting a bit worried about whether they're going to be able to put this one to bed."

"Yeah, the word around the courthouse is that this was a tough one, though I'm told you worked some magic in there."

"Yeah, well, we'll see what gets pulled out of the hat."

The DA laughed sympathetically. "Can we set something for tomorrow and then adjust if necessary?"

"That would be fine. Where do I go?"

"No problem, I'll come to your office with my investigator tomorrow afternoon at two. See you then and, good luck in the meantime."

Matt sat back in contemplation. He was pleased to hear that they may be going after Conti. The guy was definitely an evil menace, but he wondered how much he could really offer their investigation. Also, there was a part of him that really just wanted to keep a low profile and try to keep his practice alive. Sometimes it wasn't so wise to keep wandering about with your head above the bulwarks when the bad guys were after your scalp.

Emily and Mary Beth suddenly appeared in the doorway. "Matthew, they've got a verdict."

They stared at each other for a second in shock. He felt a stab of adrenaline shoot through him like a bolt of lightning. "Call Adrianne and the Gleasons."

"I already did—on their way." He grabbed his coat and briefcase and raced out the door.

In the courtroom, the two defense lawyers were already there. Anderson was pacing like a caged animal and Murphy sat in rigid anticipation, trying to look casual. Matt had a quiet word with Todd and Debbie while waiting for word that the jury was on its way. Matt looked around the room and realized the spectator section was almost full of lawyers and the curious. He noticed two newspaper reporters in the front row. In the back, a few empty seats on either side, sat Hairy Harry. Just then, Conti strolled through the swinging doors and sauntered to the counsel table to take a seat. He gave Matt a long, cold smirk. He looked like he already knew the result. Matt realized that in this town, it was definitely a possibility.

Adrianne slipped into the seat next to him. He caught her eye. She looked back at him and sighed but said nothing. Matt sat and waited. Finally, the judge came out and everyone rose. "Be seated. Sandra, tell the bailiff to bring the jury in, please." She picked up the phone and whispered into it. When she hung up, she gave Matt a stricken look. He felt the sweat dripping and his hands were clammy. He pressed his quivering hands flat on the table. The door opened and the bailiff stepped inside. The jury filed after him and into their respective seats. Matt followed them, searching for a clue. Not a one of them looked his or Adrianne's way or at Todd and his mother. Matt's heart sank. He had seen juries that looked like this before. The Olsen jury had looked like this.

The judge looked at the jurors. "Can the foreperson please stand?" Matt wasn't surprised to see the banker, Addison, rise from his seat. "Does the jury have a verdict?"

Addison looked down at the paper in his hands. "Yes, we do, Your Honor."

The judge sat forward. "Can you pass the verdict form to the bailiff, please?"

The paper was handed to the bailiff, who in turn handed it up to the judge. The black-robed man read it carefully with an impassive expression. Without looking at anyone in the courtroom, he passed it back to the clerk. "The clerk will read the verdict of the jury."

Matt could hear the clicking of the stenographer catching up as the clerk stood and first read the form to herself. Matt could see her hands shaking and felt the muscles of his body quiver uncontrollably with his pent-up nervous tension.

Finally she looked up. "We, the jury in the matter of Todd Gleason versus The Conti Law Firm and Salvatore Conti et al., find in favor of the plaintiff, Todd Gleason, and against the defendants, The Conti Law Firm and Salvatore Conti."

Matt's eyes widened and he heard Debbie gasp. He looked at the jury, but they were still staring straight ahead. Matt knew this was only one piece of the puzzle. There were a number of questions to answer and any one of them could reduce Todd's verdict to roadkill.

"We the jury, give our answers to the following questions:

1. We find the defendants were negligent in the handling of Todd Gleason's case.

2. We find the defendant's negligence to be a proximate cause of damage to the plaintiff.

3. We find the neurosurgeon to be negligent in the underlying medical care.

4. We find the emergency room doctor to be negligent in the underlying medical care.

5. We find the radiologist to be negligent in the underlying medical care."

Matt felt the tension in him ratchet up to the breaking point. The next answer was the whole case. If they didn't hold the hospital liable, the case was essentially lost because there would never have been enough coverage anyway.

6. We find the hospital to be negligent in the underlying medical care."

Oh God, they had done it! Matt realized he had been holding his breath as he felt the air begin to escape from his lungs. Now his muscles were tightening in anticipation of what had suddenly become the most important portion of the decision. They had won, but how much?

The clerk looked up from the verdict and looked right at Matt. He could feel every muscle in his body quivering. "We, the jury in the above entitled case, find damages for the plaintiff in the amount of twenty million dollars." Matt reeled back in shock. The courtroom erupted. Matt could hear Debbie crying and Todd saying, "My God" over and over. Murphy and Anderson were on their feet shouting, "Poll the jury, Your Honor." Conti bolted for the exit.

The judge rapped for control of the courtroom. The jury was polled one by one to determine if each of the findings were valid and supported by at least nine of the twelve. It was a unanimous verdict on all points. Matt sat there, stunned. How was it possible they had won so overwhelmingly? He looked at Adrianne. He wanted to hug her so badly. She had been instrumental in this astounding victory. She was really the only one who had encouraged him to go for it. A huge smile lit up her face.

Finally, the judge thanked the jury for their service and excused them. The trial was over. Matt turned and wrapped both of his clients in a huge hug, all of them crying. After a moment, Matt stood and realized the jury was still there. They were all standing in a circle around them, smiling. He looked at them, still in shock. "You weren't even looking at us when you came in—I thought we had lost."

The foreman, Addison, gave a broad smile. "We decided to do that on purpose. We wanted you all to be surprised." He looked at Todd and Debbie. "You are the bravest people we know. We want you to know we'd rather have made you better, Todd, but since we couldn't, we wanted you to have the best life you could have. We know you'll use this wisely." He smiled happily as the Gleasons cried and thanked them. Then he looked at Matt and Adrianne and gave another huge smile. "We all also agreed that if we ever need a lawyer, you guys are the ones."

Matt spent another half hour talking to the jurors, many of whom didn't leave right away. He found out that most of the time their deliberations had been about the negligence of the neurosurgeon. Finally the group that didn't think he was negligent had conceded. The rest of the decisions had been relatively easy, except for damages. They all had wanted to spend enough time on that issue to be sure they were doing the right thing. The twenty million dollars had actually been a compromise between two strong-willed factions. When he and the defense lawyers had finished talking to the jurors who had stayed in the courtroom, he went to the table and packed up his briefcase. He suddenly realized he hadn't even called the office to tell them. As he looked toward the clerk's phone, he caught Sandra's eye. She gave him a big smile. "I figured you were busy and would want to let Emily know. I called her. Congratulations, Mr. Taylor."

Matt thanked her and turned to escort his clients out. He noticed Adrianne in the back of the courtroom. He was surprised to see she was talking to Hairy Harry. He saw Harry hand her a folded note and wink at her. They walked out together. What could that be about?

As he pushed through the swinging door separating the central arena from the spectators, he found himself facing Murphy and Anderson. They both stuck out their hands. "Hell of a nice job, Matt. Pinned our ears back, big-time." Murphy gave a half-hearted laugh. "That'll teach the carrier what happens when you play games and withdraw an offer." He gave a questioning smile. "I bet you would have been tempted to grab the money if it had still been on the table about the third or fourth day the jury was out."

Matt wondered. He might just be right. He shook both defense law-yers' hands gratefully. They had been tough adversaries and gentlemen throughout the whole process. He told them so. Finally he walked Todd and Debbie out of the courtroom. They had a real celebration to plan. When they got to the hallway, he found two more people waiting patiently.

"Congratulations, Mr. Taylor. As you know, the two of us represent the *Chronicle* and the *Examiner* newspapers." The reporter smiled broadly. "We want to know how it feels to have obtained the largest jury award for an individual in California history." The reporter looked at Todd. "Mr. Gleason, we would certainly like to get pictures of you and your mom. We especially want to hear about your reaction to this remarkable verdict." Behind them, Matt saw two photographers and there were three TV cam-eras and reporters with mikes approaching. He couldn't believe this was happening.

59

Matt met MJ at eight and sat at the bar for fifteen minutes talking with Michel Elkaim, the owner of Chez Michel. Michel was a French Moroccan and had presided for years over one of the best continental cuisines in the city, at the corner of North Beach and Hyde.

"So, Matt, now that you're famous, will you still come here to see us?"

Matt laughed. "Good luck on getting rid of me, Michel."

"Thank you so much for coming here with everybody the other night. It was a real honor you chose us for the celebration." Michel threw his arm around Matt's shoulders. "Such a nice young man. So sad he is so badly injured. And his mom, such a special woman." Michel gave him a serious look. "They were very deserving, but oh so lucky to have you and Adrianne looking out for them. Congratulations, again." He turned to MJ. "A pleasure to see you again, lovely lady. Enjoy dinner, you two."

They sat at their table with their wine and both gave a simultaneous deep breath of relief and contentment. MJ spoke first. "I can't believe I was out of town teaching when this happened. I turned on Dan Rather and there you were on the six o'clock national news. In the morning, it was in all the newspapers. I want to hear every little detail!"

Matt's body shivered with the sheer joy, relief, and huge reduction in tension that had accompanied the win. He had been smiling so much in the last few days that his cheeks hurt. "I don't know where to begin."

She was pleased with how relaxed he looked. "Start at the beginning. We've got the whole evening."

MJ relived with him the long deliberation and his fear about what it meant. He described the verdict itself in exquisite detail. They laughed over the jury's decision to surprise him and how well it had worked. She commented on the great news coverage and how good he looked with the clients on TV and in the newspaper pictures.

The topic finally came around to his practice and how things were doing financially. His expression was completely amazed. "The defense lawyers in three cases I had coming up for trial called and wanted to talk settlement. Two of them settled immediately for more than I thought possible. I've also picked up ten potentially good new cases in the last two days."

"Amazing what a record verdict will do for an insurance carrier's attitude, huh?" MJ savored a sip of her wine. "What about that big loan that was due in a few months?"

"That mean old banker called me up." Matt laughed in delight. "After he congratulated me, he offered to turn the loan into an additional line of credit. I've got it for as long as I'd like. I just have to rest it once a year." He replied to her questioning look, "I didn't used to know what it meant either. It means to pay it off for at least thirty days each year. Some people call it a 'clean-down.'" There again was that silly smile that wouldn't go away. "With these two recent settlements, and if the third one settles, I can probably pay the line of credit off in a couple of months."

"From bankruptcy to solvency in days. Wow!"

"Well, I'm not exactly rolling in it, but able to pay the rent and alimony and keep going for now, anyway. The line will actually be handy to smooth out these constant up and down cash flow issues. The nature of my beast, you know—feast or famine, financially."

"What about the verdict?" Her expression brought a modicum of reality into the discussion. "What are the chances of collecting on that? Will they appeal?"

"Well, I think we should be all right." He sipped his wine as he collected his thoughts. "The judge tried a very clean case and there weren't a lot of issues. Actually several key rulings went their way. I'm sure they will make a motion to reduce the damages and try to get a reversal of the verdict. I don't think he'll reverse anything, but I suppose a remittitur is possible."

"Hey! I went to law school, but I'm a criminal lawyer."

"The judge can decide to reduce the verdict and you can either accept that or he'll grant a new trial on damages.'" He took a last bite of his dinner. "That can sometimes happen in a huge record verdict, if the judge was startled by its size or thinks the appellate court might decide to cut or reverse it." He sat back and put his arm up on the upholstered seat behind them. "There are lots of hoops a big verdict has to jump through before it gets paid. And it only takes one stumble." He brightened. "One good thing is that I sent the defense a reasonable offer to settle about a year ago. That means the judge could tack on about ten percent in interest since then, plus all our expert expenses. That would take the verdict up to about twenty-two million dollars with costs."

"Does Conti have enough coverage for that?"

"He's got a fifteen million dollar policy and the amount of this verdict with this possible add-on amount creates some major leverage." Matt gave a wicked grin. "His personal lawyers are going to be beating the insurance company over the head to try and get this paid so he and his firm aren't hit with the extra amount over fifteen million to pay personally. If the company refuses to settle and the Conti firm ends up having to pay the extra, that could be called bad faith."

"So? I'm dense maybe, but I don't get it."

"So, the idea is that his insurance company has to treat him fairly. If they refuse to settle this and stick him with the excess that is owed, maybe Conti could get punitive damages against the insurance company."

The light came on. "Big time leverage!"

"Yep. It adds a lot of pressure to deal with us and not appeal the verdict. At ten percent interest, a two or three year appeal of this large a verdict is *very* expensive!"

"What about Conti? Is he going to get off scot-free from all this after what he did to you?"

"Not exactly. There is no guarantee we will accept his policy limits in settlement. His company may have to pay more than the limits and Conti may have to kick in some real money." Matt raised his index finger. "Also, the State Bar has filed a complaint against him for destruction of evidence and they have accused him of violating the Canons of Ethics by soliciting Jim Olsen to file a claim against me. There may be suborning perjury charges too."

"My God. The worm has certainly turned."

"That's not all." Matt wagged his finger. "I spent an hour talking to the DA about those two guys who were after me. He had been trying to see if there is a connection with Conti, but he hadn't been able to turn anything up."

"But it's so obvious Conti was the guy behind all that!" MJ declared in frustration.

"There's more. Right after the verdict, a homeless courthouse character came up to Adrianne and gave her some information. It turns out this guy was once a lawyer in Conti's office back in the day. I suspect he blames Conti for the loss of his law license and the fact he's homeless now. He was able to give us some key info and a name. Adrianne gave that name to Clint, our investigator, who jumped on it." He gave a happy laugh. "It turns out this witness is a former local gang member who can make a solid connection between Conti, the thugs, and what happened to me. This guy apparently also has a reason not to be happy with Conti anymore." He lifted his glass in salute. "Here's to that turning worm!"

They ordered dessert and worked on finishing their wine. While waiting for it to be delivered, she asked about Adrianne. He told MJ about Adrianne leaving. "So how in the world are you going to handle all these new cases and the Conti motions and appeal by yourself?"

He looked uncertain. "I've done it before. I dunno, maybe you might be ready to stop putting people in jail and start making money?" He looked at her hopefully.

"No way, Matt. I love what I do. You know that." She watched him drink the last in his glass. "So, what do you think about what she said?"

"Who?"

"You know damn well who." She threw her black hair impatiently. "She's right, you know." He feigned puzzlement. "You were that way with me—drove me crazy—then when I didn't fit the image, we drifted apart. It was probably something like that with Lena too." His head movements indicated complete disagreement.

"No, really," MJ insisted. "I think that's a way you have of holding people back from your life—your real life."

"I don't see it that way at all." He folded his arms across his chest.

"Take Susan." Her lower lip thrust in thought. "A beautiful person, inside and out, smart. But she didn't fit your ideal of the perfect mother or wife, right?" His brows knotted. "No, wait. Let's take Lena, brilliant and funny, a real character and I know you had great chemistry—gorgeous even. Why didn't she fit your fantasy?" She held up the last of the wine in her glass to the light. "Matt, I know there've been lots of interesting women, but these particular ones are all special people you connected with." She speared him with her look. "Why'd you shut yourself away from all of them?" She watched him with obvious affection. "Maybe I should say 'us'?" She laughed at his startled expression. "Don't get nervous. I'm happily involved."

They enjoyed their dessert quietly.

"Matt, have you called Adrianne or heard anything from her?"

"I haven't." He looked guilty. "I wanted to, but I thought she wouldn't want to hear from me."

"Did she leave right after the verdict?"

"Well, yeah. She left by that weekend."

She held out her hand, flipping her fingers toward herself encouragingly.

"She came to the party here the night of the verdict, and then left town when she'd finished packing stuff up, I guess."

"And did you talk to her before she left?"

"Not really."

"Why not, Matt?"

He exhausted a deep breath and played with his chocolate soufflé.

She voiced a thought. "I know you were kidding about me coming to work with you."

"Not really." He looked at her wryly.

She ignored him and went on. "Adrianne was very good, clearly. You need a law partner—she's good material."

"You're not telling me anything there. She was awesome. But, she's abandoned me." His look was vulnerable. "What kind of a potential law partner does that?"

"I would hardly call it that." She almost sneered at how obtuse he was being. "She's obviously in love with you, Matt. She couldn't handle staying here even a minute longer once she recognized your pattern." MJ's features pulled back reproachfully. "She's not the kind to leave while the jury's out, metaphorically or otherwise. She waited and then took off. It's an unbearable matter of the heart." She affected pity at her friend. "She was hurting, Matt, and all this stuff with Jake just made it overwhelming."

MJ reached out and put her hand on his. "She couldn't handle it and ran away. That's not a rational response. Its pure emotion." She willed him to connect with what she was saying. "Whether she knows it or not, she's waiting to see what you do about it." She squeezed his hand and then sat back.

"So, what *are* you going to do about it? You going to use her leaving as an excuse to move on, *again*, or finally start changing the patterns of a lifetime?" She smiled in sympathy at his look of confusion. "Is she worth it?" She added sadly, "Or do you even know her well enough to know the answer?

* * *

Matt stared out the window. So much had happened in the last week. The defense motions were being prepared and he was already preparing his response. Conti had his personal lawyers demanding the insurance company offer more than their policy limits. Appellant lawyers were happily billing by the hour to read the trial transcript. Matt had heard that a Grand Jury indictment of Conti was soon to be announced and Matt had been notified to appear at the Bar's action against his nemesis. The Olsens had even called and asked him to represent them against Conti because the appeal rights on their case had lapsed.

Matt had given interviews for articles in *Newsweek* and *Forbes*. Cases were pouring in, but the money was short, of course. It would remain short until the Gleason case could be closed out. He hoped the case he had set for trial next week would settle. That would definitely help the finances. Some things never change. Susan had gone to court to seek an increase in the alimony and support payments—predictable. Grant had been chosen for the school soccer team. He was almost as excited as his Dad!

Things were almost back to normal. The defense lawyers were being as difficult as always and Emily was bitching about lack of money. Jake had brought in some lawyers to help his partner keep the practice going and had vanished somewhere on a sabbatical. Matt was looking for new office space. Roger at Fog City Diner had finally stopped asking about Adrianne. Matt had found a sensible shrink he could talk with. The first visit they had started to look at some of the things that made him tick, or not, as the case may be. He was starting to feel at peace with his life and how things were turning out. It was a pleasure to have a professional person make sensible observations, instead of having to listen to all those amateur psychologists.

Matt leaned back in his seat and felt his eyes get heavy. It was nice he could let himself be sleepy instead of feeling he had to jam through the paperwork stacked in front of him. The sound of the jet engines slowly lulled his consciousness. As he drifted in the twilight of sleep, he wondered what she would do when he showed up at her door. He hoped she would be home and that she didn't slam the door on him.

The End

Acknowledgments

I had always planned on medical school, coming from a long line of medical people (no lawyers!). When I gave up on that and ended up in law school, I was lucky enough to get a summer job at the best trial law firm west of the Mississippi. As a law clerk, and then a young lawyer, I was mentored by Bruce Walkup, who many considered the finest civil law trial lawyer in the country. It was through my observation and emulation of him and other illustrious lawyers in that firm that I gained my love and respect for the fascinating business of representing seriously injured people in a court of law.

Becoming a voracious reader of legal fiction, I noted there were very few novels about civil trials as opposed to criminal. Probably tired of hearing about this, my wife signed me up for a course on novel writing at one of the local universities. There I met my writing professor, Barbara Rose Brooker, an extraordinary novelist, and my writing journey began. She, and the small group of serious writers who met for a year thereafter, provided the inspiration to make this book a reality.

Once the bare bones were completed, I then had the benefit of extensive suggestions from my partner, Erik Peterson, as well as our wonderful office staff, Kate Schwering, Jed Thompson, Pratibha Sampson, and Sonia Del La Fuente. Many talented trial lawyers read the manuscript as well and provided additional ideas and encouragement: William Whitehurst, Jeffrey Raynes, Raymond Tam, Jan Baisch, Jerry Palmer, Judy Pavey, Ron Rouda, John McGuinn, Gary Blum, Glenn Stanford, Cynthia McGuinn and Nina

Shapirshteyn. *Acts* also benefited extensively from terrific early editing done by Melissa Atkinson and Kathlynn Lear (aka "the Comma Queen"). I am so lucky to have had their help and encouragement.

For medical help, I am grateful to my good friend and extraordinary Stanford neurologist, Bruce Adornato M.D., who read the manuscript carefully to be sure the medical details were accurate. Any mistakes in the final version are mine alone.

Walter "Skip" Walker III is a friend, famous trial lawyer, and best-selling novelist. He was good enough to read one of the later edits and give me the benefit of his extensive expertise as well as a very kind recommendation which appears on the jacket.

A few years ago, Jeff Apple, a former client and movie producer, (*In the Line of Fire* starring Clint Eastwood, among many other famous movies) read the book. He introduced me to my two awesome agents, Joel Gotler in Los Angeles and Ed Breslin in New York. They encouraged further editing and revisions which helped reduce the book to its present length. Thanks to their efforts, I acquired my remarkable team at Post Hill Press, which includes Anthony Ziccardi, Maddie Sturgeon, Kate Post, and John Bogdal. Many thanks also to Sung Kim, an extremely talented San Francisco artist who is responsible for the beautiful paintings illustrating the front and back covers of the book.

None of this could ever have become reality without the detailed editing, suggestions, and years of encouragement of my children, Brenton, Grant, Blake, Taylor, and Carter as well as my daughters in law, Keezia and Kari. Of course, the one that got all this started, read chapters late at night, and edited exhaustively, was the love of my life, Marti Phillips—my wife. Marti's insight, humor, thoughtful criticism, and patience made all this possible.

Finally, I want to acknowledge and thank the many talented and remarkable legal adversaries I have had the pleasure to work with and learn from over the decades of my legal career. The overwhelming majority of them were not only challenging opponents but always incredibly well-prepared. There is nothing more inspiring than knowing you are facing a well-armed warrior whose mission is the complete destruction of your case and your client. The best of them invariably conducted themselves in accordance with the highest ethical standards.

About the Author

James S. Bostwick is a nationally recognized trial lawyer with over forty years of experience representing catastrophically injured people throughout the country. In this first novel, he uses his vast experience to provide a rare glimpse into the world of civil trial lawyers, what motivates them, the enormous risks they take, and the choices that define them professionally and personally. Bostwick is an invited member of the Inner Circle of Advocates (limited to the top 100 plaintiff's trial lawyers in the U.S.), and is a past President of the International Academy of Trial Lawyers (limited to the top 500 plaintiff and defense trial lawyers in the U.S.). He has received many honors and awards for his work as a civil plaintiff's trial lawyer. Bostwick has obtained several record results for his clients over the years, including the largest medical malpractice jury verdict in U.S. history. He is a father of five. He practices law with his son and with his law partner of over twenty years. His office is in the San Francisco Bay Area where he lives with his wife and their two dogs.